Hunting

for

Silence

HUNTING

FOR

SILENCE

Robert Thier

2019

First Printing: 2019

ISBN: 978-3-962600600

This book is also available in eBook format.

Dedication

I would like to dedicate this story to all the amazing fans and readers who are still sticking with this series after five volumes. Thank you for your fabulous support!
Another round of special thanks goes to my spiffing proofreaders who've been helping to edit this series for all this time: Iris Chacon and Svasti Sharma. Proofreading five volumes in a row, that's what I call dedication!
Pun very much intended.
Thank you, everyone!

CONTENTS

A TAIL WITH A BEARD

'Psht!'

'What?'

'Psht, be quiet! I think someone is following us!'

Glancing around at my best friend Patsy, I rolled my eyes. Someone following us? Ridiculous!

Yes, absolutely ridiculous. That fool got himself caught again! The third time in a row!

As inconspicuously as possible, I tried to wave away the tip of the brightly coloured turban sticking out from behind a nearby rosebush.

Shew! Shew! Begone!

'Surely you're just imagining things,' I told Patsy with a bright smile. My hand was still waving behind my back like a mad windmill. 'I mean, who would follow us? That would be silly.'

Go home, you big oaf! Go!

The turban didn't listen to my mental urging. But at least it fully submerged behind the rosebush. Branches cracked, and a Punjabi curse rose into the air.

'What was that?' Patsy whirled around, trying to locate the noise.

'What?' I asked, the picture of innocence drawn by a blind, arm-amputated artist.

'That noise! Someone said something. Sounded foreign to me.' Suspiciously, Patsy peered at a mother passing nearby with a stroller, considering her as a serious candidate for tropical profanity.

'It's probably that Italian count,' Flora sighed, a dreamy look in her eyes. 'Don't you remember, Patsy? He was quite taken with you at the ball the other night. Maybe he has fallen madly in love with you, and now he is drawn inextricably towards the love of his life.'

'Madly in love, eh?' Hefting her parasol, Patsy surveyed the peaceful surroundings as if they were the fields of Waterloo just before the big attack. 'Well, I'm a charitable person. I would love to cure him of his mental illness.' Gently, she stroked her parasol. 'And I think I know the right medicine.'

I did my best to join the others' laughter, while simultaneously gesturing frantically at the turban, which had once again partially resurfaced from behind the rosebush. Damn the man! Couldn't he keep hidden for five minutes? Although, I had to admit, as a nearly seven-feet-tall, turban-wearing, sabre-swinging Indian in the middle of a public London park on a Sunday afternoon, that task did present some challenges.

'All this talk of romance has given me an appetite!' Eve proclaimed with her customary lack of logic. 'Want to come and find something to eat?'

'You go ahead,' I said, nodding at my three friends. 'I, um...have to go. I've...noticed a flower in that rosebush I'd like to admire.'

1

'Admire away,' Patsy told me. 'I agree with Eve. I need something to eat. Where is that picnic we brought?'

The others flitted away, looking for a nice place to spread a picnic blanket. I, meanwhile, walked over to the rosebush.

'Hm...what have we here?' I mused in the manner of a botanical expert. 'A rare specimen of *Rosa Annoyinga Bodyguarda*. I wonder, should I pluck a few of your petals?'

'*Allah* have mercy on you if you try,' Karim growled.

I gazed down at the big bodyguard kneeling behind the bush. His trousers were dirty, his turban sat askew, and a rose had gotten tangled up in his enormous beard. He looked like he'd tried to dance a tango with the vultures in the Sahara.

'You don't have to do this, you know,' I offered hopefully. 'You can just stay at home, comb your beard and polish your sabre. I'm sure I'll manage on my own.'

Karim's face stayed as wooden as a hundred-year-old oak. 'Ambrose *Sahib* told me to protect you, so that is what I am going to do. You need have no fear, *Sahiba*. No one shall dare to threaten your life while I am with you. I shall not leave your side for one instant.'

'Oh,' I sighed, trying my best to smile, and failing miserably. 'How wonderful.'

So I'm stuck with him. Great. That's one more thing to put on the list.

The list.

The list of things I was keeping. The list of things I would be discussing with Mr Rikkard Ambrose the moment I saw him again. It would be a long list, and an intense discussion, preferably with a shotgun in my hand. My dear employer deserved a round or two of buckshot on his derrière
for all the things he had done.

First and foremost among which is leaving me behind.

Pain, short and sharp, flared in my chest. It still hurt to think about it, damn him! We had been through everything together! We'd traversed wastelands, climbed mountains, hacked our way through jungles, and even through the London East End. He had always trusted me to have his back. Maybe even his heart. We had been a team. And now, out of the blue, he had work to do which was 'too dangerous'.

'Dangerous?' I murmured, marching away in search of my friends, ignoring the big shadow darting from tree to tree somewhere behind me. 'I'll show him what's dangerous! Just you wait until I get my hands on you, Rikkard Ambrose! You won't know what's hit you!'

Or maybe he would. He should be pretty familiar with my right hook, after all.

~~**~*~*

The picnic with my friends didn't last very long. I wasn't really in the mood for a leisurely Sunday afternoon in the park. With Mr Ambrose an ocean away, facing God only knew what kinds of dangers, all I wanted to do was grab the picnic blanket, tie it to the nearest mast, and sail off after him.

Instead, I returned home. At least this was one place where I didn't have to deal with my overgrown bearded shadow. Karim stopped short of sneaking into my house and hiding in my aunt's closet. I think he had originally intended to, but then caught sight of my aunt and thought better of it.

'There you are, girl! Where have you been?'

Hester Mahulda Brank strode towards me, her eyes flashing like daggers in her vulture-like face. 'I've been looking all around the house for you!'

'Oh. Then maybe I should have stayed out longer.'

'Don't you get smart with me, young lady!'

'Too late. I'm already extremely intelligent. What's up?'

My dear aunt gave me a look of supreme disdain. 'Only the prime social event of the year, that is 'what's up', Missy! Have you forgotten that the Duchess of Bedford's ball is in two days?'

I gave her a cheery smile. 'No. You can't forget what you never bothered to find out in the first place.'

My aunt opened her mouth—but she had apparently run out of comebacks. Pity, since I still had about a dozen left. But then, on the other hand, I did have better things to do than to spar with my aunt. Skipping up the stairs, I raced towards the room I shared with my sister Ella. Just before I reached the door, she pulled it open a crack and peeked outside.

'Ah, it's you! Get in! It's here!'

My heart made a leap.

'Really?'

'Yes, and I didn't let aunt and uncle see it, just like you asked. I snuck it out from under Leadfield's nose just as he was about to bring it in. Thank the Lord he's as blind as a bat!'

Thank the Lord indeed. If my aunt had gotten hold of the content of that letter, the Duchess of Bedford's ball would have been the least of my worries. Rushing inside, I snatched the battered envelope out of Ella's hand and threw myself onto my bed.

'Not that I want to pry,' Ella said in a tone that screamed *I want to pry! I want to pry so badly!* 'but why are you suddenly getting letters from France of all places?'

Sniffing the letter, I grinned up at her. 'They're love letters from my secret admirer, the richest, most powerful man in the entire British Empire.'

'Lill!' Poking my shoulder, Ella gave me a reproachful look. 'Stop jesting with me! Love is a serious matter.'

Gazing down at the letter as if I could see through the envelope, through the letters, all the way to the man who had written them, I swallowed.

You have no idea how right you are, little sister.

'Well, all right. If you don't want to tell me, you don't have to.' She patted my shoulder. 'I'll just go and leave you to enjoy your "love letter" in peace. But if it's a bill, remember uncle won't pay for it.'

3

I didn't see her go. I was still too mesmerised by the letter in my hands. When the door closed with a click behind her, I tore open the envelope, pulled out the letter, and started reading.

Dear Mr Ambrose,
You're probably surprised at receiving this letter. After all, you somehow happened to forget to mention the address where you would be staying in Paris. Quite an oversight on your part, considering how much I know you love writing long, regular letters to all your loved ones. But not to worry! I squeezed the information out of Karim. So here it is, my first official...

Wait a minute.

I lowered the sheet of paper, frowning. This wasn't a letter from *him*. This was *my* letter, which I had dispatched to him several weeks ago! What did he think he was doing, just sending it back to me?

Hurriedly, I read on. This had to be a mistake! It had to be!

...letter with us as a couple. Because we are still a couple, aren't we? I'm telling you now, if you've found some French coquine *over there, you had better stay in France, or I won't be responsible for the consequences! I'll rip your head off, do you hear? I'll rip your head off and stuff it down your throat!*
Have I mentioned how much I love you?

Hm. All right, maybe my style wasn't that polished yet, but I was new to this writing-love-letters thing. Actually, I was new to love altogether. It was exhilarating and frightening, and...and...

And *why the heck was there only my letter in the envelope?*

He couldn't have just sent it back without a reply! He couldn't! Did that mean he no longer loved me? Had he really found someone else? Damn that bloody son of a bachelor! If only I'd never fallen in love with that stone-cold cad! How could he do this to me! He said he loved me! I was going to kill him! Kill him very dead and use his guts for garters!

I was just about to crumple up the letter and throw it away, when something tickled at the back of my mind.

What would the average gentleman do if he received a love letter from his lady? Well, he'd probably go out to buy expensive pastel paper and write a long reply, full of protestations of love and oaths of eternal fidelity.

Only...Mr Ambrose was not the average man.

So what would *he* do?

I pondered the question for a moment—then sighed. Of course.

I turned around the letter. And there, on the formerly empty back of the page, in Mr Ambrose's clear, neat handwriting, stood the words:

Mr Linton,
Stop wasting ink.
Rikkard Ambrose

Warmth spreading inside of me, I pressed the letter to my chest. He replied! He replied! Didn't he write the most wonderfully romantic love letters?

But the wonderful, warm feelings inside me were tainted with something dark. No matter how hard I tried, I couldn't forget the reason why Mr Ambrose and I had to write letters to each other instead of being face-to-face, of holding each other, of never letting go. He had left me behind. Had left me behind because he was going into danger.

There wouldn't be any need for love letters if the bloody idiot had just taken me with him! Damn and blast! He was in danger! He was in danger, and I was helpless to do anything about it! What should I do? I...I...

I needed to talk to someone.

But to whom? My sweet little sister Ella? If she knew that I really had an illicit love affair with a ruthless business mogul and wanted to go join him on his latest dangerous endeavour, smack-dab in Paris, the city of sin, she would faint and not regain consciousness until I'd sworn a vow of chastity. If I told Patsy and my regular crew of friends that I had fallen in love with a man, they'd try to tie me down and exorcise the spirit that had taken possession of their friend. Who else was there? Who could I possibly trust to understand and—

Suddenly, a grin spread over my face.

Two minutes later, I was down the stairs and out the door. Outside, I hailed a cab, jumped inside and stuck my head out the window to tell the driver where I wanted to go. When he heard the address, the man's eyes went wide, and he blinked down at me.

'Um...Miss? Are you sure *that's* where you want to go?'

'Yes, of course. Is there a problem?'

'Well, err, it's exactly, um...well, I...' He gave up. 'No problem, Miss. I'll take you there directly.'

'Thank you.'

Retreating into the interior of the cab, I leaned back and sighed. The cab started to roll and, only about a quarter of an hour later, came to a halt in a familiar dingy street. Exiting the carriage, I pulled out my purse to pay the driver. He glanced up at the façade of the house in front of which we had come to a halt.

'Err...are you really sure this is where you want to go, Miss?'

'Certainly.' I smiled. 'I come here all the time.'

'Y-you do?' The driver's eyes bulged. 'Well, I never...! Um...sorry, Miss, I...well, that is to say, I have to go.'

Grabbing his money, he wheeled his horses around and raced off as if the very devil were behind him. Shaking my head in bemusement, I tucked my purse away.

'What in the name of *shayatan* are you doing here, woman?' growled a voice behind me. I turned around to be confronted with the familiar scowl of Karim, my round-the-clock, beard-bristling watchdog. 'This is the East End! Do you have any idea how dangerous it is for a lone woman to be here? What could you possibly want in a place like this?'

'Calm down.' Patting him on the shoulder, I pointed at the sign over the door of the nearest building, which proudly proclaimed:

The Pussycat Palace—A Gentleman's Paradise

'I'm just going to visit a friend.'
And with that, I started towards the brothel door.

PLANS FOR THE FUTURE

It took a bit longer to get inside than I anticipated, due to the fact that my bodyguard dragged me off and tried to stuff me into the nearest cab. Apparently, he for some reason took the 'guard' part of 'bodyguard' to include guarding his employer's lady friend from strolling around seedy East End brothels. Eventually, by use of logical arguments and a sharp-tipped parasol, I managed to convince him to let me go—but not before I had found a place to change from my lady's garb into the trousers of my male alter ego.

I guess I could see his point. It might create a bit of a stir if an underage girl marched into the *Pussycat Palace* and demanded some special time with the lovely Amy.

'Mr Linton!' The madam greeted me with a beaming smile when she saw me enter. 'So happy to see you again, dearie!' Then her face darkened. '*He* isn't with you, is he?'

I could guess the reason for her tone.

'Mr Ambrose doesn't tip well, does he?'

'Ha! Forget the 'well', and you've the truth of it, dearie.' The madam pulled a face. 'Oh well, the less that's said about 'im, the better. Are ye 'ere to see Amy again, love?'

Behind me, I practically heard Karim's beard bristle.

'*Again?*' he hissed. 'You've been here before?'

I batted my eyelashes up at him. 'And you didn't even notice. You're slipping. Must be old age setting in. How's your rheumatism?'

'You...you...!'

I turned back towards the madam. 'Yes, I'm here to see Amy.'

'Lovely!' The madam clapped her hands. 'Ye know, dearie, she's quite taken with you. That smile, every time you pop up...I think she's hopin' ye'll make an honest woman out of her one of these days.'

'She doesn't. She really, really doesn't. Trust me.'

'Oh, well, if ye say so, dearie. Come, let's go up. She's probably heard ye and is already waitin'.'

'Certainly.' I gave the middle-aged woman a smile. 'And while I amuse myself, would you mind keeping my companion entertained? I'm sure you could find some interesting way for him to pass the time.'

From behind me, I heard a strangled noise.

'Certainly, certainly, dearie! Go right up, ye know the way. And as for you, my big, handsome man...'

'Avaunt, woman! Do not soil me with your tainted touch!'

'Oh, I won't touch ye.'

'You won't?'

'No, silly! My girls will take care of that. Sally! Rose! Elsie! Come here! I've got a customer for you!'

Smiling contentedly, I marched upstairs, while from behind me came the sounds of a man being overrun by superior forces. Poor Karim. But then again, he did volunteer to be my bodyguard. People who do reckless, foolhardy things like that should learn the consequences early.

Upstairs, I quickly found the door to Amy's room and knocked.

'Come in,' came a sultry voice from the other side.

Putting a hand over my eyes, I stuck my head in through the door. 'Are you only moderately indecent? How much, on a scale from one to ten?'

'Lilly!'

The silly sultry tone vanished in an instant. A vice-tight hug engulfed me— Bloody hell, that girl had strength for someone who lay on her back all day!— and pulling me inside, she kicked the door shut behind us. Carefully, I peeked between two fingers and saw fabric. That was encouraging. I opened a few more fingers, revealing more fabric, hair and...

'Get that hand away from your face, you silly goose! I'm dressed!'

'Ha!' I snorted. 'Silly, my arse! Do you remember what you looked like last time I came in here?'

'Hm...' She scratched her head. 'I don't really know. I can't remember anything at the moment.'

'That was exactly it. *Not anything.*'

'Oh, well...' She shrugged. 'It ain't like you saw anything you didn't know was there, right?'

'Amy.' Shaking my head, I grinned at her. 'I've missed you.'

'Me too. Me too.'

We hugged again and settled down on two chairs by the window. Keeping our voices low so as not to be overheard through the paper-thin walls, we exchanged all the latest gossip. Amy and I led lives that were about as different as they could be, and so neither of us ever grew tired of hearing about the other's latest adventures. But we had one single, all-important thing in common: both of us were single women without inherited wealth, trying to make a living for ourselves in a world ruled by men. That had created a special bond between us. That, and the solid chocolate I brought with me on every visit.

Sadly, our discussion couldn't last long. The madam was a suspicious old fox. If she'd gotten wind of Amy wasting time talking while she could be doing other, much more expensive things, she'd have a fit. So, after a few minutes of gossip, we got up on the bed.

'It is time, my love,' Amy declared dramatically, falling back, and throwing her arms wide. 'Have your wicked way with me!'

I slugged her in the face with a pillow.

'How dare you!' She grinned. 'I thought you loved me! I shall be avenged!' And, grabbing the nearest pillow, she aimed a blow for my head. I ducked and hit back right away.

We managed three rounds of pillow fights before collapsing gasping on the bed. Amy had won two-to-one, but right now I didn't care. I hadn't had this much fun all week. Plus, we had done a pretty convincing performance for the madam. With all the creaking and screaming that had been going on, she'd probably charge me double. Ah, the price of friendship...

'You wore me out!' Amy groaned. 'I'm gonna complain to that man of yours when 'e's comin' back.'

'By all means, tell him I've been visiting a brothel in his absence. I'll write you a nice obituary.'

'Ha! I can defend myself. If anythin', it's 'is obituary you'll have to write.'

My first instinct was to laugh—but the laugh caught in my throat. Would I be writing his obituary soon? A shiver went down my back at the thought. It was less impossible than I hoped. I had no idea where exactly he was right now or what he was doing. All I knew was it was damnably dangerous. He could be lying in some dark alleyway bleeding from a bullet wound, for all I knew.

'Lilly? Lilly, did I say something wrong?'

Amy's voice intruded on my silly panic. Because that's what it was. Silly. Yes. Mr Ambrose was fine. Perfectly. Maybe if I told myself that often enough, I would even believe it.

'I...it's nothing, Amy. I just...' I swallowed. 'I...he...'

And the dam broke. The whole story just burst out of me—how Mr Ambrose had left me behind, and how I had no idea whether he still loved me or not, how annoyed I was at how much I bloody cared, and, and...

'...and I don't know what to do, Amy.' I looked at her and knew that if I were to look in the mirror instead, I'd see something in my eyes that I was not used to seeing there: fear. 'I just don't know what to do. We've been in danger before, yes—but back then, we were together. I could watch his back. Now...now it all just feels wrong. What should I do?'

Amy looked at me with eyes far too wise for her tender age. 'Ye already know what ye should do, don't ye?'

~~**~*~*

When, ten minutes later, I descended from the upper floor, Karim was waiting for me in the foyer beside a smiling madam. His turban sat askew and his beard stood on end. There was a rouge stain on the tip of his nose.

'I shall have my vengeance on you one day,' he said with a face as grim as a grimoire. 'When you least expect it, I shall strike!'

'How lovely. I had a very nice time, too, thanks for asking. Shall we go?'

In reply, Karim muttered something incomprehensible (and probably life-threatening) and followed me out the door. After finding a place to change back into my lady attire once again, I returned, full of thoughts and plans. But I had no time to execute any of them.

'Lill! Thank God you're home!' Ella rushed towards me before the front door had even closed and grasped my hands. 'Aunt has gone completely mad! She's dead set on finding husbands for us at the Duchess's ball! "A last ditch effort" she called it! If we don't find suitable men to marry, she's threatened to give us to the next best man she can get her hands on!'

'So what?' I demanded. 'No matter what she says, she'll still need us to say yes at the altar.'

Ella shuddered. 'Yes, but if your guardians demand it of you, who would be brave enough to say no?'

I refrained from giving the obvious answer—'Me!'—because it wouldn't be of much use to my dear little sister. She wasn't like me. And I didn't even want her to be. She might have the backbone of a sickly little daisy, but she was the sweetest, kindest girl on earth—especially to me. The times in my early days when she had bandaged me up after one of my shenanigans had gone awry were too many to count, and never had she told on me to my aunt or uncle. True, half of the time she had still accidentally given me away, because she blushed like a tomato and was the worst liar in the world, but it was the thought that counted. I wouldn't judge her for being who she was. Well, not much.

'And anyway,' Ella continued, 'if we don't agree, she could turn us out of the house.'

She had me there. If Aunt and Uncle threw us out, we'd be homeless.

Or we would have been, said a little voice in the back of my mind, *until recently.*

'So what?' I demanded impulsively. 'Let her go the devil! We don't need her. We can rent a flat.'

Ella's eyes went as wide as extremely scared, forkophobic dinner plates.

'Rent a flat? You're mad! How? With whose money?'

Mine. I've been saving for over a year now. I could do it.

The realization that I was no longer in my aunt's power was almost scary.

'I'd find a way,' I said aloud. One day I would tell her the truth. One day. But not today. Today, after my talk with Amy, I had too much on my mind. Too much to do to waste my time with my aunt's stupid schemes.

'You *are* mad,' Ella concluded. 'Or sick. Let me feel your forehead. Do you have a fever? Do you feel hot?'

'I am perfectly fine. And I'm telling you the truth, Ella. I would be able to support the two of us somehow.'

She didn't look as if she believed me. And I didn't dare tell her the truth. If my aunt squeezed it out of her, she would lock me up in my room and not let me out for a year. I might be moderately independent, from a financial point of view, but I was still a minor. Only on my twenty-first birthday would that old vulture lose all control over me, and that was still far in the future. Ella's even farther. I couldn't leave her alone to fend for herself. I had to help her somehow.

She gave me a sad little smile.

'Thanks for trying to cheer me up, Lill. But I can't run away. It's not me. I just can't!'

'Ella, I—'

9

'I know what you'll say! That I'm being a bad, disobedient child, and that I should be grateful to her for all the good she's done for me.'

No, that was actually not what was I was going to say. That sounded more like the kind of nonsense she would spout on occasion.

'And I suppose I am being ungrateful, Lill, but I just can't help it! I...there's something you don't know, and...' She was squirming like an eel on trial for being too slippery. 'I cannot say. I've sworn to keep it secret, but there's something...Oh, this is torture! If only I could tell you! But...no, I can't! I just can't! I...I don't know what to do, I—'

'Oh, put a sock in it already, will you?' I interrupted. 'I know all about you and Edmund.'

Ella blinked.

'You...know?'

'Yes.'

'You can't know!'

'Edmund. Piano tuner's son. About this high, brown hair, brown eyes. Lives next door. Occupation: piano tuner. Hobbies: classical music, the occasional flutter, and smooching my little sister in the moonlight.'

'You do know!'

'Yes.'

'Everything?'

'Well, let me put it this way—there was this one time when you went to his house in the middle of the night, and he fell down while trying to climb out of the window, and you grabbed him, and pulled him in for a great, big—'

Ella's face flushed beet-red. I hadn't seen her looking so guilty since she was five and I had caught her with her hand in the cookie jar. She hadn't actually taken any cookies, of course, but to make up for the sin of contemplation, she baked us fresh cookies three times in a row.

'So you do know! But...how?'

I patted her on the back. 'Sisterly intuition.'

Also, I had been listening in on her secret garden rendezvous from behind the nearest bush for, oh...how long had it been? One year?

Ella gazed up at me with tear-filled eyes. 'What should I do, Lill? Aunt has her heart set on me making a good match, and yet...I can't. I just can't marry anybody else. I love him.'

A year or two ago I would have scoffed. I would have told her that without men, the world would be a much simpler place. Now, however...

The world would be a much simpler place without solid chocolate, too. Did that mean I wanted it to disappear to keep my butt from getting bigger?

Hell no!

Hugging my little sister to me, I murmured meaningless, comforting words.

'What should I do?' she repeated, gazing up at her big sister as if I had all the answers in the universe. 'What can I do?'

What could she do? Nothing. Absolutely nothing. Against Aunt Brank's greed and social aspirations, Ella was helpless.

What *I* could do, on the other hand – well, that was a totally different matter. There wasn't a second to waste. It was time to get down to business.

THE GREAT REVEAL

'Lill? Lill, what are you doing? You can't just march over there and—'

'Of course I can. The pavement is perfectly even and good to walk on. Try it.'

'That's not what I meant, Lill! I—'

Ignoring my dear little sister with the consummate skill of an experienced older sibling, I marched up to the door of the neighbour's house and hammered on the door.

'Hey, you there! Assorted strummers, jinglers and tinklers! Out with you!'

'Lill!'

'What?'

'Where are your manners?'

'I left them in my purse at home. The damn things are too heavy to carry around all the time.'

Hurried footsteps approached from the other side of the door. It opened a crack, revealing the anxious, familiar face of a certain young man.

'Oh, it's you.' I smiled, pushing the door open the rest of the way. He stood there in the doorway like a lost puppy, blinking at me and Ella standing on his doorstep. 'Good. That simplifies things. You're in love with my little sister, aren't you?'

'Um,' said Edmund, the piano-tuner's son.

'Bravo! How very eloquent. Just the kind of intelligent reply I was hoping to get from a future brother-in-law. Are you sure you love her? Really sure? Because if you break her heart, I'll cut off your bollocks and...well, you don't really want to know what I'll do with them afterwards. Are we clear?'

'Err,' said Edmund.

'Spiffing! I'm so glad we're getting along. I can feel the beginning of a wonderful friendship here. Now, as to this whole marriage thing, I don't have a lot of time—I have to leave on a little trip soon—so I was hoping we could get it wrapped up in a day or two? I know the two of you like to languish in lovelorn agony for months on end, but I'm afraid I haven't got time for that anymore. I've got other engagements that cannot wait, so you'll just have to postpone the lovelorn agony until after you're married. Do you think you can manage that?'

'Um,' said Edmund.

'Wonderful, wonderful. Now, I think my aunt has a dressmaker scheduled to come tomorrow morning, so this whole marriage thing will have to wait to the afternoon. Could you perhaps look in on us at, say, two pm? I'm sure we could get the whole matter wrapped up then. What do you say?'

'Err...' said Edmund, 'Who are you?'

'Dear me, right, we haven't been officially introduced yet. Ella?' I waved at my little sister, who stood beside me, her face for some reason covered by her hands. 'Explain, will you?'

'This is my sister, Lilly,' Ella said in the tone you'd use to say, 'This is my darling pet dog, Fluffy. He doesn't bite, trust me, and I'm so sorry he just peed on your carpet.'

'Oh.' His eyes went big. 'So this is...'

'Yes.'

'And she really...?'

'Yes.'

'And the time you told me about, when she...in public?'

'Yes, that, too.'

'Hello?' I waved a hand in the air. 'Anyone remember I'm standing right here?'

Shaking himself, Edmund came out of his daze. 'Of course. Forgive me, Miss Linton, where are my manners?'

'I don't know. They're yours.'

'Um. Yes. So...you know about the two of us?'

'Yes.'

He straightened. 'Well, let me assure you that my intentions are nothing but honourable. I mean to marry your sister.'

'And how's that working out so far?'

'Lilly!' Ella hissed.

'What?' I hissed back. 'He's been at it for nearly two years. It's a legitimate question.'

Edmund, who by now was as red in the face as a virgin tomato on its wedding night, cleared his throat. 'There have been some difficulties in gaining the consent of her guardians for Ella's marriage, Miss Linton.'

'Such as the fact that you haven't actually asked yet.'

'Lill!'

'True, Miss Linton. However, the doorstep is hardly the right place to discuss this. Would you like to come in to have a cup of tea? My parents will be back in half an hour, so I'm afraid you cannot stay long, but—'

'Oh, half an hour will be plenty of time to wrap this little matter up. I have lots of other things to do today, anyway.'

He stared at me for a moment—then nodded and stepped aside.

'Very well, Miss Linton. After you.'

I entered the modest home. The brick house was almost an exact replica of Uncle Bufford's. Whoever had built these things had not possessed a great deal of creativity. Edmund led us to a small sitting room, where we sank into two plush armchairs while he busied himself with the tea kettle in the kitchen. Ella turned her head from left to right, gazing at everything as if this were the Palace of Versailles and we were two poor peasants taken on a tour as a last treat before our execution.

'What's the matter?' I demanded.

'I...well...it's just so overwhelming, seeing it for the first time.'

'Wait a minute...for the first time? You've never been here before?'

She looked shocked. 'Of course not!'

'You've been sneaking around with this fellow for nearly two years, and you've never seen the inside of his house? What if he had a collection of previous wives stacked in the cellar?'

'Lill!'

'Should I check? Just in case?'

Edmund returned, with two tea cups in his hand and a helpless little smile on his face. 'Um...one lump of sugar, Miss Linton? Two?'

I took a look at his honest smile on his honest face, stuck between his honest ears.

'Forget what I said,' I sighed in Ella's direction. 'We don't need to check.'

We all settled down around the little table in the centre of the sitting room.

'So, Miss Linton.' Edmund cleared his throat. 'Am I to gather from your appearance here that you approve of my interest in your sister?'

'Not really,' I told him. 'I think you're a bit of a wimp, and she could do much better.'

'Oh.'

Under the table, Ella gave me a kick.

'But it's not really my opinion that matters,' I continued, kicking back and making her yelp. *Ha! Take that. No one bests me in a kicking contest!* 'It's hers.'

'True.' Edmund's expression brightened. 'So...do you have a plan to help us?'

They both looked at me like starving bunnies at a gardener specializing in lettuce.

'Yes, I have. Listen closely.'

And I proceeded to explain to them what I had in mind. When I was finished, they gazed at me with eyes widened by admiration. I'm not ashamed to say I preened a little. It wasn't often I got to bask in unbridled admiration of my genius.

'Can it really be that simple?' Edmund whispered.

'It can be, and it is.'

They glanced at each other. Without a word, they reached to take each other's hands, and squeezed in silent agreement. The sight sent an unexpected shard of pain through me, as I remembered a hand that had once held mine like that. A hand that was now far, far away.

Soon, I told myself. *You'll just have to wrap up this little matter, and then....*

'All right,' my thoughts were interrupted by Edmund, who, for once, sounded uncharacteristically determined. 'I'll do it.'

'Very well.' Rising, I nodded. 'Just remember to be at my uncle's house tomorrow afternoon at two. Oh, and also remember, if you break her heart—'

'...you shall remove, um...certain extremities. I remember.'

'Good.' I beamed. 'I might learn to like you after all. Now, let's go, Ella, shall we? I've got some preparations to make.'

~~**~*~*

13

The next day, my aunt went insane. Well, she was pretty crazy most of the time, but that morning, she went completely off the rocker, down the stairs and into the metaphorical coal cellar to paint pink guinea pigs on the wall, so to speak.

What, you may ask, had her in such a spin?

You've got three guesses. But you'll probably only need one.

'Hurry, girls, hurry! If you tarry like this, you'll never be ready in time for the duchess's ball! Get moving, get moving!'

The duchess's ball was all she could talk about. She was racing through the house like a rabid vulture, bonnets and trinkets and ribbons in hand. I hadn't seen so many pretty non-essentials in this house since a package meant for a seamstress three houses down had accidentally been delivered to our house. Aunt had even, bless her stingy, social-climbing little soul, ordered a dress-maker to come to the house to create a special ball gown for Ella, thus bringing the entire number of dresses owned by her to a staggering total of three. Apparently, my dear aunt had high hopes that her niece's stunning beauty would attract a great catch.

Did I mention I didn't get a dress? Surprise, surprise.

'Would the pink ribbons be better, or the blue?' Aunt Brank demanded, buzzing around Ella with arms full of accessories.

'Why not the grey?' Maria suggested sweetly. 'They match her personality.'

'Wonderful!' I said. 'Then you can take the green, Maria. They'll match your envy.'

Maria sent me a death-glare across the room, which I shrugged off without blinking. When you've been glared at by Mr Rikkard Ambrose, an evil twin sister is easy to deal with.

'Take this one,' I whispered, pressing another, brand-new blue ribbon into Ella's hand. 'It'll match your eyes.'

'Lill! You shouldn't have!'

'I know. But I like doing stuff I shouldn't do. It's so much fun.' Before she could protest any more, I tied the ribbon into Ella's hair. Aunt Brank elbowed me out of the way, grabbed the ribbon and shifted it approximately a quarter of an inch to the left.

'There! Now you look just perfect!' She beamed. Not the way a lamp does, but involving an actual, honest-to-God smile. Wonders never cease. 'Looking like that, you'll be able to catch yourself a baronet, or maybe even a duke!'

Just then, the clock in the corner struck two pm. A moment later, the door-bell rang downstairs. Aunt Brank frowned. 'Who could that be? It's not yet time for the dressmaker to arrive, is it?'

'I'll go and see,' I volunteered with an innocent smile.

Poor Aunt Brank. She was so swept up by her dreams that she didn't even notice the abnormality of me volunteering to do something to help her. She just waved her hand.

'Yes, yes, do. Ella and I have more important things to take care of.'

I doubt that. Now then...Let's have some fun.

Turning to go, I winked at Ella. She nearly toppled off the stool she was standing on for her dress fitting. Her face was alternately flushing and draining of colour.

'Hold still, girl! What is the matter with you?'

'N-nothing, Aunt. Absolutely nothing.'

Grinning, I sauntered down the stairs. This was going to be interesting.

Downstairs, I opened the door to find a sweating piano-tuner's son on the doorstep.

'You look a little flushed,' I commented. 'Have you changed your profession to plumber?'

He eyed me dubiously. 'It just occurred to me...if I marry Ella, I'm going to have you as sister-in-law, aren't I?'

I gave him my most magnificent smile. 'Indeed.'

'And there's no way around it?'

'No.'

'Oh. Mhm. Well...' He swallowed, hesitated—and nodded. 'Well, lead on. Where are they?'

'Upstairs. Follow me.'

He did. At a safe distance.

When we entered the room upstairs, nobody glanced our way at first. But then Lisbeth turned to reach for another ribbon and caught sight of Edmund. Her eyes widening, she tugged at Anne's sleeve. Anne turned, an annoyed expression on her face, which melted into curiosity when she caught sight of the newcomer, and instantly switched to malignant delight when she saw his gaze fastened on Ella. Quickly, she tugged Maria's sleeve, and soon, the whole room was staring at us – except for Aunt Brank. She was far too deeply lost in dreams of social aspirations.

'Oh yes, Ella, my dear! With this dress you'll catch yourself a really remarkable man! Only, make sure not to focus too much on wealth, and more on position. Money is there one day and gone the next, but a seat in the House of Lords is forever! You can't go wrong with...What's the matter, girl? Why aren't you listening? What are you staring at like th—?'

Finally, she saw him. Her eyes narrowed.

'Who are you?'

You had to admire her for achieving such a level of callous carelessness. We'd had the same neighbours for the last ten years, and she still didn't know their names.

Edmund cleared his throat. 'My name is Edmund, Ma'am. Edmund Conway. I live next door.'

'Then what are you doing here?'

If she'd hoped to get rid of him by being rude, she was about to be disappointed. Stiffening his spine, Edmund met her gaze head-on.

'I've come to ask for your niece's hand in marriage.'

Aunt Brank blinked. Then her eyes went back and forth between Edmund and me—and a smile spread across her face. Twice in one day? I had to remember to mark today red in the calendar.

'By all means, take her hand, and the rest of her. When will she be out of the house?'

Edmund's eyes widened, and his head snapped around to stare at me. I might have been a bit offended by the undisguised horror in his expression if I wasn't close to bursting out laughing.

'Um...I'm afraid you misunderstand me, Mrs Brank.'

'Don't tell me that you're planning on a long engagement. If Lillian's going to marry, I'm going to rent her room out, and I need it quickly.'

'Err, no, Ma'am. That's not what I was referring to. I meant that it's not Miss Lillian I wish to marry.'

The smile vanished from Aunt Brank's face. 'Oh. Are you sure?'

'Yes, Ma'am.'

'And there's nothing I can do to change your mind?'

'No, Ma'am. I wish to marry Miss Ella.'

In an instant, my aunt's demeanour shifted. Where, a moment before, she had been glowing with anticipation, she now switched from -cipation to -pathy.

'Are you a duke?'

Edmund's honest eyebrows shot up. 'A duke? No.'

'A marquess? Earl?'

'No.'

'Viscount? Baron? Some other kind of lord?'

'I'm afraid not.'

'Then what are you?'

'I, um, am training to become a piano tuner.'

'A piano...*out!*'

'Pardon, Ma'am?'

Raising her hand, she pointed a trembling finger at the door. 'Out! Out of this house, now! You'll marry Ella over my dead body!'

'How kind of you,' I took the opportunity to cut in. 'Over there is a nice, open window. It should be quite high enough to bash your head in.'

My aunt gave me a dour look.

'This is your doing, isn't it.'

I tried to look innocent. Unfortunately, it was an art I had never completely mastered.

'Well, whatever you're up to, missy, it stops here! It's not you who has the power to decide Ella's future. It's me! And I'm saying no.'

Edmund's face paled. But before he could lose what remained of his courage, I gave my aunt a smile and fired back.

'Actually, that's not entirely true, is it? If there is someone who could decide, it is Uncle Bufford. After all,' I said and internally begged forgiveness from all the feminists who had gone before me, 'he is the man of the house, isn't he?'

Gertrude nodded. Lisbeth nodded. Quickly, Ella inclined her head. Even Anne and Maria managed a grudging nod.

My aunt opened her mouth—then closed it again. Her eyes flashed with venom. Ha! I had hoisted her on her own petard. Opening the door, I performed a bow.

16

'Gentlemen first.'

A slightly dazed Edmund walked through, followed by a fuming aunt, a pale Ella, and a gaggle of curious sisters. We marched down the corridor, coming to a halt in front of Uncle Bufford's room. Raising my hand, I knocked.

THE PRICE OF LOVE

'Go away!' came his jovial greeting from inside.

'But Uncle,' Ella dared to protest. 'We need to speak with you.'

'Then *especially* go away. I don't have the time to bother with women's problems.'

'There, you see?' Aunt Brank raised her chin triumphantly. 'He doesn't want to be bothered. It seems I shall have to be the one to decide the matter after all.'

'Let me try,' I suggested with a brilliant smile. Stepping forward, I knocked against the door. 'Uncle? It's about money.'

There was a momentary pause from within, then...

'Come in.'

Sometimes, I truly loved my uncle.

We stepped inside. The room was as dingy as I remembered. Although it was a bright spring day outside, only slim slivers of light fell into Uncle Bufford's study, due to the heavy curtains that covered most of the windows. Coins, receipts and bank notes in bundles still covered every available surface. The piles seemed to have grown about two inches since my last visit. Uncle Bufford sat, as he always did, behind his massive wooden desk, most of his face, apart from his sharp little eyes, concealed behind a ginormous beard. The instant we entered, those eyes focused with unerring speed on Edmund.

'You. I know you. You're the Conways' boy.'

Edmund swallowed. 'Yes, Sir.'

'Are you the one who wants money from me?'

'No, Sir.'

'Then what do you want?'

'Um, well...'

'What are you waiting for? Speak up, young man!'

'I, um, came to ask for your niece's hand.'

'Which one? There are so many running around here I can hardly keep track.'

'Ella, Sir.'

'Ella? Hm, hm. Ella.'

'And I, of course, said no!' Aunt Brank cut in. 'Ella is a charming young girl, who, with a bit of luck, could marry into any of the highest families of the land! To give her to a half-baked, piano playing nobody—'

'Tuning,' Edmund corrected.

'What?'

'Tuning, Ma'am. I tune pianos, I do not play them.'

17

My aunt gave him a look that suggested where he could stick his well-tuned pianos. 'As I was saying, to give her to this nobody of a nincompoop would be beyond ridiculous. It would be the height of folly!'

'B-but Aunt!' Ella stepped forward, wet her lips and, with a blush taken straight out of a gothic romance, whispered, 'I love him.'

My aunt stared at her. My uncle stared at her. I stared at her. For Ella, this was rebellion. For Ella, this was dancing naked on the rooftop while the house burned down. She had actually *voiced her own opinion*—and not while hiding in a broom closet. Just goes to show: wonders never cease.

Uncle Bufford sent me a grumpy glare. I knew what that glare meant.

You've lured me into this under false pretences, young lady! You said we would be talking about money. And now I have to deal with marriage, and love, and other kinds of mushy female matters that make me want to hurl. Just you wait. This will have consequences.

I gave him a bright smile.

Oh yes, it will. Just you wait, you old buzzard.

'Well?' Aunt Brank demanded. 'Aren't you going to say anything?'

'Why would I?' her loving husband replied. 'You talk enough for both of us.'

But he turned once more towards Edmund and scrutinised him from under his bushy eyebrows. The young Romeo paled under the old man's scrutiny, but didn't back down.

'So, you want to marry my niece Ella, young man?'

'Yes, Sir.'

'How long have you known her?'

'What does it matter?' Aunt Brank cut in. 'He's obviously unsuitable—'

Uncle Bufford raised a finger—and Aunt Brank shut up. I blinked at my uncle, flabbergasted. How had he been able to keep this secret from me all the while? My uncle had superhuman powers in his index finger!

Uncle Bufford returned his attention to Edmund. 'Well? How long?'

'I've known her casually ever since we moved in. But we've...grown closer over the last three years, Sir.'

Turning to Ella, Uncle Bufford lifted an eyebrow. She nodded, quickly.

'It's true, Sir. We've had an attachment for quite some time.'

'I see.' Leaning forward, my uncle focused on Edmund again, and his face grew serious. 'Are you serious in your wish to marry my niece, young man? Have you thought about what it would mean? Can you support her?'

'Support her? I, well...um...'

There was a moment of silence. Then...

'I don't know, Sir.'

'Let me put it this way, young man—do you have an income of your own?'

'Not yet, but—'

'Do you have steady work? Some occupation that could support my niece? Or, if it comes to that, a family?'

Edmund opened his mouth—then hung his head. 'No.'

Uncle Bufford closed his eyes for a moment, and nodded. 'Then there's your answer.'

Edmund opened his mouth again, wanting to protest, but then he looked into Bufford's eyes and saw implacable resolve there. Ella rushed to him, and together they hurried outside. The door slammed, and I could hear my little sister sobbing from behind the thin wood.

Aunt Brank looked as if she'd just been elevated to Duchess of Somerset. It seemed like the matter was closed. Once it was made up, no one could change Uncle Bufford's mind.

Well, you've always loved trying the impossible, haven't you, Lilly?

Clearing my throat, I stepped forward. 'I wonder whether I might have a word with you, Uncle?'

Instantly, all heads in the room turned to me. Aunt Brank narrowed her eyes. 'Why?'

'Excuse me, Aunt, but it's not you I was talking to.' I looked straight at my uncle, praying I wasn't wrong about him. 'Uncle? Alone, please?'

He hesitated for a moment—then nodded.

'Bufford!' Aunt Brank protested. 'You can't—"

He flicked his finger again, and her mouth snapped shut. I *really* had to get him to teach me how to do that. With a last venomous look from my aunt, and not-too-friendly ones from the twins, everyone filed out of the room. Only Uncle Bufford and I remained.

'Well, girl? What do you want?' Steepling his fingers, he regarded me from under his bushy eyebrows. 'I hope you're not going to plead or cry or some silly female nonsense like that.'

'Please don't insult my intelligence,' I told him. 'You'd be about as likely to be moved by tears as a mountain by an ant fart.'

He nodded approvingly. 'True.'

'No, I don't want to cry or plead. I simply want to point out some arguments in favour of Edmund you might not have thought of before.'

'You mean there are actually arguments in favour of him?'

'Surprising, I know. But yes, there are.'

'Pray tell.'

'Well, to start with, Edmund's father is quite old. Soon he'll be too old to work. Young Edmund might not have an income now, but he's good at what he does. The moment his father retires, he'll inherit a profitable business that would be more than sufficient to support a family.'

One bushy eyebrow rose, decorating the upper half of Uncle Bufford's head with a little bit of hair for the first time in decades.

'Which isn't much good to him now, is it?'

'True. But who says Ella needs to marry him right away? She's young. Besides, many couples choose an extended courtship or a long engagement. A tacit agreement could be formed, without any public announcements, and when Edmund takes over from his father, we could make things official.'

'True, that would work, girl. But he'd still only be a piano tuner. Ella could do much better.'

'Ah yes, all those barons and marquesses...' I smiled. 'You've never married off a female relative, dear Uncle, so you might not be aware of this, but there's a custom in our fine country called a 'dowry'. It's a substantial sum of money paid by the father—or guardian—of the bride to the prospective husband.'

Uncle Bufford's face turned to stone. His hands clamped around the armrests of his chair.

'If Ella marries some baron or marquess, or, God forbid, a Duke, he is going to expect a dowry. It could be, oh, I don't know...' I let the sentence trail off, suggestively looking around the room at all the heaps of coins and banknotes in view. Uncle Bufford couldn't suppress a shudder of horror. Inwardly, I smirked. Time for the last strike.

'Plus, there will be a big wedding—which someone will have to pay for.'

My uncle's beard twitched. 'You don't think that...'

'Oh yes. I do.'

'Hrumph.'

'On the other hand, if Ella were to marry Edmund,' I continued quickly, 'I'm sure they'd want a humble, private ceremony. And if there were problems with money, I could help out.'

That caused another eyebrow-elevation.

'Help? How?'

'With money. I have...some funds of my own.'

'Do you, now?' He stared at me for a moment, as if trying to penetrate my secrets. Finally, he asked, 'Is that all?'

I thought hard for a moment. Wasn't that enough? I had done my very best. What else could I do? What on earth could convince him that this was the best, the only choice for Ella?

Finally, inspiration hit.

'I also,' I added, with a big smile, 'would like to make you a small present of, um...ten shillings to thank you for being such a kind, considerate uncle who always thinks of his nieces before himself.'

He cocked his head. 'Ten?'

'Err...fifteen?'

'Thirty.'

'Twenty-five. My last offer.'

'Done.' Uncle Bufford nodded. 'I do love being a kind, considerate uncle.'

Not betraying a hint of how my heart was hammering in my chest, I stepped toward the door with a little curtsey. Done. I had done it! I had saved my little sister. And for half as much as I'd expected to pay. Mr Ambrose would be proud.

'A pleasure doing business with you, Uncle.'

Turning, I slipped outside, closed the door behind me and walked until I was out of hearing distance—then I leapt up and punched the air. 'Yay! I did it! I did it!'

Leaning against the corridor a bit farther down, I noticed a picture of misery that was quite a convincing portrait of my little sister.

'Cheer up!' I told her, thumping her on the back.

'Lill!' She sent me an accusing gaze. 'How can you smile at a time like this?'

'The question is, how can you not?' My grin broadened. 'Or don't you want to marry your piano-tuner anymore?'

Ella blinked. 'Marry? Marry Edmund? But Uncle Bufford said....'

'He changed his mind.'

'But how...?'

'I appealed to his generous nature.'

It told you a lot about my little sister, practically everything you needed to know, that she swallowed this lie hook, line and sinker. A beatific smile spread across her face, and the tears on her face sparkled like diamonds, making her only look more beautiful than ever.

'His generous nature? Oh, that dear, dear old man. I've got to thank him! I could weep at his feet in gratitude all day!'

'Don't,' I advised. 'We don't want him to change his mind again.'

'But Lill—'

'Besides,' I added, 'shouldn't you go tell Edmund? He's probably languishing in horrible heartache or something silly like that right now.'

'Oh my goodness, you're right!' Clapping her hand over her mouth, Ella whirled and rushed towards the stairs. 'I must go to him at once! Oh, poor, poor Edmund!'

I had a feeling poor, poor Edmund wasn't going to feel so poor anymore in a few minutes. Smiling, I gazed after Ella as she rushed off to meet her future. Now it was time for me to go find mine.

˷˷**˷*˷*

When Aunt Brank heard that Uncle Bufford had changed his mind about Ella's marriage, she immediately got it into her head that it was my fault. I thought this quite unfair. Of course it *was* my fault, totally and completely, but she couldn't know that, could she? Where would we be if a suspected criminal could be thrown in jail even if his crime wasn't proven, just because he happened to be guilty?

'Just you wait!' she hissed when she settled herself down next to me at dinner that evening. 'I'm going to get you for this. You're going to rue the day you were born.'

I didn't dignify that with a response, but I decided I would have to look up what 'rue' means in a dictionary. I wasn't really worried. I mean, what could she try to do to me that she hadn't done before?

The next evening, I got my answer. We were preparing for the Duchess of Bedford's ball. Edmund had arrived to escort a beaming Ella, and I was just about to go upstairs and fetch my one and only ball gown, when my aunt appeared behind me like the spectre of doom and held something out towards me.

'Oh no, my dear,' she simpered. 'We wouldn't want you to wear that ugly old thing now, would we? Take this.'

'But that's—'

'Ella's new gown, yes. I thought the matter over and came to the conclusion she won't really need it anymore, now, will she?' Her eyes flashed with venom. 'After all, she's soon to be engaged. So I had it altered to fit you. I'm sure with

21

such a beautiful dress, you'll attract plenty of attention from gentlemen looking for a bride.'

You had to give it to her—she was a master at being nasty. Genghis Khan couldn't hold a candle to her. I put on the dress, and it fit me disturbingly well.

'At this ball,' she whispered to me when I left my room, dressed and prepared, 'we are going to find a husband for you. I don't care if it's the bastard brat of the Duchess's second gardener. In fact, that would be just what you deserve. I'm going to make sure you get what's coming to you.'

It was very, very hard not to smile. Poor Aunt. I didn't have the heart to tell her that all her malevolent schemes would be futile in the end. The time when I feared her was long past. And besides—in this case, I didn't even have a reason to. I wouldn't be around to be caught in her trap.

That evening, we all got in the coach that had been rented for the occasion and drove off towards the duchess's town house. Nobody noticed that I had my largest purse with me, which appeared rather fuller than usual. They were all too busy staring at Ella and Edmund, who sat in a corner, gazing into each other's eyes as if they could read a riveting novel there. Gertrude and Lisbeth seemed happy for them. Anne and Maria looked torn between derision (because Ella was going to marry a man without money or a title) and envy (because in spite of her misfortune, she had the audacity to be happy). And Aunt Brank...well, she looked like Aunt Brank, which was bad enough in itself.

We arrived at the ball just as a big, fancy coach deposited several gentlemen and drove away to find a parking spot. The sight seemed to fan the flames of my aunt's rage. Gentlemen. Probably wealthy and respected gentlemen, whom Ella now would never get to marry. She threw me another look promising vengeance, and I returned a smile. She had no idea what was coming.

At the door, we were greeted by a swarm of scurrying servants who escorted us inside. There, at the door of the ballroom, the duchess awaited us, greeted us as if we were old friends, and very elegantly glossed over the fact that she didn't know our names. I didn't take it personally. To judge by the droves of people already milling around the ballroom, half of London had been invited.

'Well, well...' My aunt gave me a smile that, a year or two ago, would have sent a shiver of fear down my back. 'Looks like there are plenty of eligible bachelors here, my dear Lillian. Why don't you go and mingle? We would hate for you to miss this opportunity, now, wouldn't we?'

'Yes, quite so,' I agreed merrily. 'I'll just go powder my nose before I venture into the thick of things, all right? I wish to look my best for the gentlemen. After all, I might find my man tonight.'

'Do that, dear.' Her eyes sparkled with suspicion. 'I'll wait here in front of the door, so you don't accidentally lose your way and leave. That would be too bad.'

Like an army sergeant, she took up her post in front of the door as I slipped inside. I had expected no less. No matter. Quickly, I walked past the room intended for gentlemen, farther down the corridor, and entered the powder room reserved for ladies.

There was only one other lady inside, and she seemed eager to get back to the dance floor. She didn't seem to notice I took rather longer to powder my nose than usual and rushed out with pink cheeks and an excited shine in her eyes.

The instant she had left, I opened my purse and pulled out a nice, big, floppy hat. It was the work of a moment to slip out of my dress and reveal the tailcoat and trousers I wore underneath. Quickly, I put on the hat and pulled it as deep into my face as it would go. Stepping out of the powder room, I strode down the corridor.

For one moment, I hesitated in front of the gents' room. Hm...in all my time as Mr Victor Linton, I had never set foot in one of these. Should I? It would make a nice story to share with Amy. And with Ella, if I ever wanted to make her faint on the spot.

Shaking my head, I strode on. Maybe another time. Tonight, I had more important things to do.

Pushing open the door, I stepped out into the ballroom and tipped my hat to Mrs Hester Mahulda Brank. She didn't even glance at the stranger with the floppy hat. Trying my best not to burst out laughing, I marched past several ladies, taking care to bow politely every time. I was a gentleman, after all. And I was quite a success with the ladies. Several of them smiled at me and waved their fans.

Outside, no coaches were standing around at the moment. What was standing around, however, was a big, bearded mountain of a bodyguard with a turban on his head. Good God! Had he followed me all the way here on foot?

Of course he had. Ambrose *Sahib* had commanded it, after all.

Thanking my lucky stars that I'd been clever enough to buy a new tailcoat and hat for this little subterfuge, I headed towards Karim. Why oh why did he have to be just there, in my way? I couldn't get down the street without going past him.

Please don't let him recognise me! Please don't let him recognise me! Please!

If Karim noticed it was me, the game would be up. He would never allow me to go against the order of our dear employer. For some reason, he laboured under the strange delusion that orders from employers had to be obeyed.

I was approaching the corner. Soon. Soon, I would be out of sight and out of danger. Only ten steps.

Five.

Four.

Three.

Two

O—

'Lilliiaaaan!'

Crap!

The harpy's screech from inside the duchess's residence froze my bone marrow—but, thank the Lord, not my feet!

'Hey, you there!' I heard Karim's growl behind me. 'You there with the ridiculous hat! Stop!'

I broke into a run.

MY FIRST TIME

'Pfft...! Pffft...!'

Panting like an asthmatic steam engine, I leant against the brick wall of the house behind me and peered around the corner. No Karim. No aunt. Yay! I had managed to outrun them. If I was especially lucky, they had run into each other, and Aunt Brank would by now be busy trying to marry Karim off to Anne or Maria.

Indulging for a few moments in that sweet fantasy, I gave myself a bit of time to rest. Then I set out towards the Charing Cross Coaching Inn. I suppose I could have embarked towards France straight from the London docks, but that was what Karim would be expecting. Besides, there would be very few passenger ships departing to France at this hour of the night, if any. Yet there would be no shortage of coaches travelling down towards the coast, heading for Dover. Dover was the big port for channel crossings. If I wanted a fast way to get to Mr Rikkard Ambrose, it would be from there.

Halfway to the inn, I stopped at a bank that offered storage, not just in safe deposit boxes, but bigger lockers as well. I had stored a getaway suitcase there a while ago, in case I would ever need to run from my aunt's marriage schemes. Now it would serve a different purpose.

Plus one case and minus one floppy hat (the bloody thing had been a bit too cumbersome), I approached the coaching inn, my heart pounding. For a moment I didn't know why. Why would there be beads of sweat on my forehead?

Then I realised—this was the first time. The first time I had ever been completely on my own. I had been to Brazil and Argentina, to Egypt and the North of England (which is a lot more foreign, than Egypt, trust me). But never once in my life had I been completely on my own. Mr Ambrose had always been with me, and if he hadn't been, Karim had. God! Could it be that I was actually missing that big, bearded mountain?

Get a grip, Lilly! You've only just managed to escape his clutches. Now isn't the time to get soft.

Still—being alone was a scary thought. I didn't even have Ambrose the camel for moral support and face-spitting.

You're a strong woman, Lilly! You can find your way without a camel to spit in your face!

Raising my chin, I marched down the street and knocked on the inn's door. A moment later, it was opened by a portly man with an apron around what had once been a waist, but now was more of a barrel. He smiled down at me from an impressive height.

'Good evening, Guv, good evening! What can I do for ye?'

I cleared my throat. 'Good evening to you, too, Sir. I was wondering whether there's a coach departing for Dover soon.'

'You're in luck, Guv. One's about to arrive 'ere in just 'alf an hour or so. And...wait a minute, let me check my logs...' Bustling over to his counter, he started leafing through a tattered, grease-stained book. 'Ah yes, 'ere we 'ave it! Three seats in the Dover coach are still empty. Looks like there's gonna be plenty of room.'

Breathing a sigh of relief, I hurried over to one of the tables scattered throughout the room and settled down. I hadn't dared to use my disguise twice to reserve seats for me on the coach. If Karim had seen and followed me, my whole plan would have been ruined. It had been a bit of a gamble, hoping that there would still be empty seats. I guess I was in luck that France wasn't as popular a destination nowadays as it had been during the Napoleonic Wars.

'Here you go, Sir.' The innkeeper hurried over and placed a tankard of ale in front of me. 'It won't be long.'

'Thank you.'

In my quiet corner, I watched and sipped my ale while more and more people filed into the inn's common room. Some came from outside, some from rooms on the upper storeys, where they had obviously been staying. Trying not to be too obvious, I scanned the people with whom I would be spending the next few hours. There was a clerk in a cheap suit and bowler hat and a harried look in his eyes that I remembered seeing in the mirror on busy work days, several ladies, a travelling salesmen who made his rounds through the common room trying to sell everyone brushes and cheap perfume, and a grumpy old fellow who muttered to himself in French. None of them looked overtly menacing or dangerous. Still, I was glad I had my revolver in my pocket. You never knew.

'Excuse me, may I sit here?'

Looking up, I saw the harried-looking young man, who was clutching a briefcase in his arms. He glanced anxiously over his shoulder towards the other tables, where the ladies sat scattered, talking animatedly, and gave a little shudder. 'I can't sit anywhere near them. They keep talking like hyperactive parrots, and that salesman is constantly trying to sell them the latest perfume from Paris. I guess he hasn't realised yet that most of us *are going* to Paris.'

'By all means.' I patted the chair next to me. 'Sit down.'

'Thanks so much!' Breathing a sigh of relief, he dropped into the chair. 'I need a spot of sanity among all those females.'

Pulling open his case, he removed multitudes of documents. Without wasting a moment, he started scribbling, his eyes hectically flitting from left to right.

Leaning forward, I glanced over with professional interest. 'Sorry to interrupt, but that should be 21, not 12.' I pointed at the offending line.

'Oh dear! Thank you! Thank you so much. I don't know what Mr Wallace would have said if I'd gotten that wrong.'

'My pleasure. You're doing balance sheets?'

The young man's eyes lit up with the recognition of one tortured soul in hell spotting another sinner. 'Yes! Are you a bank clerk, too?'

'No.' I grinned. 'Worse. Private secretary.'

'Keeping a calendar is torture, isn't it?'

'You have to do that, too?'

'Yes. But Mr Wallace calls me clerk instead of private secretary so he can pay me less.'

'I have a feeling our employers would get along well with each other.' I extended my hand. 'Linton. Victor Linton.'

He took it and shook it. 'Edgar Phelps.' His little chicken chest puffed out with pride. 'I work for Mr Wallace at the Bank of England. And you?'

'Oh, no one that special,' I said, wiping a stray dust moat from my tail coat. 'You may have heard of Rikkard Ambrose?'

He nearly dropped off his chair. I'd had no idea that name-dropping could have such literal effects.

'*The* Rikkard Ambrose?'

'Yes,' I said, glancing down at my fingernails with humility that was about as genuine as an antique statue sold in the East End for two shillings and thruppence.

'My goodness! Working for him must be so interesting.'

A series of scenes flashed before my inner eye—*Mr Ambrose Ambrose pulling me against him in his office and kissing the breath out of me, Mr Ambrose and I bare-skinned under a Brazilian waterfall, Mr Ambrose gazing into my eyes and asking me to be his forever....*

I felt a little tug at my heart.

'You have no idea.'

He sighed. 'I wish I had seen what you have seen. I wish I had experienced what you have experienced.'

I choked, the mental images in my head suddenly not quite so pleasant and a lot stranger than before. 'No, you don't. Trust me, you *really, really* don't.'

'I don't know about that. I bet you can learn so much from a man like Mr Rikkard Ambrose.'

'Definitely. Among other things, how to do sums in your head because he doesn't want to waste paper.' I pointed at a row in his calculations. 'That should be two hundred seventeen, not sixteen.'

'Oh. Blast! Thank you, Mr Linton.'

'Don't mention it. So you're on your way to Dover. Will you be going to Paris, too?'

'Yes.' He beamed, seeming pleased by the idea. 'Mr Wallace had some confidential papers he needed delivered to our branch in the city, so I immediately volunteered.' His eyes took on a dreamy hue. 'It is the city of love, after all.'

I blinked. 'It is?'

'Oh yes. They say even the most hard-hearted of men will behave like a romantic fool in Paris.'

'Do they, now?' I leant back, trying hard not to smile. That was interesting information. This trip might end up being more interesting than I had expected.

Mr Phelps and I continued to chat for quite a bit, and by the time the innkeeper brought us another round of drinks and I had done most of his balance sheet for him, we were fast friends. And, apparently, we were about to become even faster.

'Ladies and gentlemen?' The innkeeper came in from the yard. 'I see the coach arrivin' outside. Please check if ye 'ave any baggage left be'ind. Once the coach is 'ere, the driver will want to leave quickly to keep his schedule, and there won't be no chance to turn around.'

I swallowed.

Right then and there, it sank in. I was really going to do this. I was going to travel several hundred miles, half of that through a country whose bloody language I didn't speak, without a single person to watch my back.

Get a grip, Lilly! He's in danger. He needs you, even if he'll never admit it himself. Go get your man!

We all started climbing into the coach. Luckily, the innkeeper had been right. There indeed was plenty of room. I could even stretch my legs a little. On my left sat Mr Phelps, and on my right was an empty spot just waiting to be used for a little nap later. This was going to be a comfortable ride.

'Is that everyone?' the driver asked. 'Well, then—'

'Wait! Wait for us!'

Turning to the coach's window, I saw two figures rushing towards us. Women—one middle-aged and one younger one, with expensive-looking dresses and ridiculously large cases.

'Do you have reservations?' the driver asked, annoyed.

'No, but we do have money,' the middle-aged woman panted, pulling a purse out of her pocket.

The driver, not one to argue with the root of all evil if it had the face of the queen stamped on it, pulled open the coach door.

'Welcome to the party, ladies.'

Smiling at each other with relief, the two women stepped up to the coach and looked up at the passengers inside. The younger woman, for some reason, seemed to focus her eyes on me. She was pretty, I supposed, with pale skin, a slim figure and light brown hair that fell all the way down her back, but the way she was staring at me was rather creepy. I nodded at her and smiled. Still, she didn't look away. She wiggled her eyebrows. Then she cleared her throat.

My brow furrowed in concern. 'Are you ill? Would you like a cough drop?'

Mr Phelps nudged me in the ribs. 'I believe,' he whispered, 'she wishes for a gentleman to help her into the coach.'

'She does? So why aren't any of them moving?'

'Um...well...'

Oh crap. Right. *I* was a gentleman.

Well, 'man' maybe, in this getup. I didn't know about 'gentle'. Still, I extended my arm and helped the two ladies climb up the steps they would have been perfectly able to climb themselves if they'd just set their minds to it. Then I saw that their luggage was still standing outside.

'You forgot your suitcases,' I pointed out helpfully.

The older lady gave me a cool look. I looked back. Mr Phelps gave me another nudge in the ribs.

'I believe it's a gentleman's duty to help a lady with her luggage.'

'Oh, it is, is it?'

Sighing, I slid out of the coach. The old dame gave me a triumphant look, and the girl chirped, 'Thank you so much, Sir. We are ever so much obliged to you.'

'No problem,' I told her, took hold of her suitcase—and instantly revised my opinion. It was a problem. A bloody heavy problem.

'What the heck did you put in there? Half a brick house? A collection of medieval suits of armour?'

The older lady gave me a supreme look that reminded me of Aunt Brank. Flicking open her fan, she gave me a wave that said, 'Get on with it, will you?'

God, did I miss being able to be rude!

Groaning curses in several languages that I hoped the ladies couldn't understand, I dragged the cases towards the luggage rack at the back of the coach. Bloody hell! Being a gentleman was too much for any sane person! Why did those women have to be such lazy, good-for-nothing parasites, who were nothing but a bane on the life of an honest, hard-working man and—

Then I realised what I was thinking and dropped a suitcase on my big toe.

'Ouch! Ow! Damn and blast it to hell!'

That, to judge by the outraged whispers coming from the carriage, the older lady had heard and understood. Right now, I didn't care. She could go boil her head in wine sauce, if she wanted!

Huffing and puffing, I pushed the last case into its place and returned to the carriage door, wiping sweat off my forehead. Only when I sank down in my seat and wanted to lean back for a nice little nap did I notice that the seat beside me was now occupied. The girl smiled up at me.

'Thank you so much, Mr...?'

'Linton,' I panted and then realised that she'd just finagled an introduction out of me. Damn! 'Victor Linton. How do you do, Miss...?'

'Emilia Harse. A pleasure to make your acquaintance, Mr Linton.' The girl gazed up at me with big adoring eyes. I don't really know how she managed it, seeing as she was technically taller than I was. Impressive. 'I'm so glad we have a big, strong man like you along with us on this journey.'

The older lady—probably her mother—gave a sniff. 'Yes, very strong indeed, Emilia. I hope you did not break anything in my suitcase when you dropped it, Mr Linton. There are some very precious valuables in there.'

'Don't worry,' I reassured her with a saccharine smile. 'Luckily, its fall was broken by my foot. Although it felt the other way around.'

She sniffed again and hid her face behind an issue of what I'd like to do it. *Punch.*[1]

The girl—Emilia—glanced over at me. She looked as though, for some reason, she wanted to talk to me. So I quickly turned towards Mr Phelps and started a conversation about balance sheets, guaranteed to bore anyone within a radius

---

[1] There actually was a magazine called *Punch* in Great Britain during the Victorian period. It proved to be quite a long-lived publication, shutting down only in the 1990s. *Punch* was one of the earliest publications of its kind and helped to create the principle of political caricature.

of fifty yards to death. The strategy worked. Soon, young Emilia appeared to have lost all interest, and I could settle down for the nap I so badly needed. The excitement of my flight had taken its toll, and despite the rumbling of the coach, I drifted off quickly.

When I awoke, jolted awake by a pothole, we had left the city behind us. Emilia and her mother both seemed as sleepy as I had been before my little rest. Mr Phelps was still frantically calculating, and the other passengers were dimly staring into the emptiness that develops wherever people are squeezed together who don't know one another well enough to talk.

Outside, a moonlit landscape was whizzing past. With every passing minute, we were moving farther away from home. I glanced at the other people in the carriage. I didn't really know any of them. Not even Mr Phelps. And it was a long way to France.

Suddenly, I felt very alone.

Instinctively, I leant over to the window and looked back to where the glittering lights of good old London Town were just visible in the dark. A shiver went down my back. The thought of being hundreds of miles away, completely on my own...

Don't be ridiculous, Lilly! I told myself. *You're still in England. This isn't the South American jungle, where jaguars could leap at you from behind every bush! This is a civilised country. What could possibly happen?*

That question was answered a moment later, when the coach came to a screeching halt, and someone stuck a pistol through the window.

'Hands up!' A gruff voice demanded. 'Your money or your life!'

A LADY'S HERO

Your money or your life...

It told me that maybe I had been spending a bit too much time in the company of Mr Rikkard Ambrose that I actually had to think for a moment about which to pick.

Finally, I decided: neither. But before I could grab the arm of the bandit and slam it against the wall, a horrific scream pierced my ear drums and I instinctively clapped my hands over my ears. Bloody hell! That Emilia Harse had a set of lungs on her!

'Stop screaming!' came a slightly panicked voice from outside. Whoever was trying to rob us, didn't seem exactly to be an expert. 'Don't move! Hands above your head! Get out of the coach!'

I raised a hand. 'Um...which first? Don't move, or get out of the coach?'

'Shut up! Get out of the coach, now!'

The ladies immediately jumped to their feet—just what I had been hoping for. Behind their voluminous skirts, I could safely duck down, pull the revolver out of my pocket and conceal it in my sleeve. Thank God I had opted for the handy, purse-sized model.

'Out!' the highwayman demanded. 'Move!'

Of course. Happy to oblige.

The doors swung open, and we all climbed out into the cool night, the ladies wailing and pleading all the while for the bandit to have mercy, and the salesman pleading not to be deprived of his precious sample case. I, on the other hand, was keeping silent. My eyes were sweeping over the mounted figure with the gun. He truly was the real deal. Dark clothes, a fashionable hat, a black cloth tied in front of his face—a real, honest-to-God highwayman.

'Raise your hands, all of you!'

Mr Phelps raised his hands.

Miss Harse raised her hands.

I raised my hand—the one with the gun in it. I aimed.

Bam!

Beside me, Miss Harse screamed again. But this time, she wasn't the only one. Bellowing like a skewered donkey, the highwayman clutched his shoulder and slid off his horse. He hit the ground with a dull thud. Instantly, I rushed forward, kicked away his weapon and aimed the barrel of my gun between his eyes.

'Don't move, you lowlife scum! One twitch, and I'll bow your head off!'

I'd always been dying to say that. The heroes in Western adventure novels you could buy on the street corner for a few pennies always said that when they had bested the villain. All I was missing was a sheriff's star on my chest.

'Ladies and gentlemen?' I glanced at my fellow passengers, who were all still standing with their arms in the air and their mouths wide open. 'Would one of you be so kind as to fetch the miscreant's weapon?'

Nobody moved.

'Get the gun! Now!'

Mr Phelps staggered forward and bent to retrieve the weapon with two fingers.

'It helps if you put the safety back on,' I advised.

He yelped, dropped the gun, and when it didn't go off, bent to pick it up again and carefully put the safety in place.

I cocked my head at him. 'Let me guess—you're not a gun expert.'

'Never touched one in my life! This is a civilised country, Mr Linton. Who needs to be armed in this day and age?'

'We,' I pointed out.

'Oh. Um...I suppose that's right.'

Turning back to the highwayman, I gave him a friendly kick in the ribs.

'Hey, you!'

He gave a yelp of pain, clutching the spot on his pretty coat where blood was beginning to seep through the cloth.

'You shot me!' he exclaimed, as if he'd never heard of anything so scandalous in his life. After all, who could possibly consider doing something as crass as shooting a dangerous criminal in self-defence? 'You shot me!'

'Yes, and there are still plenty of spots without holes to aim for. So get up on your feet, will you? Chop, chop!'

I had never seen a man jump to his feet so fast, with the possible exception of Rikkard Ambrose when he smelled charities or creditors approaching. Jabbing my gun into his back and feeling quite fabulous about myself, I forced the man to climb onto the roof of the coach.

'What now?' he demanded.

I grinned.

'Someone,' I called down to the others who were still standing there gaping up at me. A few still hadn't lowered their hands. 'Throw me a bit of rope!'

Soon, the cursing highwayman was secured, with both arms tied to the luggage rack on top the carriage. Jumping down, I wiped my hands on my trousers—and only then noticed the looks of my fellow passengers. They were gazing at me as if I had sprouted horns and a spare set of muscular arms.

'Um...and you're sure you are a secretary?' young Mr Phelps enquired.

'Of course.' I twirled my revolver. 'Do you doubt my qualifications?'

'Not at all! Not at all!' Raising his hand again, he quickly retreated a few steps. 'I doubt nothing whatsoever. Everything is perfectly fine.'

'Good. Well, I suppose we'd better continue then. We've lost enough time as it is. We don't want to have too much of a delay. I'm sure the carriage company would prefer us not to derail their schedule, eh?'

I nudged the leg of the coachman who, during all this time, had been sitting on his box, frozen as a statue.

'Err...um...schedule? Right. Schedule. Of course.' He cleared his throat. 'Everyone, please get in. We'll be continuing on our way.' His eyes darted to me, and to the gun I realised I was still holding in my hand. 'That is, if that's all right with you, Sir. I mean, we can wait here a little, or have a picnic, if you prefer.'

I grinned. 'Maybe later. Right now, I think we should be going.'

'Of course, Sir! Right away, Sir!'

Sir...

My grin widened until it nearly split my face apart. Ah, what a sweet feeling. Did Mr Ambrose feel like this all the time? No wonder he insisted on tyrannising his employees. Being the tough man was fun. Even if, technically, you didn't possess all anatomic requirements for the job.

Whistling, I got into the carriage, and it set off. I was in such a good mood that it took me a few moments to realise not all my fellow passengers were gazing at me with a mix of fear and apprehension. There was one among them who had a very different look on her face.

'Oh...oh, Mr Linton!'

Crap. No, please don't let this be what I think it is! Crap, Crap, Crap!

Miss Emilia Harse, her big eyes shining with adoration, leant across the bench towards me. 'Mr Linton, you were so brave! You acted when nobody else had the courage to protect me.'

'Well, I wouldn't say I was protecting *you*, per se. It was more about—'

'And modest, too!' A blush rose to her cheeks, and she gifted me with a smile I would dearly have liked to return to the gift shop. 'Oh, Mr Linton. You're the first true man I've met in my whole life.'

'Then I pity you,' I told her earnestly, edging away. 'From the bottom of my heart.'

She didn't exactly get the intended meaning.

'No need.' Ignoring her mother's indrawn breath, she reached out to touch my hand. 'Not now that I've met you.'

Oh God, please help me. I know I've never believed in you, but please prove me wrong and work a miracle. A nice thunderbolt to strike me dead would do, thanks.

How could it possibly get any worse than this?

A moment later I found out, when Mrs Harse leant forward and smiled at Emilia and me, motherly love shining in her eyes.

'I must say, I am also very glad that fate caused our paths to intersect, Mr Linton. At first I wasn't sure about you, but you've shown yourself to be a fine man.'

Her eyes wandered from me to Emilia and back again, and she nodded in approval. In *approval*!

Satan, if God can't help me, maybe you're available? I need help now!

Thank heavens we would be going our separate ways soon. They'd be going wherever they were planning to, while I'd be off onto the channel ferry. The sooner I put an ocean between me and Miss Emilia Harse, the better!

~~**~*~*

'Do Re Mi Fa Sol La Ti Do....Do Re Mi Fa Sol La Ti Do...'

Groaning, I pressed my hands over my ears and tried to ignore the pounding in my head. An ocean between me and Miss Harse wasn't nearly far enough! She had been going on like this all morning, and I desperately wanted to catch a few more hours of sleep before the ferry's departure. Normally, I would have marched down the coaching inn's corridor, kicked open the door to Miss Emilia Harse's room, and sung, *'Do Re Me The Fa Vor To Shut Up!'*

But, considering the adoring way the girl had gazed at me as we'd exited the coach a few hours earlier and the authorities had come running to pluck the highwayman from the roof, I had better keep my distance from Miss Emilia. If I came to her bedroom at this hour, she might just get the wrong idea.

What was the bloody girl singing for, anyway? Was she training to be a banshee?

Stuffing my head under the pillow, I tried to ignore the noise and think about more pleasant things. Like what would happen when I saw Mr Ambrose again.

Can't you guess, Lilly? He'll be overjoyed! What man wouldn't be when unexpectedly seeing the girl whom he loves most in the world, and who just turned down his proposal like a plate of cold porridge?

All right, maybe I had better think about something else. How about...how about...Ella! Yes, Ella was a safe topic. She would be with Edmund, probably, blissfully happy, anticipating a long and happy life together with the man of her dreams.

Which is a lot more than you'll have, seeing as you turned down yours.

Sometimes I really hated my inner voice.

'Do Re Mi Fa Sol La Ti Do...'

But not quite as much as I hated some other voices.

Finally, blessedly, the singing ceased, and I was able to drift off into an uneasy sleep. I dreamt of Rikkard Ambrose singing a tragic aria in soprano about his faithless love, who had left him for her feminist principles. When I had awakened and thanked God on my knees that it had just been a horrible nightmare, I cautiously snuck to the door and listened. No noises. No voices. Nothing. Apparently, Miss and Mrs Harse were doing what I had done—taking a well-deserved nap before the next stage of their journey, wherever they were going.

This was it. This was my chance!

Jumping up and stuffing all my things into my suitcase, I carefully opened the door and peeked outside. No one in sight.

Cautiously, I tiptoed down the corridor. Thank heavens I had broken Mr Ambrose's cardinal rule and paid the landlord in advance. It was worth it if I could get out of here without a teary goodbye scene with Miss Emilia Harse.

The inn was quiet. While most of Dover was already up and about, most passengers, to judge by the noise coming through some of the thin doors, seemed content to snore the day away. I reached the front door without encountering anyone. Outside, the dull grey sky of a beautiful English morning greeted me, accompanied by the smell of freedom, seaweed, and rotten fish. Following the latter, I easily found my way to the harbour.

I'm coming, Mr Ambrose!

Several steamships lined the docks, interspersed with smaller fishing boats and cutters. Rising above the smaller masts, like castle towers above the treetops, I could even see the huge masts of a great sailing ship. My eyes wandered up and, there, at the mast, I saw flying the flag of the East India Company.

Shuddering, I quickly turned away. That was one ship I would not be boarding.

Turning my head this way and that, I wandered down the docks, searching. After only five minutes, I spotted it: a small steamer painted in cheerful blue and green, on its side emblazoned the name the innkeeper had told me: *Rob Roy*,[2] Scottish hero, and today, my hero as well, if all went as planned.

Hastily I marched up to the guard beside the gangplank.

'Please tell me that you're going to France and you're weighing anchor soon,' I demanded, throwing an anxious glance back at the inn. No sign of Emilia yet. 'Please!'

'Err...aye, we're leavin'. In about fifteen minutes, guv.'

'Wonderful! Brilliant! You're my saviour!'

And, pressing my ticket into his hand along with a tip that would have made Mr Ambrose faint, I hurried onto the ship and ducked behind the closest funnel. Sinking against the heated metal, I let out a sigh of relief. Safe!

---

[2] There actually was a channel ferry of this name. It was the first steam boat to ever make the crossing, and was later bought by the French postal service, renamed 'Henri IV' and put to use as a passenger ferry between England and France.

Well, almost.

With bated breath I waited while more passengers streamed on board, and sailors loaded bags of mail. The same bags that, not so long ago, must have contained my own letters to Mr Ambrose. Finally, a bell sounded, and the captain stepped out on the upper deck.

'Ladies and gentlemen, please step back from the gangplank. We'll be casting off soon. If any passengers are still on land and do not wish to miss the ferry from Dover to Calais, please board now. We shall be departing in approximately five minutes.'

A harried-looking little man sprinted on board, but everyone else seemed to be ready for departure. Especially me.

Get it over with! Go on! Move!

Finally, the bell sounded again.

'Ladies and gentlemen, please step away from the gangplank and hold fast. This ferry from Dover to Calais is now departing. May we have calm seas and fair weather.'

With a deep rumble, the steam engines sprang to life. Smoke spewed from the funnel high above my head. The sailors raised the gangplank, and slowly, ever so slowly, we started to drift away from the docks, gathering speed, wind blowing ever faster in my face.

It's really happening. I'm going. I'm leaving, all on my own.

Stepping out from behind the funnel, I slowly approached the railing and gazed back at the quickly receding city of Dover, its beaches, docks and white cliffs gleaming in the sun. A broad smile began to spread over my face. I had done it. I had gotten away and was heading towards France. Towards Mr Ambrose. And far, far away from Miss Emilia Ha—

'Mr Linton! What a pleasure to see you here!'

I froze.

Slowly, torturously slowly, I turned around. I didn't want to see what I knew I would see once I faced towards the ship—but as usual, the universe didn't give a flying fig about my preferences.

'So you're on your way to France, too?' Beaming with happiness, Emila Harse rushed towards me, little hearts blinking in her eyes. 'How wonderful! I was so terribly upset when we had to board the ferry this morning, thinking we were leaving you behind. And now look what's happened! Isn't this splendid?'

'A pleasant coincidence,' the mother agreed, a calculating look in her eyes that I knew all too well from my Aunt Brank. It was the same look she directed at eligible bachelors. I nearly jumped over the side of the ship. 'A pleasant coincidence indeed.'

'Coincidence?' Stepping towards me, Emilia touched my hand. Why shouldn't I jump over the side? Surely it couldn't be so hard to swim to Calais? Wasn't there a fellow who had tried to swim the English Channel and only drowned just before he reached the shore? That was a risk worth taking, surely! 'It must be fate that has led us together.'

Fate, I'm going to kill you.

FEEDING THE HOMELESS AND THE BLACKMAILERS

As a child, I loved playing hide and seek. We had our own special family rules, and they were quite simple: I would put a frog in my aunt's boot. Her screech was the signal for the game to begin. I would hide, and she would seek (screaming with rage and waving a carpet beater). The thought made me smile. Ah, what fun times we had as a family...

Now, however, things were different.

'Mr Linton? Yoo-hoo, Mr Linton, where are you?'

Holding my breath, I cowered behind the lifeboat and prayed she wouldn't think to look there.

Just let her walk by. Just let her walk by, please...

The tarpaulin over the lifeboat lifted just a bit and a curious pair of eyes peeked out.

'Are ye a stowaway, too?' whispered a voice that hadn't encountered puberty yet.

'No,' I whispered. 'I'm a passenger! Please, can I come hide in there with you?'

The eye blinked. 'Err....why?'

'Yoo-hoo, Mr Linton? Come out, come out, wherever you are. You're such a tease. I love that about you.'

'Long story!' I hissed. 'Can't explain now. Please, just please! Let me hide in there?'

The young stowaway considered.

'Two shillings,' he finally decided. A hand emerged from the tarpaulin and opened.

'You expect me to *pay* you?'

'Hey, Mister, ye're the one who's wanting to share me hiding place.'

'*Your* hiding place? You are the stowaway here! I could just call the captain and—'

'—draw attention to yerself,' the boy finished. He sounded as if he was enjoying himself. 'And I'm sure we don't want that, now, would we? Two shillings and sixpence.'

'*What?* You conniving, greedy little—'

'Two shillings and eightpence.'

'All right, all right! But only because you remind me of someone I know.' Quickly, I dug around for a few coins in my pocket and pressed them into the greedy little hand. It withdrew with admirable speed, and I followed, crawling under the tarpaulin. Inside, I encountered a shadowy little form with a dirty face and gap-toothed grin.

'So...' enquired the boy. 'If ye ain't no stowaway, why are ye hiding? Smuggling? Murder? Piracy?'

He sounded hopeful.

'God, no! Nothing like that.'

'Oh. Um...but maybe you know some smugglers or pirates? I'd love to be a pirate one day! If you could tell me where to join—'

'Be quiet, will you?' I hissed. 'She'll hear us!'

'She? We're hiding from a *girl*?'

Just in time, I lunged forward and grabbed him by the scruff of the neck, or the little brat would have stuck his head out from under the tarpaulin and given us away.

'Let me go!' he protested. 'I can't hide from a girl! That's cowardly. Girls are harmless.'

'You, young man,' I told him, 'have a lot to learn. Now keep your mouth shut!'

'Or what?'

'Or you won't get the other shilling I've got in my pocket.'

That did the trick. Grumbling, he fell into reluctant silence. So did I, and we waited while Miss Emilia Harse passed by outside, calling my name. When she was gone, I waited another few minutes, just to be sure, then slid out from under my hiding place and handed the boy his shilling.

'Can I come hiding here again?' I asked. 'Things are rather desperate.'

He grinned up at me. 'Depends. 'ave you got more money?'

'Yes, but you won't get any! Wouldn't do you any good, anyway. You're heading to France, you little worm, remember? They don't use pounds and shillings over there.'

'Oh.' His face fell. 'Right.'

'But,' I continued, 'I might have something even better for you.'

'Better than money? What's better than money?'

I grinned. 'Can't you guess?'

~~**~*~*

A quarter of an hour later I sauntered into the ferry's dining room and settled down at a nice, quiet corner table. A waiter came hurrying towards me.

'Good afternoon, Sir. Have you made your choice yet?'

Cocking my head, I studied the menu. 'That depends. Is the food included in the ticket price?'

Looking up, I saw the waiter gave me a considering look. A look that said, *How much could this little fellow eat, after all?* He smiled. 'Yes, of course, Sir. All included in our service.'

'Very well. Then I would like...the roast duck, as an appetizer, next the French pie and the chicken fricassee, then the tomato salad, the strawberries in cream, and the steak and kidney pie, followed by the hare soup, without any hairs in it, please, and the mutton cutlets, the braised beef, the turbot in lobster sauce, the spring chicken, the roast quarter of lamb – or all four quarters, if you have them – and, as a little dessert, two apple pies and a chocolate cake, please.'

I glanced up to see the waiter standing there with his mouth open.

'Well?' I enquired. 'What are you waiting for?'

The poor waiter hurried off towards the galley to make the cook into a galley slave.

The rumbling of a stomach came from under the tablecloth. 'How long will it be until the grub comes, guv?'

I kicked the table. 'Be quiet, you little greedy-guts. You'll get your food.'

'Aye aye, Sir!'

The table fell silent.

I was just about to lean back in my chair and pop open the bottle of wine waiting for me on the table when the doors to the dining room opened, and in stepped Miss Harse. Her eyes found me and lit up with joy.

My first instinct was to jump up from the table and out the nearest porthole.

Stay where you are, Lilly! You don't run. You've got backbone, and if you don't, you'd damn well better get some! You're safe here. She wouldn't dare to maul you in front of all the dinner guests.

Probably.

Well...hopefully.

The lady approached my table with a broad smile. I forced an answering smile onto my face, for the first time in my life understanding why it was so hard for Mr Ambrose to do that he didn't bother most of the time.

'Miss Harse. What a pleasure to see you,' I lied.

The table giggled. I gave it another kick.

Miss Harse blushed. She damn well *blushed*! And then—bloody hell!—she stopped in front of the table.

'Yes. A true pleasure for me as well, Mr Linton.'

And she still stood there, without showing a sign of sitting down, although she clearly wanted to. Why not?

'Ask her to sit down, you dummy!' hissed my table.

'What was that?' Miss Harse asked.

'Nothing. Nothing at all.' I shook my head and felt like slapping myself. *Of course! Those gentlemanly rules again. She's probably waiting for me to ask her to sit down, and to pull her chair out.*

Well, time for me to do the thing I was simply fabulous at: being rude.

Leisurely crossing my arms behind my head, I leant back and gave the lady a charming smile.

'Wonderful weather we have today, don't we?'

She blinked, and looked from me to the chair and back. This was not what she'd been expecting to hear.

'Err...yes.'

'Oh dear me, where did I leave my manners? Won't you take a—'

'Yes, please!'

'—nut?'

She froze in mid-motion.

'Pardon?'

'A nut.' I reached for the bowl of nuts and grapes standing on the table and held it out to her. 'As a little appetizer.'

'Oh. Um. Yes, thank you.'

Still she remained standing, unable to sit down, but clearly unwilling to walk away. With severe difficulty, I managed to suppress a grin. Boy, this was fun! More than that, it was genius! Why hadn't I thought of this before? I could just be abominably rude to her, and soon enough she would leave me alone.

You're a genius, Lilly! Just act like an arrogant, patronising, chauvinistic son of a bachelor. After all, who in their right mind would want to be with a man like that?

With an arrogant smirk, I crossed my legs under the table. Something tugged at my trousers. Damn! I didn't need a street urchin and stowaway trying to remind me of my gentlemanly manners! Especially not since I had only just gotten rid of them. With my foot, I gave the squirt a gentle shove, telling him to keep his nose out of my business.

Time to start your career as a chauvinistic bastard, Lilly!

'I'm really looking forward to seeing France again, you know.' I informed Miss Harse.

'Again?' The girl's eyes widened. 'You mean you've been there before?'

'Of course. I've been all over the world.' Dismissively, I flicked a speck of dust off my tailcoat. Heck, being arrogant was fun! Time for a bit of chauvinism. 'But France is one of my favourite places to be. French girls are simply...*oh la la.*'

'Mr Linton!' The scandalised girl covered her mouth with one hand, a fierce blush rising to her cheeks. 'You shouldn't say these things in front of a lady.'

I gave her an arrogant smirk, the kind of which usually earned my suitors a kick on the shins. 'Well, as the French say, *Vous êtes une botte asymétrique liée à une courgette.*'[3]

'Mr Linton!' Blushing furiously, she took a step backwards. An impressive result, considering I was quite sure she had no idea what I had just said, and incidentally, neither had I. 'You wicked, wicked man.'

Her blush deepened. Oh yes. I was making quite a good start in my career as a blackguard, rake and general arsehole. Only...why hadn't she run away yet? She was still standing there, her eyes resting on me with strange fascination. I supposed I would have to use more drastic measures.

'Well, it's been nice chatting with you. But now run along little girl, will you?' With one leisurely hand, I waved her off. 'I think my meal is coming, and you're blocking my view of the ocean.'

Wow. I really was talented at being a chauvinistic arsehole—almost as though I had rehearsed the role. How could that be?

Oh well, who cared? As long as my patented arsehole method would get rid of Miss Emilia Harse, what did it matter?

'Y-your view?' The girl blinked. 'Oh. Of course.' Giving me a shy smile, she curtsied. 'I'll go find my mother. I hope we meet again, Mr Linton. Very soon.'

And with another blush, she hurried away, while I stared after her, dumbfounded. She hoped we'd meet *again*? *Very soon*?

Why?

'Gorblimey!' A dirty little head emerged from under the table, gazing after Miss Harse. 'She's got it bad for you, guv. You played her good!'

---

[3] You are a skewed boot tied to a zucchini.

'What do you mean, I played her?' I blinked at him. 'I was an arrogant bastard! My manners were worse than those of Attila the Hun with a hangover. She would have to be insane to want to spend another minute in my company.'

The little boy glanced up at me—then gave a cackle. 'You're serious guv, aren't ye? Ye God! Ye've got a lot to learn about women.'

I glowered at him. 'Get back under the table before I change my mind about the food.'

He stuck his tongue out and vanished with another grin.

Shaking my head, I grabbed for a paper and put up a dignified wall between me and insolent stowaways. Me, not knowing anything about women? Ha! Ridiculous!

'Sir?'

Lowering my paper, I spotted the approaching waiter swaying under the weight of my meal. 'Here you are, Sir,' panted the poor man, dropping the first three courses in my lap. Somehow, I managed to slow their descent and steer them onto the table.

'Thank you.'

Straightening, the waiter wiped sweat off his forehead. 'Will you be needing anything else, Sir?'

I gave him a smile. 'Well, yes. The next course, in about ten minutes.'

'*Ten minutes*?' With wide eyes, the poor man stared down at the three humongous plates in front of me, stuffed to the brim with food. 'But...'

'Oh, that?' I glanced at the plates while a small hand sneaked out from under the table and, unbeknownst to the waiter, snuck a slice of French pie from my plate. 'Don't worry. I have a feeling it'll be gone quite soon.'

'Y-yes, Sir. As you wish, Sir.'

The waiter stumbled away, and I took a sip of soup. From under the table came the sound of energetic chewing, reminiscent of a beaver determined to fell a whole forest. Soon, the last bite was gone, and a small hand appeared to snatch another slice of pie.

'That young drapery miss really fancies you, mister.'[4]

I gave the table a censorious look. 'Shut up and eat.'

'So,' he said, completely ignoring my order, 'have you prigged her yet?'

'*Excuse me*?'

'Prigged. You know? Docked her, done the beast with two backs—'

'I know what it means! The question is, how do you? How old are you exactly? And no, I haven't! And I'm not going to!'

'Oh.' For a moment, thoughtful silence reigned under the table. 'Do you mind if I give it a try, then? She's quite easy on the eyes, and maybe...'

I kicked the table.

'Eat! And be quiet!'

'Yes, Sir! Right away, Sir.'

---

[4] Drapery Miss – a Victorian expression, defined by the poet Lord Byron, as 'a pretty, a high-born, a fashionable young female, furnished by her milliner with a wardrobe upon credit, to be repaid, when married, by her husband'.

I put the rest of my 'be-an-arsehole' plan into effect that very day. When I met Miss Harse and her mother on the promenade deck later that day, I gave no greeting, but instead marched past them in sullen silence.

'Mr Linton!'

I turned. Apparently, my egregious lack of manners wasn't sufficient. Oh well...time to fire a bigger calibre.

'Mr Linton, have you heard? The captain said we'll reach the French coast tomorrow. Oh, I'm so excited.'

'Well, I'm not,' I snapped. 'And neither should you be!'

Taken aback, she retreated a step. 'Mr...Mr Linton?'

'France isn't as safe as England.' *Where you get robbed by highwaymen on public roads.* 'Two women travelling alone? It would be insupportable!' I let my derisive gaze slide over them, channelling every chauvinistic bastard I had ever heard. 'Women are weak. Women are defenceless without a strong man to protect them. You should turn around the moment we land in France.'

Wow. It was amazing how easy it was to spout this sort of nonsense while you were wearing this getup. Maybe it was something about the big pair of socks stuffed down the front of my trousers. They seemed to have taken on a mind of their own.

Regardless of where they'd come from though, I could see that my words were having the desired effect. Emilia's cheeks had paled, and her mother had taken a step backwards.

'Mr Linton...Mr Linton, are you...'

A total and utter asshole? Yes!

'...concerned for me?'

What? No! No, no, nononono!

'That's so sweet!' Not giving a damn that people were watching, Emilia rushed forward and hugged me as if I were a big piece of solid chocolate. Good God! If she felt the socks...

'Oh, Mr Linton!' Glancing up at me, her cheeks reddened, and a smile tugged at the corners of her mouth. 'You rogue!'

I want to die. I want to die right here and now. Spontaneous combustion would be nice. Or maybe some kind of horribly painful, quick-acting poison?

'Don't worry,' she whispered. 'I won't be travelling through France alone. I'll have you to protect me.'

And with a wink and a giggle, she scurried away. Her mother sent a beneficent smile my way, and I felt a sudden yearning for the good old days, when prospective mothers-in-law had despised me at first sight. Good God! Did I make for a better son-in-law than a daughter-in-law? Would I have to get a permanent pair of socks?

Shrugging off the horrifying thought, I quickly made my way across the deck. As soon as I was out of sight of the two harpies, I started to run and didn't stop until I reached my destination. Panting, I kicked the side of the lifeboat.

The tarpaulin lifted a fraction of an inch. 'Yes?'
'Move over!' I commanded. 'I'm coming in.'

I sat in the dark, happily breathing in the smell of rotten fish. The time in the lifeboat, in spite of the smell and the boy's sharp elbows, was a blissful respite. Yet sooner or later, the problem of Miss Emilia Harse would have to be dealt with. What could I do? She had me backed into a corner. She was a woman on the prowl, and I was nothing but a poor, hapless gentleman, defenceless in her clutches.

My last hope was that, surely, the two ladies weren't planning on going to Paris, like I was. After all, there were hundreds of towns all over France, and a whole continent of people beyond. What were the chances of them going to the same city I was?

I couldn't deal with distractions like this now. Mr Ambrose was in trouble, and that was what I had to focus on. I had to concentrate on getting to him, not getting some infatuated country damsel to keep her hands off my extra pair of socks!

Surely, they wouldn't go to Paris.
Surely.
Probably.

THE ADMIRAL'S OPERATION

'Mr Linton! What a happy surprise! We didn't know you would be travelling to Paris, too.'

Excruciatingly slowly, I raised my eyes until, through the coach window, I gazed into the beaming faces of Miss and Mrs Harse. The sight led me to revise my earlier plans. I wasn't just going to kill Fate. I was going to throw the witch into a deep, dark dungeon and think up some nice tortures for her before ending her misery.

'And I'm here, too.' Stretching up, Mr Edgar Phelps waved at me over the ladies' heads. Winking at me and pointing at Emilia, he mouthed, *I think she really likes you. Go for it!*

'How fabulous,' I groaned. 'And here was I thinking this was going to be a boring trip.'

Beaming, Mr Phelps slid aside, making room for me between him and Miss Emilia Harse. How nice of him. I wondered, was it legal to shoot people for good manners?

'So,' I said, for lack of anything better to say as I settled in the only free seat. 'I heard correctly? You're travelling to Paris, as well?'

Please say no. Please say no. Even if it means that my hearing was malfunctioning earlier, please say no!

'Yes.' The girl beamed up at me, stars sparkling in her eyes. 'I don't know whether you heard...I...well...'

A blush rose to her cheek.

'Heard what?' I enquired, curious against my better judgement.

'My singing,' she said with downcast eyes. 'I was singing in my room the other day.'

'Oh, that.' I nodded, a painful grimace flicking over my face. 'Trust me, I heard.' *And so did half of Dover, probably.*

'Well...' Taking a deep breath, she raised her eyes again, and suddenly there was fire in her gaze and steel in her backbone. I blinked, taken slightly aback. I hadn't seen this side of her before. 'I *love* to sing. Especially opera. It's my dream to become a prima donna and sing on the great stages in the city of love. To perform *The Marriage of Figaro* or *Fidelio* in front of all of Paris...'

She gave a dreamy sigh.

I considered her words carefully.

'You want to become a famous singer? In France?'

She nodded earnestly. 'The French operas are the best.'

'And, um....' How to put this? She obviously had not yet considered the re-percussions. 'You don't think there will be any problems when a French gentleman steps onto the stage and announces that Miss Emilia Harse will be singing for them next?'

She was still looking at me, complete innocence in her eyes. 'Problems? What problems?'

Oh my God. The poor girl had no idea.

'Err...none. None whatsoever.' Clearing my throat, I struggled mightily not to burst out laughing. Had she ever heard a French accent before? Probably not. Oh the poor, poor, girl. Still, who was I to ruin her dream?

I patted her shoulder encouragingly.

'Go to Paris.' I told her with a smile. 'Sing to your heart's content. Every girl should live her dream.'

Her eyes lit up with joy and...crap! More than just joy. Lots more. 'You really think that?'

Crap, crap, crap! Why couldn't I keep my trap shut? I was supposed to be an arsehole! An overbearing, arrogant, dictatorial male asshole! I couldn't suddenly start being nice and reasonable to females. To judge by the look she was directing at me...*crap!*

'Oh, Mr Linton, I can't tell you how much it means to me that you believe in me. Aside from my dear mother, you're the only one, the only one who's ever...'

Trailing off, she gently touched my hand, making her meaning abundantly clear. Groaning, I sank back into my seat. This was going to be a very long drive.

~~**~*~*

'...and three hundred divided by six makes fifty.'

'By Jove, you're right! I can't imagine how I missed that mistake.'

Neither could I. But I was kind enough not to mention that. Although he didn't know it, Mr Phelps was doing me a huge favour by leeching off my math skills. Nothing was so effective at putting people to sleep as watching other people solve complex math problems. Miss Harse's eyelids were already drooping, and the rest of the passengers had long since started snoring. It wasn't long before the young lady joined them, and Mr Phelps did, too.

'Oh dear.' Blinking, I gazed down on his head, resting on top of my calculations. I hadn't reckoned on my strategy working quite this well. Carefully, I shoved him aside so he slumped against the door, and concentrated on the math again. It was soothing and familiar, and kept my mind—at least for a while—from the thing it really wanted to worry about.

Him.

With every passing minute, I was getting closer. With every passing mile, the moment was approaching when I'd have to face him, and whatever trouble he was in. Math was a welcome distraction, filling my head with number after number.

Finally, the last one was deducted, the last zero dealt with, and I was left only with the snoring of the other passengers and the landscape rushing past outside to distract me. A landscape which, I noticed, was already growing considerably more urban. We were quickly approaching Paris and, along with Paris, Mr Rikkard Ambrose.

A shiver travelled down my spine as I remembered our last exchange.

'*Mr Ambrose, where are you going? Where?*'

'*It's better if you don't know, Miss Linton. Dalgliesh will be waiting for just such a chance. Where I'll be going...he'll be lying in ambush.*'

'*And you think that argument will convince me to let you go?*'

'*No. It'll tell you why I cannot take you with me.*'

With a grim smile, I glanced down at the slip of paper in my hand onto which, under threat of horrible torture, Karim had scribbled an address. An address that was only ever meant for me to send mail to—not to visit in person.

Ha!

I'm not that easy to get rid of, Mr Ambrose. I'll have your back, whether you want it or not. And, since your derrière is attached to your back, I'll use the opportunity for some long overdue kicking!

Still, my desire to be with Mr Ambrose, and my foot's desire to meet with his backside, didn't mean that I wasn't terrified. I knew perfectly well what Lord Daniel Eugene Dalgliesh was capable of. What I didn't know was what kind of devilry he had cooked up this time. What kind of danger could Mr Ambrose be in? It had to be something really bad for him to leave me behind. We had tracked through jungles and deserts, fought our way through bandits and rebels together. What could possibly be in store for me in the capital of France that was bad enough for him to leave me behind?

Taking a deep breath, I put my calculations away and raised my chin, staring belligerently out at the French landscape, as if daring it to be dangerous. I might have no idea what kind of perilous situation I would be walking into, but no matter what, I would fight for him tooth and claw!

Outside, the sun slowly sank towards the horizon. As the sky turned darker, my thoughts of Mr Ambrose slowly turned into daydreams, and then the day disappeared, and only dreams remained, which gradually faded into darkness.

I was jerked awake when we hit a bump in a road. Blinking, I glanced outside and saw a sea of lights below. We were driving down a shallow hill, and below us, twinkling lights stretched out as far as the eye could see, separated by a glittering band of darkness.

'Is that...?' I whispered.

Mr Phelps nodded, rubbing the sleep from his eyes. 'Paris. The dark band in the centre has to be the Seine.'

He reached out towards Miss Harse to shake her awake.

'Wait!'

He glanced at me, taken aback. 'But won't the ladies want to see it?'

'Err...no.' I cleared my throat. 'Best let them sleep. They've had an exhausting journey. Why not let them rest until I've had time to esca– um, I mean until I've fetched someone to help them into the posting inn.'

'Oh, well, if you think so.' He patted me on the back. 'I'm sure you know better what's best for Miss Harse, eh?'

And he winked at me.

Winked!

I had to find Mr Ambrose. Firstly, because I had to save him from Lord Dalgliesh. And secondly, and most importantly, because I needed to be saved myself. Urgently.

We plunged towards the lights below. Racing past buildings growing ever taller, we fast approached Paris. The first suburbs started to appear on either side, and the smells and sounds of a foreign city began to engulf us.

'*Citrouilles! Citrouilles fraîches!*'[5]

'*Je te déteste, trou du cul!*'[6]

'*Sais-tu combien de temps ta mère prend pour chier? Neuf mois!*'[7]

'Ah,' Mr Phelps sighed. 'French, the language of love. It sounds so romantic. If only we knew what they were saying.'

'Yes, um...' I cleared my throat. 'If only.'

Passing under a great arch, we entered the city proper, and the noise exploded around us. I could already tell that in one respect, this city was going to feel just like London—it never slept.

Is Mr Ambrose sleeping? Or is he wide awake right now, just like me?

The coach slowed. Gradually, it came to a stop and, glancing out, I saw what was undoubtedly a coaching inn.

'Well,' Mr Phelps sighed. 'Time for something to eat, don't you think? Are you as eager as I to taste the French *cuisine*, Mr Linton?'

'No.' Abruptly, I rose. 'I just remembered that I have some very urgent business to take care of. Very urgent indeed.'

---

[5] Pumpkins! Fresh Pumpkins!

[6] I hate you, you asshole!

[7] Do you know how much time your mother needs to take a shit? Nine months!

Mr Phelps looked startled. 'In the middle of the night? Surely Mr Ambrose wouldn't mind you taking a little time to rest.'

Even though, inside, my heart was hammering against my ribs in anxiety, I couldn't keep a smile from spreading across my face. 'If you think that, Mr Phelps, you don't know Rikkard Ambrose. *Au revoir.*'

And with that, I jumped out of the carriage, past the startled landlord and his big moustache, out onto the street. Grabbing my suitcase from the coach, I squared my shoulders, triangled my self-confidence and octagonalled my meagre knowledge of French. Then I set out into the strange world of wonder that was Paris at night.

I had progressed about five yards into this wonder before a street vendor tried to sell me a bowl full of snail soup. The other offers were more tempting – paintings, postcards, toys, souvenirs, and, oh, the flowers, how many flowers! Sir Philip Wilkins would have fainted with joy at the sight, but I ignored it all, forging ahead, only one single goal in mind.

Get to him. Get to him. Get. To. Him.

Approaching the first kind-looking face in the crowd, I bowed before the old lady and enquired

'Um… Excoosay ma, poo way woo me dear commaw…?' Pulling the precious piece of paper out of my pocket, I glanced at it, tried to form the words—then decided to forget about it and just showed her the damn thing.

Her eyebrows rose.

'Oh, vous êtes admirateur de l'opéra?'[8]

My mouth went dry. Good god! Someone was being operated on? Had someone been shot? But it couldn't be Mr Ambrose, right? She said something about an admiral. What the heck was a naval officer doing posing as a doctor? And had he gotten his hands on Mr Ambrose yet? I shuddered. Whatever dark, twisted intrigue was going on here, I was putting a stop to it!

'Where?' I demanded, grabbing the lady's wrist. *'Où? Où?'*

Startled, she drew back and pointed down the street. I whirled and sprinted in the direction she had indicated. As I ran, a thousand dark scenarios flashed through my head. Was I going to march into some kind of murderers' den? Who was the admiral? And what did he have to do with Mr Rikkard Ambrose? Pumping my legs like never before, I raced down the street like a favorite at the Ascot races. Every now and again, I stopped and waved the scrap of paper with the address under someone's nose. But always they pointed farther ahead, always I had to run on and on and on, until—

'Là.' The portly man pointed to the other side of the street. *'Juste là.'*

'Merci bon coup!' I squeezed his hand. *'Merci bon coup d'etat!'*

Turning, I faced the building he had pointed out—and gaped. If out of all the buildings in Paris I'd had to pick one place that I would least expect to find Rikkard Ambrose in, this would be it. No, that wasn't quite true—the donation office of the biggest Paris orphanage would probably be topmost on my list, but this would come in as a close second. The building was magnificent. The façade

---

[8] Oh, you are an admirer of the opera?

in baroque style was majestic and at the same time playful, with tall columns topped by curly decorations cut from stone and elegant arches connecting the row after row of pillars. Above rose a majestic dome, supporting glittering golden statues of ancient gods and goddesses.

Golden statues.

Luxurious decorations.

And Mr Ambrose was supposed to be *in there*? Had the world gone mad?

I was just contemplating whether or not to pinch myself—just to check if I was still in the coach, fast asleep and caught in some strange dream—when from inside the building, a terrible, ear-splitting scream erupted. The scream of a woman in terror. Instinctively, my hand went to my revolver.

Not a dream, Lilly. Just a nightmare. Time to face it!

And, pulling my revolver, I dashed forward, up the steps and into the building.

THE TRUTH

I can tell you, the doorman seemed pretty surprised when an armed man dashed past him into the building. Not nearly as surprised as I was, though, to meet a doorman at the entrance of a villain's lair. What kind of bloody place was this? The Villain Hotel for Megalomaniacs and Masterminds?

Another scream ripped through the air. If I'd had any doubt left that there was danger threatening in this place, it was gone now. Whoever that poor woman was, she sounded as if she were having her toenails pulled out with hot tongs. I had to find her! I had to find Mr Ambrose!

Following the distant sound of voices, I rushed down a corridor, the door-man's shouts echoing behind me—but I was too fast for him to catch up! Soon, I reached a big set of double doors, and in front of them—damn! Another door-man!

'Out of the way!' I ordered.

'English, *n'est-ce pas*?' The doorman smiled, extending his hand. 'Tickets, please.'

Tickets? *Tickets?* What kind of sick show were they running in there? Were they demanding money so people could watch some poor woman being tortured?

I raised my revolver. 'Out of my way. Now!'

The doorman paled and ducked behind the nearest column. Pushing open the double doors, I ran on, past a staircase, up another, through a door, and...

Light and sound engulfed me.

My chin dropped. Flabbergasted, I stared at the sight before me. I stood at the entrance to a huge room, a hall really, decorated in gold, silver, brocade and every imaginable luxury—more than I had ever seen squashed together in one place, except maybe Buckingham Palace. Seats stretched out as far as the eye could see, an ocean of people filling them. On the gold-decorated walls, boxes with velvet drapes half hid the richest patrons, but from the shadows, pearls shone and diamonds sparkled. At the opposite end of the room from me rose a stage, and on the stage stood two people. A handsome man and a woman, clasped in his arms. The woman parted her lips and screamed.

No.

Not screamed.

Singing. She was *singing*. The fancy building. The doorman. The audience.

Oh, vous êtes admirateur de l'opéra?

Bloody hell. How could I have been so stupid?

By not learning French, Lilly. That's how.

But...wait just a minute.

Opera?

Opera?

That thing where performers stood at fake balconies for hours upon hours and sang about how lovesick they were, and how they couldn't live without the one man/woman/weird creature they were destined for? The thing that people attended as a pastime, with absolutely no thought of earning money in the process?

And Mr Rikkard Ambrose was supposed to be *here*?

Listening to an aria about...

'*Porgi, amor, qualche ristoro,*

Al mio duolo, a'miei sospir!'

About *amor*.

I didn't know much Italian, but even I knew that word. Rikkard Ambrose was here, listening to *this*?

No.

No, that couldn't be possible. It had to be a mistake. Maybe I'd entered the wrong building. Maybe I had...maybe...maybe...

Slowly, inevitably, as if by magic, my gaze was drawn upward to one of the boxes. There, among the shadows, in one of the best seats in the house sat a tall, dark, ramrod-straight figure, his hands curled around the armrests of his seat hard enough to dent metal. I couldn't see his face, but I could see those hands of his. The left little finger was twitching.

No.

No.

No, no, no. It couldn't be, could it?

The sound of hurried footsteps from behind tore me from my daze. I had just enough presence of mind left to duck behind a decorative curtain before the two doormen burst into the room, looking around wildly. The audience didn't notice them. They were too focused on the stage. And I...

I was still too damn focused on Mr Ambrose. Mr Rikkard Ambrose. At the opera. Listening to people singing in Italian about lo—

I couldn't even think it.

The doormen whispered to each other in frantic French. Their searching gazes swept over the crowd, but couldn't find any sign of the lunatic with the gun that was yours truly. I could only follow the gist of the hurried conversation in French, but after a while, they seemed to agree that whatever they had seen, it probably wasn't a gun after all, and if it was, and some rich bugger got shot tonight, it would be better for both of them not to have seen a gun, and not to have let an assassin run past them without raising so much as a finger. With that agreement reached, they nodded to each other and returned to their posts, once more staunch guardians of the opera.

I, meanwhile, stood behind the curtain and waited. Waited as the people on the stage sang about eternal love and devotion, and as Mr Rikkard Ambrose's little finger twitched ever faster. Finally, the opera drew to an end. The curtain closed, opened once more for a final round of applause, then closed for the last time last time.

So did the curtain up in the box of a certain someone.

Without even thinking about it, I launched myself from my hiding place and sprinted towards the nearest staircase. Around me, thunderous applause roared. I didn't give a damn. Quick as a flash, I dashed up the stairs, down the corridor, around a corner, and...

There!

Two mint-condition ten-year-old coat tails vanishing around another corner. I ran faster. By the time I rounded the bend, no one and nothing was to be seen—except a closed door, with a plaque on it saying

ACCES INTERDIT!
Bureau du propriétaire

Hmm...

What could *'acces interdit'* possibly mean?

Probably 'please come in right away'. And of course, kind lady that I was, I would oblige. Marching forward, I pushed open the door.

It took a few moments for my eyes to adjust to the gloom. When they had, I saw before me a sparsely lit – and sparsely furnished – room, filled with stacks of papers. Lists, accounts, numerous books of music and song...the selection was varied and vast. A lone candle flickered on a rickety table. And in the light of the candle I could just make out a tall, dark form silhouetted against the window.

'Leave the papers I asked for on the table,' Mr Rikkard Ambrose commanded, not bothering to turn around. 'Then go and get me something to drink.'

'No.'

He stiffened. There was a long, long moment of silence. Slowly, so slowly it could almost be called a waste of time, he turned around to face me. His familiar, cold, sea-coloured eyes, the eyes I hadn't seen in far too long, met mine, and I felt a tugging in my chest.

His eyes narrowed infinitesimally.

'I am going to kill Karim when next I see him.'

I lifted an eyebrow. 'Don't blame him. I tortured the address out of him.'

'I surmised as much. And I pay him not to crack under torture.'

'You...!' Eyes narrowing, I took a step forward and stabbed a finger in his direction. 'You are not exactly in a position to go around criticizing people, Mister I'm-going-to-a-place-so-dangerous-I-can't-take-you-along Ambrose!'

He cleared his throat. 'Ehem. Well...as to that, Mr Linton...'

'What "danger" were you referring to, exactly?'

'Well, I...'

'I knew it. I bloody knew it!' Eyes flashing, I took a step forward. 'There is no damn danger is there? The only bloody reason you didn't want me along is because you didn't want me to know you own a goddamn opera in Paris, wasn't it? And you certainly didn't want me, the dastardly female who just dared to turn you down like a ton of bricks, to sit next to you while you mope and listen to a lady sing love songs in Italian!'

His little finger twitched and...was that the tiniest blush on his chiselled cheeks? Surely not! Inwardly, I grinned. Outwardly, I didn't want to lose my job.

'Don't be ridiculous, Mr Linton,' Mr Ambrose told me coolly, tugging at his lapels, which had been absolutely straight already. 'You did not "turn me down". Nobody has ever turned down an offer of mine.'

'Oh, I didn't, did I? Out of curiosity, Sir...what would you call the answer "no" in response to a proposal?'

He considered for a moment. Finally, he decided:

'A delay in negotiations to be solved at my earliest convenience through the application of alternative strategies.'

'Indeed?'

'Yes, indeed, Mr Linton.'

You had to hand it to him—he might be full of crap, but it was high-quality, perfectly delivered crap.

'Then, pray tell me...' I took a few more steps towards him, not taking my eyes off him for a second, 'if you aren't hiding out here, soothing your bruised megalomaniac male ego, what are you doing?'

'Why the interest?' he enquired coolly. 'If you have, as you say, "turned me down" like a large amount of building material?'

'Ha!' Crossing the last bit of distance between us, I jabbed my finger into his chest—not a wise move, since I nearly broke my finger. 'Ouch! I knew it! I knew you were hiding out here drowning your sorrows over your broken heart.'

He looked as outraged as it was possible for a stone statue with money constipation to look. His dark, sea-coloured eyes flashed at me with a stormy light.

'I am not in the habit of drowning anything. But I might make an exception for you.'

'Hit a tender spot, did I? Well, deal with it!' Slapping his chest, I grabbed him by the collar. 'You bloody well deserve it! Do you have any idea how worried I've been?'

'Indeed?'

It was just an instant. A moment so short it hardly existed—but for that moment, triumph flashed in his eyes.

'Don't you dare smile, you bloody son of a bachelor! This is no joke!'

'Smile?' One eyebrow lifted infinitesimally, daring to play innocent. 'I do not waste time or facial musculature on such wasteful activities, Mr Linton.'

'No, you don't, you bloody block of stone! You just somehow smirk with your coat tails while keeping your face perfectly straight. It's bloody infuriating!'

'I have no idea what you could possibly mean, Mr Linton. I don't—'

I hit him. Not hard—the episode with my finger had reminded me what kind of obstacle I was dealing with—just hard enough to get his attention.

He blinked. A bit like a giant who wasn't quite sure whether a mouse had just been stupid enough to stab him in the foot. There was a moment of total silence as he gazed into the distance. When he lowered his eyes to look at me and opened his mouth, he found tears in my eyes.

His mouth closed again.

'I was afraid for you.' The words tore from my throat. I told myself that my voice didn't quiver. Not the tiniest bit. Not the tiniest little bit! 'You pretended to be in danger, and I was bloody afraid for you!'

'Mr Linton...Lillian, I...' Slowly raising a hand, he touched my cheek, his fingers so careful and tender one might think I was the most precious object in the world. Until he grabbed me hard and pulled me towards him.

Our mouths clashed like a prima donna and her manager, both wrestling for control and ignoring the fact that they bloody needed each other. My hands were suddenly in his hair, holding him tight, so tight it felt as if I could meld us together forever. And, dammit, that's exactly what I wanted! I didn't want marriage. I didn't want to swear obedience. I just wanted him! Was that so hard to understand?

Well, since it's Rikkard Ambrose you're talking about, yes, probably.

Why couldn't I have fallen in love with a nice, compliant egghead?

Then he kissed me again, and I remembered why. I remembered exactly. His lips were....oh...they were hotter than a furnace, stronger than a hurricane, and sweeter than chocolate melting on your tongue.

Well, maybe not the last, but that would be a bit too much to ask for from anyone. So I asked for something I knew he was willing to give. I asked for more. With my mouth, I begged for it, and for the first time in his life, Mr Rikkard Ambrose gave freely. Very freely indeed.

When we finally ran out of breath, I reluctantly released his hair from my grip. Placing a last searing brand on my lips, he broke the kiss.

'All right,' he panted. 'You may have been correct.'

'I? Correct? And you admit it?' I raised an eyebrow. 'Goodness gracious! Where is my calendar? I must mark today in red for all eternity as a memorial to this momentous occasion.'

Silence.

'So, tell me, Sir...in what regard was my correctness so correctly correct today?'

A muscle in his jaw ticked. 'The things I told you about Dalgliesh—they were made up. There is no danger here.'

'Ah! I knew it!' I tapped an accusing finger against his chest. 'I knew that everything is fine here, and nothing bad is happeni—'

It was then that the high-pitched scream of a woman pierced the air.

THE IFRIT AND THE BANSHEE

It wasn't difficult to find out where the trouble was happening. All we had to do was follow the ear-piercing screams. And they were screams this time, Mr Ambrose assured me, not high notes in a Mozart aria. Personally, I couldn't tell the difference, but then, I was an expert on opera the same way a squid was an expert on mountain climbing.

'Over there!'

Mr Ambrose pointed down a corridor, at the end of which a banshee seemed to be getting strangled. We started to sprint forward, and the farther we got, the more people joined us. It's interesting how people always run away from danger when they're being chased, but run towards it if they aren't. One of the many proofs for the essential blockheadedness of humankind.

Finally, we reached a door with a name plaque on it that I didn't bother to try and pronounce. To judge by the women crowding around the entrance and the shrill screams still issuing from inside, it was easy enough to deduce that there was a lady in there, but other than that, I had no idea what was going on. The women were blocking the way.

'Stand aside!' I ordered.

They ignored me.

I glanced sideways at Mr Ambrose. 'Maybe they don't speak English?'

He gave me a look.

'Stand aside!' he commanded. Instantly, the crowd parted for him, and the ladies curtsied as he passed. I followed, grumbling something not very flattering about arrogant, chauvinistic men. I hated them even more now that I'd been one of them for a while.

Inside the dressing room, a voluminously voluptuous lady stood plastered against one wall, screaming with the stamina possessed only by professional singers and crazy demagogues on Speaker's Corner. To her right, a girl in a maid outfit stood pressed against the wall, her face white. And on the other side, nestled into the chaise longue...

'Holy Moly!'

Mr Ambrose cocked his head. 'Indeed.'

There on the chaise longue, bold as brass, as if it were perfectly at home here and a well-known native to Paris, lay a coiled snake, its colourful scales shining in a poisonous pattern. As if feeling the attention, the reptile raised its head and hissed. Screams erupted all around in a high-pitched cacophony that was loud enough to ring my skull like a bell.

I gave a derisive snort.

God! And these ninnies called themselves women? The snake wasn't even doing anything! It was just sitting there and hissing.

'Calm down, will you?' I called, cutting through the kerfuffle.

'Calm down?' the maid squashed against the wall exclaimed. "ow should I calm down? Sere is a snake in madame's room! A great, big poisonous snake, c'est vrai!'

'No, no.' I waved her concerns away. 'I know this snake. I've seen it before in South America. It isn't poisonous.'

'It isn't?'

'No.' I patted her hand. 'It just wraps around its victims and squeezes them to death.'

Maybe, I realised as renewed shrieks threatened to rip apart my eardrums, I shouldn't have said that last part out loud.

'Well, Mr Linton?' Cocking his head, Mr Ambrose gave me a look.

'What are you looking at me for?'

'You got them screaming again. You get them to stop.'

'And how am I to do that?' I demanded.

'It might help if you removed the snake.'

'Fine, fine!' I sighed, pulled out my revolver and shot the snake through the head. And you know what? Those ninnies still didn't stop screaming! If anything, the din got louder!

'Parbleu!' the prima donna exclaimed. 'C'est scandaleux!'

'You shot it!' the maid shrieked. 'You shot it!'

'Well, of course I did. You wanted it gone, didn't you?'

Annoyed, I turned towards her—unfortunately forgetting that I still had a smoking gun in my hand. That ratcheted up the screaming to new and unexplored levels. Wincing, I raised my hands to cover my ears. Luckily, Mr Ambrose picked the gun out of my hand before I accidentally shot myself through the head.

'Out!' he commanded, cutting through the screams like a hot knife through foie gras. The assorted singers and dancers scattered. Only the prima donna and her maid remained plastered to the wall. I could only assume they had never dealt with Rikkard Ambrose personally before. Silently, he lifted one finger to point first at them, then at the door.

'Mais...mais Monsieur Ambrose...'

'Dis is Madame's room!' the maid protested. 'You cannot just—'

'Out. My secretary and I will attend to this problem. You will be notified when this room is once more ready for your use.'

The young woman's eyes widened. 'Our use? Mon Dieu, you cannot expect Madame to return to this place after what has just 'appened and just pretend that—'

Mr Ambrose took a step towards them and gave them one long, hard, cold look. The words died in the maid's throat, and she curtsied.

'Oui, Monsieur Ambrose. Tout de suite, Monsieur Ambrose.'

Half a second later, they were gone. Shutting the door behind them, Mr Ambrose strode over to the coil of limp scales on the bed, grabbed it as if it were a shawl, and lifted it up. Through narrowed eyes he examined the animal.

'Hm. What do you think, Mr Linton?'

The question, as simple as it was, touched something deep inside of me. A year and a half ago, he wouldn't even have considered asking it. But now...

He cared what I thought. More than that, he respected my opinion.

'Well...' Taking a step closer, I gazed at the snake. I had been right before. It was indeed a South American specimen. One, in fact, that I had nearly stepped on more than once during our travels across the continent. Seeing it this close up made me very glad I hadn't. 'I think we can both agree that this little charmer isn't native to France.'

'Indeed, Mister Linton.'

'So the question is—how did he end up here?'

'She.'

'Pardon?'

'She.' Mr Ambrose pointed to the snake's tail. 'This snake was a lady.' Glancing at me, he lifted one eyebrow infinitesimally. 'You really shouldn't make chauvinistic assumptions, Mr Linton. It is unbecoming of a gentleman, I've been told.'

The...the nerve of him!

Suddenly, I felt the strangest urge to throw myself on him, wrestle him down to the chaise longue and kiss him silly. But since the chaise longue was spattered in snake blood, I refrained, and instead gave him a cool look that told him exactly what I thought of his attempt to turn the tables.

'Well, we still have to ask ourselves how this *lady* ended up here. I doubt she came over from Brazil because she's an opera enthusiast. Could she have escaped from some kind of zoo or ménage?'

Mr Ambrose shook his head. 'If there were something like this anywhere near my opera, I'd know about it.'

'Is there someone who could have left this on purpose? Someone who hates the prima donna that much?'

'Yes.' Mr Ambrose nodded. 'The prima donna's understudy, the understudy's understudy, the choir, the managing director, the orchestra, and half of the two dozen men who are in love with her.'

I blinked. 'But if they're in love with her...?'

'They're French.'

'Oh. I guess that explains it.' I hesitated. 'But could any of these people have gotten hold of such an animal?'

'Maybe. But for them, there would be far easier methods to achieve the same goal. A bucket of dirty dishwater balanced on the door, a bit of paint splashed over a costume—it does not take a deadly snake to upset a prima donna. And if the purpose was not just to play a trick on her, but to kill—why not simply shoot her? It doesn't make sense.'

'You...' I hesitated. 'You don't suppose it was Dalgliesh after all, do you?'

He whipped his head around to look at me sharply. 'What makes you think that?'

'When I think of Dalgliesh,' I told him darkly, 'I think of a snake. Besides, this smells of something bigger than some spat between opera singers. There's a vicious mind behind this, with resources at its disposal.'

Mr Ambrose considered it for a moment – then shook his head. 'No.'

'So he doesn't have an opera house in Paris?' I probed. 'Any place that might be in competition with this one?'

'Yes, he does. But the mighty Lord Daniel Eugene Dalgliesh would never stoop to concerning himself with the day-to-day running of such a small operation. Dalgliesh likes to plan great intrigues and play at politics. I am the one who has the hands-on approach.'

'Oh, trust me,' I told him with a wink, 'I've noticed.'

The look he had on his face for a moment—just a moment—was priceless.

'Yes. Um. Well...' He cleared his throat. 'Back to the business of the attempted murder...'

'Must we?'

'Yes, we must, Mr Linton.'

'Too bad. Since you're sure Dalgliesh is not behind this, I was hoping I was going to get to see more of this beautiful city. Maybe with some company?' Sidling up to him, I put my arm around his waist. He, fervent romantic that he was, responded by holding a dead snake under my nose.

'Well, then you shall get your wish. I will put the investigation of this incident into your capable hands, and to ensure you'll have plenty of company, you'll start by questioning all the opera staff.'

My eyes nearly bugged out of their sockets.

'I *what*?'

'Oh, and this...' He dumped the dead snake into my arms. 'Take it to an expert, will you? Find out where exactly it came from. Preferably without threatening anyone with a firearm.'

'You...I...how...what...?'

'Quite adequate questions to begin with, Mr Linton. I'm sure you will be a success as an investigator. Good day.'

And, turning, he strode out of the prima donna's dressing room. I, for my part, stood there in silence for a moment—then looked down at the snake.

'You know, I think I understand your choice of lifestyle. Strangling people to death is so much more satisfying that just poisoning them with a little bite.'

~~**~*~*

My first interview with a member of the opera staff went something like this:

'Good morning, ma'am. Could you please state your name, and then describe in your own words as closely as possible what happened a few hour ag—'

'Mon dieu! C'est scandaleux! J'exige de voir le gérant, ou du moins je l'aurais fait s'il avait été là, mais ce bloc de pierre appelé Ambrose l'a envoyé en vacances parce qu'il n'avait pas besoin de de le payer pendant qu'il était là, n'est ce pas? Cet homme me rend fou! Mais pourquoi suis-je entrain de vous le dire? Vous êtes son fidèle laquais, un homme dont il faut se méfier! Vous n'oseriez jamais remettre en question les précieux ordres de votre maître, n'est-ce pas? Allez au diable! Allez en enfer et prenez votre bloc de glace de

patron avec vous! Peut-être qu'il va fondre et faire de ce monde un meilleur endroit! Et puisque nous sommes sur le sujet de l'enfer...'[9]

'Um...yes. Thanks.' I held up both hands, just about managing to halt the flood of words from the big-bosomed prima donna. 'That's a very great description. Now—could you repeat it in English, please?'

'Pourquoi diable tu m'as appelé ici? Et pourquoi est-ce que tu continues de parler en anglais? Je ne comprends pas un mot de ce que tu dis. Honnêtement, je m'en fiche, mais j'ai de meilleures choses à faire plutôt que de m'asseoir là à écouter. Est-ce que Ambrose va déduire de mon salaire le temps passé ici?'[10]

I perked up. That last part I might actually have kind of understood!

Ambrose de déduire cette temps de mon salaire...

What could that possibly mean? Take three guesses.

'Yes.' I nodded emphatically. 'He will absolutely deduct this from your salary. This and anything else he can think of.'

The prima donna slapped a delicate hand on the tabletop between us.

'Merde!'

I beamed. She had understood! We were making huge strides in interlingual communication.

'Yes, absolutely *merde*,' I agreed, patting her hand. 'Don't worry, I know the feeling. I've had a few *merde*-moments with Mr Rikkard Ambrose myself.'

'Cet homme est une tête de nœud!'[11]

'Yes, absolutely. He definitely is a tait du noid, whatever that may be.'

'Hm...' The prima donna gave me a considering look. *'Pour un homme, vous n'êtes pas trop mal. Surtout pour un anglais.'*[12]

'Thank you—I think. If that was was a compliment. You're not too bad yourself, as long as you aren't screaming or singing.'

Reaching into her humongous collection of petticoats, the prima donna removed a small flask and held it up.

'Voulez-vous partager?'

Ah, the international language of getting completely wankered! This was one I definitely understood. With a broad grin, I snatched up the bottle, unscrewed the top and took a big gulp.

---

[9] This is outrageous! I demand to see the manager-or I would, if the manager were here, but that ice cold block of stone called Ambrose had to send him on vacation because there was no need to pay him while he was here, was there? That man drives me insane! But why would I tell you this? You're his loyal minion, and a man to boot! You would never dare to question your precious master's orders, would you? Go to hell! Go to hell and take your ice block of a boss with you! Maybe he'll melt and make the world a better place. And since we're on the subject of hell...

[10] Why the hell did you call me in here? And why do you keep on jabbering in English? I don't understand one word you're saying. Honestly, I don't really care, but I've got better things to do than sit around here listening to nonsense in a foreign language. Will that cheapskate Ambrose deduct this time from my paycheck?

[11] That man is a complete dickhead!

[12] For a man, you aren't too bad. Especially an Englishman.

'*Hou la la! Ralentissez, petit gars, ralentissez!*'[13]

'Ooo la la is right!' A broad grin spread across my face, and I handed her the bottle. She grabbed it, and took a gulp even bigger than mine.

'*Voila!*'

'Ha! That's the best thing you can do? Give me that bottle!'

'No way! If I do, it be empty in three gulps!'

I froze. Then, slowly, I raised my eyes to meet hers. She clapped her hand in front of her mouth. '*Merde!*'

'You can say that again, Lady! How come you suddenly speak English?'

She gave me a sullen look. 'I thought you call me to reduce my pay. That *enfoirè* Ambrose try to do that twice since he arrived. So I simply pretend I not understand. Simple solution be the best, eh?'

'Genius!' I slapped the table. 'I wish I'd had that idea.'

A corner of her mouth twitched. 'He try with you, too?'

Oh, he tried lots of things with me—most of which succeeded.

'Um...something along those lines. But, you know, I'm not here to announce a pay cut.'

She nodded. 'I gather from what you say.'

I frowned. 'Then why did you keep on pretending?'

Her smile blossomed into a full-blown naughty grin. 'It be so much fun to watch you wrestle with *Francais* and lose.'

'You...you devious little...!' I jabbed a finger at her, while the inner me stood up and applauded. 'As punishment, you will serve as my translator! I need someone to help me find out what is happening here. And since you're the victim, you're pretty much the only one I can trust to tell the truth.'

'Translator. New job, *oui?*' She held out an open hand and raised a delicate eyebrow. 'How much it pay?'

'You'll do it, or I'll inform Mr Ambrose about this little scheme to avoid him.'

'*Qu'est-ce que vous avez dit? Je crains que je ne comprends pas un mot que vous dites. Je ne parle pas anglais. C'est un langage tellement compliqué, et je ne suis qu'une chanteuse idiote.*'[14]

'Really?' I gave her a long, hard look. 'You're really playing that game again?'

She smiled at me with an innocence not even my little virgin sister could have matched.

'*Excusez-moi? Qu'est-ce que vous avez dit?*'[15]

My shoulders slumped. Crap! Or, as the French would say, *crêpe suzette!* What was I going to do now? I needed someone impartial to translate, or I would never get anywhere in this damn investigation. How could I possibly change her mind and make her help me? How could I convince her?

My gaze swept over the well-endowed prima donna—and then, as if led by a helpful alcoholic divine entity, landed on the bottle. An idea popped into my

---

[13] Wow! Slow down, little guy, slow down!

[14] What did you say? I'm afraid I don't understand a word you say. I don't speak English. It's such a complicated language, and I'm just a silly singer.

[15] Excuse me? What did you say?

head. An idea that, I was sure, Mr Ambrose would not like. Which of course meant I had to try it immediately.

A smile spread over my face, and I leant forward, towards my soon-to-be interpreter.

'Listen. I have an offer for you...'

THE RETURN OF THE YELLOW PIGGIES

I stopped in front of Mr Ambrose's door. Or, to be more exact, my mind stopped. The rest of me needed a moment or two of wobbling to catch on. For a moment, I gazed consideringly at the three doorknobs on the door. Finally, I grabbed my favourite, before it disappeared, and turned it. It actually stayed substantial.

'Yay! Victory!'

Triumphant, I pushed open the door and swung into the room with it, dangling from my trusty friend the doorknob. It really was a nice doorknob. I should come visit it more often in future, maybe start exchanging news on women's rights and brass polish...

'Mr Linton?'

My philosophical reflections on human-doorknob relations were rudely interrupted by a familiar cool voice. Glancing up, I saw a tall, dark figure standing at the window. Or maybe two. Or three. Math was so difficult to deal with when some nefarious character had stuffed your head full of cotton wool. The Ambrose(s) stood with their back to me, not moving an inch.

'You've concluded your interviews for today, Mr Linton?'

'Yep!'

'And? Did you find out anything?'

'Y-yep!' I announced, cheerily. 'I f-found out that those French singers carry some s-strong strong stu...stubledywubledy...stuff.'

He stiffened. Hm...was he tense? Did he need a backrub?

Slowly, so slowly he could have counted the dust moats in the air, Mr Ambrose turned around, his dark eyes flashing.

'No. No. Not *that* again.'

'Hello!' With a bright smile, I waved at him, then turned a bit to the left, towards the yellow piggies dancing in the corner. 'Hello to you, too! I've missed you! Where've you been?'

'I've been here the whole time, Mr Linton!'

'Not you! I'm talking to my friends over there. And psht!' I held an admonishing finger to my lips. 'You'll interrupt their performance.'

Mr Ambrose turned to glance into the corner, then turned back to me. 'Mr Linton—how much alcohol exactly did you consume?'

'Enough to be completely rat-arsed,' I announced proudly.[16]

'Mr Linton!'

---

[16] Rat-arsed: another one of those lovely British expressions for 'drunk'.

'Funny expression, that, isn't it? Rat-arsed? I mean it's not as if tipple came out of a rat's arse. Or maybe it does? I've never seen alcohol be made. Hm...I wonder if someone ought to look into that...Only not too closely unless they want their nose bitten off.'

'Mr Linton! Cease talking immediately!'

'Why?'

'Because I told you to!'

'That's no reason!' I told him, raising a hand to wag an accusing finger in his face. 'You can't tell me what to do. You can't—'

Unfortunately, the hand I had raised to admonish him was the one I had used to cling to the doorknob before. Without its friendly support, my face decided it was time to French kiss the floor.

'Ow!'

'Mr Linton!'

Suddenly, strong arms were around me, lifting me up, holding me close.

'Oh, sure,' I muttered into a comfortingly warm chest. '*Now* you rescue me, after I've rammed my head into the floor. Very gentlemanly, I'm sure.'

'Rescue you?' Icicles were hanging from Mr Ambrose's voice. 'I gave you the task to undertake an important investigation, Mr Linton, a very important investigation—and you return to me dead drunk. I don't think you're in a position to throw around accusations. Besides...' Fingers slid down my cheek. Fingers that felt hard as steel and at the same time unbelievably gentle. 'I've been reliably informed that women have just as much right as men to smash their heads into the floor. It's called equality.'

The insult I wanted to throw at the hypocritical son of a bachelor was muffled by his tailcoat. Struggling free, I bent my head back until I could meet his gaze and jabbed a finger against his chest.

'D-dead drunk? Ha! I'm just a little tipsywipsy. Besides...how do you know I didn't start on your investigigi...investititty...investic nation?'

Dark, sea-coloured eyes seared into mine.

'I would say that the fact you cannot pronounce the word "investigation" is a pretty strong hint.'

'Ha! That's where you're wrong, Mr Ambrose, Sir!' I thumped his chest. 'I made huge leaps in the investiture...investmentality...in...in...oh, heck! In my job!'

'Indeed?'

'Oh yes indeed, Sir!' I beamed up at him. 'I persuaded a very nice lady to translate for me when I interview the staff tomorrow.'

'And how did you do that?'

'I drunk her under the table,' I announced proudly. 'Bloody hell, those French singers can drink a lot of plonk![17] But I beat her! She's sleeping the sweet sleep of approaching hangover. Which reminds me...maybe someone should scrape her off the floor.'

---

[17] British English for cheap wine.

'So let me recapitulate.' Mr Ambrose was as deadpan as a skillet that had just committed a tragic suicide by hurling itself into a furnace. 'You got drunk on the job in order to do the job.'

'Yep!' I grinned up at him, proud of myself at having found such fabulous reason to be nefarious. The yellow piggies clapped and applauded, their cute little tails wiggling. 'I absolutely did. Tomorrow morning, I'll have a translator, and I'll be able to investimalate to my heart's content.'

His grip tightening around me, he pulled me up until I was standing on my feet—or at least wobbling.

'I usually do not make predictions based on feelings, Mr Linton, but I have a feeling that tomorrow morning, you will be busy with other matters. Ones that involve a bucket and an icepack on the forehead.'

I was about to respond when, suddenly, the floor lurched beneath me. Heck! Why did the bloody floor insist on acting up every time I took a little drink?

Of course! The floor was a temperance activist![18] That was it! The evil floor wanted to outlaw my drink and banish the little yellow piggies!

Well, I couldn't allow that, now, could I?

I kicked the floor.

'Bad floor! Bad! Take a drink yourself before you judge.'

'Err...Mr Linton?'

'Bad floor! Bad! Just because drunk people always end up drooling on you, that's no reason to be vindictive. How could you want to hurt those cute little piggies? Can't you see how well they dance?'

'Mr Linton, I think I'd better get you upstairs to your room.'

'No! I need to have a serious talk with this floor.'

'There's plenty of floor upstairs, Mr Linton.'

Really? Damn! This was a conspiracy. 'Is he a bloody teetotaller, too?'

For some reason, Mr Ambrose seemed to take this perfectly harmless question as reason for concern. In one swift movement, he bent down, knocked my wobbling legs out from under me and caught me up in his arms.

'Woah! What are you doing?'

'I'm taking you upstairs.' His tone brooked no argument. 'Now.'

He started forward, and his long legs quickly ate up the distance to the door. With the heel of his foot, he pulled the door open and marched through, towards the stairs.

'P-put me down!' I protested. 'I'm not some helpless camel...camsel...damsel!'

---

[18] Temperance activists were (often religiously motivated) people who wanted to reduce the general consumption of alcoholic beverages. In some countries and at some times, this included the outlawing of alcohol. Although temperance movements already started during the 19th century in response to the high alcoholism and domestic violence of the Victorian Age, it only gained true popularity with the general populace of some countries in later years. The prohibition in the USA from 1920 to 1933, for example, was the result of the efforts of the temperance movement.

'Agreed. You're missing a hump.'

'So you're going to put me down?'

'No.'

'Do it now!'

'No.'

I tried to find the strength to protest again, but it felt so nice being snuggled against his warm, hard chest, and my head was feeling a bit woozy.

'You're a tyrannical son of a bachelor,' I accused.

Mr Ambrose snorted, and murmured something too low for me to really understand. Something about a pot calling the metal back?

We ascended the stairs in silence, all the way up the opera house that was long asleep by now. No voices of singers rose from below, no chatter of dancers flitted through the corridors. The only things to hear were Mr Ambrose's quiet footsteps and the ringing of a church bell in the distance.

A church bell.

Mr Ambrose stopped on the last step.

'Is that why you said no to me? Because I'm a tyrant?'

I thought about it.

'Yes,' I finally admitted. 'And no.'

'That doesn't make sense, Mr Linton.'

'I'm drunk,' I reminded him happily. 'I don't have to make sense.'

'Oh yes. Yes, you do.' A powerful hand caught my chin in its grip and lifted my head. Blinking the drowsiness out of my eyes, I gazed up at Mr Rikkard Ambrose, his icy gaze boring into me. I felt like whiskey on the rocks. Lots of alcohol with a bit of ice mixed in. 'I know you—and I know you want me. I told you when I left for France, I'm not just going to walk away from you. I'll make you mine, one way or another.'

'There!' I waggled a finger in his face. 'That's what I meant by tyrannical. When a woman tells you no, you have to accept it!'

'Even if she doesn't mean it?'

'*Especially* then. Agonizing over potentially idiotic decisions is one of the most precious rights of womankind.'

Muttering a low oath, Mr Ambrose continued on his way, and I snuggled back into his chest.

'You're impossible!'

'I'm your little *ifrit*,' I grinned up at him. 'That's my job description.'

Wordlessly, he pulled me tighter against him and lowered his face into my hair, crushing it against his lips. Not loosening his grip for an instant, he carried me along a corridor, the walls of which seemed rather wobbly and colourful for a scarcely lit house in the middle of the night.

'W-where are we?' I murmured.

'The attic.'

'You're going to store me in the attic?'

'Yes, with the brooms, buckets and old costumes.'

But, contrary to his words, a moment later he pushed open a door and stepped into one of the most beautiful rooms I had ever seen. True, it was a bit dusty, and there was actually a broom leaning in the corner—but the rest?

I sucked in a breath at the sight.

High, high above us, the two slanting sides of the ceiling med above an intricate labyrinth of rafters. Between the rafters, cobwebs hung like velvet drapes, glittering in the silvery moonlight that fell in through the window.

Oh, and the window...

It was big. It was high. And it was beautiful. Through it, I could see lights glittering as far as the eye could see. In the distance, a dark band cut through the luminous magic of Paris. The Seine. I gazed, unable to look away. If the view was this amazing in the middle of the night, what would it look like in the morning?

'Up here you won't bother anyone,' Mr Ambrose said, his voice cool and detached, while his fingers gently stroked my cheek. 'And I can lock you in when I need to stop you from causing trouble.'

I gazed once more at the beautiful room—then looked up at his face, only inches away, and pressed a gentle kiss on his cheek.

'That's so considerate of you. It's been some time since I had leisure to practice my lock-breaking skills.'

Making an indistinct noise at the back of his throat, he marched over to the window, to a cot that was already waiting there. A cot without the barest hint of dust on it. This hadn't been standing here a long time, like everything else in the room, a realization surfaced in my befuddled mind. He'd had it brought up especially for me, long before I'd stumbled drunk into his office downstairs. Warmth rose in my chest. Yet as I looked up into his eyes, I saw nothing but ice there. Quickly, he looked away.

'Here,' he said, gruffly, and lowered me onto the cot. With one quick jerk, he pulled a blanket over me. 'Sleep it off. I need you alert in the morning, and ready to continue with the investigation.'

Ready to be out of your way, you mean.

'Why can't you look at me? Why do you want to avoid me?' Would I normally have asked such a question straight out? Probably not. But in my pleasantly befuddled state, it seemed the logical thing to do.

His eyes flashed.

'I could ask you the same thing. Why, Lillian?' His voice was like a knife, cutting straight to the chase, and through it, straight into my heart. 'Why did you say no?'

I flinched. There was no need to ask what he was referring to.

'You know why.' Gently I reached up to touch his cheek, but missed and bumped his nose instead. Oh well, who said I couldn't invent the romantic nose-bump?

Capturing my hand between both of his, he stared at me, cold, controlled rage in his eyes. 'Just because of a few stupid words in a wedding vow? *Honour and obey?*'

'Words you would hold me to.'

At least he didn't try to deny it. Turning away, he gazed out through the dirt-stained window.

'Why did you leave?' It was an audacious question. A question about pain, and secrets of the heart. A question I'd probably never have asked if I were sober. Luckily, I was still completely sloshed.[19]

For a moment or two, he didn't reply. The silence was deafening. But then...

'When you said no to me, I...'

'Yes?'

At his sides, his hands balled into fists.

'It was the first time I wanted to punch something without having a debtor in front of me. Even when directed against a valid target, violence is mostly a waste of time. And there was I, wanting to punch without knowing whom or what or why! And every time the logical part of my mind told me I should probably try punching you, I felt like punching myself, and there is nothing more bloody illogical in the entire world!'

There was a thunderous thud. It was over so quickly, I had hardly time to blink. Had that really just happened? Had I just seen Mr Rikkard Cool-As-An-Icecube Ambrose *punch the wall*?

'I needed to get out of there.' His voice had sunken to an arctic whisper. 'I grabbed the first file from my "problematic business" pile, and jumped into a carriage. And as the non-existent deity of fate would have it, the business I ended up giving a thorough examination was this one. Do you have any idea what I've had to suffer through the last few weeks? If I have to hear one more romantic aria sung by an overweight fool in a parrot costume...!'

'My condolences. But, you know, my life back in London hasn't been exactly a picnic, either.'

'Indeed?'

'Oh yes indeed, Mr Ambrose, Sir. Can you imagine how hard it is to make up excuses for why you're being followed everywhere by a turban-wearing mountain wearing a giant beard and sabre?'

'I don't have to imagine. I know the feeling well. And I always say he's here to cut the throat of anyone who thinks of harming me.'

'Well, for some reason, that wasn't something I wanted to tell my lady friends over afternoon tea.'

We lapsed into silence again. And in the silence, in the dark of this dusty attic in Paris, the sadness and hurt between us shifted and morphed into something else. Something warm. Something that drew us together.

'I missed you,' I whispered into the darkness.

Silence.

Silence which for once, wasn't cold.

'I missed you, too.'

---

[19] Another British English expression for being drunk. Britons have quite an amazing collection of these, it seems.

I bit my lip. Was it cruel to tell him this? I'd said no. I'd refused his proposal, and he had made it clear he wasn't interested in anything less than marriage. Would it only hurt him to tell him?

Oh, to hell with it!

'I love you.'

Silence.

Silence for a long, long moment, that stretched and—

Suddenly, he whirled around to face me. In a blink, he was at my bedside and grabbed hold of me. Digging his fingers into my hair as if it were the thread that connected him to life, he pulled me against him and kissed me, hard, fast, heady.

Holy hell! If this is his punishment for being drunk and disorderly, maybe I should do it more often!

When he finally broke away, he was panting. His eyes held mine captive, ice swirling in their sea-coloured depths.

'Likewise.'

Wasn't it wonderful how sweet and loving Mr Rikkard Ambrose phrased his romantic declarations? He should have become a poet.

'Move over,' he ordered.

I obeyed him, because it was always a good idea to stay unpredictable. Lifting the covers, he slid into bed beside me and wrapped his arms around me like iron fetters. Only iron wasn't quite as hard.

'So, we've established the basic parameters, Mr Linton. We both possess mutual affection for one another.'

'Yes, Sir.'

'And we both want to be together.'

'Yes, Sir.'

Gripping my shoulders, he turned me around. I lay there, gazing up at him. Darkness was starting to encroach on my vision, heralding the approach of sleep. But even if I'd been as drunk as the whole House of Lords, I would still have seen his stone-hard face, and his eyes, burning with sincerity.

'So have you changed your mind? Will you be my wife?'

I considered for a moment, then glanced over at the solitary little yellow piggy that had coiled itself up in a comfy corner of the room and was watching us with interest.

'What do you think?'

'Oink,' it said, and wiggled its tail.

'Good advice,' I agreed—and promptly dropped into unconsciousness.

INVESTIGATING

Have you ever tried to get a hungover French prima donna out of bed at seven in the morning? No?

Lucky you.

Now try imagine that, only while your head is hurting like the devil rammed his favourite pitchfork through your left ear, and you'll have a vague idea of how I felt the next morning. I didn't exactly feel like conducting an in-depth investigation. However, I decided it was better than trying to face Mr Rikkard Ambrose, since I was not entirely certain whether last night had been a weird dream, or whether I had really answered his renewed marriage proposal by oinking.

'*Merde! Vous, les Anglais, vous êtes complètement fou! Personne ne devrait pouvoir se promener à cette heure de la matinée.*'[20]

'Oh, come on Claudette,' I told the prima donna. We had gotten to a first-name basis last night. It was amazing what you could achieve while completely wankered. 'Put a *chausette* in it.'

She wrinkled her nose.

'What would I want with a ordinary, filthy sock? I only wear se most finest silken stockings.'

'Oh, just be quiet and come along. You know as well as I what we have to do.'

She continued grumbling in her native language, but she followed after me and settled herself down beside me in the room that had been declared our official centre of operations.

'And?' I asked her. 'Ready to investigate? Remember, you are my translator, so you'll have to pay close attention.'

She gave me a look of polite disinterest, and made a 'pouah' noise in the back of her throat that was as uniquely French as you could get. Sighing, I turned towards the door.

'Oh, well. Here goes nothing.' I cleared my throat. 'Send the first one in!'

The door opened, and a lady rushed in, a few music sheets in her hands and a dangerous glint in her eyes.

'*Est-ce que Ambrose va déduire ce temps de mon salaire?*' she demanded.

Claudette and I shared a look.

'Do you need me to translate sat?' she enquired, one corner of her mouth twitching.

I sighed and pulled out a list of prepared questions. I could see this was going to be a long investigation.

I turned out to be right, and wrong in a way. Right because I had not the least difficulty finding people who harboured a grudge against my new friend, the temperamental prima donna. In fact, the first two dozen people I interviewed gave me extensive and detailed plans of what they'd like to do the stuck-up witch, never mind that the stuck-up witch in question was in the room translating for them.

'*Pourquoi voudrais-je mettre un serpent dans sa chambre? Si je voulais nuire à la chienne, je lui aurai juste tiré dessus! Elle m'a volé le rôle principal dans les trois derniers opéras effectués dans cette décharge! Elle mérite de mourir! Le serpent l'a mordu?*'

---

[20] Shit! You English people are completely crazy! No one should be allowed to walk around awake at this hour of the morning.

64

'Why would I put a snake in her room?' Claudette translated. 'If I wanted to harm the bitch, I would just shoot her. She stole the leading role from me in the last three operas performed in this dump! She deserves to die! Did the snake bite her?'

Thoughtfully, my translator inclined her head. 'I have to admit, she has a point.'

'Err...you do? She has?'

'Absolutely. That's what I would have done if she had gotten the leading roll. Shot her, I mean. Oh, and regarding the "bitch" comment...'

She turned back to our suspect. '*Vous pouvez prendre votre arme à feu et tirer sur votre propre cul, misérable petit cafard!*'[21]

'Err...what did you just tell her?'

Claudette gave me a bright smile. 'I told her that we appreciate her honesty and cooperation, of course.'

'Of course you did.'

I asked the lady a few more questions, and Claudette translated (hopefully) faithfully, although I had the niggling suspicion that she tagged on a few less than complimentary remarks here and there. But who was I to prevent people from insulting each other? I was a firm proponent of freedom of speech, after all, as long as that didn't include beating someone to death with a volume of famous speeches.

One after the other, more members of the opera staff filed in, and with each and every one, the proceedings went more or less the same. I'd ask if they had put the snake into Claudette's changing room, and the answer would be...

Well, let me just give you a few examples.

'*Pourquoi utiliser un seul serpent? Et qui n'est pas toxique? Cela n'a aucun sens!*'

'Why would I use just one snake?' Claudette translated, nodding approvingly. 'And one sat isn't poisonous? Sat does not make any sense! You know...she's quite right, actually. If I'd gone for snakes, I'd 'ave used more than one, *certainment*.'

Or, the next one:

'*Un serpent d'Amérique du Sud? Pourquoi d'Amérique du Sud? Ma cousine Monique a utilisé un serpent local lorsque son mari était grossier, et cela a bien fonctionné pour elle, à en juger par la taille de son pied. Comment oses-tu suggérer que je serais antipatriotique au point d'utiliser un serpent étranger? Vive la France et notre roi Louis Philippe!*'

'A snake from South America?' Claudette translated. 'Why from South America? My cousin Monique used a local snake when her husband was being rough, and it worked perfectly fine for her, to judge by the size his foot swelled to. How dare you suggest I'd be so unpatriotic as to use a foreign snake? Long live France and our king Louis Philippe!'

And finally, my favourite:

---

[21] You can take that gun of yours and shoot it up your own arse, you miserable, slimy little cockroach.

'Mettre un serpent dans le vestiaire de la prima donna? Je ne ferais jamais une telle chose! Non, ce que je voudrais lui faire c'est coller une carotte sur sa tête, la peindre en argent et lui faire jouer une licorne sur scène devant tout le monde.'

'Put a snake in the prima donna's dressing room? I would never do such a thing! No, what I would like to do is glue a carrot to her head, paint her silver and make her play a unicorn on stage in front of everyo...really?' Breaking off, Claudette turned to the vindictively grinning, middle-aged janitor that sat facing us. 'Sat's the best you can sink of, Francois? You need to sink of somesin' a lot better if you want to get back at me because of the incident with se brooms, *mon ami!'*

At the end of a very long morning, I sagged back in my chair and stared at Claudette.

'Does anyone in this place not want to see you dead?'

'The mice under the floor?' she suggested, as if she wasn't entirely sure about them.

'I don't quite understand. How have you managed to get this many enemies? Do you have some nefarious alter ego that I have yet to meet?'

The prima donna gave a soft laugh, and looked at me with a mixture of pity and fondness. 'Oh, my dear *Monsieur* Linton, you don't actually sink sat sis has anythin' to do with 'ow I behave or w'o I am inside, do you?'

'It doesn't?'

'Of course not! I am se prima donna! Everybody wants me out of se way. Sey want my job, or sey want revenge for my taking se job from them, or from their mother, cousin, daughter, grand-niece twice removed...you take your pick.'

'Then how are you still walking and breathing?'

'Se *bon Dieu* likes me,' she said with a cheeky grin—which slowly disappeared from her face. 'Or at least I thought so until yesterday.'

'So...if everyone here wants you gone, how are we supposed to find out who put that snake in your room?'

Claudette shrugged, as if it were a matter which could still be solved tomorrow if we didn't get to it today. But spending a lot of time in the company of Rikkard Ambrose had given me an eye for looking beneath the surface. I could see the little twitches in her face that betrayed her hidden emotions. And among those emotions, one rose high above the others: fear.

Reaching out, I squeezed her hand.

'We're going to get them. Whoever they are, we're going to get them.'

She gave me a weak smile.

'Thank you, *Monsieur* Linton. You are a good man.'

Why did people keep telling me that? It always made me want to answer 'Not according to my crinkum-crankum[22].'

'Let's see...' I bit my lower lip and concentrated, trying to see our problem from all angles. 'We can't discover who has a motive, because practically everybody does. What else is there? Hm...We could gather the entire choir and...no,

---

[22] A Victorian expression for a woman's ladyparts.

that won't work. We could get the music director in one room with a gorilla, an axe and...no, that won't work either. We could...yes! Yes, that's it!'

I snapped my fingers. Sitting up straight, I grinned at Claudette.

'I know how we can find out the truth. Go and get Mr Ambrose! I've got a task for him.'

Claudette blinked. 'You 'ave a task for '*im*?'

'Yes.'

'And you want me to... *fetch* 'im?'

'Yes.'

'You have plate armour and a gun for me?'

'Ha, ha. Very funny.' I waved her off. 'Go! And hurry! We don't have much time.'

She jumped up and ran, and—wonder of wonders—truly returned with Mr Ambrose in tow only a few minutes later. He did not look pleased. Not at all.

'Mr Linton? I was told that told that my *assistant* required *my assistance*?'

Oh. I hadn't thought about it in those terms before. Maybe I should have gone myself after all. I cleared my throat.

'Well, um, err...yes.' I sat up straight. 'I know how we may be able to find out who's behind all this. But I need your help.'

Even though I might have oinked at you last night. You wouldn't mind that, would you? After all, it's a perfectly acceptable response to a proposal in most porcian families.

For a moment, I was sure he would tear me a new one. For a long, silent moment, I was sure he would just turn around without a word and march out of the room. But instead, he looked at me and said: 'How can I help?'

I felt a warm tug in my chest.

Maybe there was no oinking after all. Maybe, in response to his renewed proposal, I just passed out in a drunken stupor. Yay!

'I'm going to call the staff in again, one after another. And while I've got them in here and am squeezing everything I can out of them, I need you to go search their rooms.'

One stony eyebrow lifted infinitesimally. 'You want me to go and...what? Dig through dresses and note paper for clues?'

'I want you to search for a cage. Or a basket. Or anything else that could have been used to bring a snake into this place. Unless, of course, you think whoever did this brought it in here wrapped around their neck, disguised as a shawl?'

'Somewhat unlikely.' Mr Ambrose gave a slow nod. 'I see your point, Mr Linton. Adequate. I will go inspect the rooms in question, while you keep the suspects occupied.' He gave us both one last, hard, ice-cold look. 'Do your job well.'

Then he turned and was gone.

Beside me, Claudette raised a few sheets of music and fanned herself. '*Oh là là!* That man is simply...well, I know you are a man, so you would not understand, but trust me, he is...*oh là là!*'

'Oh, I think I understand what you mean,' I said, my voice rather fainter than usual.

We called in the first employee, and I pelted him with renewed questions, this time focusing on any contacts they might have to shipping companies, zoological gardens, geographical societies or any other place or organization that might somehow grant them access to rare South American serpents. This proved to be a far more fruitful line of enquiry than my previous attempts. By asking the staff members about each other and comparing their statements, I was able to eliminate most of them from my list of suspects. In the end, only three remained. I sent a messenger boy to inform Mr Ambrose who was under suspicion and where their rooms where located, and then detained them with further aimless questions. I was just starting to wonder how long I would have to keep them occupied when, from outside, a loud screech cut through the everyday noise of the opera house, followed by a resounding slap.

'Stay here!' Jumping to my feet, I pulled my revolver and raced to the door. Claudette, the stubborn idiot, acted as if she hadn't heard me and stayed right on my heels. Ha! A woman after my own heart.

Racing down the corridor, I swerved around a corner, approaching the epicentre of the commotion. To judge by the sound of it, a minor French Revolution was going on somewhere in the opera house, involving mostly female revolutionaries. I was ready for anything when I came around the last corner.

Or at least I thought I was, until I saw Mr Ambrose striding towards me, three red streaks down his cheek, and the rest of him covered in rouge and pink feathers. I stopped in my tracks, my eyes nearly popping out of their sockets.

'W-what happened to *you*?'

'The directions you gave me to the last suspect's room, Mr Linton—were they "left corridor from the entrance hall, two doors down"?'

'Yes.'

Mr Ambrose's eyes glittered with frost. 'Interesting. I wonder how it is, then, that when I opened that door I appeared to have stepped into the ballerinas' dressing room.'

My eyes, if possible, went even wider. 'The ballerinas'...!'

'Yes.'

'Oh dear.'

'Indeed.'

I eyed his decorated state. A tiny part of myself wondered if I shouldn't feel jealous that Mr Ambrose had entered a room full of scantily clad women. But the bigger part of me felt only one thing when looking at him right now: a burning need to burst into maniacal laughter.

'Mr Linton?'

'Y-yes?' I managed.

He raised a warning finger. A stray feather fell from his fingertip. 'One word. Just one word, and I...'

I whirled away, ducked through the nearest doorway and managed to slam the door behind me before succumbing to the inevitable.

~~**~*~*

68

Once Mr Ambrose had cleaned up, and I had managed to regain control of my facial muscles, we met with Claudette in Mr Ambrose's office for a strategic conference. Having told him about my three suspects, I expected him to have news for me after searching their rooms. And he did. Only not quite the news I was expecting.

'None of those people had anything resembling a basket or a cage in their rooms, Mr Linton.'

I frowned. 'You're sure? Did you look everywhere? Did you—'

'I checked every cupboard. Every wall. Every loose floorboard.'

'Couldn't you have missed—'

He gave me a look. 'I spent years in the colonies with little money in my pockets and only my wits to defend it. Trust me when I say I know how to hide something.'

I closed my mouth and nodded. A little shiver went down my back. Every time he said things like that I realized how little I actually still knew about Mr Rikkard Ambrose. Yet...how were you supposed to question a man like him? It was more likely you could open a safe with a can opener.

Focus, Lilly! You've got more important things to do right now.

'Well, then...what now?'

We exchanged looks. None of us seemed to know what to say, with the exception of Mr Ambrose, who knew how not to say anything.

'I suppose I'd better go back to re-interviewing the staff,' I sighed, finally. 'Maybe there's something I overlooked.'

The next few hours I spent once more cooped up with Claudette in our impromptu interrogation room, grilling one opera employee after another. But after an exhausting afternoon of endless questions, I still was no closer to discovering the truth. Finally, I slumped in my chair, utterly spent. Unfortunately, there were no yellow piggies to distract me. My eyelids, far too heavy to hold up anymore, slid shut.

'Do you have any more of that fabulous plonk with you?' I appealed to Claudette. 'I could use some right about now.'

'I'm afraid not, *mon ami*. Your dear employer confiscated it.'

I muttered something about Mr Rikkard Ambrose I would not be able to repeat in polite society—just as, without a knock, the door opened.

'I didn't quite hear that. You were saying, Mr Linton?'

Cautiously, I half-lifted one eyelid. There he was. Mr Rikkard Ambrose. 'I, err...I was just discussing the current state of our investigation with Claudette, Sir.'

'Indeed? So you have something to report?'

In answer, I sank deeper into my chair and groaned.

'Not really,' explained Claudette, my trusty translator.

Mr Ambrose opened his mouth, probably to fling some criticism at me—and then hesitated. His gaze slid over me, and a muscle in his jaw twitched.

'Hm. Well...I can't have you wasting the entire day with this. I am here in Paris for more than just this little opera house, you know.'

I groaned again, letting my eyes slide shut. Honestly, at the moment, I just couldn't find the energy for a rebuttal.

'Miss Allard?'

'Yes, Sir?' Claudette enquired.

'Go.'

'But—'

'Go *now*. I have things to discuss with Mr Linton.'

Shrugging, Claudette rose from her chair and left the room, leaving me behind under the intense scrutiny of Mr Rikkard Ambrose. With all my might, I managed to lift one eyelid.

'What? Are you going to give me a lecture on not doing my duties?'

'No.' He continued to watch me, his intense gaze sending a shiver down my back. 'How long have you been working, Mr Linton?'

I thought of saying something like, 'Not long enough, Mr Ambrose! I must get back to work immediately. After all, knowledge is power is time is money!'

But in the end, I just went with the truth.

'Too long for someone with a hangover,' I admitted, resisting the temptation to sink down onto the table. For a solid oak surface, it looked extraordinarily comfortable right now.

'Is that so? Hm.'

He regarded me for a moment—then seemed to come to a decision.

'Get ready!' he commanded.

'For what? More work?'

'No. To leave. Meet me at the front door in ten minutes.'

My head, already halfway down to the tabletop, came up again.

'The front door?'

He gave me a supreme look. 'Do you think that this measly little opera house is the only business in Paris I have to attend to? I cannot waste all my time investigating an incident that might have been nothing but the random act of a jealous singer. I have more important things to do. There are some interesting real estate investments I want to examine while I am here, and I need someone to accompany me through the city. Be sure to make the cantina cook give you something edible to take along. The real estate evaluation will likely take up the rest of the day.'

It took a few moments for his words to sink in. When they did, I felt a tingle rise inside me. My one open eyelid rose a little higher.

'This "real estate evaluation"...would it involve us walking through Paris? Making a tour of the city?'

'Probably.'

'And would it also involve us passing some popular tourist attractions?'

He gave a jerk with one shoulder, that might have been a shrug. 'Quite possibly. These are difficult to avoid here.'

'And we'll be feeding pigeons?'

'If you want to waste your lunch, be my guest.'

'Mr Rikkard Ambrose...!' A grin started to spread across my tired face. 'Are you asking me on a *romantic rendezvous* to take my mind off things?'

'Certainly not!' His spine stiffening, he sent me an arctic look. 'I am here for business purposes and require my assistant, Mr Linton. So get moving, will you? Knowledge is power is time is money!'

My grin widened. 'Yes, Sir! Right away, Sir!'

CITY OF LOVE, BACON, AND EGGS

I waited in the candlelit entrance hall, nearly jumping with excitement. I was going on a rendezvous with Mr Rikkard Ambrose! In Paris! And also in trousers. I would have put on a dress, but I had been expecting to march into mortal danger when coming here, and so hadn't even bothered to pack one. Maybe I would remedy that at some point in the future, but for now...

I grinned at the sound of footsteps behind me and turned to face Mr Rikkard Ambrose marching towards me.

'Good evening, Sir. Ready for your rendezvous?'

He gave me a cool look. 'This isn't a rendezvous, Mr Linton. This is a business matter.'

'Of course, Sir. Certainly.' I lifted the wicker basket I'd brought with me. 'I brought a picnic, just as you asked.'

'Marching rations, Mr Linton. Those are marching rations.'

'Of course, Sir. Just as you say, Sir.'

I pushed open the door, and together we stepped out into the mild Paris evening. In passing, I smiled and nodded at the doorman, who was halfway into nodding back—when suddenly, his eyes widened with recognition, he gave a squeak and jumped backwards to duck behind the nearest column.

Mr Ambrose looked from me to the doorman and back again. One eyebrow lifted about a quarter of a millimetre. I acted as if I didn't notice and, whistling, strolled off into Paris.

We made our first stop at a beautiful, wrought-iron bridge spanning the Seine. For several minutes, we just stood there, gazing over the water glittering in the last light of the sinking sun, and taking in the fact that we were both here, side by side, in this beautiful place. Finally, the little *ifrit* in me reared its head and asked:

'So...what are we here to inspect?' One corner of my mouth lifted. 'What real estate do you want to buy?'

Mr Ambrose's little finger twitched. Quickly, he glanced around from right to left, and then said, as if that should be evident to anyone and he was surprised I'd asked, 'This bridge, of course.'

'You want to buy the...what is it called?' Doubtfully, I glanced at the massive iron construction connecting two public roads. Couples were strolling up and down everywhere, holding hands, enjoying the fresh evening air.

'The *Pont des Arts.*'

'Pardon my saying so...but won't the city of Paris object to your buying a public bridge?'

In answer, he pulled a measuring tape out of his pocket and started examining the bridge, mumbling and taking notes in a little notebook. I looked on with a little smile and let him be. Firstly, because it was adorable how hard he was trying to be businesslike, and secondly, because there was a tiny chance that he was actually planning to buy up all of Paris' public bridges. This was Mr Rikkard Ambrose were talking about, after all.

'Where next?' I enquired when he put his measuring tape away.

Mr Ambrose pointed across the bridge, to where an imposing two-wing palace with a lavish park rose high above the Seine.

'There.'

'Err...Mr Ambrose?'

'Yes?'

'Pardon me if I'm mistaken, but isn't that the Louvre?'

'Yes.'

I blinked. 'The Louvre is part of your real estate inspection tour.'

'Indeed.'

'Just so I get this right – you want to *buy* the *Louvre*.'

'I am not in the habit of repeating myself, Mr Linton. The building in question is prime real estate near the waterfront that wastes a lot of space — space that could be used as building sites — on greenery and open spaces.' Cocking his head, he gave the museum a critical look. 'Also, I have heard that for some reason, a number of eccentric people consider the contents of the building to also be of considerable value.'

Covering my eyes, I gave a dismissive wave. 'Forget I asked.'

'Well, what are you waiting for, Miss Linton? Let's go.'

He marched off towards the Louvre, and I followed. I had to say, it was quite an interesting visit. It was probably the first time that the museum's guides and curators had been asked questions like 'How thick is the wall behind that ugly painting there?' and 'How much rent does an average flat bring in this quarter of the city' or 'Excuse me, is that a water pipe behind that chunky statue? How much would it cost to get running water in this whole place if you partitioned the rooms?'

Of course, most of the conversations happened in French, so I wasn't really sure what was said most of the time, but I could deduce pretty much everything from the way the curators' faces turned first white, then red, and maybe even a little bit blue in a fit of enraged patriotism. One of these artistic gentlemen finally tried to have Mr Ambrose removed from the building after he started to check the wall behind the Mona Lisa for structural soundness. I, meanwhile, leaned against a column next to an ancient Greek fellow in a marble bedsheet, watching the whole scene with relish. This was exactly what I needed to relax.

'And?' I asked innocently when Mr Ambrose came over, his lips tight and his hand clenched around his measuring tape. 'How is the wall behind dear Lisa?'

'Mr Linton?'

'Yes, Sir?'

'Be silent!'

'Yes, Sir.'

'Follow me.'

'Right away, Sir. Bye!' Waving to my Greek friend and to the curator who was still mumbling about mad Englishmen, I hurried after Mr Ambrose.

Our next stops were the *Champs-Élysées* and the *Arc de Triomphe*. By the time we had switched directions and were heading towards the Cathedral of *Notre Dame*, Mr Ambrose had pretty much given up the pretence of reviewing possible real estate for purchase and development—which was good, because I don't think the Catholic Church would have been happy. I heard the Pope can be difficult about things like levelling cathedrals to build apartment buildings. We climbed all the way up to the top (after Mr Ambrose stared at a priest who said we couldn't, and the little man hurried off to pray) and stood at the stone railing, looking over the city of Paris in the setting sun.

For the first time in a long while, I was away from all work, from all noise, breathing in clear air. It made me feel free. I gave a sigh.

'I could stay up here forever. Too bad I don't have a hump on my back.'

Mr Ambrose stared fixedly ahead into the sunset. Or...did his eyes flicker over to me for just a millisecond?

'I cannot say I feel similar regret over that particular lack, Mr Linton.'

Mr?

I jabbed his ribs.

'Oh, come on! We're at the top of a church, hundreds of yards away from anyone, in a city where the people don't speak English! Even if I'm wearing trousers, I think you could call me Lillian without risking a scandal, don't you?'

'No.' Still, he would not look at me. 'I can't. Because if I were to call you Lillian, if I'd let myself think and feel what you really are to me, I would do something that *would* cause a scandal. *Especially* in a church.'

'Oh.' I felt heat rush to my cheeks. Thank God it was fast getting dark. 'Mr Ambrose, I...'

Suddenly, he whirled to face me, and, in the last light of the setting sun, his usually cold eyes seemed to gleam with fire.

'You haven't given me an answer yet.'

I didn't even pretend not to know what he was talking about. His question still echoed in my mind, haunting me at every opportunity.

So, have you changed your mind? Will you be my wife?

I swallowed.

'You know I didn't say no the first time because of you, don't you?' Whose voice was this timid, whisper? Who was speaking? Surely not I. I was a strong and independent woman, and I bloody well sounded like one!

Silence was the only answer I got.

Quickly, I turned towards him. 'You do, don't you?'

More silence. Cold. Hard. Icy. Silence. Grabbing his beautiful face in both hands I stood up on tiptoe to press my forehead pressed against his. Our breaths mingled in the cool evening air. Revelling in the feeling, I closed my eyes.

'It's not because of you,' I whispered. 'I love you. But...those vows...I...I...can't...'

I can't swear to obey a man. Not even you. And you won't take me unless I do.

Opening my eyes, I gazed up at him, hoping he would read in my face what I couldn't put into words right then.

His left little finger twitched.

'Maybe we could come to some kind of...compromise.'

Pardon?

Screech! Pull the brakes. Halt the universe for a moment. Had I just heard correctly? Had Mr Rikkard Ambrose, Mr I'll-grind-you-into-the-dust-before-I-shift-an-inch-from-my-conditions Ambrose just offered to *compromise*?

'Did I fall off the cathedral, break my neck and go to heaven?' I enquired.

To judge by the look on his face, he didn't appreciate my attempt at humour. His eyes narrowed infinitesimally. 'Not that I'm aware of, Mr Linton. However, that can be arranged.'

'Ah. I must be dreaming, then.' Dropping all humour, all defences, everything that stood between the two of us, I slid my arms around him and pulled him close.

A compromise. A compromise! What does it that mean?

Should I dare hope it meant he wanted me more than he wanted to own me?

He hesitated for a moment—then roughly pulled me against him and held me so tight I almost couldn't breathe. I didn't complain.

'And what a dream it is,' he whispered. 'What a dream.'

'In a dream, we could be together forever.' My grip on him tightened even more, as if I never wanted to let go. 'Just imagine it...no society, no judgements, no laws, no stupid vows of obedience...just the two of us, able to do whatever the heck we want.'

His grip tightened, too. Now I really couldn't breathe—but for the moment, I didn't care. I'd always thought about starting a career as a Caribbean pearl diver. Didn't they have to hold their breaths for over eight minutes?

'Adequate.'

'So...how do we make this dream reality?'

Loosening his grip, he took my chin in one hand and made me look up at him.

'I'm master of my fate,' he told me, and his cold, hard face had never looked as beautiful as in that moment. 'Making dreams reality is what I do.'

'I thought that was making massive amounts of money.'

He raised one eyebrow about half a millimetre. 'As I said—making dreams reality is what I do.'

I narrowed my eyes. Suddenly, a very important question occurred to me. A question which, all things considered, I probably should have asked before now. 'Which is more important to you—me or your money?'

He considered the matter for a moment. And another moment. And another. Finally...

'Is that a trick question?'

I stomped on his foot.

'You...you...bloody son of a bachelor!'

'Language, Miss Linton. Language.'

'Just shut up and hold me.'

He did. And so we stood there, high above Paris, watching the sun set, safe in each other's arms. And deep, deep inside, I didn't need to hear the answer to my question, because I already knew with a hundred percent certainty which of the two was most important to Rikkard Ambrose.

Well...ninety-nine percent. But that was all right.

Soon, the sun had disappeared behind the horizon, and the cool blanket of night spread across Paris. Still—neither of us felt like returning home already and breaking the spell of the evening. So we went to the Luxembourg Gardens[23] and settled down in a quiet corner of the magnificent park. Spreading out a chequered blanket, we unpacked our dinner and tucked in. For entertainment, we had a little disagreement.

'No,' Mr Ambrose said, his face immovable, 'it is not.'

'Oh, come on!' I jabbed my elbow into his ribs, nearly giving it a bruise. 'How can you say that?'

'Quite simply. It. Is. Not.'

'Mr Ambrose—we are in the middle of a beautiful park, which by the way we have nearly all to ourselves at this late hour—sitting on a chequered blanket, eating sandwiches and watching the stars glitter in the night sky. How does this *not* qualify as a romantic picnic?'

'Easy. It is merely a simplified work dinner. It relieves one of the need to expend money on useless items such as chairs, tables, knives, forks and plates. I am actually considering implementing a similar eating environment at my various offices and factories.'

'I'm sure your staff will be thrilled.'

In answer, Mr Ambrose pulled out a baguette and started cutting it into neat, equal slices. Somewhere in the distance, a nightingale started to sing. Other than that, there were no sounds audible here, deep in the park, shielded by the trees and the night.

We're totally alone.

As if sensing my thoughts, Mr Ambrose glanced up. He didn't stop his preparations for his simplified work dinner, his hands continuing to move with the effortless precision of someone who'd had to make his own meals many a time. His eyes bored into me.

We're even more alone than we were on top of Notre Dame. *Nobody else is in the park at this hour. All the fine people of Paris are probably preparing to go to the opera, looking forward to hearing sweet songs about love.*

The nightingale sang again, this time closer. Mr Ambrose put the knife aside and leant towards me.

I don't think I'm going to need to go to the opera.

'Miss Linton?'

'Yes?' I breathed.

'Hand me the bacon.'

---

[23] A beautiful park that is a popular tourist attraction today. In spite of its name, it is not located in the country of Luxembourg, but in the city of Paris. Its name originates from the fact that it was originally owned by the Duke of Luxembourg.

I blinked. 'Pardon?'

'The bacon. To put on the baguette. And the bowl of scrambled eggs.'

What the...? Was he serious? He wanted to *eat*? And, even more disturbing...

'You're out on a romantic midnight picnic in the middle of Paris, and you brought *eggs and bacon*?'

'This is not a picnic. And certainly I did.'

I reached into the basket and pulled out the bowls with the eggs and bacon. For a moment, I considered smashing them over his head—but then concluded that would probably hurt the bowl more than him.

Doesn't he know? Doesn't he feel what's happening between us?

Before I could fling the questions or the bowls in his face, he reached out to take them. And when his fingers touched mine, I realized: he *did* know. He *did* feel. He was just very good at hiding underneath a hard shell of ice.

Heat surged between us as our fingers brushed against each other. His hand lingered. One moment. And another. And another.

'Let go of the bowls, Miss Linton.'

'You let go of my fingers.'

He didn't.

I let go of the bowls.

He still didn't.

A branch cracked nearby, and we started apart, relaxing only when the shadowy form of a bunny raced across the lawn. If someone saw two gentlemen in tailcoats having a romantic picnic in the moonlight, probably not even the liberal-minded Parisians would be willing to look the other way. Still, I couldn't seem to make myself care. It felt as we were in our own little world, as if the night around us was protecting us and our special moment.

Opening the bowls, Mr Ambrose started to prepare sandwiches. I didn't really feel hungry anymore. Not for food. But when he lifted one tasty morsel into the air and held it out towards me, that didn't keep my mouth from watering.

His eyes met mine.

'Come here!' he ordered.

I shook my head. 'No. You come here.'

A muscle in his jaw twitched. But...it wasn't the usual kind of twitch. 'Maybe we could meet in the middle?'

A smile tugged at the corners of my lips. 'You mean...like a compromise?'

'Yes,' he said, leaning forward. 'Exactly like that.'

I leant forward, too, and by the time we reached each other, food was long forgotten. Our lips met and we clung to each other, in the silence and the dark, not needing anything or anyone except each other. Deep inside me, a beautiful, inescapable knowledge settled.

This is the beginning. The beginning of us.

DALGLIESH'S PLAN

Most couples would probably have strolled back from their rendezvous hand in hand, exchanging kisses. The two of us marched back at top speed, exchanging arguments about Paris real estate prices—and I loved every single minute. Who the heck said you had to be like other couples, anyway? I was myself, and he was he, and neither of us would make apologies. The fact that he still wanted me, that he valued me, meant a thousand times more to me than any conventional romantic gestures.

He's willing to make a compromise. A compromise!

We reached the opera house just as the show for the evening performance was opening. People were standing in a line that reached all around the block, which Mr Ambrose promptly ignored. Someone opened his mouth to protest as my dear employer cut in line—until he met Mr Ambrose's eyes and shut up faster than I could blink. We reached the door with minimal fuss. This time, the other doorman I happened to know was standing there, smiling at the crowd— a smile that disappeared the instant he saw me.

'Hello there.' I winked at him.

The man gave a yelp and jumped behind a nearby potted plant, cowering down, out of the line of fire.

'A very nice evening to you, too!' I called as we stepped inside. Turning, I met the piercing gaze of Mr Rikkard Ambrose.

'Something the matter, Sir?' I enquired innocently.

'What is the matter with those men?' He jabbed one finger at the spot where, a moment ago, the doorman had stood. The trembling cap of the man was still peeking out from behind the potted plant. 'This is the second time today! Have they lost their senses?'

I gave him a sweet smile, and flexed my non-existent biceps. 'Can't you tell? They find me intimidating.'

Mr Ambrose gave me a look. One of *those* looks.

'This is no time for jests, Mr Linton.'

And, whirling, he marched away. I, meanwhile, glanced back at the doorman who was just peeking out from behind the potted plant. Raising my hand, I pointed a finger gun at him and mimed shooting. Quickly, the poor man ducked down again. Giggling to myself, I hurried after Mr Ambrose. The poor man. If he only knew what he was in for in the years to come...

Hurrying across the entrance hall, I caught up with Mr Ambrose.

'What is being performed tonight?'

'Some new thing by a local composer.' He gave a dismissive wave.

'Can we see it?'

He gave me a startled glance. 'I've already watched one performance, Mr Linton. That was sufficient to assess the capabilities of the performers and remove the inadequate ones.'

'I meant,' I said in the tone of someone explaining the meaning of 'entertainment' to a granite boulder, 'watch it *for fun.* You know, fun? That thing where you do something to enjoy yourself?'

'That, Mr Linton, would be a complete waste of time and—'

Batting my eyelashes, I looked up into his eyes.

'Mr Linton!'

'Yes, Sir, Mr Ambrose, Sir?'

'Cease that immediately!'

'What, Sir? I'm not doing anything.'

'Cease looking at me like that!'

'Like what, Sir?'

He held out for another three impressive seconds—then gave an indistinct noise in the back of his throat and turned around.

'Maybe I should assess the performers' capabilities a second time, just to be sure.'

'I think that's an excellent idea,' I agreed primly, and followed him up the stairs to the box he had apparently reserved from himself. I wondered if I should start whistling in triumph, but decided that would probably be pushing things a little too far.

We settled in the luxurious box, and my derrière got to enjoy the rare experience of sitting next to Rikkard Ambrose on something that wasn't a bare plank of wood, the hump of a camel or a slab of stone in a South American ruin. Sighing contentedly, I leant back and prepared to enjoy the show as the curtains opened.

Since I didn't understand much French besides *merde*, the plot was a little difficult to follow. If I grasped matters correctly, the heroine was in love with a gentleman who was in love with another lady who was in love with a man who was in love with the heroine. Everyone was very brave and noble and suffered in silence, except for the villain, who was villainous and sang for about a quarter of hour about how he was going to kill everybody, not seeming to care that the heroine was within hearing distance, and so on, and so on.

I must admit, the performance wasn't quite what I had been hoping for. I had been expecting a little bit more intrigue, more passion, more action on the stage. But all I got was another aria about two characters in the woes of love. I was about to lean over to Mr Ambrose and ask how long the performance would still last, when suddenly, a body dropped from the higher levels of the scenery and hit the stage with a thud. Gasps rose from the startled audience, and a bit of fake blood trickled down from a stab wound on the actor's chest.

'Now this is what I'm talking about!' Clapping my hands, I leant forward. 'Finally! I was waiting for something exciting to happen. It's done so well! Especially the fake blood. How did they get it to look so realistic?'

Slowly, Mr Ambrose leant over. His face seemed even stonier than usual.

'This,' he informed me, 'is not part of the performance.'

It took a moment for his words to sink in. My eyes flicked back to the prone actor on stage and the fake—or maybe not-so-fake—blood trickling from his stab wound. A cold tingle travelled down my spine.

'Oh.'

'Indeed, Mr Linton.'

For one single moment, there was fateful silence. For a moment, everything hung in the air. What would happen? Screams? Chaos? A scandal that Paris would never forget?

Then one of the violinists struck up a timid note. Others joined in, rising in a sinister crescendo, and the singers on the stage resumed their aria, sounding slightly shriller than before.

'They're singing! Why the heck are they singing?'

Mr Ambrose cocked his head, listening to the French words. 'Ah. Apparently, the clandestine romantic meeting of the two characters has been interrupted by the ghoul of a former lover, who, in his undead wrath, has decided to haunt them and bleed on their shoes. An innovative storyline. Perhaps I should suggest to the playwright that he incorporate this into his libretto.'

'They put the *corpse* in the *opera*?'

Mr Ambrose gave me a look. 'You might have heard of a saying that is popular among performing artists, Mister Linton: the show must go on. Especially when the man paying your wages is watching.'

'I don't quite remember that second part.' I still couldn't tear my gaze away from the dead man on the stage. The pool of blood was widening, and the actors were having increasing difficulties not stepping in it while they finished their aria about the woes of love.

'Innovation is everywhere, Mr Linton. Especially in the opera.' Leaning forward, he raised an opera glass to his eye. 'Ah. Apparently, even in the face of this daunting haunting, the two protagonists remained faithful in their unending love. How romantic. And profitable.'

'There's a dead body on the stage. A *dead body*!'

In the audience, tears sparkled and handkerchiefs were raised to eyes. Here and there, some noses were cleared, and applause rose as the aria came to its climax. With an energetic kick, the lady singer kicked the corpse off the stage. With a thump, it fell down into the opera pit on top of some hapless tuba player, and to frantic applause from the audience, the two lovebirds sank into each other's arms, kissing passionately. The curtain closed, and several people rose to their feet, shouting '*Da capo! Da capo!*'

'That was a truly ingenious ending wasn't it?' an elderly Spanish lady in the box next to ours said to her friends, who nodded energetically.

'Oh yes! I haven't seen such a marvellous opera in a long time. This fellow Berlioz will go far.'

Again, shouts of '*da capo, da capo*' rose from the audience. Wasn't that Italian for 'again'? Cautiously, I glanced at Mr Ambrose. If a paying audience was calling for opera with mayhem and murder, would he...?

'Cease looking at me like that, Mr Linton.'

'Like what?'

'Like you're concerned I'll start snatching people of the streets for a realistic re-enactment of the French Revolution in operatic form.'

'I would never think such a thing of you!'

Actually, I had been thinking rather along the lines of Hannibal and the Battle of Cannae.

'Just in case you are not clear about this, Mr Linton,' he told me, his icy eyes boring into me, nailing me to my seat, 'I'm not pleased about what happened. Not at all.'

I blinked. 'You aren't? But I thought...'

'Oh, I'm pleased about the *outcome*.' He nodded at the happily chattering audience that was slowly getting to its feet and filing out of the hall. 'No one noticed what happened. There wasn't a hint of scandal. But am I happy about what occurred?' Slowly, he flexed his fingers, as if wrapping them around an imaginary neck. 'Most assuredly not. And you can trust me when I say that, once I find out who is behind this, they are going to pay.'

'In pounds or francs?'

'Mr Linton?'

'Yes, Sir?'

'Shut up, and up on your feet!'

'Yes, Sir!'

'Let's have a look around the stage, shall we?'

While the audience was still happily chatting about the wonderful performance and the singers returned to the stage for a second round of bows, Mr Ambrose and I slipped out of our box. He started down the corridor, his long strides eating up the distance, and I hurried after him, nibbling at the distance as best I could. Inside, my mind was whirling. A murder! An actual murder! Was it Claudette? Had they gotten to her?

Damn! Why did she have to offer me a free drink? It was practically guaranteed we'd be friends after that. And now I was worried sick for the woman. Damn her and her delicious bottle.

Calm down! It's not Claudette. It can't be.

Even from a distance, it had been pretty clear the victim was a man—or at least had dressed like one. Unless she'd taken a leaf out of my book and taken up cross-dressing, Claudette was perfectly safe. But if it hadn't been her they were after, then who? There couldn't be this many intrigues and unscripted murder plots in this opera house, could there?

Shouts and curses came from up ahead.

Or maybe there could.

'Faster, Mr Linton. Faster!'

'Coming, Sir!'

This was beginning to look more like something other than a simple rivalry. Something much more sinister. Had we misjudged the situation from the start? What the heck was going on?

We rushed around another corner, and finally stood in front of a large door marked STAGE. Well, actually it was marked *SCÈNE*. I just hoped that was French for 'stage', and not 'gentleman's lavatory'.

Without hesitation, Mr Ambrose shoved open the door. Thank God the curtain was already closed again, or *Monsieur* Berlioz would have gotten another unscheduled addition to his latest opera. A group of people in colourful costumes was standing in a circle, whispering to each other, a motionless leg sticking out from their midst.

'What,' Mr Ambrose demanded, his voice as cold as a glacier having a good time in the middle of the ice age[24], 'is going on here?'

Everyone whirled to face him. The moment she caught sight of him, the mezzo-soprano's eyes flashed, and she stormed towards him.

'I quit!' she declared, waving her fingers in her face. 'No good pay? Fine! Philistine *patron* who understand nothing of opera? Fine! But dead *cadavre* interrupting my scene? *Non, merci beaucoup!'*

Slamming her feathery hat into Mr Ambrose's face, she marched off stage, muttering under her breath.

With two fingers, Mr Ambrose picked the offending object off his stony visage.

'Well?' he enquired, staring at the wide-eyed remaining staff. 'I am waiting for an explanation.'

Instinctively, everyone took a step back. Not one of them said a word.

Stepping closer, I pushed them aside to look at the unfortunate victim—and sucked in a breath. 'Mr Ambrose, you need to come and look at this!'

Instantly, he was by my side. There was a moment of silence, then... 'Hm. I see what you mean, Mr Linton.'

'He must have been dead for a while. Look at his face!'

'Definitely not well-preserved.' He sniffed. 'To judge by the smell, the flies have been at him.'

One of the remaining ladies gave a dramatic sigh and collapsed into a well-practiced decorative faint with no risk of injury. This was the opera, after all.

I frowned down at the red stain spreading on the stage. 'But if the corpse is that old, why is he still bleeding?'

Instead of answering my question, Mr Ambrose bent and, with the careless attitude of a man who'd lived off dead rats and dry bread crusts for several years of his life, dipped a finger into the red liquid and tasted it.

'Tomato juice,' he stated.

Another lady fainted in a decorative manner.

'*Tomato juice?*' Claudette, who had been silently watching so far, strode forward, pushing through the other onlookers. '*Moi*, I do not understand sis! What kind of maniac would use a tomato juice to make a fake corpse bleed?'

'Se prop master?' suggested someone.

'Except for him, you *idiot!*'

Mr Ambrose's eyes met with mine, and silent agreement travelled between us.

---

[24] Just in case you are wondering whether it is historically accurate to be referencing the ice age in a book set in Victorian times—the first modern scientific theory of a widespread ice age was developed by the Danish-Norwegian geologist Jens Esmark in the early nineteenth century. So it is quite plausible for such a comparison to occur.

'I don't think this corpse was the work of the prop master,' I told the assembled singers.

'No indeed.' Mr Ambrose looked grim. 'This was the work of someone who wanted to cause a scandal with minimal danger to themselves. Nobody could convict someone of murder for leaving a body that had been killed weeks ago, and probably dug up from a vagrant graveyard.'

'But for the opera house...' I continued his thought, and he nodded.

'For the opera house, it would have been another matter entirely. A dead body on the stage? That's the stuff that scandals are made of. Scandals the like of which could break this place.'

'Kind of like a deadly snake in the prima donna's changing room?'

'Exactly like that.'

'But w'o?' Claudette demanded. 'W'o could want to ruin sis entire opera house? We shust sing 'ere! We are no danger to anyone!'

'Hm...' I stroked my chin, pretending to think. 'Who do we know that would love to ruin each and every business venture of Mr Rikkard Ambrose...let me think...do we know such a person?'

'I told you, it's not Dalgliesh.' Mr Ambrose gave an aggravated headshake. 'He wouldn't concern himself with a little matter like a single opera house, unless—'

Suddenly, he cut off.

'*Guizot!*' he hissed.

'Whatever kind of curse that is,' I told him, 'I'm sure it's not fit for ladies' ears. What does it mean?'

'It's not a curse, Mr Linton. It's a man.'

'Oh.'

'François Guizot, the French foreign minister.'

My brow furrowed. 'I don't understand. What does this have to do with Dalgliesh?'

'I think we'd better discuss that elsewhere, Mr Linton.'

It was only then I realized that everyone around us was listening intently. Even several people who I—up to that point—had believed didn't speak a word of English seemed to be quite interested in our discussion. A cold shiver went down my spine.

'You there! You! And you!' Mr Ambrose pointed at a few of the male singers. 'Grab this—' He jabbed the corpse with a boot, '—and dispose of it. Quietly. You, Mr Linton, come with me.'

He strode away and left Claudette to translate to her colleagues that they had just been promoted from famous singers to corpse-removers.

Mr Ambrose marched me off the stage and to the closest door, which he immediately pulled open.

'Inside!'

'That's a broom closet!'

'Which means nobody will find it worthwhile to listen at the door. Inside. *Now.*'

I did as he ordered, and Mr Ambrose stepped in after me, closing the door behind us. I had to silently congratulate him on originality. I had envisioned quite a few scenarios that could motivate Mr Ambrose and me to sneak off into a broom closet—but discussing corpses and French politics had not been one of them.

'What is this all about?' I demanded of the darkness. 'What has this Guizot fellow to do with Lord Dalgliesh?'

Mr Ambrose muttered something else in French which—this time—I was pretty sure was a curse word.

'I was a fool! I should have seen it sooner. Guizot, as foreign minister, is the driving force between the peaceful coexistence of France and England. It was his appointment that soothed tensions and maybe even averted war in the wake of the Far East Crisis.'

I nodded. 'Averted war. Sounds good.'

Even in the complete darkness surrounding us, I could feel the tickle of Mr Ambrose's cool look.

'Not for someone whose business thrives on war, and on the expansion of the British Empire, Mr Linton.'

Something went *click* in my head. Mr Ambrose must have felt me stiffening, because I heard him take a small step towards me.

'Yes, Mr Linton. Dalgliesh is not at all pleased with *Monsieur* François Guizot. He would love for the man to simply disappear. Or maybe even die.'

I felt a cold shiver travel down my spine.

'So what? What if he wants that politician gone? This has nothing to do with our dead man on the stage, surely?'

'Don't you see, Mr Linton? Guizot is protected. He rarely makes public appearances, and when he does, it is in heavily guarded, secure government locations. He knows very well there are plenty of people who'd like nothing better than to see him dead. But there are some things a minister cannot avoid. One of them is attending his king at public events—when he holds a parade, visits the theatre, or sometimes...the opera.'

I swallowed.

'And how many opera houses are there in Paris?'

'Many. But few of them large and prestigious enough for people like Guizot, let alone the king. Only two come to mind. I own one of them.'

I smiled weakly into the shadows. 'Do I get three guesses to find out who owns the other?'

'If you need three guesses for that, Mr Linton, I have considerably overestimated your intelligence.'

I didn't give him a sharp retort, or even a kick on the shin. My mind was still busy whirling from the implications of what he'd just told me.

'So...Dalgliesh is trying to bring this opera into disrepute? Why? So next time some government minister watches the opera at his place?'

'Yes. At his place, with his armed men everywhere, and his hands holding the keys to all the doors. Imagine how many accidents could happen in such an environment.'

'Holy moly! You don't mean...?'

Was he honestly suggesting that Lord Dalgliesh was planning to assassinate the minister of a foreign government? And not just any foreign government, but Britain's bitterest rival, who, just a few decades ago, had nearly brought this country to its knees?

'Doesn't he realize what will happen?' I had to clutch the wall, I felt so dizzy. 'If the wrong people are suspected of this assassination, the French king will have no choice but to take action! There will be war. Not just a battle here and there, but real, actual, full-out war, all across the continent. It would be Napoleon all over again! He can't be planning that! He can't!'

A firm hand landed on my shoulder.

'As I said,' Mr Ambrose's cool voice reached my whirling mind. 'Lord Dalgliesh does not concern himself with small endeavours.'

A choked sound came out of my mouth. Maybe it was a laugh. Maybe not. I didn't know.

'Not that the goings-on on the continent are why he is planning this,' Mr Ambrose continued.

I blinked. 'He isn't?'

'Of course not. Remember, Mr Linton. What happened the last time Britain and France fought? What happened during the Napoleonic Wars?'

It took a moment for the penny to drop. Probably because it was one of the pennies in Mr Ambrose's purse, and he was loath to let it go.

'The English fleet devastated the weaker French fleet, and France was cut off from all its colonies!'

'Exactly. Imagine a repeat performance of that, all those colonies without supplies, without reinforcements. There will be no other big colonial power to balance Great Britain, and Lord Dalgliesh will be in India, with the largest army of the world not tied down in the continental conflict, free to do as he wishes, the world as his personal plaything.'

I did try to imagine it. But I stopped when I nearly had to hurl.

I had only one question. Grabbing Mr Ambrose by the collar, I pulled him towards me until I knew that, even in the dark, I was staring directly into his eyes.

'How do we stop him?'

NEW ARRIVALS

How do we stop him?

Mr Ambrose had answered the question only with silence. And really...I couldn't blame him. Morals aside, it was comparatively easy to shoot someone through the head, especially if you had Dalgliesh's kind of power. It was a lot harder to prevent someone from being shot through the head if you didn't know when the shot was coming and where it was coming from.

For days and days, while we quietly disposed of the corpse, cleaned the stage and tried to keep rumours to a minimum, we both brooded over this question.

Finally, inspiration hit! I had an idea. A brilliant idea!

Only...I was pretty sure it was one Mr Ambrose was going to detest.

Still, I had to try. We couldn't be sure that we had guessed Dalgliesh's plans correctly—but it all fit so horribly well. Mr Ambrose had told me the king and foreign minister were set to return from a trip to Versailles next month and, by all reports, the king liked to show his face in public whenever he came back, to be cheered along and reassure himself another revolution wasn't just around the corner. And, of course, his favourite minister would be there.

It might be possible that we had misread the situation. That Dalgliesh wasn't after Guizot at all. But with Lord Daniel Eugene Dalgliesh, it was always wise to assume the worst. I had to tell Mr Ambrose what I'd come up with. If there was only the slightest chance to avert what we feared was coming, I had to let him know.

Marching up to his office door, I knocked.

'Enter,' came his commanding voice from inside.

I pushed open the door and stepped inside, finding Mr Ambrose pouring over thick piles of papers. They weren't bills or sheets of music for the next performance. Oh no. Even upside-down, I could spot words like 'surveillance' and 'report' before he hurriedly put the papers away.

'Yes, Mr Linton?'

'You're keeping an eye on Dalgliesh, aren't you?'

The look he gave me was so cold it was almost scary. Only almost, though, because of the words that next came out of his mouth. 'You stay away from Dalgliesh! He's dangerous.'

Warmth flooded my heart. He cared. He cared if I was in danger. The arrogant, chauvinistic asshole! He should know that I could very well take care of myself. How could any one person make you feel so mushy and pissed off at the same time?

Concentrate, Lilly!

Clearing my throat, I stepped closer to the desk.

'I may have an idea of how we can prevent Dalgliesh's plans, Sir.'

'Indeed, Mr Linton?'

'Yes indeed, Sir.'

I explained my idea to him. He listened calmly and patiently until I was finished, and then he nailed me to the wall with his cold gaze. By the looks of him, he was contemplating fixing me in place there permanently, if that could stop my crazy plans.

'No!'

'Just think about it!' I cajoled.

'You can't be serious, Mr Linton!'

'But it would work. I'm sure it would.'

'Dropping Dalgliesh into a volcano would also work. That does not mean it is a feasible plan.'

'But it would be a darn interesting one.' I tugged my ear. 'Are you sure there aren't any volcanos around here?'

'Mr Linton!'

'All right, all right. Back to my original plan, then.'

He didn't seem much more pleased about that. His eyes narrowed. 'Ah yes. Your "original plan". Correct me if I am mistaken, Mr Linton. Your plan consists of finding the saboteur here in my opera house...'

'Yes.'

'...and then,' he continued, icy derision dripping from his voice, 'offering His Majesty King Louis Philippe, his entire court and all the cabinet, as a sign of my *generosity* and *love for the French people, free seasonal tickets* for my opera?'

'Err...yes?'

The glower he sent me could have frozen a volcano in mid-eruption.

'Do you have any idea how much an opera ticket costs, Mr Linton?'

I didn't, actually—because he had forgotten to charge me for the earlier performance. I decided not to mention that fact at the present moment, however. Better to annoy him with it in a month or so.

'No, Sir.'

'And do you have any idea how many members the king's court has?'

'Um...a dozen?' I guessed.

His glower become even frostier.

'Two dozen?'

I could feel my toes starting to freeze. Swallowing down my misgivings, I raised my chin.

'Do you have any better ideas?'

Silence.

More silence.

And another teaspoonful of silence.

Finally...

'No.'

I thought as much.

Accompanied by the noise of grinding teeth, Mr Ambrose reached into his drawer, pulled out some official-looking writing paper with pre-printed letterhead. In his precise, small, and murderously neat handwriting he penned a few quick words, and signed the note with a flick of the wrist. Then he pulled a bellpull, and waited until a messenger boy peeked his head through the door.

'*Oui, Monsieur?*'

Mr Ambrose threw him the letter. '*Pour que Sa Majesté, le roi Louis Philippe, soit livré immédiatement.*'[25]

The boy's eyes went as wide as saucers. '*Oui, monsieur! Tout de suite, monsieur!*'[26]

He shut the door, and I could hear him running down the corridor at breakneck speed.

---

[25] For his Majesty, King Louis Philippe, to be delivered immediately.

[26] Yes, Sir! Right away, Sir!

At the desk, Mr Ambrose sat down heavily in his chair and gave me a stony look.

I sent him back an encouraging smile. 'It's to prevent a horrific war and untold amounts of bloodshed.'

By the looks of him, that wasn't a great consolation.

~~*~**~*~*

While Mr Ambrose brooded over how much money he was going to lose and mobilized his forces to spy on Dalgliesh, I had been ordered to receive my punishment. As vengeance for forcing him to spend money, it was to be my task to interview the opera staff once again, but this time with a new perspective. We weren't just dealing with some petty rivalry between artists. We were dealing with a traitor—both from Mr Ambrose's perspective and, if we were right, from the perspective of the King of the French.[27]

And everything depends on detective inspector Lilly Linton. Huzzah!

I didn't share the new direction of the investigation with my translator, however, when she asked why the heck we were starting the interviews all over again. Considering what we suspected now, it was entirely possible she was the architect of the whole plot, and had placed the snake in her own changing room to throw us off the scent. I didn't like to think my drinking buddy could be the force of evil we were trying to root out, however, she was definitely sneaky enough. It was the reason why I liked her.

'*Monsieur?*' a boy stuck his head in through the door. I nodded and waved at him.

'Let them in.'

He disappeared, and a moment later, the first suspect entered the room. I tried my best to ask new questions without being too obvious about what we suspected, like: Have you worked here long? Have you ever worked for other operas in Paris? Are you satisfied with the wages Mr Ambrose pays you? (The last being more of a rhetorical question.)

My particular focus was on the men and the larger women. I doubted very much one of the pixie-like ballerinas would have been able to drag a days-old corpse halfway through the opera house undetected. Still, I couldn't afford to leave anyone out. So the day dragged on and on, filled with endless questions, until finally the sun sank beyond the horizon.

Once again, the messenger boy stuck his head in the door and said something in quick French.

'He says there's someone outside asking for an interview,' Claudette translated, 'and—'

---

[27] The title of the king in France at that time was indeed 'King of the French', and not 'King of France'—the reason being that King Louis Philippe had just replaced the branch of the royal family who originally (and legitimately, as regards succession) held the throne. Therefore, he was trying to legitimize his kingship not through descent and legal ownership of land, but through assent by his people.

'Let them in, let them in.' I waved a tired hand. 'I've conducted dozens of interview today, one more won't hurt.'

'Err...I don't think he meant that kind of interview. I think he meant—'

The door opened.

'Good evening,' an eerily familiar voice said. 'I've come to apply for the post of—Mr Linton! Good Lord, Mr Linton – is that *you*?'

Slowly, I lifted my gaze, dread rising inside me, to see standing in the doorway the slender, beaming figure of Emilia Harse.

~~**~*~*

Bam! Bam!

'Let me in!'

Bam! Bam!

'Let me in, blast you!'

The door opened, and I nearly fell into Mr Ambrose's office. His arms shot out to catch me before I hit the floor, and he pulled me upright.

'Mr Linton! What is the matter?'

'I need an advance on my salary!'

He blinked. 'Pardon?'

'I need money! Right now! Please!'

His eyes narrowed infinitesimally. 'My ears must be deceiving me, Mr Linton. I could have sworn you just demanded money. From *me*.'

'Yes!'

'After already making me spend an enormous sum today.'

'Yes, yes! I need the money now! Please!' I sank to my knees in front of him. To hell with pride and feminism! This was an emergency! 'Right now! It's a life and death matter. Please, I'm, begging you!'

Ice flashed in his eyes, and he grabbed my hands. 'What is it? Has someone threatened you? Has someone dared to lay a hand on—'

'No! No, nothing like that.'

'Then what is it? What do you need the money for?'

I cleared my throat. This part I wasn't eager to confess. 'I need it for a dress!'

There was a long moment of silence.

Then another.

And another.

'You have barged into my office,' Mr Ambrose said, coolly, 'nearly broken down my door, gotten on your knees and begged me for help in a life and death situation, and now you tell me you want money for *the latest Parisian ladies' fashion*?'

'Yes! Yes, please, I'm desperate!'

He cocked his head.

'Well, well, Mr Linton...Paris has managed to do in a few days what I have been trying for years now: to turn you into a normal woman.'

I would have dearly liked to kick his shin right then and there, but unfortunately you can't do that sort of thing while kneeling on the ground pleading for help. So I punched him in the leg instead.

'Be serious!'

'I am absolutely serious. I am even slightly impressed. If I had known Paris would have such a positive effect on you, I would have brought you here sooner.'

I punched his leg again.

'I haven't suddenly become fashion-crazy! I need the dress as a disguise, you bloody son of a bachelor! I need a cover!'

'A cover?' His eyes wandered over me in a way that made my cheeks heat. 'What, pray, do you need to cover?'

I broke down. I broke down, and told him all about the burgeoning passion between Miss Emilia Harse and Mr Victor Linton, and how Mr Victor Linton wanted to please please please switch genders in order to put a stop to any further burgeoning. If, at any time in the past, I had doubted that Mr Ambrose's capability to keep his face stoic and stony approached the superhuman, those doubts were now eradicated. Not once during my entire tale did he even so much as hint at a smile.

When I had finished, and gazed up at him with the big, pleading eyes of a tortured soul searching for an escape route from hell, he simply cocked his head, his eyes glittering, and said:

'I see.'

My finger twitched in the desire to strangle him.

'And?' I demanded. 'Will you let me have the money?'

'No.'

'But Mr Ambrose, Sir! I—'

'In fact,' he continued, stroking his chin thoughtfully, 'I have decided to appoint you the temporary head of the human resources department here at the opera house.'

'What?'

Eyes blazing, I jumped to my feet.

'Ah. Eager to go to work, I see? I appreciate your enthusiasm, Mr Linton. This great responsibility is a sign of my trust in you. It means that you will be in charge of hiring and firing all the major staff members. Some singers have quit their jobs over that little incident with the rotting corpse.'

I had a horrible feeling where this was going.

'No. No. No, nononono!'

'Since you are already practised in interviewing people,' he continued mercilessly, 'you might as well interview potential candidates for those positions. I'm sure that Miss Harse will appreciate having a friendly face on the committee that will decide her fate.'

Rushing forward, I grabbed him by the collar. He gazed down at me, as cool as if I wasn't contemplating smashing his head in.

'This is revenge, isn't it?' I growled. 'Revenge for the free tickets! You bastard son of a bachelor!'

'I have no idea what you are talking about, Mr Linton.'

Tightening my grip, I pulled him down towards me, or myself up towards him, who the hell cared, and slammed my lips to his, kissing him fiercely.

'I hate you!' I whispered against his mouth.

'Indeed?' he whispered back, catching my cheeks in his hands.

'If you say "indeed" one more time, I'm going to clobber you over the head with a wooden prop sword!'

Releasing him, I took a few steps back and raised a threatening finger. 'I shall be avenged! Be on your guard. It may take months. It may take years. But one day, when you least expect it, I will appear from the shadows and wreak my vengeance upon you!'

'I think you will make an excellent head of human resources, Mr Linton. You obviously have a talent for the performing arts.'

Tempted to stagger under the weight of my fate, but holding myself proudly, I marched out of the door, away from the cruel, cruel man who was going to let me suffer through this and who I most certainly did *not* love, no matter the evidence to the contrary. As I marched down the corridor and towards the lovestruck girl who was my worst nightmare, I was only cheered by one single thought:

Wait till Miss Harse is introduced to the first French person. Just wait. It'll be worth all the trouble...

THE SINGING BUTT

'*Do Re Mi Fa Sol La Ti Do...Do Re Mi Fa Sol La Ti Dooooooooo...*'

'Thank you, *Mademoiselle* Monette.' I waved, wincing. 'Thank you for the, um...memorable performance. Your application will be considered.'

I waited for Claudette to translate and, once the girl had disappeared, leant over towards her. 'What do you think?'

'*Zut!*' Sticking one finger in her ear, Claudette wiggled it experimentally. 'I sink I need to invest in earplugs.'

'Oh, thank God!' I took a deep breath. 'I thought it was just me.'

'It's not.' Claudette patted my hand. 'Trust me, *Monsieur* Linton, for every good singer out sere, sere are a 'undred people who cannot wait to drive metaphorical nails into your ears.'

Another figure stepped from the door that led backstage, dressed in a white gown and a brilliant smile that widened at the sight of me.

'Speaking of nails,' I groaned. 'Here comes one to my coffin.'

Claudette raised one eyebrow. 'What is se matter? She is pretty girl, *non*? And she appears to be quite fond of you.'

'That *is* the problem.'

'Ah.' Claudette's eyes lit up with sudden understanding. 'You are...how they say it in English...queer, *oui*?'[28]

My eyes nearly popped out of my head.

'What? No!'

'It is all right.' She gently patted my shoulder. 'I'm not the same as all the stuffy English people. I no judge.'

I opened my mouth to reply, but Miss Harse had already reached us, and I shut it again. Clearing my throat, I bowed to her.

'Welcome, Miss Harse.'

'Good morning, Mr Linton. It's so wonderful to see you again!'

'You, too,' I said with my fingers crossed behind my back. 'This is Claudette Chantagnier, the prima donna here at the opera house, who is going to advise me...'

'A pleasure, Madame.' Miss Harse bowed to the prima donna, while Claudette scrutinized her intently. Poor girl. In a way I pitied her. Even though I wanted nothing so much as to get as far away from her as I could, I knew that singing in the opera was her dream, and I also knew that there was no way she was going to get a job here in France. Not after the introductions were over.

'...and this,' I continued, gesturing at the man on my other side, 'is *Monsieur* Louis Joyal, the music director. *Monsieur* Joyal, meet Miss Emilia Harse.'

Emilia did another shy curtsy. 'A pleasure to make your acquaintance, *Monsieur* Joyal.'

It was coming. The end of the poor girl's music career in France. Any second now. Any second...

'Good evening,' the music director said in heavily accented English. 'Welcome to Paris, Miss 'arse.'

I nearly choked myself trying to stifle the sound of my laughter. My knees trembled, trying not to collapse.

'Yes,' Claudette agreed, inclining her head. 'Welcome, Miss 'arse. I hope you will enjoy your stay in Paris. For a lovely young thing like you, sere are so many fascinating opportunities in sis great city.'

Wheezing, I had to support myself against a nearby column. Claudette glanced over at me, one eyebrow raised.

'Is something se matter, Mr Linton?'

'N-nothing! Nothing at all!'

I'm just thinking about all the fascinating opportunities that Paris could offer to a young 'arse!

Grabbing on tightly to my column, I just about managed not to collapse from laughter. I wasn't quite sure the opera audience, on the first night when Miss 'arse would make her debut, would be so lucky.

---

[28] Before 'gay' became the commonly accepted euphemism for 'homosexual', the word 'queer' (which originally meant 'strange') was used in such a way. Although not in common use today, it played quite a big role in the gay rights movement, as in the famous slogan 'We're here! We're Queer! Get used to it!'.

'Well, mademoiselle.' Waving a well-manicured hand, Claudette gave the girl a tiny little smile. 'Go on and show us what a 'arse can do.'

I lost my hold and slid down the column.

'Thank you, *Madame*! And...' Emilia's gaze flitted over to where I lay wheezing on the floor. 'And thank you, Mr Linton, for giving me this opportunity. I'll never be able to thank you enough. Whether you accept me or not, this is a dream come true.' Blushing, she sank into another curtsy, and hurried onto the stage. I pulled myself back up onto my seat and raised my fingers to my ears, ready to stuff. A moment later, she opened her mouth...

And sang.

And it did not sound like the harpy's screech I'd been expecting.

Maybe she'd had a sore throat that morning I had first heard her. Maybe I had just been annoyed as hell she'd kept me awake. It didn't matter. What did matter was: the girl could actually sing!

Which meant I couldn't toss her out on her apostrophised English 'arse. Damn!

Conspiratorially, I leant over towards Claudette.

'Tell me she's bad!' I whisper-pleaded. 'Please? Please tell me that in your professional opinion, she's horrendous, and my philistine ears are deceiving me!'

'Hm...' The prima donna tapped her chin with a long, manicured fingernail. 'Sorry to disappoint. She's a little rough, per'aps, but with a little training...'

'Don't say it! Don't say it!'

'...she could become quite the famous singer. I think we should consider 'er, *mon ami*.'

I buried my face in my hands. Peeking out from between my fingers, I glanced at the music director. He had an expression on his face as if he'd just seen one of the three muses walk on stage and start giving him a private performance. I was doomed. Doomed to eternal misery.

Emilia sang three entire songs for her captive audience. Finally, the echoes of the last note subsided. She ran down from the stage and rushed towards us. Or at least I think that was what she did. I wasn't too sure, because I was still hiding behind my fingers.

'Mr Linton! Oh, Mr Linton, I can hardly express what it means to me,' she whispered. 'To see that my performance moved you to tears...!'

'Oh. Um...yes. Tears. Of course.'

Quickly, I lowered my hands, wiped my dry eyes and tried to look as moved as possible for a person sitting perfectly still.

Shyly, Emilia turned towards Claudette and *Monsieur* Joyal. 'What did you think?'

The prima donna gifted the young girl with a rare smile. 'In my personal opinion, you did very well, child. But of course I am not se one who will make se final decision.'

'I agree.' *Monsieur* Joyal nodded enthusiastically. He looked as if both his ears had fallen irrevocably in love. 'But I'm not se one with se power to decide, either, *Mademoiselle*.'

They both looked at me.

I cleared my throat. 'Um...well...I'd have to say that...well...'

Claudette stepped on my foot.

'Ouchesss!'

'Pardon?'

'Yes! I mean yes. You are hired.'

'Oh, Mr Linton!'

Rushing towards me, Emilia threw her arms around my neck and hugged me. Her lips dived towards me.

Hell no! No, no, nonono!

I dived to the side just in time. Her mouth hit only empty air.

'Thank you, thank you, thank you! You're so wonderful! Oh, Mr Linton, if there's ever anything I can do for you, if ever you need something, I'll do anything, I promise, I'll—'

'No!' I squeaked, somehow managing to slither out of her stranglehold. 'No need! It was a pleasure! The platonic kind of pleasure! And there won't be a need for you to do anything whatsoever, not ever! Except sing, occasionally. But that's none of my business. If you would excuse me...'

I fled. As I ran for my life through the corridors of the opera house on the search for a safe hideout, I swore to myself: Mr Ambrose was going to pay for this!

Dashing around a corner, I started towards his office. I didn't knock. The moment I reached the door, I kicked it open and marched inside.

'Now listen here, you—'

That's about how far I came.

Not because Mr Ambrose interrupted me.

Not even because I chickened out.

No, I fell silent because of the man with the matchbox in his hand, about to set fire to the oil-soaked floor.

˷˷**˷*˷*

'*You?*'

The doorman whirled to face me, and his eyes went wide at the side of me.

Quick as a flash, before even thinking about it, I pulled my revolver and pointed it at his head.

'Drop it!' I growled.

'Err...' The doorman lifted an already burning match, which I hadn't noticed so far. 'Really?'

My eyes flicked down to the oil-soaked floor. 'On second thought, don't drop it.'

His shoulders sagged with relief.

'It's you,' I whispered, gazing around the room. It was a complete chaos. Papers were strewn everywhere. Big packages of music sheets that had arrived just earlier today for new performances were lying close to a particularly large puddle of oil. So was a heavy box that was probably full of cash. It was a good

93

job I had found the fellow first. If Mr Ambrose had gotten his hands on a cash-burner, he'd probably have shot him on sight. I lifted my gaze to the doorman again. 'You're the saboteur.'

'Please don't kill me! I'll do anything you want. Just please don't kill me.'

'Put out the match. Go on! Now!'

Instantly, he did as I said.

'Face the wall! Put your hands against it! Legs apart!'

'Err...why?'

'So I can do this,' I told him, and kicked him in the bollocks.

'Rrrrrrgh!'

'That was for poor Claudette, you bastard son of a bachelor! Do you have any idea what you put her through with that bloody snake?'

'I'm s-sorryaarrrnnng!'

'And *that*,' I said, lowering my knee for the second time, 'was for getting that damn singer to quit and my having to hire a replacement. Do you have any idea what I'll have to endure from Miss Emilia 'arse in the coming days and weeks?'

'Gnrgldrgl...'

'No, of course you don't. Let's see how you like singing soprano!'

'Slfnnk!'

'Now, down to business.' Quickly and efficiently, I searched the man for any more weapons or combustible objects. 'No weapon. No nothing.' Shaking my head, I slapped my hand onto the man's shoulder, pushing him into the wall. 'How stupid are you, exactly? You just thought you could come in here and ruin this place without anybody noticing?'

'H-he said nobody would notice,' the doorman groaned. 'He said nobody would be here but musicians with their heads in the clouds. He never said nothing about maniacs with guns! And the money he paid was just so—'

'He who?' I interrupted.

The doorman's mouth snapped shut as if I'd threatened to force-feed him acid.

'Never mind.' My grip on his shoulder tightened, and I pulled him away and whirled him to face the door, pressing my revolver into his back. 'I can guess. Let's go.'

'W-where?'

'I'll be the one asking the questions here, if you don't mind. Move!'

Just before we left the room, I pulled the bell pull. As we stepped outside, a messenger boy was already rushing down the corridor. Mr Ambrose had apparently trained his minions well. The little fellow's eyes widened when he caught sight of the revolver in my hand.

I thought for a moment. I didn't know French, but surely I could get one single point across?

'*Monsieur* Ambrose!' I snapped at the boy. '*Dépêche-toilette!*'

He blinked—then his eyes flickered to my gun again. Without a word, he turned and ran. Hopefully to get the right person. I would have kept my fingers crossed, if I hadn't needed them for the handle and the trigger.

I hardly had to wait a minute before the sounds of rapid footsteps met my ears. An instant later, Mr Rikkard Ambrose rounded the corner, thunder and lightning in his eyes. If my dear friend the saboteur had looked scared of my gun before, it was nothing compared to what he looked like in the face of Rikkard Ambrose's wrath. Sweat was running down his face, and his knees trembled. Although that might also have been a side effect of my triple bollocks blaster.

'*Monsieur* Lamarque,' Mr Ambrose said, coming to a stop only a few yards away. 'As I recall, you were begging for this job a few years ago, when you had nothing but the rags on your back. Interesting how you chose to repay me.'

'Please, *Monsieur* Ambrose, Let me explain—'

'You don't need to explain things to me.'

The saboteur blinked, taken aback. 'I...I don't?'

'No. You need to explain things to *him*.'

Mr Ambrose snapped his fingers—and from around the corner emerged a giant figure armed with beard, sabre and turban, striding towards us with determination. Or maybe I should say towards me?

'Six days!' Karim's voice was like the rumble of a volcano. The saboteur jerked back and cowered behind me, not realizing that he wasn't the object of the bearded mountain's wrath. 'Six whole days I had to rot in that *Rōṭa dē mōrī*[29] of a prison cell before they let me out!'

In prison? That was the first I'd heard of it. But then...it did explain why he had taken so long to appear.

'You were thrown in chokey?[30] What did you do?' I asked, curious. 'Kiss a statue of the queen? Decapitate someone important?'

'I was observed,' the big bodyguard ground out between clenched teeth, 'running after a young man, shouting and apparently armed too heavily for the liking of the English police. They put me in a cell to, as they put it, "cool off".'

'Oh dear.'

'Do you have any idea what indignities I've had to face? What kind of dregs of society I was forced to tolerate, and—'

He was cut off abruptly when I threw my arms around him and squeezed.

'I missed you, too.'

The only answer I got from Karim was a kind of gurgling noise you'd expect from a suffocating porcupine. Somewhere in the background, Mr Ambrose cleared his throat. That seemed to rouse Karim from his shock-induced paralysis, and made him realize he was in the arms of his *Sahib's* intended, in front of the aforementioned *Sahib*, and at least one other witness.

'What are you doing, woman? Release me!'

I smirked up at him. 'I thought you had already been released six days ago? Or are you only out on probation?'

'I...you...that's not what I...!'

---

[29] Rat's hole.

[30] A British English expression for 'prison', originating from the Hindi term 'caukī'.

'Don't worry.' I patted his beard. 'I've been on the inside, too. We're fellow jail birds now. Isn't that sweet?'

In response, he only uttered an incomprehensible Punjabi curse.

Taking pity on the poor man, I squeezed him one last time, patted his furry cheek, and stepped back. Instantly, Karim grabbed the saboteur, and gave him a if-you-ever-repeat-what-you-saw-I'll-kill-you look.

'You! You dare to go against the *Sahib* and injure those in his service?'

The doorman fainted.

Turning towards Mr Ambrose, Karim stood as straight as a drill sergeant who had swallowed a ruler. 'Fear not, *Sahib*. I shall squeeze every last bit of information out of him. When I'm done with him, we shall know every detail of Dalgliesh's plans, and we will be able to move against him.'

Mr Ambrose nodded. 'Indeed.'

A moment later, Karim had disappeared, and we were left alone in the room, scrutinizing each other.

'I do not appreciate,' Mr Ambrose told me coolly, 'your throwing yourself at other men.'

'Oh, come on.' I couldn't help the grin tugging at the corners of my mouth. 'You have to admit it was worth it, just to see the look on his face.'

Mr Ambrose was not in the habit of admitting anything, just in case a tax collector happened to be nearby. But the non-expression on his face told me everything. He took a step towards me. I took a step towards him.

'We did it,' I whispered. 'The saboteur is caught. Out of pure dumb luck, true, but what the heck? We did it.'

'Indeed.'

Another step.

'I never thought it would be over this quickly.'

'Neither did I.'

And another. We were almost close enough to touch.

'Now all we have to do is wait for the King to accept your gracious invitation, and we've won.'

A muscle in his jaw twitched. 'Don't remind me.'

'Don't worry.' Reaching up, I caressed his cheek with the back of my hand. 'The expense will be worth it.'

'Indeed, Mr Linton?'

'Well...' Smiling cheekily up at him, I sidled closer until our lips were nearly touching. 'How about if I make it worth it?'

'Ahem?'

At the sound of another voice, we jerked apart. Whirling around, I saw Claudette standing at the end of the corridor, her eyes twinkling.

'I...we...errr...were just...'

'Not worry.' Winking, she hustled over towards us. 'Your secret is safe wis me, *mon ami*.'

Under my hand, I felt Mr Ambrose stiffened. He stared at me intently and mouthed, 'She knows?'

I simply nodded and prayed to God he never found out what it was she knew, or thought she knew, about me, and now, by extension, about him. Oh dear. If he ever found out...

Best not think about it.

At all.

Never.

''ere.' Claudette handed me a folded piece of paper she'd been carrying. 'A messenger boy arrived at se front door with sis for you when I was passing by. It sounded urgent.'

I reached for the paper, but—surprise, surprise—Mr Ambrose snatched it out of her hand before I could get there. Flipping the paper open, he started to read...

And he froze.

Not stiffened. Froze. Under my fingers, he became a statue of ice, burning with cold fire. Fear surged inside me.

'What is it?' I demanded. 'What does it say?'

He said nothing. He just handed me the note which, thank heavens, was written in English!

A moment later, when I saw what it said, I wanted to take that back. I wish the note had been in French, or better yet, Bellarussian or Cechua, so I would never ever understand it.

Dear Mr Ambrose,

His most August Majesty, Louis Philippe, King of the French, regrets that he cannot accept your generous invitation. We have already received a similar offer from Lord Daniel Eugene Dalgliesh, and have accepted in the hope of fostering better relations between our two great nations. His Majesty extends his invitation for you to join us in his permanent box at Lord Dalgliesh's opera house, where he will be happy to receive you into his royal presence.

Yours Truly

M. Blanchard
Royal Secretary

OFFENCE IS THE BEST DEFENCE

'What now?'

It was about an hour after the receipt of the note. Mr Ambrose had sent it off to his Paris headquarters, to have its contents confirmed. A few minutes earlier, the answer had arrived: the note was genuine. The signature was indeed that of the royal secretary. So now Mr Ambrose and I sat around a small table in my attic room, while one floor down, oil was being mopped off the floor of

Mr Ambrose's office, and a few floors farther down, Karim was mopping the floor with our own personal traitor.

'What now?' I repeated.

Mr Ambrose stroked one long, powerful finger along his chiselled jaw. For a long moment, there was nothing but silence. Then he said something that took me completely by surprise. Something that, for the first time since we'd discovered the swamp of plots and secrets we'd stumbled into, gave me hope for the future.

'What do you think?'

He was asking *me*.

He was *trusting my opinion*.

And I had no intention of letting him down. Taking a deep breath, I met his cool gaze—then plunged forward. 'I say we take the battle to Dalgliesh!'

One eyebrow lifted infinitesimally. 'Indeed?'

'Yes, indeed, Sir.' My eyes flashed. 'I'm sick and tired of always being on the defensive. That bastard is a killer and a tyrant, and he deserves to go down for what he's done—not to mention what he's planning to do! If we can save millions of lives, we have to try!' I flashed him a grin. 'And if we also could destroy your biggest business rival into the bargain...who can say no to an offer like that?'

Mr Ambrose reached across the table, something shining in his dark eyes that made me feel all warm inside.

'I always knew there is a reason why I love you.'

Taking hold of his hand, I held it fiercely for a moment, then lifted it to my lips and gently kissed his open palm. 'Likewise.'

'But the question remains, how do we proceed?'

I considered the question for a moment.

'Can we warn the king?'

Mr Ambrose gave me a look. 'Warn him that a Member of the British House of Lords is about to assassinate his foreign minister? If he's in the right mood, that alone would be cause for war. That would rather defeat the purpose, correct?'

Biting my lip, I nodded. He was right, dammit! But what else could we do? Our hands were tied. If we didn't warn them, the king and the foreign minister would be inside Lord Dalgliesh's building, surrounded by his men, blissfully ignorant of the lion's den they had entered.

Suddenly, out of nowhere, an idea struck me. It was like the spark that started a bushfire.

'Lord Dalgliesh doesn't know we're here...' I began slowly.

'Yes. We already established that, Mr Linton.'

'But,' I continued, 'the King does.'

Reaching for the unfolded message on the table, I tapped the words *His Majesty extends his invitation for you to join us in his permanent box.*

Mr Ambrose's eyes narrowed infinitesimally.

'What are you suggesting, Mr Linton?'

Slowly, a wicked grin spread across my face.

'This. Listen closely...'

I told him my idea. Just when I was finished, the door opened and Karim entered the room, his face grim.

'He confessed to his misdeeds, *Sahib*, and to the identity of his employer. But I failed to obtain any useful information about Dalgliesh. I fear I cannot provide a feasible option to stop whatever he is planning.'

Mr Ambrose and I exchanged looks.

'No matter,' Mr Ambrose told him. 'We have a plan. But we're going to need some help.'

~~**~*~*

'*Bon Dieu*, this is exciting! I've never been to the opera before.'

'You go to the opera every single day,' I reminded her.

Claudette waved that little unimportant detail away. '*Taratata*. Sat is just business. I've never gone for my own amusement, *c'est frai*! And I certainly have never gone out clothes shopping just for such an occasion. Oh, what shall I wear?'

'You do realize that an evil genius is planning an assassination to start a gigantic war, right? Fashion is probably not that high on the list of most important things right now.'

Another unimportant detail Claudette dismissed with a wave of the hand.

'It is always important to look your best, *Monsieur* Linton.'

'But people won't even realize it's you! You have to dress up as...you-know-what.'

'Even more reason to look my best. I never disappoint an audience when I perform.'

We were heading towards the exit of the opera – now lacking one doorman – when quick, light footsteps approached from behind. I started to speed up, but too late.

'Mr Linton! Mr Linton, wait. It's me!'

I know, blast it! That's why I'm running!

I turned to see a smiling 'arse rushing towards me. Taking the last few steps, Miss Emilia reached out and attached herself to my hands like a fashionable limpet.

'Have you heard? I'll be singing my first performance tonight! Just a small role, because *Monsieur* Joyal wants to see how I do on stage, but I'll be singing! In front of hundreds of people!'

'That's wonderful,' I told her and tried to detach my hands. It didn't work. They were stuck. Darn! How did she have this much strength in those tiny little fingers? 'Now, if you'll excuse me...'

'Will you be there? Will you watch and be my good luck charm? Please say yes! Please, please.'

I considered how to answer that diplomatically. *No, thanks, I have to go stop a bloody murder and prevent the end of the world as we know it?*

That probably wouldn't go over well.

'I'm sorry.' Once again, I tugged on my trapped fingers—to no avail. 'I, um...err...'

'Mr Linton has promised to help me pick out new costumes for a performance we are planning to stage soon,' Claudette cut in, giving the girl a broad smile. 'There will probably be a very interesting part for you, too.'

Emilia let go to clap her hands in delight. I immediately wrenched mine back and hid them safely behind my back, out of her reach.

'Will there? Oh, that's wonderful. Thank you!' She threw her arms around Claudette, and hugged her—and before I could leap back, she submitted me to the same horrific torture. 'And thank you, too, Mr Linton! All my good luck is due to you, I'm sure.' Love-struck eyes gazed up at me. 'I'm more certain than ever that fate has brought us together.'

Fate can go kiss my generous feminist 'arse!

Behind me, I heard Claudette snort, and I sent her a look that told her all too clearly what I thought of her. Finally, I managed to disentangle myself from my destined lady love, grabbed Claudette by the arm and rushed out of the door. I didn't slow down until we were at least three streets away.

'Phew!' Wiping the sweat off my forehead, I sagged against the closest wall.

Claudette took up a position beside me, one eyebrow lifted in curiosity. 'So...when are you going to tell 'er you're actually a girl?'

I nearly fell on my butt.

'You...you *know*?'

The prima donna rolled her eyes. 'Oh, please! I 'ave been playing pants roles in se opera for over a decade! You don't really suppose they leave the acting of boy roles to actual, pimply little boys, do you, *mon amie*?'[31]

'But...you asked if I was...and when you saw Mr Ambrose and me together, you said....'

She grinned. 'A girl 'as to 'ave some fun now and again, *non*?'

To that, I replied with some inventive language I'd heard from one of the janitors who squashed his thumb in a door. Claudette listened and, when I was finished, nodded appreciatively.

'Not bad, *mon amie*, not bad. Your French is improving.'

'I'm glad to think so! Maybe you can help me and tell me what "You're a bloody devious witch and I hope you burn in hell!" means in French?'

'That would be *"Ma tête est une pomme de terre pourrie"*.'

'*Ma tête est une pomme de terre pourrie!*'[32]

She gave me a grave nod. 'I'm sure it is, *mon amie*.' She patted my shoulder. 'Don't worry. I won't 'old it against you.'

---

[31] This is actually true, creating an interesting dichotomy between theatre and opera. While in theatre, for a long time in history female roles were played by boys dressed up as ladies, in opera, it was the other way around, with ladies playing the roles of younger male characters. The reason for this was that teenagers are at the age where they go through their change of voice. So teenage boys were (and still are) unable to play singing roles.

[32] My head is a rotten potato.

Deciding to take her translations with a pinch of salt from now on, I strode down the street towards our goal. We still had an assassin to catch and a war to prevent,

I spotted the building we were heading towards at the end of the street.

'Claudette! There! Is that it?'

'Yes, *mon amie*.'

The place was a luxurious three-story building with large, arched windows, pretty columns and gilded decorations. It almost looked like a small palace. And to judge by the sumptuous gowns, tailcoats and coats displayed in the shop windows, its owners considered themselves to be the kings of Parisian fashion.

'*Mon Dieu!*' Claudette gave a longing sigh at the sight of some of the dresses.

'Don't get any ideas, Claudette. You know what we're here for.'

'*Oui*, but your *beau* is quite well-to-do, *n'est-ce pas*? And he loves you very much. Couldn't we just put it on the bill, and...'

Taking a step closer, I took a look at the price tag. 'Trust me—he doesn't love me *that* much.'

Claudette gave me a pat on the back. '*Ne dis pas de bêtises!* You are underestimating your attractions, *mon amie*. I'm sure if you went about persuading him the right way....'

I gave her a look. 'I have no interest in persuading him. I have, however, an interest in stopping a megalomaniac from plunging Europe into war. Could we concentrate on what's important here?'

She gave an impish smile. 'It's all a matter of perspective.'

'Yes. And my perspective is: war is more important than clothes.'

'Ah, you English! Philistines, the 'ole lot of you!'

'Come on. Time to get down to business.'

As we stepped into the shop, the doorbell above our head tinkled like a fairy's laugh. Not surprising, considering the room we stepped into looked like something straight out of fairyland. Gold, silver, brocade, jewels, silk, satin—everything that was soft, sumptuous or sinfully expensive was gathered all around us, beckoning and whispering: 'Buy me. Buy me. I might not be on sale, but your soul is, and it'll surely be worth it to part with that annoying little thing to pay for me.'

'*Bienvenue! Bienvenue, Monsieur et Madame, à Leclercq et Lacroix, les meilleurs modistes en France.*'[33]

A short, wrinkly man came hurrying around the closest rack of clothes, his eyes alight with the glitter shared by hunting sharks and sales assistants who have just spotted a new customer.

'*Anglais, s'il vous plaît?*' Claudette told the assistant with an apologetic smile.

'Of course, *Madame*.' He bowed deeply. 'We often get customers from the British Isles in our establishment. And for good reason. After all, our handiwork is famed throughout the world.'

'A reputation which I'm sure is not undeserved.'

---

[33] Welcome! Welcome, Sir and Madam, to Leclercq and Lacroix, the finest fashion designers in France.

'You're too kind, *Madame*.'

'Not at all, not at all. Now, if you would be so good as to show as some of your wares...'

'Of course, *Madame*. What would you and your husband like to see?'

My eyes went wide. 'Oh no, no, nononono! We're not married.'

The shop assistant blinked owlishly. 'You are not?'

'No.'

'Brother and sister, then, *oui*?'

'No. No, definitely not.'

'Oh. Well...err...' For a moment or two, the poor man struggled for words. You could almost see the cogs turning in his head as he tried to figure out our connection. Young aunt and nephew? Lady and her chubby gigolo? The latter obviously didn't suit his taste very well. He cleared his throat. 'My apologies. It is none of my affair, *Monsieur et Madame*. What items would you like to see?'

I gave him a bright smile. 'We're going to the opera.'

'Ah!' The old shopkeeper's face brightened at the sound of something so respectable and familiar. 'Of course. How wonderful. What may I show you? Accessories only, or a whole wardrobe?'

'We need everything, please. A beautiful dress fit for the best of society, up to and including royalty, and a tailcoat and trousers of the same quality.'

'Royalty?' The little man's eyes went wide. 'You don't mean...?'

'Yes.' I nodded. 'We expect to be introduced to His Majesty in the course of the evening.'

Now the little tailor was beaming. Surely, if we were going to see royalty, we had to be respectable people, right?

'Don't you worry, *Monsieur et Madame*!' He clapped his hands. 'I shall make you a tailcoat that Jupiter himself would not be ashamed to wear. And for you, *Madame*, I shall make a dress the likes of which the world has never seen.'

'Oh, no, no,' I hurriedly clarified, my smile widening. 'The dress is for me, and the tailcoat is for her.'

~~**~*~*

'Aaah! Safe at last.' With a sigh of bliss, I let the dress settle around me.

Behind me, Claudette chuckled and started buttoning up the back.

'This is the first time I have heard that response to putting on a gown from Leclercq & Lacroix, *mon amie*. Stunning? *Oui*. Beautiful? Absolutely. But safe? What do you think it is? A plate armour?' She sounded highly amused. 'It will not protect you from bullets, you know.'

'Not from bullets,' I agreed, 'but from Emilias.'

'Ha! *Oui*, of course she will be the biggest danger you'll encounter tonight.'

'You think you're joking.'

Making a derisive French noise at the back of her throat, Claudette closed the last button. 'There. *Tout est prêt*.'

'Hey! Why did you call me a prat?'

'Because we still need to work on your French, I think.'

'Hm.' Ignoring her jibe, I tugged at my dress. 'How do I look?'

She scrutinized me. 'Utterly and completely non-male.'

'Good. That was what I was going for.'

'And also…'

'Yes?'

'*Magnifique.*'

A slow smile spread across my face.

Claudette patted me on the shoulder. ''e will be blown away.'

'He?' I fluttered my lashes. 'Who could you possibly mean?' Turning, I examined Claudette. 'You clean up pretty nicely, too.'

'Why, thank you.' She bowed, the long tails of her tailcoat billowing behind her. Elegantly, she extended one arm to me. 'May I escort you down the stairs, *Mademoiselle?*'

'You may, *Monsieur.*'

Once we reached the landing, we saw Mr Ambrose standing down in the entrance hall of the opera, Karim and the pale figure of the saboteur beside him.

'…was your meeting with Dalgliesh?' Mr Ambrose was asking. 'Did he seem suspicious?'

'N-no, Sir, Mr Ambrose, Sir. Not at all.'

'And you stored the items we discussed exactly where I told you to?'

If possible, the face of the little worm went even paler.

'Y-yes. B-but what do you intend to do with—'

Mr Ambrose raised one finger.

The saboteur shut his mouth.

'Adequate. Now, if you have done everything you said, you might—emphasis on *might*—get out of this with your head attached to your body. If not…' Mr Ambrose tapped his pocket. 'I have your signed confession right here, and the other two copies are in the hands of capable people who know what to do with them. If the police get their hands on them, you'll be spending a decade or two behind bars. Understood?'

'Yes, Sir, Mr Ambrose, Sir!'

'Adequate.'

Just then, Mr Ambrose looked up. His eyes swept over the stairs for a moment—then he saw me.

One of his eyebrows lifted about half a millimetre.

'Ah. Miss Linton.'

'Err…is this what his version of "blown away" looks like?' Claudette whispered from behind me.

I grinned. 'This is what his version of everything looks like.'

'My poor dear. You 'ave my condolences.'

I didn't really hear her. I was already rushing down the stairs. Mr Ambrose had hardly enough time to fully turn towards me before I crashed into him, flinging my arms around him.

'Miss Linton! What, pray, are you doing?'

'Hugging you,' I whispered into his chest. 'It's the first time in ages I've been able to without having to wonder if anyone is watching. I've missed it. I've missed you.'

For a moment, there was nothing but startled silence. Then his stiff form relaxed just a tiny little bit, and his arms slid around me. That was all the response I needed. I leaned into him, not giving a damn if anyone was staring. Finally, I relaxed my grip and looked up at him, a fierce grin spreading across my face.

'Shall we go kick Dalgliesh's arse?'

His eyes met mine and held them for a moment that felt like forever.

'Let's go, Miss Linton.'

MEMORABLE MOMENTS

'I have to admit, his opera looks better than yours. Did you skimp on decorations?'

Mr Ambrose gave me a cool look, then turned back to the massive building in front of us. I had spoken the truth. It did look better than Mr Ambrose's opera house—if you measured beauty in pomp and luxury. But at a second glance, you could see where Dalgliesh's architect had used just a little bit too much decoration, just a little bit too much gilding and glitter. There might be less pomp at Mr Ambrose's building, but there also was a lot more style.

And fewer murderous plots, probably, as well.

'Well?' I asked, slipping my arm into Mr Ambrose's and smiling up at him. 'Shall we go give His Lordship a nice surprise?'

'We shall. Let's go.'

'Yes, let's!' came an excited voice from behind us. 'Oh, sis is going to fun!'

Followed by Claudette, Mr Ambrose and I climbed the front steps to the arched entryway. The doorman at this place looked a whole lot bigger and more intimidating than the one Mr Ambrose had had the misfortune to employ.

'*Des billets, s'il vous plait?*'

'Do you speak English?'

'Yes, but—'

'Read this.'

Mr Ambrose held out the king's note.

'Sat is not a ticket, *Monsieur*.'

'Read it.'

Frowning, the doorman unfolded the note and started to skim it—when his face suddenly paled.

'*Mon dieu! Monsieur*, you are truly here—'

'—on the personal invitation of His Majesty King Louis Philippe? Yes. I am afraid his invitation arrived at too short a notice to procure tickets for ourselves. We can, of course, come back another time, if you would be so kind as to give His Majesty our apologies and explain to him why we could not—'

'Oh, no! No, *Monsieur*! I wouldn't dream of it. Please, come in. Guests of 'is Majesty the king are always welcome. He 'as the best box to himself, after all, and can do with it as he sees fit.'

'Adequate.' Tugging the royal note from the doorman's motionless hands, Mr Ambrose pocketed it and strode inside. 'We'll find our own way.'

When we were inside and out of hearing distance, I squeezed his arm and beamed up at him.

'I'm proud of you.'

'Indeed?'

'Yes. Even on a deadly mission with the fate of the entire world at stake, you still find time to cheat your enemies out of the price of three tickets. That's what I call staying true to yourself.'

Claudette gave the two of us a look and shook her head. 'One sing is for sure. Nobody will ever write an opera about se two of you. Nobody in the audience would be able to figure out when you're flirting and when you're insulting each other.'

'We do both at the same time,' I told her, grinning up at Mr Ambrose. 'Knowledge is power is time is money, right?'

I felt his fingers give my arms a gentle squeeze.

'Indeed.'

The entrance hall was brightly lit and filled with excited chatter—about tonight's performance, and much more besides. Apparently, we weren't the only ones to know that His Royal Majesty the King would be present tonight. Gentlemen were walking extra stiffly and correctly, and ladies were checking and re-checking their hair and clothes in the floor-to-ceiling mirrors

The three of us proceeded in a tight group towards the grand stairs that obviously led to the upper levels and the best boxes in the opera, our heads lowered. It wouldn't be smart to be recognized too soon, in case any of Dalgliesh's goons were here. Once we reached the top of the stairs, Mr Ambrose nodded to Claudette in her male costume.

'You'll find the items you need in the third bin down the hall in the west corridor. If that little snake of a saboteur didn't do as told and they aren't there, signal us by coming to the royal box and knocking on the door three times short, one time long. Understood?'

'*Oui, Monsieur!*' Grinning, Claudette gave a mock salute. She was obviously having the time of her life. 'Do I get a bonus for this?'

'Yes. A bonus of one tailcoat and one pair of trousers from Paris's foremost fashion designer, completely free of charge.'

'*Sacre bleu!* How generous. You take my breath away.'

'I'm in a generous mood, so you can keep it. Get to work.'

Hand in hand, we stood there and watched Claudette bustle away.

'Maybe we shouldn't have involved her in this,' I murmured.

'Why not, pray, Mr Linton?'

'Because she could get shot or arrested!'

'Do you know another Parisian with sufficient acting skills we can trust to keep their mouth shut afterwards?'

'Well, I don't think we can trust her to keep her mouth shut entirely—'

'*Except* for when she's singing.'

'Oh. Well, in that case, no I can't think of anybody else. But still—'

'Adequate. Then that is settled.'

Taking a tighter hold of my arm, he started to steer me down the corridor, and I let him, because, honestly, I had no bloody clue where we were supposed to be going. We took a turn, and then another one, climbing another set of stairs. The farther we went, the more luxurious our surroundings became, and the more guards were everywhere. I had to keep myself from jerking back the first time I saw a soldier in the uniform of the presidency armies.[34] Lord Dalgliesh's personal lackeys were everywhere, and they made my skin crawl. Another one was just coming around the corner, and I felt my mouth twist in disgust—until I saw his face.

'Crap!' The word escaped me as a hiss.

Mr Ambrose froze. 'What is it, Mr Linton?'

'I've met him! He knows my face!'

Mr Ambrose froze. 'Are you certain he will remember?'

'The way I smashed the butt of my gun into his ugly mug was pretty memorable!'

'I see.'

He was on me before I could even blink. Grabbing my shoulders, he whirled me around into an alcove, blocking out the light from the corridor.

'What the heck are you doing?' I hissed. 'Don't you realize we'll only attract more attention if we try to hide and—mmmmph...'

My words were abruptly cut off when his hands slid up to take hold of my face, and his mouth came down on mine.

Holy...

Thank God for violent criminal kidnapping thugs in the service of megalomaniacal evil masterminds! You are fabulous! The world needs more of you!

'Are you satisfied with my deception techniques?' he murmured against my lips. 'Or do I need to get more inventive?'

No! No, please, or I'll have a heart attack.

'Yes!' I breathed. 'Do! Now!'

What do you know? My mouth was getting emancipated.

'Indeed?'

That was all he said. Just that one word. His one hand tightened its grip on my face, while his others moved down over my cheek, splayed fingers caressing my face, my neck, my...

Oh my.

---

[34] In spite of the name, these troops have nothing to do with any president, especially not an American one. They were the official troops of the East India Company, the British conglomerate which at this time controlled the Indian subcontinent, including some countries and regions that today are not part of India, such as Pakistan.

Somewhere very, very far away, footsteps passed by. I didn't really pay any attention.

Mr Ambrose renewed his attack on my mouth. He was merciless. Without the slightest hint of pity. My knees started to tremble below me, and one strong arm came around my waist to pull me against him, so close the heat of his skin almost burned me and—

And then he let go.

'Wbldb?'

I blinked in the sudden light. Mr Ambrose had stepped out of the alcove and was peering around the corner.

'He is gone,' he announced coolly. 'We can proceed.'

Proceed? Hell yes, I wanted to proceed! I wanted to proceed all night and into the small hours of the morning, preferably on a comfortable bed!

'Miss Linton?' He snapped his fingers in front of my face. 'King? Minister? Assassination, remember?'

Lifting my nose into the air, I slapped his fingers away. 'Of course I remember! I was just considering our strategy.'

'Of course.'

In a very gentle and loving way, I stomped on his foot.

'Drop that smug tone, mister!'

'I have not the slightest clue what you could possibly mean, Miss Linton.'

'Of course you don't.'

He offered me his arm, and I took it as the peace offering it was. Arm in arm, we continued down the corridor.

'So, Miss Linton—what exactly in regard to our strategy was it that you were considering?'

I thought quickly—or as quickly as I was capable of at the moment, with my mind still fogged. What to say? Well...there was actually one point I had meant to ask about, a daunting possibility that had preyed on my mind for some time.

'What if the assassination is already planned for tonight?' I whispered.

'Assassinating the King of the French on the very first night after inviting him to his private opera house? I don't think even Lord Daniel Eugene Dalgliesh would be so bold. If there is anything that man prizes more than power, it is his public image. He would not risk suspicion falling on him for such an inane reason as haste.'

I smirked up at him. 'You would. You'd want to get it over with as quickly as possible.'

'True.' He looked over at me, and his eyes were so cold it sent a delicious shiver down my back. 'But if I wanted to start a war between two countries, I wouldn't have to kill to do it.'

I wasn't quite sure which was worse—the fact that I believed him, or the fact that his words, horrifying though they might be, made me want to grab him and kiss him senseless.

'*Monsieur? Madame?*' At the sound of the strange voice, I glanced up and saw a man in uniform. My heart filled with ice-cold fear—until I realized it wasn't a uniform of the presidency armies. It was a French uniform. Sagging against the wall, I gave a sigh of relief, probably the first any English man or woman had uttered at the sight of a French soldier since that little matter with Napoleon.

'Yes?' Mr Ambrose cocked his head at the soldier.

'Oh. *Vous etes...*English? *Anglais, oui?* I am sorry, *Monsieur.* But I cannot let you pass 'ere. This 'allway leads to se royal box of 'is Majesty. I cannot let anyone srough.'

'Maybe you'll make an exception for us,' Mr Ambrose told him, handing him the note. The soldier's eyes flicked over it, and quickly, he bowed. 'Yes of course. Pardon me, *Monsieur.* I was unaware you had been invited. Jaques!'

He snapped his fingers and another soldier appeared around the corner, this one with fewer stripes on his uniform and more pimples on his face.

'Jaques, conduct sis lady and gentleman to 'is Majesty se king immediately, please.'

The young man saluted. *'Immediatement, mon colonel!'*

'My thanks, colonel.' Mr Ambrose nodded at the officer. 'A young associate of mine may drop by to deliver an important memo sometime during the evening. *Monsieur* Claude is his name. Would you mind letting him through?'

'Well...' The Frenchmen hesitated. 'Is sis memorandum of interest to the king? Otherwise, I would not very much like to disturb him unnecessarily.'

'Trust me,' Mr Ambrose said, his face as deadpan as a whole collection of suicidal cooking pots. 'My business here tonight is of great interest to His Majesty.'

'Very well, sen. I shall send him srough se minute he arrives.'

The colonel stepped aside and we proceeded farther down the corridor, past several more soldiers, until we finally reached an ornate door. The soldier beside it snapped his heels together.

'Names, please?'

Mr Ambrose pulled out a card and silently extended it.

'Very well, Sir. And your companion?'

'Miss Lillian Linton.'

The soldier knocked against the door. *'Monsieur* Rikkard Ambrose and *Mademoiselle* Lillian Linton to see 'is Majesty se King.'

There was a momentary pause. Then...

'Entrer!'

Holding my breath, I watched as the door started to swing open. We had discussed all sorts of scenarios before coming here. There was a distinct possibility that Dalgliesh would be waiting in that box. I perfectly remembered the last time we had met. It was difficult to forget being kidnapped and held hostage in a lonely cabin in the middle of nowhere. I had no idea how he was going to react if he was there. More importantly...I had no idea how I was going to keep myself from scratching his face off.

Calm down, Lilly! I told myself. *Calm down. You've got a mission. And it's not killing Dalgliesh. At least not tonight.*

The door opened, and...

Dalgliesh was nowhere to be seen.

But there were a few other mildly interesting people.

Louis Philippe, King of the French, was sitting in a luxurious blue and gold armchair near the railing. He looked a bit like your favourite friendly shopkeeper, who had been on his luck recently, but didn't let it get to him too much. His round face was pretty unremarkable, except for the ginormous nose that hung like a zucchini in the middle of his royal visage. Worry lines were carved into his face, especially at the corners of his mouth, but there was a glimmer in his eyes that told everyone this old royal horse had still plenty of life left in him.

Minister Guizot, on the other hand, looked like he had still plenty of death in him. If the man beside the king was, in fact, Minister Guizot, and not an undertaker here to take the king's measurements before the assassination. The tall man was dressed from head to toe in black, with a high collar and beak-shaped nose that gave him the appearance of a hungry bird circling above his favourite corpse. Add to that his pale face and sharp, intelligent eyes, and he didn't exactly look like the broker of international peace Mr Ambrose had described.

I leaned over towards Mr Ambrose. 'Are you sure that saving him will help world peace?'

'Yes, Mr Linton.'

'Oh dear. Poor world.'

At the sound of our approach, the king turned around and, suddenly, his lined, heavy face was lit with a broad smile designed to put everyone at ease. Meanwhile, the foreign minister lurked behind his monarch, making sure everyone stayed uneasy.

'*Monsieur* Ambrose! What a pleasure to see you here. When I sent my invitation I didn't know you were going to answer it so promptly.'

'It was a spontaneous decision, Your Majesty. I hear tonight's performance is going to be something special.'

'You did, did you?' From behind his king, Minister Guizot's eyes bored into Mr Ambrose. I had to give the man credit. His stare was almost as intimidating as that of my dear employer. No wonder he was able to keep several nations dancing to his tune.

'Yes.' Mr Ambrose met the minister's gaze unblinking. 'It might be a little shocking, but very beneficial in the long run. An operatic catharsis, you might say.'

'Like in ancient Greek tragedy?'

'Yes.'

'But didn't everyone die in ancient Greek tragedy?'

There was a long moment of silence, as the two powerful men stared at each other.

'Only on the stage,' Mr Ambrose told him.

'I see.'

'Where are my manners? I'm so forgetful tonight.' The king clapped his hands. He seemed to have noticed nothing of the tension in the air. 'Please, sit down, *Monsieur, Madame*. You, *Monsieur* Ambrose, take the seat of honour on my right, and you, my dear *Madame*...?'

I dipped into a perfect curtsy. Aunt Brank would have been proud of me. 'Miss Lillian Linton, Your Majesty.'

'Charmed. Please, take a seat, *Mademoiselle* Linton.'

We sank into our seats, Mr Ambrose and Minister Guizot still eyeing each other intently without the king noticing a thing. Down in the orchestra pit, the musicians began tuning their instruments.

'So, what brings you to our beautiful capital city?' the king enquired.

'Yes.' The minister's eyes switched from Mr Ambrose to me, on the search for a weaker target. 'I would very much like to know that, too.'

'Well, originally I only came here for business reasons, Minister, Your Majesty. But then I happened to meet Miss Linton, and well...'

His hand landed on mine, taking hold of it. A distinctly possessive hold. It took a moment or two for me to realize that he had just as good as announced his intentions. Announced his intentions to the *king of bloody France*! My eyes flew to his, and he gazed back, completely implacable.

'Oh, that's how it is, *oui*?' The king chuckled. 'Yes, Paris can have that effect on people.'

'So that is why you still are in Paris?' The minister's eyes were narrowed. 'For the romantic atmosphere?'

'Indeed.' Mr Ambrose nodded, looking about as romantic as a constipated rock. 'That and...'

The door opened.

'My apologies, Your Majesty,' came a voice from behind us that I knew all too well. A voice that made my spine stiffen and my skin crawl. 'I was somewhat delayed, because I was engaged in planning a little surprise for you later in the evening.'

'What a coincidence!' Half-turning, the king beamed across his whole face. 'We have a surprise for you as well, Your Lordship.'

'You have?' Lord Dalgliesh asked, striding around to towards the seat right next to the king.

'Yes,' Mr Ambrose told him as he rose from that very seat, cold eyes sparkling. 'He has. Good evening, Your Lordship.'

THINKING INSIDE THE BOX

Lord Dalgliesh froze.

'You two know each other?' The king seemed delighted. 'What a happy coincidence!'

'Yes.' The foreign minister's eyes were darting between Mr Ambrose and His Lordship. 'What a coincidence, *vraiment*.'

Slowly, Dalgliesh came out of his paralysis. Somehow he managed to force a smile onto his face. 'Mr Ambrose. I was not aware you were in Paris.'

Mr Ambrose cocked his head. 'Sometimes fate just puts one in the right spot at the right time.'

He extended his hand. Looking as if he was being forced to swallow an adder whole, Lord Dalgliesh reached out and shook it. It was obvious that, whatever he had planned for tonight, meeting Mr Rikkard Ambrose was not high on the list. I couldn't help it. I grinned from ear to ear. Apparently broadly enough for Dalgliesh to notice me.

'Miss Linton. What an...unexpected pleasure.' His eyes glittered. 'You left so suddenly last time we met.'

My smile didn't even flicker. 'I found the surroundings somewhat constricting.' *Particularly the locked door and armed guard in front of my cell.* 'But I hope that sometime soon, I'll be able to repay your hospitality in kind.'

One of Dalgliesh's eyebrows rose. 'Is that so, Miss Linton?'

'Yes,' Mr Ambrose said from right beside me, his voice as cold as the frost on an polar bear's bottom. 'Now sit down, will you? The show is about to begin. And what a show it'll be...'

'So you've seen this opera before, Mr Ambrose?' the king asked, intrigued.

'No, Your Majesty. But I have a feeling it will be a life-changing experience.'

As Lord Dalglesh slowly sank into his seat behind Mr Ambrose, I caught another glimpse at the foreign minister. He was scrutinizing everyone intently, his sharp eyes focusing particularly on Mr Ambrose and His Lordship. When his gaze strayed to me, I winked at him.

He blinked.

By the looks of him, I had been the first one to ever do that. Poor man. I waved at him, just for the fun of it.

Out of the corner of my eye, I noticed a motion. Lord Dalgliesh was leaning forward, towards Mr Ambrose.

'What,' he hissed, too low for anyone else to hear, 'are you planning?'

'Shh.' Mr Ambrose raised one long finger to his lips. 'Can't you hear? The performance is about to begin.'

'Tell me now! Or I'll...I'll...'

'I'd be very cautious with what you say.' Mr Ambrose's voice was low, cool and controlled, but no tiger's roar could have been more threatening. 'Remember where you are, Dalgliesh, and in whose company.'

'The king can't—'

'I wasn't talking about the king.'

Dalgliesh shut his mouth. He was seething, but he was silent. He had no idea whether Mr Ambrose had come alone or brought a battalion of men with him. No one knew. Not even I. Just as Mr Ambrose wanted it.

'Relax. Be patient. You'll soon find out what I have planned for tonight.'

Never in my life would I have thought I'd hear Mr Rikkard Ambrose tell someone to be patient. And never in my life would I have thought I'd enjoy the experience so much. The look on Dalgliesh's face was priceless.

'Your Majesty.' He leaned forward abruptly. 'I just recollected some urgent business I have to take care of. Would you excuse me, please, to—'

'Psht! Not now, Dalgliesh. The performance is starting.'

Gritting his teeth, the mighty Lord Dalgliesh sank back into his chair, in his box, in his opera house, unable to move an inch from the spot. God, this was good! Who knew opera could be this much fun?

Down on the stage, things seemed to be getting started. A bunch of people in oriental costumes were singing in a choir and brandishing cardboard sabres. My grin widened. Oh, if only Karim were here to see this. Or better yet, if only he were here to *be seen*. I had a feeling that after taking one good look at him, the actors would work to make their performance feel a whole lot more authentic.

Out of the corner of my eye, I glimpsed a movement. Glancing up, I saw that, to the left, all the way across the room, the heretofore closed curtains of another box had shifted. A figure was moving behind them. Touching Mr Ambrose's arm, I got his attention, and he followed my gaze to where I was looking – just in time to see a hand reach out between the curtains, giving us a thumbs up.

'What was that?' Lord Dalgliesh demanded, craning his head to see past us.

'What?' I enquired, innocently.

'That over there! I saw a movement.'

'I didn't see anything,' Mr Ambrose lied with a more convincing poker face than a marble bust.

'Psht!' The king raised a finger to his lips. 'It's getting interesting!'

And it was—though not on the stage, where an unhappy man was just singing about how some villainous sultan had kidnapped and enslaved his beloved, while the bodyguards of the aforementioned villainous sultan danced happily in the background. I was far more interested in the subtle movements across the room. The thumbs up had been the signal. Our friend had found the necessary equipment. Tonight's opera wouldn't be in three acts. The climax would come a whole lot sooner than anyone suspected.

'Your Majesty...' The minister leaned forward, squinting. Apparently, I wasn't the only one who had noticed something was going on. 'I think—'

'No interruptions, Guizot! This part is brilliant.'

'But Your Majesty, I think we should call some soldiers in here right now. There, on the other side of the room is—'

Bam!

The explosion tore straight through the music. Everything went silent. The orchestra. The audience. The singers. Everything. It took people one or two seconds of shock to realize that the shot hadn't come from the stage, from the cannon of some fictional sultan. This was very real. Slowly, they raised their eyes to where, far to our left, from behind the curtains of a certain box, the smoke of gunpowder rose towards the ceiling.

'Down!' Guizot yelled, throwing himself against the king's chair. With a surprised yelp, the king toppled to the floor and said hello to the carpet in typical French fashion.

'Grgs! Blg!'

Bam! Bam!

Chaos erupted below us. People jumped up from their seats, rushing towards the exits, climbing over the backs of chairs and each other to be faster, to get out, to get as far away from this place as they possibly could.

'Where are they coming from?' the minister yelled over the racket. 'The shots?'

'Box!' I called back. 'Other side of the room.'

'We have to—'

Mr Ambrose was already up on his feet and moving to the door. 'Consider it handled. Stay here. Guard the king.'

'Yes, Sir!' I said and planted my behind next to the King's nose, smiling down at him. 'Comfortable down there, Your Majesty? Don't worry, Mr Ambrose will handle everything.'

The king's only answer was a confused little noise from the back of his throat. Outside, Mr Ambrose's commanding voice rang out over the din.

'You, you and you! Stay behind, guard the king! You there and you, come with me! We've got a gunman to catch. *Suivez-moi!*'

The sound of trampling footsteps headed away. A moment later, two soldiers appeared in the doorway.

'Good evening, Gentlemen.' I smiled up at them. 'I'd suggest that you—'

Bam! Bam

'—duck.'

Yelping, they threw themselves to the ground and landed right next to me.

'Well, well, isn't this a nice get-together,' I mused, then glanced over to Lord Dalgliesh who was cowering against the wall, a little paler around the nose than usual for a megalomaniacal tyrant. 'Want to come and join the group hug, Your Lordship?'

'No, thank you!' he hissed, his eyes promising fiery retribution. I didn't give a crap. Tonight, he wasn't in charge. This was our show.

Dalgliesh, however, didn't seem to agree with that. His face suddenly set in determination, he half-rose, carefully keeping his head below the top of the balustrade.

'I'm going to see what is going on out there. Maybe I can find some reinforcements to help protect the king.'

My spine stiffened. Any 'reinforcements' he would find would be his own men. And I could imagine only too well what kind of protection they would offer. I could still remember the horrible first seconds of awakening in Dalgliesh's captivity.

Instinctively, I moved to stop him, but he already was on his way to the door, and—

—and froze in his tracks when he heard heavy footsteps from outside. A moment later, the door swung open, and Rikkard Ambrose, followed by a single soldier, marched into the box.

'Mr Ambrose!' Minister Guizot almost jumped to his feet before remembering that could get his head blown off. 'What is happening out there? Was it truly an assassin?'

'I'm afraid so.' Mr Ambrose's face was set in a grim mask. So, basically, it looked just the same as any other time. 'We saw him with our own eyes. We chased him through the opera house.'

Guizot's eyes flicked to the soldier, who nodded, quickly. '*Oui, oui! C'est vrais!*'

'Who was he? Did he bear any insignia?'

'No.' Mr Ambrose shook his head darkly. 'But he didn't really need to. His allegiance was quite clear from the way he shouted "*Vive la Revolution!*"'

The soldier nodded and, forgetting for a moment where he was, spat on the ground. '*Sans-culotte!*'

Over in the corner, Lord Daniel Eugene Dalgliesh had suddenly become very quiet and very pale.

'A revolutionary agitator?' the king demanded, half-sitting up. 'Did you catch him?'

'I regret to have to answer in the negative, Your Majesty.' Mr Ambrose bowed his head. 'We chased him down three corridors and into a powder room, but the only thing we found in there was a terrified lady and an open window. He must have jumped. There are bushes below that could have cushioned his fall.'

'*Mon Dieu!*' the king exclaimed. 'Poor lady. 'ow terrible it must have been for her, to have her privacy invaded by such a monster. Was she much disturbed by the event?

'*Madame* Chantagnier is somewhat in shock, but recovering. I left one of the soldiers with her, and sent another to alert the gendarmes.'

'Thank you, *Monsieur* Ambrose. If that scoundrel can still be caught, it will be thanks to your quick and decisive actions. We owe you a great debt.'

Mr Ambrose bowed more deeply than I had ever seen him do before. It was amazing what feats that stiff stone spine of his was capable of. 'It was my pleasure, Your Majesty.'

What, not 'Then pay it back right!'? You're slacking, Mr Ambrose.

It was hard to keep a grin from spreading all over my face. Our plan was working perfectly. Now all that remained was for the king to take the bait...

'Do you realize what that means, Guizot?' the king demanded, turning to his foreign minister.

The minister was eying Mr Ambrose and Lord Dalgliesh, his eyes wandering between the two. 'To be honest, not quite yet, Your Majesty. But I will soon.'

'*Alors!* It is not so difficult to understand, *n'est-ce pas?* The revolutionists are stirring again! We must send envoys to Britain and ensure ourselves of their good will and support in case of another revolt. If ever we've needed good relations with our neighbours, it is now.' His head whipped back towards my dear employer. 'What do you think, Mr Ambrose? You are an influential person in your 'omeland. Do you believe the Queen would be amenable to deepening relations?'

'I'm quite sure Her Majesty would be delighted.'

'Excellent! Excellent! And you, Lord Dalgliesh, would you be inclined to facilitate such an improvement of our diplomatic relationship?'

You could almost hear Dalgliesh's teeth grinding. 'Certainly, Your Majesty. I shall do all that is within my power.'

'That is a relief.' Rising to his feet, the king went over to Mr Ambrose. 'Thank you for being here tonight, and for acting so quickly. You shall always be welcome at my court.' Then he turned to Dalgliesh. 'And thank you, too. If you hadn't invited me to the opera, the assassin might 'ave struck at a less opportune time, and I might not have survived.'

Not bursting into laughter is a true art. And sometimes, that art is really difficult. With relish, I watched the changing expressions on Dalgliesh's face.

'You're welcome, Your Majesty. I am delighted that I was able to serve you in some small manner.'

Heavy footsteps sounded outside again, and more soldiers started to file through the door, mixed with gendarmes. They surrounded their king, some cheering, some shaking Mr Ambrose's hand, but all keeping a vigilant eye on what was going on in the rest of the opera house.

'Well, My Lord, *Messieurs, Mademoiselle...*' The king gave us all a nod and a smile. 'I won't go so far as to say it's been a pleasure, but it has definitely been an interesting evening. I think I shall turn in for the night. Tomorrow is likely to be a busy day.'

There were bows from all around, except from me, because (A) I was a woman and (B) I was still sitting on the floor. This carpet was really quite comfortable. Nobody really seemed to mind my taking it easy. With a last smile at Mr Ambrose and me, the king left the box.

'I shall be retiring as well,' Lord Dalgliesh informed us. He did *not* smile. 'His Majesty is right. Tomorrow will be a busy day.'

And with that ominous statement, he stepped into the corridor. His footsteps receded, which left Mr Ambrose and me in the company of the Minister Guizot.

'*Mademoiselle?*' Stepping forward, the thin Frenchman offered his hand to me.

'I'm quite comfortable down here, thank you.'

'Pardon?'

'Well, I deserve a little break after all this excitement, don't you?' And I leaned back against the balustrade, crossing my arms behind my head.

'Assuredly, *Mademoiselle.*' The minister's thin lips twitched in a humourless smile. 'Unfortunately, I 'ave a feeling that I myself will not be getting one in the near future.'

Stepping up to the balustrade, he peered over to the other side of the room, to the box from where the shot had come.

'It is not so far away.'

Mr Ambrose and I exchanged looks.

'Interesting, *n'est-ce pas*, that an assassin, whom you would presume to be an expert marksman, missed from such a close distance.' He whirled around and strode over to the wall. Eyes narrowed and nose flaring like bloodhound on a scent, he began to examine the walls, the columns, any and all surfaces he could get his hands on.

'*Très interresant…*'

'Minister?'

'*Monsieur* Ambrose, you are a man of the world, are you not? An experienced man, who has 'andled firearms? I even believe you own a company that produces them?'

'More than one, Minister.'

'Excellent. Then perhaps you can help me understand.' Turning towards us, the minister sent Mr Ambrose a penetrating stare over his hawk-beak nose. 'Can you explain to me how an assassin could fire several bullets from a vantage point that is quite close to 'is target, and yet not only miss, but, even more astonishingly, fail to leave leave a single bullet 'ole be'ind?'

Silence.

A long, long empty silence.

Finally, Mr Ambrose lifted one shoulder high enough for a shrug of a corpse in rigor mortis. 'Perhaps he was a very bad assassin.'

'Per'aps.' The minister's stare became even more intense. 'Or perhaps he was a very smart assassin, sent 'ere by an even smarter man.'

'Or woman,' I piped up from the floor.

They both ignored me.

'Perhaps,' Mr Ambrose allowed.

'It seems,' the minister mused, 'that, miraculously, the political situation has shifted to my advantage. The attack of a revolutionary will silence my critics. All those who 'ave been railing against an alliance with England will be eager to support my efforts now, or will at least be too cautious to speak up against it.'

'Indeed.'

A smile tugged at one corner of Guizot's thin mouth.

'It occurs to me that maybe I should thank you, *Monsieur* Ambrose.'

'Maybe you should.'

'It also occurs to me that maybe I should 'ave you arrested for meddling in state affairs.'

The room temperature sank several degrees. 'Indeed?'

'Unfortunately, I do not 'ave sufficient evidence for the latter.'

Mr Ambrose's right hand shifted slightly, coming to rest over the place where I knew, beneath his tailcoat, he kept his trusted revolver. 'Or fortunately, depending on how you look at it.'

'Quite so.'

The two men stared at each other. On the one hand, the French Foreign Minister, a man of power, experience, and with eyes as sharp as his mind—on the other, Mr Rikkard Ambrose, cold, implacable, as immovable as the Colossus of Rhodes. Silence expanded between the two as they measured each other. Long moments passed. And some more of them. And more.

I cleared my throat. 'Are you quite finished?'

Mr Ambrose's little finger twitched. I got the feeling he would have dearly liked to give me a cool look, but he couldn't very well do that without being the first to end the staring contest.

'I believe the lady has a point,' Monsieur Guizot said.

Well, well, look at that. A sensible man. And I only had to travel a few hundred miles from home to find him.

'I myself shall retire for the evening. I would appreciate, *Monsieur* Ambrose, if you were to call on me at the ministry tomorrow. I would like to discuss this matter further with you.'

Mr Ambrose gave a curt not. 'So would I. There are things you need to know, Minister.'

'I shall look forward to hearing them. *Au revoir, Monsieur* Ambrose. *Au revoir, Mademoiselle* Linton.'

The minister turned and walked towards the door. He was just stepping outside, when...

'*Monsieur Guizot?*'

At the sound of Mr Ambrose's voice, the minister froze. 'Yes?'

'Be cautious of Dalgliesh. He is not all that he seems.'

The minister gave a dry laugh. '*Personne n'est, Monsieur!*' Then, with a final nod he strode out of the box.

'What did he say?'

Silence.

'Mr Ambrose?'

'He said: nobody is.'

'Oh.'

Smart man.

Turning, Mr Ambrose gazed over at me.

'I believe our business is finished here, Miss Linton. Agreed?'

'Yes, Sir.'

Striding over to me, he held out a hand. Without even thinking about it, I took it, and he pulled me up with an ease that might be due to the strength in his arms, but was still very good for my ego. Those strong arms of his slid around me, pulling me close.

'My, my, Sir,' I whispered, batting my eyelashes up at him. 'Aren't you brazen! I will have you know that I am a decent young lady who is not in the habit of compromising her reputation.'

Dark, sea-coloured eyes glittered down at me, their depths swirling, drawing me in. 'You're a bad liar, Miss Linton.'

'No I'm not!'

'To me you are,' he told me, one hand taking hold of my jaw, drawing me up towards him. 'I see you. I know you. All of you.'

Fierce heat rose inside me. Sliding my arms around his neck, I pulled him close and crushed him against me for one hard, sweet second.

'Me too,' I whispered. 'And I'll never look away.'

My arms loosened at the same instant his did, but we never let go. Holding on to each other, we stepped out into the corridor. No one was left out there. The soldiers had escorted their king and minister back to the palace, and the audience had long since made themselves scarce. In silence, we descended the stairs, heading towards the exit.

'Where's Claudette?' I asked Mr Ambrose when we reached the bottom.

'Probably at home locked in a room with thick walls, laughing intensely. For some mysterious reason, she seemed to find it quite amusing to play the revolutionary assassin.'

I grinned up at him. 'I can imagine.'

'What perturbs me, Miss Linton, is that yes, you probably can. Remind me to take your gun away before we return to England, will you?'

'Ha! You just try that and see what happens.'

We had reached the entrance by now, and I pulled open the door, giving a slight curtsy. 'Gentlemen first.'

He gave me a stern look, but he did step out first. Which meant that when Lord Dalgiesh's arm lashed out of the darkness, it was not me he grabbed.

PLOTS WITHIN PLOTS

Mr Ambrose reacted faster than the eye could blink. In the fraction of a second, he had twisted out of Lord Dalgliesh's grip, and his hand was on his revolver, ready to draw. I, unfortunately, was a little bit farther behind, my hand furiously rummaging around for my weapon in the folds of my dress. Bloody hell, I should have worn trousers and damn the consequences!

'No need for weapons, Lord Ambrose,' Lord Dalgliesh said, his eyes glittering. 'I'm not here to kill you.'

A muscle in Mr Ambrose's jaw twitched at the sound of the title he hated, the heritage he despised. 'Now why do I find that difficult to believe?'

'Oh, I will destroy you. Just not here. Not tonight.'

'Indeed?'

'Yes, indeed.' Dalgliesh took a step closer, his steel-blue eyes gleaming in the darkness. Mr Ambrose glared back, the air between them freezing. If the staring contest between Mr Ambrose and Minister Guizot had been bad, this was on a totally different level. Mr Ambrose and the minister had merely been testing their mettle. These two were testing their hatred. And there was lots of it to go around.

'I'm warning you,' Dalgliesh whispered. 'Leave Paris. Leave now—or you won't like the consequences.'

'*You* are warning *me*?' Mr Ambrose's voice was soft. Soft of as the footfalls of a Siberian tiger on fresh snow as it stalked its prey. 'Have you forgotten who it was who sabotaged my business, who put my people at risk?' He took a step forward. 'I'm not going to warn you, Dalgliesh. I've done that before, with little result. The time for warnings is past. Now it's time for war!'

His hand moved in a flash. There was bang, and I jumped forward, expecting to see a bloody hole in Lord Dalgliesh's waistcoat—but there was nothing. Mr Ambrose's smoking revolver was pointing in a totally different direction.

'Arrrh!'

My eyes swivelled towards the noise, and I saw a dark shape drop from a roof, in the direction Mr Ambrose had aimed. It crashed onto a cart of cabbages parked in the street and writhed, cursing loudly. A rifle fell from its hand, clattering to the ground.

'Do not,' Mr Ambrose told His Lordship, his smoking revolver still out in the open, 'try that again. Next time, I'll shoot to kill. And not just your henchman.' He extended his hand to me. 'Miss Linton?'

I quickly put my hand in his, hoping nobody would notice I'd just pulled it out of my knickers, still in search of the missing gun.

'Let's go.'

'Yes.'

We slowly moved away down the street, feeling Lord Dalgliesh's eyes on us the whole way until, finally, the shadows swallowed us.

The nocturnal streets were extremely lively, even by Parisian standards. Everywhere, people chattered excitedly, gesticulating with both hands, and sometimes both feet. I didn't understand a word of what was going on, but I didn't really need to. It was all too clear what was happening. The news of the assassination attempt was making the rounds. People were burning to know who the dangerous revolutionary was who had dared to take a shot at the king.

Not long after, we reached Mr Ambrose's opera house, and the door was opened by an exuberant dangerous revolutionary.

'Sat was the most fun I've 'ad in years!' Claudette exclaimed, tearing the revolutionary hat with the tricolour[35] from her head. '*Sacre bleu!* I should 'ave done somesin' like sis ages ago.'

I nodded gravely. 'Yes, because killing kings is so much fun. Particularly the executions afterward are said to be fascinating.'

'Oh, shut up and come 'ere, you!' Grabbing me, she pulled me in for a crushing hug. 'Everysin' went all right, *oui*? That detestable man who owns se oser opera 'ouse got his comeuppance?'

'Yes, he did. But how do you know he's detestable?'

''e did not 'ire me, of course. Sat's 'ow.' She gave me a look as if that should have been obvious. 'Instead, 'e 'ired that dreadful Louise Blanche. I can shatter glasses with my beautiful voice. She only shatters eardrums with 'ers. *Pfoui!* Someone wis such bad taste does not deserve to own a temple of se arts. I wish I 'ad aimed at 'im.'

'You do know that the gun wasn't actually loaded, right? There was just gunpowder inside.'

Grinning, she slid a hand into her pocket and, when she pulled it out again, displayed several shiny metal objects. It took me a moment to realize what they were.

'Claudette!'

---

[35] A 'tricolour' is any insignia with the colours red, white and blue (in France, not the USA). It was the official emblem of the French Revolution and later became the flag of the French Republic, a rather ironic fact if you take into consideration that the white part of the flag stems from the white banner of the House of Bourbon, the very monarchs of France who were beheaded during the Revolution.

'A lady should always be prepared, *n'est-ce pas?*' She patted my shoulder. 'No need to worry, *ma petite*. I did not use sem.'

'I did sort of deduce that from the live king I just said goodbye to.'

'Are you quite finished?' came a familiar voice from behind me. When I first met him, his impatient tone would have riled me to snap back. But now I only could think about what he might be impatient for. Of what was still awaiting me tonight. A smile tugged at the corners of my lips.

'Yes, Sir!'

'Adequate. Claudette, I shall await a full report in the morning.'

And with that, he took me by the arm and swept past the prima donna turned hobby assassin, towards the stairs. Stairs that led up to my room.

'You know,' I sighed, leaning against him, 'it was fun, but I'm glad it's over.'

It wasn't until we were halfway up the stairs that he replied.

'I'm not sure it is.'

I stiffened. 'What? What do you mean?'

'Remember how Dalgliesh warned us away?'

'It would be hard to forget.'

'Why would he do that? If his plans had all failed and his business in Paris was finished, why would he want us out of the way?'

His words sent a shiver down my back. They made far too much sense for my liking. I would have to think about them.

But not tonight. Tonight was for reserved for other matters. I had decided it was past time I had a little chat with Mr Rikkard Ambrose. There were things we needed to talk about.

Pushing open the door, he stepped into the room, me at his side. The moonlight fell in through the big windows and illuminated the little cot that had been my nocturnal nest ever since my arrival in Paris. In silent agreement we approached and sank onto the mattress. For a long time we just sat like that, leaning into each other and gazing out across the moonlit city of Paris. Finally, our eyes met.

My mouth felt dry. How on earth was I going to say what I had to say? How?

I cleared my throat. 'We make a pretty good team, don't we?'

'Indeed we do, Miss Linton.'

Cautiously my hand reached out to touch his, and I licked my lips.

'And with that in mind...'

'Yes?'

'I've thought some more about what you said. You know, about finding a compromise?'

His left little finger twitched.

Ah. So he has thought about it, too. Onward, Lilly! Do it! Tell him!

Taking a deep breath, I turned towards fully, raised my chin and said:

'I'll marry you.'

His mouth dropped open.

'Y-you will?'

It was the first time I had ever heard Rikkard Ambrose stutter. The first and probably the last. He reached out towards me—but then his hands stopped in mid-air, and his eyes narrowed infinitesimally. 'Wait a moment. This is what you consider a "compromise"? Not that I object, mind you, but what about your misgivings in regard to certain parts of the marriage vow? If we marry, you will have to swear to obey me in front of a priest and an entire church full of witnesses. There is no way around that.'

'Oh, I know.' I beamed. 'I've found a solution.'

'You have?'

I nodded proudly. 'I'll swear to always obey your orders,' I promised, 'if you swear to never to give me any.'

He stared at me for a long, hard moment of utter silence. It was impossible to read the emotion in his dark eyes.

'You're serious, aren't you?'

'Of course. Why not?'

Another moment of silence.

Then he suddenly grabbed me. Before I knew what was happening, he had pulled me into a vice-tight embrace.

'You're mad!' he growled, crushing me against him.

'I know,' I wheezed.

'I love you.'

One corner of my mouth curled up in perfect bliss. 'I know that, too. So...do we have a deal?'

His grip tightened until I couldn't breathe, and didn't mind a bit.

'My little *ifrit*,' he murmured. 'Mine. Forever.'

That was answer enough for me.

~~**~*~*

The French Ministry of Foreign Affairs was located in a rather cramped, drab little building for such a lofty institution. Mr Ambrose, Karim and I—in my male persona, with my gun in easy reach, just in case—approached the door, and as soon as he spotted us, the uniformed man at the door saluted and indicated that we should follow him.

'Be careful,' Mr Ambrose warned in a low tone. 'I do not believe Guizot considers us a threat, but he is a powerful man, and if he does...'

He didn't finish the sentence. Probably because he realized he'd just committed the grievous sin of admitting out loud in the presence of witnesses that he cared. Inside, I was beaming. Outwardly, I simply squeezed his hand.

'Don't worry. I certainly don't.'

And I didn't. I didn't care about Guizot. I didn't care about Dalgliesh. I wouldn't have cared if there were fifty powerful maniacs out to get us. Something had shifted. Something had changed. I was no longer alone. Alone, I'd taken on the world. Together, we'd take the world. Together, there was nothing we couldn't accomplish.

Besides, I thought with a smile at the sound of familiar heavy footsteps behind me, *I doubt anybody is really dangerous in comparison as long as a certain bearded someone is around.*

'Monsieur Ambrose? *Suivez-moi, s'il vous plaît.'*

The uniformed doorman handed us over to a servant in livery, who led us through a labyrinth of narrow corridors until we finally reached a dark wooden door with Guizot's name on it. The servant knocked.

'Venez!'

The door swung opened, revealing the foreign minister behind a desk on which high stacks of paper were arranged in meticulously precise order. Every other surface seemed to be filled as well, with documents and memorandums, pens and pencils, maps and notes, and any other weapon a bureaucrat and diplomat could think of. Careful not to nudge anything over, he rose and bowed in greeting.

'Monsieur Ambrose. What a pleasure to see you again. Please excuse the clutter. I am trying to convince 'is Majesty to provide us with new premises, but as yet 'e 'as not seen fit to agree.'[36]

Mr Ambrose gave a curt nod-shrug, a reply that at the same time signified 'What a waste of money!' and 'Why the heck should I care?'

'My secretary, Mr Victor Linton,' he said, gesturing to yours truly. 'You met his sister last night at the opera.'

Guizot's aquiline eyebrows lifted for a moment. 'Sister? Oh, yes, I remember. Good morning, Mister Linton. I hope you won't take this amiss but I 'ave to enquire: 'ow much of Mr Ambrose's dealings are you privy to? That goes for the bearded gentlemen as well.'

We both understood the true meaning of the question all too well.

'Karim,' Mr Ambrose said slowly and distinctly, icicles growing on his voice, 'is completely trustworthy. I trust him with my life.'

'And your secretary? You'd trust 'im with your life as well?'

'Better. I trust him with my money.'

Deep inside, I felt a surge of warmth at his words. We really *were* going to make it. This had to be true love, right?

Apparently, *Monsieur* Guizot had done his research on my dear employer. He understood the gravity of Mr Ambrose's words and didn't question my presence further. Instead, he reached for a folder on his desk and let it fall open.

'The officer in charge of the investigation into last night's incident has presented me with 'is findings.'

'Indeed?'

'He concluded that it was the work of a lone gunman. A revolutionary or anarchist.'

'You don't say.'

''owever, he does not preclude the possibility that there is a larger movement, and that the assassin was just the tip of the iceberg.' Closing the folder, Guizot met Mr Ambrose's expressionless eyes. 'It seems my best course of action

---

[36] A few years after this book, the Ministry of Foreign Affairs did in fact change premises from its old headquarters to number 37 Quai d'Orsay in Paris, where it still is located today.

would be to reinforce my policy of stronger amiable connections with 'er Majesty's Government in the United Kingdom.'

Mr Ambrose gave a small nod. An important nod. 'Taking into account Lord Dalgliesh, Minister, that would indeed be the wisest course of action. I would pursue it with the greatest possible speed.'

Guizot's eyes narrowed.

'What, pray, does 'is Lordship 'ave to do with the matter?'

'Things tend to...happen where Lord Dalgliesh is involved.'

'Hm.' The minister considered for a moment—then nodded. 'The king's guard will be reinforced.'

'A wise measure.'

'And also—not that I am under any obligation to tell you this, mind you—I shall send a special envoy directly to my colleague in London and see what we can do about deepening relations. As for appearances of His Majesty in public...does your generous offer regarding free tickets to your opera still stand?'

If Mr Rikkard Ambrose had had facial muscles in that stone mask he called a face, they would have contorted in pain. 'Yes, Minister.'

'Excellent.' The minister smiled, in a way that told me he enjoyed that moment a little bit too much. 'Then His Majesty and I will be paying your establishment a visit soon. And you may expect some other dignitaries to join us there in the near future. I must say, I am particularly glad this whole business happened before the big visit.'

Mr Ambrose froze. Until a moment ago, he had been a stone statue. Now he was a stone statue with a coating of ice. Only his eyes were flickering with fire.

'What visit?' he demanded.

'Why, the visit of the Earl of Auckland, of course.'

Mr Ambrose didn't relax. If anything, he became even tenser, and the temperature in the room plummeted.

'Would that be the same Earl of Auckland who is currently Governor-General of India, Minister?'

'Yes. Why—'

'The governor-general of the company in which Lord Dalgliesh is the majority shareholder?'

There was a momentary pause. We all exchanged dark glances. Was this part of Dalgliesh's real plan? Was this what we had been missing? Why he wanted us gone?

'Yes.'

Mr Ambrose took a step forward. 'And did you plan to show him around the city? Show him the sights? Maybe invited him to social events with yourself and His Majesty, such as...the opera?'

Shadows fell across the minister's countenance.

'Yes. I did.'

Behind me, Karim uttered a low oath and slammed his fist against the wall.

'I don't understand.' Uncertainly, I glanced from Mr Ambrose, over Karim, to the minister. 'Auckland is in Dalgliesh's pay, isn't he? Dalgliesh is going to have *him* assassinated? And, more importantly, why the heck should we care?'

Karim's only reaction was to smash his fist into the wall again.

The minister winced. 'Please, *Monsieur*, would you be so kind as to desist? I 'ave asked the king for a new Ministry of Foreign Affairs, but I would rather that this building not topple around my ears before the other is finished.'

Giving a grunt, Karim clenched his fists and crossed his arms in front of his chest, glaring at the rest of the room as if he expected the piles of documents to charge him any minute, intent on delivering deadly papercuts.

'I don't understand,' I repeated. 'Auckland *is* one of Dalgliesh's minions, right?'

My dear employer and the minister exchanged another dark look.

'What? What is it?'

'The problem, Mr Linton,' Mr Ambrose started to explain, 'is that this governor-general has actually been something of a thorn in Lord Dalgliesh's side. He was a member of the reform party during his time in parliament. His tendencies were less evident as he rose through the ranks, but when he became governor-general, he began implementing reforms in India. Building up industry, opening schools, that sort of thing.'

I blinked. 'And? Wouldn't Dalgliesh want that?'

Mr Ambrose gave me a long look. 'Would Dalgliesh want his subjects to learn how to read and write western languages, understand the works of people writing about democracy and the rights of people to govern themselves, and work in factories that make trains, cannons and guns? What do you think?'

'Oh.'

'Indeed.'

'Quite a vexing situation for 'is Lordship, I imagine.' Guizot's thin lips twitched. ''is company's PR department has done such a wonderful job convincing everyone that the true reason why the British reign over a gigantic empire that sucks the life out of the world is to educate and help the poor natives, that some of his own employees and recruits 'ave actually started to believe the lie. How annoying it must be that some of your own people are spreading dangerous ideas, when all they're really supposed to do is increase the opium production.'[37]

---

[37] One of the major branches of British trade during the 19th century was the opium trade. Opium was planted in India, and then mostly sold to China, where addiction to the drug caused severe health problems and was the origin of two successive wars against the British Empire. It would be difficult to make comparisons to modern times because of the illegal nature of today's drug trade, but it probably wouldn't be unfair to say that the British Empire was the greatest drug cartel in the history of humankind.

Karim looked as if he'd like to punch the wall again. Instead, he just muttered something in Punjabi. If I got it right, he told the East India Company to go and do something which I wasn't sure was anatomically possible for a company to do.

'I still don't quite get it,' I told Mr Ambrose, shaking my head. 'So, Lord Dalgliesh wasn't planning to kill Monsieur Guizot?'

Mr Ambrose speared me with an icy glare. Why was he looking at me like this? Why—

Oh crap.

I had completely forgotten that we hadn't shared the little detail of Dalgliesh plotting to assassinate him with the minister yet. Quickly, I threw a glance in his direction. But, to judge by the dark look on Guizot's face, my mention of his demise hadn't come as a great surprise to him. Mr Ambrose must have noticed, too, because he didn't try to evade my question.

'You don't see it, Mr Linton, do you? You don't think like Dalgliesh. For a moment, do not consider the matter to be one-dimensional. Think of a plan as a labyrinth with many facets and many possible outcomes. Who says he is only after war with France?'

It took a moment for his words to really sink in. But finally they did, and something went *click* in my head.

'Holy....no! He couldn't, could he?'

'What do you think? He's Dalgliesh.'

Thoughts raced through my head. Wild thoughts. Impossible thoughts. The governor-general, who was a thorn in Dalgliesh's side and yet had to obey his commands, coming to Paris at a time when the foreign minister, who was also a thorn in Dalgliesh's side, would be returning to Paris from a visit to Versailles. The governor-general had no choice but to come to Paris if Dalgliesh ordered him to. He was a state official. The foreign minister had no choice but to play nice and invite him out for some public event. And it just so happened that Lord Dalgliesh had presented the French king with free opera tickets. And his opera was swarming with soldiers loyal to Dalgliesh, and two men he wanted to get rid of were nicely tied down in one place...

'He couldn't! Not both of them at once!'

'Why not?' Minister Guizot sounded astonishingly calm for a man discussing his own demise. 'He could put the assassin in a British Army uniform, and then have some French soldiers spot him before he escaped. Then, when the French government sent outraged envoys to the British to demand an investigation, he could tell his fellow lords and queen that it was all a pack of lies, and that the true assassin had been an Indian rebel in cahoots with the French. Who do you think they would believe?'

Suddenly, I could understand Karim's desire to punch walls with his bare hands all too well. Too bad my hands weren't made of iron. I would have loved to slam a hole into a wall right now. But even more than that, I'd have loved to wrap them around Dalgliesh's lordly neck.

'He'd be killing two birds with one stone,' Mr Ambrose picked up the tale in a tone so cool and detached I wondered how he could keep it up. 'Or, to be precise, several million. Not only would war break out between Great Britain and France, but Dalgliesh would be granted a free hand in India to deal with dissenters as he sees fit. Britain would probably be strong enough to win the war alone, but it wouldn't even have to. Taking into account the Napoleonic wars, most European powers would likely pick any side that isn't France, just for fear of another Napoleon. And as for India, well...'

Mr Ambrose glanced at Karim and fell silent. That scared me more than anything he'd said so far.

'But we've stopped him, right?' I demanded. 'We've acted before he could even start to put his plan into action.'

'We've stopped the war with France, yes. As long as that is not an option you are considering?' One eyebrow raised infinitesimally, Mr Ambrose turned to Monsieur Guizot.

'I might be tempted.' The foreign minister's eyes glittered dangerously. 'That a member of the British House of Lords planned my assassination is not something I hear on a daily basis. But I am no fool. I won't give that man what he wants, and I most certainly won't plunge the world into war just to satisfy my ego.'

'Adequate. But that still leaves one problem. The question of India.' Once again, Mr Ambrose's eyes flitted to Karim, and, just for a moment, they didn't seem to radiate quite as much cold as usual. But when he returned them to the minister, the ice in his gaze was back in full force. 'I'm telling you this in confidence. If you betray my confidence, you will not like the consequences.'

'Understood.'

'My agents in India report that Dalgliesh is facing problems. Discontent in the population is mounting. A sense of cohesion, of unity is growing among the various peoples of the different princely states, as well as the areas under British control. Soldiers in the Indian army are less and less certain why they should uphold what begins to seem like a tyranny over their own people. Trouble is brewing for Dalgliesh—but so far he hasn't had an excuse to act. He's chomping at the bit to squash the dissenting voices in the country.'

Guizot nodded. 'That matches with my information on the subject.'

Not with mine, but that might be because I didn't have any. It really was a hardship sometimes to not be an insanely powerful megalomaniac with spies on every continent.

'And what makes the situation worse,' Mr Ambrose continued darkly, 'is that we've played right into his hands—or at least I have.'

Guizot frowned, and I didn't feel any less confused.

'How so?'

'Let's call a spade a spade, Minister. I faked last night's assassination attempt.'

Silence.

Except for the echo of the words I'd never expected to be spoken aloud. Neither, apparently had the minister, to judge by the look on his face. Still, he managed a suitable ministerial nod.

'I surmised as much.'

'I thought I was preventing war between Britain and France. But now, with a British representative arriving, the situation changes completely. Because of my actions, there has already been one supposed "assassination attempt" in the name of French revolutionaries. What do you think Britain would do if those same revolutionaries were to kill, say, the governor-general of India?'

Guizot's face hardened. He didn't even hesitate with his response. 'There would be war.'[38]

'Correct.'

Silence descended over the room. This time, it held, and held, and held. Finally, I couldn't stand it any longer.

'So what are we going to do?'

The only answer was more silence.

~~**~*~*

The door of the foreign ministry closed behind us. Karim didn't stop, but marched until he reached the nearest pillar supporting the front porch and delivered a blow to it that made me very glad indeed that I wasn't a pillar.

'Careful. Remember, the minister said he'd like the building to remain standing for now.'

He ignored me. Breathing heavily, he stared off into the distance and muttered Punjabi under his breath. Finally, he whirled around to face us. I took a step back. I had never seen him like this.

'Things are bad enough in my homeland as they are! But if the so-called "governor" were to be killed...' His paws clenched into fists. 'Oh, if only I were alone with that piece of human filth that calls himself a lord!'

Mr Ambrose put a hand on Karim's shoulder. 'Calm yourself, Karim. You and I both know that this problem is bigger than Dalgliesh. You don't kill the hydra by cutting off its head.'

The Mohammedan took a deep breath, his eyes glittering darkly. 'True, *Sahib*. We need to light a fire for that.'

Turning away from the ministry, we started on our way home—or what we considered to be 'home' in this city that suddenly didn't seem quite as hospitable and romantic as before. We were silent all the way, while around us the people of Paris chatted merrily. When we finally arrived in front of the palatial

---

[38] If you consider the possibility of a country going to war over a single death remote, think again. This is essentially how the First World War was started: the crown prince of Austro-Hungary, Archduke Franz Ferdinand, was assassinated in Sarajevo by Serbian nationalist terrorist Gavrilo Princip, which began a war between Austro-Hungary and Serbia that was joined by so many allies on both sides that, eventually, it involved nearly all the major powers of the modern world.

façade of the opera house and stopped in our tracks, I glanced sideways at Mr Ambrose.

'We can't return home yet, can we?'

'No. Not until the matter of the governor-general is resolved and the man is safely out of Paris.'

One corner of my mouth curled up in a half-hearted smile. 'Dang! And I was so looking forward to getting back home in time to ruin Aunt Brank's birthday.'

'Perhaps I can offer you something equally satisfactory.'

One of my eyebrows rose. Mr Rikkard Ambrose offering something? On his own accord? 'I'm intrigued. Pray, tell me more.'

'Not today, Mr Linton. Not today. You'll find out in good time.'

'What? And that from you, Mr Knowledge-is-power-is-time-is-money?'

He gave me a look that made me shiver all over—in a good way. 'Some things take time, Mr Linton. Some things are worth the wait.'

And with that, he turned and marched up the steps of the opera.

'Hey, wait! I want to know more! I want to—'

But he had already disappeared through the door. Muttering a curse, I hurried after him. He wasn't going to get away this easily! Pushing open the door—which didn't have a doorman anymore, I noticed—I ran through the entrance hall, towards a door at the other end that was just closing behind Mr Ambrose. I wouldn't let him get away! He would have to talk to me and—

'Mr Linton! There you are. Oh, I've been looking for you everywhere.'

Oh no.

Oh God, please no. Saboteurs and assassinations, wars and devastations I could handle, but *this...*

Slowly, I turned, dread rising in my stomach, only to come face to face with my worst fear.

'Mr Linton. Oh, how I've longed to see you.'

I managed a weak smile. 'Good afternoon, Miss Harse. So nice to see you.'

Emilia beamed from ear to ear.

'Did you hear the news?' she gushed.

'What news?' I dared to sound hopeful. 'Are you getting married to some nice French gentleman?'

'Oh no, nothing like that!' She gave a dismissive wave. 'It's my first performance. Did you hear who is coming to my first performance?'

'The King,' I guessed.

She covered her mouth with both hands. 'Gosh! How could you possibly know? I only heard a few minutes ago!'

'Let's call it fem– um, male intuition.'

Emilia's eyes started to gleam. 'That is almost uncanny. It's like we have this special connection between us that links us no matter how far away we are.'

'Oh, err...yes. Really interesting. How about we test it by getting really, really far away from each other?'

'Pardon?'

'You think it's a great idea, too? Spiffing! See you later!'

And I fled. I only stopped when I was up in my room, with the door safely barred behind me.

Even under normal circumstances, I wouldn't have been too keen on Emilia's company. But these weren't normal circumstances. Mr Ambrose was plotting something. And worse—much, much worse—so was Lord Daniel Eugene Dalgliesh.

How could we possibly stop him? Auckland was his employee. Dalgliesh could direct him wherever he wanted, he could control his movements, whom he came into contact with, and pretty much anything else. How could you possibly protect someone under such circumstances?

Plus, part of me wasn't even sure whether I wanted to protect Auckland. Even if he was better than the average minion, he was still in the service of Mr Ambrose's arch-enemy, and Karim didn't seem to like him very much, to put it mildly. I might not be a gentle, kind or considerate person, in fact I probably lacked ninety-nine out of a hundred positive character traits, but you go up against my friends, and I'll be on you faster than you can say "Crap!". Loyalty was everything. Protecting Auckland simply went against the grain.

Well, you'd better forget about your grain and come up with a plan, Lilly, or Karim's people might end up paying the price.

How to protect someone who was by definition unprotectable? How to get someone out of Paris, one of the most famed and wonderful cities of the world? What would make Auckland return immediately?

I froze.

Unseeing, I stared out of the window, an idea shimmering at the edges of my mind, just out of reach.

Make him return...

Return where?

To India, of course.

India, which was very, very far away. He had no idea of what might be going on there, did he? If something were to happen, or we could at least *convince* him that something had happened before he met up with Dalgliesh, he would have to return.

But what did we have that could convince the Earl of Auckland that we were sending a genuine message from India?

Wrong question, Lilly. Not 'what'. 'Whom'.

A grin spread across my face. Oh holy moly, what a plan. Poor Karim. This was going to be fun.

A Wolf in Jackal's Clothing

'You,' Karim said, his face as wooden as a five-hundred-year-old oak that had decided it was time to retire and petrify, 'must be joking.'

'I am not in the habit of joking,' I said in my best Rikkard Ambrose imitation. I could keep it up for about five seconds, then my face broke into a grin. 'Well, actually I am, but this isn't one of those times. I'm actually being serious.'

'You want me—*me!*—to put on one of the uniforms of the oppressors of my country, and go to the man under whose tyranny my family still lives, bend my knee before him and pretend to be one of *his men?*'

I patted his shoulder. 'You'll make a fine oppressor. You've got the physique for it. And your face...just perfect!'

To judge by the expression on his face, the compliment did not go over well.

'You'll get to lie to him,' I pointed out the bright side of things. 'You can lie until your pants catch fire.'

'What a cheering prospect,' Karim told me with a face that was just about as cheerful as that of Ah-Puch, Mayan god of death, darkness, and disaster. I had seen a few pictures on my trip to South America. Trust me when I say it wasn't pretty.

'I must say, Mr Linton's suggestion is not without merit.'

Karim's eyes widened, and he whirled to face Mr Ambrose. Our dear employer had so far stayed out of the conversation, while I had explained to Karim what my intentions were. But now he was looking at his bodyguard with a cool, determined look I knew all too well. It was the same look that had gotten me to stay for free overtime around five out of six weekdays on average.

'*Sahib!* No, *Sahib*, please. You cannot be seriously considering—'

'Do you have a better suggestion to accomplish our goal?'

'No, but—'

'Is impersonating a soldier of the presidency armies beyond your scope of abilities?'

'Of course not, *Sahib*, but—'

'Very well, then. It is decided.'

An unhealthy noise reached my ears. It took me a moment to realize it was Karim grinding his teeth. His eyes flicked from left to right, desperately searching for a way out. It was almost enough to make me feel sorry for him. Almost.

'What about the uniform?' he demanded. 'We don't have a uniform, and not nearly enough time or information to have a convincing one made.'

'Hm...' Thoughtfully, Mr Ambrose stroked one long finger along his chin. 'A valid point. Mr Linton?'

'Well...' I wet my lips. 'Actually, I have thought of a solution for this. The only thing is, it might be a teensy-weensy bit....adventurous.'

˷˷**˷*˷*

'This is what you call "adventurous", woman?'

'What would you call it?'

'I would call it "Take your foot out of my face!"'

'Oops! Sorry.'

Shifting my foot, I wobbled, and thrust my arms forward. Just before I slipped, I managed to grab hold of the iron spikes atop the wall. My feet flailed, and I kicked out, trying to find anything to stand on.

'Arrg! *Kīrī'āṁ tuhāḍī'āṁ āndhararī'āṁ vica phasa sakadī'āṁ hana!*'[39]

'I hope,' Mr Ambrose said in a voice cool enough to freeze lava, 'that was simply an expression, and not an actual idea which you plan to execute.'

'No, *Sahib!* Of course not, *Sahib.*'

'Adequate. Now stand still and let Miss Linton climb. And *do not* look up.'

'Yes, *Sahib.* Of course not, *Sahib.*'

'I'm not even wearing a dress,' I pointed out, still dangling from the iron spikes. 'And besides—'

Suddenly, I cut off. Had my ears deceived me? No! Footsteps were approaching.

'Quiet!' I hissed. 'A guard is coming.'

Instantly, Karim was at my side—or at my feet, to be more precise. He grabbed hold, and I found solid purchase on his broad shoulders. Letting go of the spikes, I ducked down behind the wall while, on the other side, the guard approached. We waited with bated breaths as his footsteps receded into the distance.

Finally, he was gone.

'This is madness,' Karim growled from a few feet below. 'The minute they notice the theft, Dalgliesh is going to know what we are planning.'

'Then we had better move quickly, now, correct?'

Glancing down, I saw the bodyguard throw one last pleading look at his employer. Mr Ambrose gave a short, sharp wave of the hand.

'Proceed.'

Resigning himself to his fate, Karim stretched as high as he could reach, pushing me up over the edge of the wall, and I quickly tied the rope I had brought around one of the sturdier iron spikes. Throwing a thick blanket across them, I slid across. Even through the padding, they jabbed my soft bits, but I gritted my teeth and slid over the rest of the way.

'I'm across!' I hissed. 'Move!'

And, wonder of wonders, they did. I would have to remember to mark today in red in my calendar. Karim *and* Mr Ambrose obeying my orders, all in one night? A special day indeed.

Thud.

A bearded boulder with a turban landed next to me. A moment later, it was followed by a shadowy figure, coat tails fluttering in the breeze.

'What now?' I whispered. 'Should I tackle one of the guards and ask him nicely to strip for us?'

Mr Ambrose sent me a frosty glare. 'No, Mr Linton.'

I gave him my best innocent smile. 'Oh, so you want to do it yourself?'

'No one shall tackle anyone, Mr Linton. Especially not the guards. If we remove one of them, people will notice as soon as the guards are changed, and

---

[39] May ants infest your underwear!

131

our whole plan would be discovered. We want to get in and out with as little fuss as possible.'

'So where do we go? Where the heck can we find clothes without people stuck inside them?'

Mr Ambrose gave me a long look—then exchanged a glance with Karim. 'You know...you were right.'

'I was? Well...thanks. About what, precisely?'

'You were never meant to be a housewife in a traditional marriage. It would never have worked.'

I blinked. 'Well...thanks for the agreement. Now can you explain what the heck you meant?'

He didn't say anything. Instead he just motioned for me to follow and, hiding in the shadow of the wall, led us around the back of the house where Lord Dalgliesh was staying. There, in the open courtyard, between beds of kitchen herbs, rose two wooden posts. And between the posts...

'Washing line,' Mr Ambrose said, gesturing towards the object in question. 'Laundry. Clothes without people in them.'

I gave him a sour look. 'I know what a washing line is!'

'Indeed?'

'You wait until we're back home, and I'll give your neck a demonstration of just how well I know how to use a washing line!'

'I look forward to it, Mr Linton.'

'Hm. Well...then let's go and—'

'Shh!'

Darting forward, he clapped a hand over my mouth. For a moment, I struggled out of instinct—but then I remembered who this was, and what he was to me. If he did this, he had a good reason.

My body went limp.

Quickly, Mr Ambrose dragged me behind a tree, while Karim made a desperate leap for the largest bush in the kitchen garden. Only an instant later, I heard someone whistling, and a rotund woman opened the back door of the house. She had an empty wicker basket in her arms and headed with determination towards the washing line. The washing line from which, I noticed only now, three bright red-and-blue uniforms dangled, just begging to be snatched. My gaze snapped back to the woman.

Oh no you don't! The laundry is mine!

A thought I'd had for the first, and probably last, time in my life.

Stooping, I snatched a pebble off the ground and let it fly. It sailed through the night and, with unfailing aim, landed straight in the chicken pen. Letting loose an unearthly racket, the animals scattered in all directions. The housekeeper—if that's what she was—swerved around and sent a suspicious glance towards the disturbance.

'Hello?'

She was speaking English. Dear me, had Lord Dalgliesh actually brought his own staff with him from England? The man really travelled in style. But the chickens were distinctly unimpressed. The only answer the housekeeper received was more panicked clucking.

'Mr Jeffries, if that's your boy messing with the chickens again, I'll spank 'im till he ain't gonna sit down for a week!'

Still, no answer. Shrugging, the woman turned back towards the washing lines—and I sent another pebble flying! Once again, the chickens erupted in chaos. Behind me, Mr Ambrose's hand landed on my shoulder, giving me an approving squeeze. I smiled.

'Gordon Bennet! What the 'ell is going on there?' Whirling back towards the chicken pen, the woman marched over, brandishing her empty basket like a club. Her back was towards us, and towards the laundry.

'Now!' I hissed.

Neither of the men moved. Both of them looked at me.

'What?' I demanded. 'You expect *me* to do it?'

'It's laundry,' Karim said as if that explained everything.

'Laundry which we'll need to prevent an assassination that could spark a global war!'

Karim considered this for a moment, then said: 'It's still laundry.'

My gaze slid to Mr Ambrose, looking for help. I guess I should have known better.

'Come on! Not you, too!'

He raised an eyebrow about one quarter of a millimetre. He didn't even need to say anything. It was very, very clear that Mr Rikkard Ambrose did not consider stealing laundry to be an appropriate way to occupy the finely-tuned money-grabbing instruments that were his hands.

Muttering a curse that wasn't very complimentary to the male species, I dashed out from behind the tree and grabbed the first bright red and blue thing I could get my hands on. Quickly, I dashed back behind my cover and ducked down into safety just before the housekeeper reappeared from behind the chicken pen.

'Here!' I hissed, throwing the bundle of cloth at Karim. 'I hope you choke on it.'

Not deigning to dignify that with an answer, the Mohammedan shook out the garment—and his eyes went wide.

Oh dear.

It took a very, very great deal of effort for me not to burst out laughing. What I had snatched off the washing line was indeed red, white and golden, the colours of the presidency armies. However, it could only be called a 'uniform' in the broadest sense of the word. Apparently, one of the officer's wives must have been feeling patriotic, and had had the fabulous idea to order a dress in her husband's uniform colours. The result was something which, in addition to bringing every fashion-sensitive person to their knees, quite literally had the power to make Karim choke. At least if he had to put it on.

'My goodness,' I said. 'Dear me.'

'Indeed,' Mr Ambrose affirmed.

'Gndrnxs,' Karim said.

Was that a Punjabi word? Probably not. For a moment, silence reigned in the backyard, except for the whistle of the housekeeper collecting her laundry in the distance.

'Well,' I finally managed, 'look on the bright side. You will definitely make an impression on the governor-general. If a seven-foot-tall bearded man came into my room dressed in that, I don't see how I would be able to help listening. Of course, I might not hear everything because I would be too busy staring.'

Karim made an indistinct noise in the back of the gravel driveway he called a throat. 'Woman?'

'Yes?'

'Not another word!'

Ordinarily, I would have had a lot to say in response to that, but in that very moment, a gasp suddenly came from behind me.

'What the—'

I whirled around to come face-to-face with a guard who had, to judge by his open fly, just come around the bushes to relief himself, only to discover the spot was already occupied. I didn't hesitate. I didn't think. I just whipped out my pistol and pointed it at the man's head.

'Don't make a sound. Hands in the air!'

The man's hands flew into the air, causing his open trousers to notice the law of gravity.

There was a rustling of cloth and a clink, as a belt buckle hit the ground.

Ugh. Not a pretty sight. But after all, we were here on a mission. You had to endure suffering for a great cause. I cocked my gun, and pointed at the man's trousers.

'Excellent. Keep going.'

The soldier blinked, uncomprehending. 'W-what?'

'Keep going. Take off your clothes.'

'Y-you want me to...'

'Yes.'

'I'm a soldier of the presidency armies!' The man's chest puffed out. 'Whoever you are, know that I will not be forced to suffer such indignities!'

I considered for a moment—then shifted my gun from the man's head to his lower parts.

'Now!'

Instantly, the man's fingers flew to the buttons of his shirt. 'I'mdoingitI'mdoingitpleasedon'tshoot!'

'Stop!'

The ice voice from behind me said just one word. One word. But it was a commandment chiselled in stone. Mr Ambrose stepped up beside me, and the man's hands froze.

'I order you, don't move another inch. Don't take any more clothes off!'

The unspoken words *not in front of her* hovered in the air. I suppressed the urge to grin.

'Err...' The poor soldier's eyes flicked between me and Mr Ambrose. 'Not to offend you, Sir, whoever you are, but that one over there has the gun. I think I'll do what he says.'

Forget about fighting the urge. This was definitely worth a grin!

'Are you certain?' Taking another step forward, Mr Ambrose captured the gaze of the soldier, focusing the full force of his arctic eyes on the man. 'If I were you, I'd consider my answer very carefully.'

'Err...um...I...well...'

'You do know that our whole reason for coming here was to obtain a set of clothes, don't you?' I asked my employer in a conversational tone.

'Irrelevant, Mr Linton! He is not stripping in front of you.'

'Oh dear...is someone jealous?'

His little left finger twitched. 'Feelings do not enter into the matter. It is a question of decorum.'

'Decorum my arse! And speaking of arses, you there, soldier boy, get yours out of the rest of your clothes!'

At a jerk of my gun, the man instantly obeyed—that is, until Mr Ambrose pulled out his own revolver. The click of the hammer sliding in place echoed audibly in the backyard.

'Don't. Move.'

I threw him a look. 'This is getting ridiculous!'

'I agree. Turn around, and we can proceed.'

'I'm not turning around!'

'Why? Do you *want* to see this man naked?' Icy eyes found mine, burning with such fierce cold that it made the hairs stand up on the back of my neck.

'What I want is for you to stop behaving like a chauvinistic son of a bachelor and start treating me—'

Thud!

The sound of the dull impact of wood on skull cut me off mid-rant. Glancing to where the sound had come from, I saw Karim standing over the prone body of the guard, the butt of his sabre held high. He noticed me staring and gave a dismissive wave. 'You go on arguing. I shall take care of this.'

I put my hands on my hips. 'Oh, so you have no problems stripping a man? It's just not possible for a manly man like you when the clothes are hanging nice and handy on a washing line?'

Ignoring, me, he bent and went to work on the unconscious soldier. Ha! Men!

I had to hand it to him, Karim was pretty quick at stripping men. Since I figured I had given him enough reasons in one day to bite my head off, however, I didn't point out that little fact. Instead I kept watch with Mr Ambrose, making sure no one else discovered our hiding place behind the bushes while Karim worked. When the bodyguard was finished, he tapped Mr Ambrose on the shoulder and showed him the rolled-up bundle of cloth in his hand.

I jerked my thumb towards the unconscious guard. 'What are we going to do about him?'

Karim, eyes glittering, started to draw his sabre.

'Oh no!' Quickly, I stepped in front of him. 'No killing!'

'Why?' The Mohammedan's eyes narrowed. 'Do you believe that man has not killed before? He is nothing but a paid thug in the service of a power-hungry maniac!'

'Yes. Which for me makes him rather easy to relate to. Besides, think for a second! This isn't a firefight in the middle of the godforsaken desert. This in Paris, in the middle of France, and killing him would be murder. A chargeable offence. Do you really want to put that kind of advantage in Dalgliesh's hands?'

'Mr Linton is right, Karim,' came Mr Ambrose cool voice from behind me. 'About both parts.'

Karim stood there for another long moment—then slowly lowered his sabre. 'Very well. What do you suggest we do with him?'

I let my gaze travel across the courtyard, looking for anything that could be used to restrain the man—until my eyes landed on something lying on the ground only a few feet away.

'I think I have an idea.'

Five minutes later, the unconscious guard was wrapped up in a red, blue and golden dress and gagged with a pair of similarly patriotic gloves. I had even placed a red and blue bonnet on his head to complete the picture.

'Doesn't he look adorable?' Grinning, I admired my work.

'Indeed,' Mr Ambrose said, his face as stony as a slab of slate. 'Let's go.'

With a sigh of regret, I followed as he stalked away in the shadow of the wall. I would have loved to have been there when the other soldiers discovered their comrade. But, I told myself, you can't have everything in life. Preventing an intercontinental war would have to be enough for tonight.

Suddenly, Mr Ambrose held up a hand. I stopped in my tracks and, at another gesture, ducked behind a fountain. A few seconds later, two soldiers emerged from the shadows and marched past us, backs straight, rifles up in the air.

'Now!' Mr Ambrose whispered when they had passed. 'Before the next patrol comes!'

Quickly, I unwound the rope from around my waist. Karim lifted me as he had before, and I clutched the wall to steady myself. I looped the rope over the nearest spike and—

'Hey, you! What are you doing there?'

Crap!

Twisting around, I glimpsed a figure in red, blue and gold, who had just stepped out of the back of the house. I didn't hesitate a second. Without even using the horse blanket I pulled myself up and flung myself over the spikes. The sharp metal tore into my hand, but I clenched my teeth and ignored the pain. This was no time to be a ninny!

'Stop! Stop, and put up your hands!' came the shouts of the fast approaching soldiers.

An instant later, Karim appeared atop the wall. In a move that was pretty risky for his manly parts, he crouched down over the iron spikes and extended a hand.

'Come, *Sahib!*'

'Move, Karim! You're a sitting duck! I'll be up there in a second.'

'Not until you're up here with me, *Sahib*.'

Bam!

The shot ripped through Karim's turban, scattering bits of cloth left and right. The Mohammedan didn't even blink an eye.

'Come, *Sahib*. Now!'

Yes, come you bloody stubborn idiot! Move your tight, money-shitting derrière! I need it! And the rest of you, too!

An incredibly long second passed—then Mr Ambrose's hand appeared above the crest of the wall. Karim clasped it and tugged.

Bam!

'Aaarh!'

I heard a dull thud, and out of the gloom above me, a few wet droplets of red hit my face.

THE PEACEFUL FRENCH COUNTRYSIDE

My heart stopped beating.

Just like that. It froze up. I froze up. Nothing worked anymore. Not my arms, not my hands, not even the smallest finger on my hand. There was only a single thought in my head, over and over again.

Please, no! Don't let him be dead! Don't let him be—

'Damnation! That hole will cost a fortune to mend!'

Thank you, God! He's alive and well!

A familiar, tall, dark figure hit the ground beside me, and before he'd even had time to straighten, I swooped down on him, crushing him to me.

'Are you all right?'

'Of course I am all right, Mr Linton. Cease this exuberant display of emotions. Knowledge is power is time is money.' A shot sounded from beyond the wall. 'Especially when people are firing at you. Move!'

'Yes, Sir!'

'And hand me a piece of cloth. I have to stop the bleeding before it ruins my whole tailcoat.'

Muttering something not very polite about skinflints, I tore a strip out of my shirt and thrust it into his hand. My feet never stopped moving. 'Here!'

'Adequate.'

'Would it kill you to say "thank you"?'

Behind us, more gunshots sounded.

'No, but the bullets might. Run!'

We dashed away, across the pitch-black street. A few moments later we heard the loud thudding of footsteps behind us, and suddenly Karim was at our side.

'They're right behind us, *Sahib*! Some have run to open the gate and pursue us on horseback. Where now?'

'Down here! Come!'

Veering off to the side, Mr Ambrose dashed down another street, and then another. Behind us, the sound of pursuit grew louder and louder. I was just about to demand where the hell he thought he was leading us, when he slid into an alleyway that even the grimiest beggar in Paris would have considered below his standards. Coming to a stop in front of a door, he knocked, four times quickly, two times slowly.

'Jacques, laisse-moi entrer!'[40]

A moment or two later, the door was pulled open a gap, and a suspicious eye appeared. When it recognized Mr Ambrose, it widened, and so did the gap. The man beyond, whoever he was, grinned from one side of his face to the other.

'Mon Dieu! C'est toi! Entrez, entrez!'[41]

The door flew open, and the fellow on the other side practically dragged us inside, while he let loose a flood of French so convoluted probably not even Napoleon would have been able to understand it. I scrutinized him, trying to figure him out—with absolutely no success. He didn't look as if he were Mr Ambrose's agent, or employee, or in any way connected with him. Dressed in baggy trousers and a shirt with enough holes to qualify as a fishing net, he looked like....well, I wasn't exactly sure what he looked like. I could only be sure what he was not: a Parisian fashion designer.

The rest of the people in the room didn't look any better. There were sailors smoking cheap clay pipes, factory workers with stains all over their clothing, children tumbling around on the floor and on each other, and a general chaos of looks, smells and people that would have been enough to make most fine ladies back in London faint with horror.

Lucky me, I wasn't a fine lady.

One thing I did notice, though. Despite the fact that their clothing was pretty drab all around, nearly everyone was carrying some bits of clothing in the bright colors red, white and blue.

I leaned over to Mr Ambrose. 'Who,' I asked out of the corner of my mouth, 'are those people?'

'Revolutionaries.'

'What?'

'Well, perhaps it is not quite correct to call them that at the moment, seeing as there currently is no revolution in progress. But these are what the French generally refer to as sans-culottes.'

'Err...naked butts?' I translated.

Mr Ambrose threw me a look. 'While sans-culotte does indeed mean "without breeches", that does not mean they run around with bare posteriors, Mr Linton. It simply means they wear long trousers instead of the breeches which, at one point, used to be the fashion among French aristocrats. These are the poorest of the poor. The most desperate, decrepit people you could find in Paris.'

'Ah. I see. So...why are we here, exactly?'

---

[40] Jacques, let me in.
[41] My God! It's you! Come in, come in!

138

'If you must know, back when I first came to Paris, I was looking for a reasonably-priced place to stay. I ended up here, at *Monsieur* Jacques' boarding house for the economically disadvantaged. For some reason I cannot explain,' Mr Ambrose said, glancing down at his ten-year-old mint condition tailcoat with its decorative scuffed sleeves, mended holes and bloodstains, 'they seemed to assume from my appearance that I was one of them. Since they offered me room and board at a very reasonable price, I saw no reason to disabuse them of their misconception.'

'Of course not.'

'You can rest easy, Miss Linton. Dalgliesh will never consider looking for us here. We are as safe as houses constructed by a competent architect.'

'Unless, of course, these nice people here find out who you really are and decide to slit the throat of the dissembling capitalist pig.'

'There is that possibility, yes.'

I made a face. 'Besides, staying out of sight won't do us any good. We need to find some way to stitch up that wound of yours, and then we've got to move! Like you said earlier, by going after a guard we've drawn attention to ourselves. Dalgliesh will soon figure out what we need the uniform for, and then he'll send a messenger to intercept the governor-general. If the messenger reaches him before we do....'

'True. But don't worry. Hiding people who don't want to be found isn't Jacque's only specialty.'

Turning to the scraggly Frenchman, Mr Ambrose started speaking rapid, concise French. It was quite amazing how, even when speaking in the language of love, he made everything sound like an ultimatum chiselled in stone. My worried gaze staying on the slowly growing bloodstains in his shirt, which neither Jacques nor any of his guests seemed to find particularly disquieting, I leant closer to Karim.

'What's he saying?'

The big bodyguard eyed me for a moment. I could tell he was struggling with whether such an outrageous demand for classified information from a nosy female was worth answering. Finally, he caved.

'He's asking for clean bandages and horses.'

I glanced around the room, which appeared to contain only one thing free of dirt: a small spot about three inches above the door lintel. Everything else was covered in various layers of...substances. Even on the cobwebs, there was growing mold. 'There are clean things in this place?'

'Apparently.'

Jacques clucked his tongue and nodded at Mr Ambrose's shot wound in a universal 'bad luck' gesture. A few quick words in French followed.

'He asked who's after us,' Karim translated.

Mr Ambrose's reply was characteristically concise. *'Des Aristos.'*

It suddenly went very quiet in the common room. Even I didn't need a translation for that one. Jacques' face, grimmer than before, shifted to sympathy as he placed a hand on Mr Ambrose's uninjured shoulder and squeezed. A few more quick words of French, and he marched out of the room.

'He says he'll bring bandages. He'll have horses for us in a quarter of an hour,' Mr Ambrose told us.

'And what was that last bit?'

'"Free of charge. Anything for the enemies of the aristocracy."'

'You told him we were being hunted by aristocrats!'

'We are. Remember the "Lord" in "Lord Dalgliesh"? He is an aristocrat, is he not?'

'Yes, but so are you!'

'Details, Mr Linton. Details. Besides, as they say: never look a gift horse in the proletarian mouth.'

It was probably better not to look it in the mouth. The horses Jacques provided might have been fast, but pretty they were not. I didn't want to get a closer look at their dental state. As for the bandages—Mr Ambrose had tried to put those on himself with his one functioning arm. I told him to hold still, and that I would get Karim to knock him over the head if he didn't do as I said. Amazingly, he did. So I sat there with a bowl of surprisingly clean water and wrapped Mr Rikkard Ambrose's arm tightly in bandages while Karim saddled our mounts.

'The minute we get back to the opera house,' I ground out between clenched teeth, trying to ignore the queasy feeling in my stomach, 'you're going to call a real doctor, and you're going to have him look you over, no matter how much it costs, understood?'

'Mr Linton, I really see no need for—'

I squeezed his injured arm, causing a hiss of pain. 'And I see no need for torturing you,' I told him with a sweet smile, 'but I might just do it if I feel like it. You will take care of yourself, understood? You are not allowed to die!'

In the shadowy corner where we sat, no one noticed as his eyes darkened, and he reached up to caress my cheek.

'You will pay the bill, of course.'

Placing my fingers gently over his, I squeezed. My eyes didn't leave his for a second. 'Of course.'

'Adequate. Are you finished? We must be on our way.'

'Nearly,' I told him—and quick as a flash leaned forward to place a feather-light kiss on his lips. When I leaned back again, his eyes were swirling maelstroms of dark ocean, threatening to pull me under.

'You know, Mr Linton...I don't know whether I'll need that doctor after all. I suddenly feel quite energized.'

'Good.' I stood. 'Then let's go kick Dalgliesh where it really hurts.'

'Admirable suggestion.' Rising to his feet as well, he marched out the back door. Outside, the horses were waiting for us, along with an impatient Karim and a joyful Jacques. As soon as he saw us, he thrust his fist into the air.

'Mort aux Aristos!'[42]

'Yes, yes.' I gave him an encouraging nod. 'Moron Aristo, absolutely.'

'Vive la révolution! Vive la liberté!'

---

[42] Death to the aristocrats.

'Yes definitely! I love going to the library.'

'Come on, Mr Linton. Let's go.' With incredible ease for a man who wasn't supposed to be able to use one of his arms, Mr Ambrose swung himself onto the back of his horse. I followed suit, with not quite as much ease.

'Where to, *Sahib*?' Karim enquired. He had a glitter in his eye that, not for the first time, made me wonder whether delivering a message was all he would like to do when he met the governor-general.

'Northeast, Karim. I've received reports Auckland is approaching from that direction.'

'How far?'

'If all goes well, he's still a good distance from Paris. Keep your eyes open for his crest, three bales of hay on a red field.'[43]

'Yes, *Sahib*.'

And we were off. Karim rode in front, because nobody would be stupid enough to get in his way. Mr Ambrose came right behind him, and I brought up the rear. I knew that Mr Ambrose thought that was because the rear was the safest place for me. But, really, I kept back because it was a place from where I could keep an eye on his bandage. A bloodstain had once again started spreading there, and although Mr Ambrose still sat in the saddle as steady a rock, I wanted to be close behind. If the worst came to the worst, I would catch him— or at least try, and be squashed underneath him. There were probably worse ways to go.

Winding our way through alleys and backyards with crisscrossing washing lines, we headed in a meandering line towards the *Porte de la Chapelle*. When we finally reached the city gate, Mr Ambrose glanced back, his stone face implacable.

'We'll be out of Paris in a minute. The moment we are, we'll speed up. We have to get a head start. It won't be long before Dalgliesh's men report back to him and he figures out what we are up to. We'll have to ride hard.'

'But Mr Ambrose, your shoulder—'

Somehow, his face grew even harder. 'No argument, Mr Linton. We ride hard.'

'Yes, Sir!'

We passed under the arch, and the darkness of the countryside enveloped us.

'Now, Mr Linton. Ride! Ride, and don't stop for anything!'

I gave him my best smirk. 'Not even if I find see a purse full of gold lying on the road?'

'Shut up and move!'

'Yes, Sir!'

---

[43] This should actually be historically correct. I took me quite a while to discover the real crest of an obscure personality from 19th-century England. I truly hope I've done my research correctly. If I'm correct, the motto to go along with the crest is '*si sit prudentia*', Latin for 'if there be prudence'.

Let me tell you—when Mr Rikkard Ambrose says 'ride hard' he really means 'hard.' I nearly broke my teeth from the staccato my horse's hooves played on the harsh cobblestones. We did, however, make excellent time. It didn't take long until the first coaching inn appeared in the distance. Mr Ambrose reined in his horse.

'Karim, stay here while I check the stables for the earl's coach.'

Karim's eyebrows drew together. '*Sahib*, that is not something you should do, especially not in your injured state. Let me—'

'Use your head, man! What if the earl sees you approaching, then riding off again, and then coming back dressed differently? You don't think he might find that slightly suspicious?'

'Oh.'

'Precisely. Now stop fussing over me. I'm fine.' And, tugging his horse around, he rode off towards the inn. I watched him go. When he was out of hearing distance, I leaned over to Karim and asked: 'How long have you been with him?'

The big man hesitated for a moment, then...

'I have been in the *Sahib*'s service for more than half a decade.'

I considered this for a moment.

'How on earth have you managed not to strangle him?'

Karim nearly fell off his horse.

'*What?*'

'Really, I'd love to know your secret. Seeing as I'm probably going to be around him for quite a bit, it could come in handy.'

The Mohammedan gave me a haughty look. Not a hard thing to do when you're two heads taller than everybody else. Three heads, if you counted the turban.

'I would never even dare to contemplate physical violence against Ambrose *Sahib*.'

I raised an eyebrow, and just waited. And waited.

Finally....

'I count, all right?' Karim admitted in a low grumble. 'Satisfied? I count to ten!'

'And that works?'

'Ten imaginary punches to the gut.'

'Oh.' I nodded. 'Yes, that would work. Thanks for sharing your experience with me. I'm glad we had this little talk and got to know each other better.'

Karim gave me a look that said, 'if anyone asks I'm going to deny this ever happened', and turned his massive back on me. Wasn't he a sweety?

Just then, Mr Ambrose rounded the corner and came galloping back towards us.

'He's not here. Let's move!'

And he rode off into the night.

'Gee-up!'

Spurring my horse, I raced after him. Behind me, Karim uttered a curse, which was answered by a protesting whinny. His horse didn't seem very pleased about having to carry twice as much as his four-legged friends.

Well, I couldn't wait for them. Not while I had my bloody employer to catch up to. And in this case, bloody wasn't even an insult! When I caught up and Mr Ambrose appeared out of the darkness in front of me, he was hunched over on his horse, clutching his injured shoulder.

'Mr Ambrose! Are you all right?'

His spine snapped straight as if it someone had shoved a ruler up his *derrière*.

'What is it, Mr Linton? We've got no time to waste.'

Why, the son of a...was he actually trying to pretend there was nothing wrong?

Maybe I *should* shove a ruler up his *derrière*. But I would first have to take out the stick that was already in there.

'You're bleeding!'

'Negligibly.'

'What a lot of horse crap! Just ask your horse, it'll probably recognize the smell.'

'Language, Mr Linton!'

Ignoring him, I grabbed the reins of his horse and pulled until it came to a stop.

'Let go, Mr Linton!'

'Of course, Sir,' I said and took a firmer hold, while with the other hand turning him around so I could see his bandage. Just as I had thought! The darn thing had come loose.

'Didn't you hear me? That was an order, Mr Linton!'

'Of course it was, Sir.'

'Then why aren't you doing what I tell you to?'

'Well...' I batted my eyelashes up at him, the picture of innocence drawn by a drunken sailor on the wall of a disreputable pub. 'Do you remember our compromise, Sir?'

'Compromise? What are you talking abo—oh.'

'Exactly.'

Beaming, I ripped off a fresh strip of cloth from my shirt and wound it around his arm. 'Ignoring your orders is really fun. Mind giving me another one so I can ignore it?'

'Be silent, Mr Linton!!'

'Thank you for obliging. You're so thoughtful.'

I finished my packaging, and just for the fun of it, gave him a kiss on the cheek. 'There. Does that feel better?'

He gave me a look that could freeze a polar bear's bone marrow.

'Let's go!'

'Yes, Sir. Or should I call you darling?'

'I can still cut your salary, Mr Linton.'

'True.' Giving a sigh, I spurred my horse. 'Oh, the injustice in the world...it's enough to make one cry.'

'Cry later!' His horse shot past me, cantering down the road at a dangerous tempo. 'We have to hurry.'

'Then let's.' Giving my horse another nudge, I shot past him again, flying into the darkness. 'Last one to the earl is a rotten egg!'

It wasn't long before we reached the next coaching inn. Unlike at our last stop, here the lights were still burning. When Mr Ambrose wanted to approach, I held him back.

'In the dark it didn't matter. But here, with the lights still on? If they see you with those bloodstains on your shirt, they'll raise such a hue and cry we'll never get to do our job.'

He considered for about a quarter of a second—then nodded.

'Go.'

I turned my horse.

'And Mr Linton?'

I stopped.

'Yes?'

'Be careful.'

I smiled.

'Yes, Sir.'

And I cantered off in the direction of the inn. Hardly had I rounded the corner of the building, though, when I realized that it had been the wrong move to make. Firstly, because there was not a single carriage in sight, let alone one with the earl's crest. And secondly, because the moment I came around the bend, I heard a sound from behind me. A sound that after all this time with Mr Ambrose, I was disturbingly used to.

Bam!

I whirled around—but there was no gunman to be seen. Then I realized—the shot had come from around the corner.

Where Mr Ambrose was.

No!

A CRAPPY FIGHTER

Mr Ambrose would really have been proud of my time-saving skills. I had my gun out and my horse at a gallop in about half a second. Still, I hadn't even come around the inn before I heard the second shot—and a cry of pain.

Don't let it be him. Please, don't let it be him!

I dashed around the corner—and froze at the sight that met my eyes.

Mr Ambrose was on the ground, kneeling behind his horse. Shot?

No, thank god! He's taking cover.

But a moment later, another shot rang out, and his horse balked, and raced off into the night, taking away with it any cover it had provided. And cover was urgently needed. Riders were streaming down the road, rifles raised, ready to fire. They weren't wearing uniforms, but with the way they were moving—swift, orderly, precise—they didn't need to.

Soldiers.

And I could guess from whose army.

The first man took aim.

My hand moved before I was even consciously aware of it. In the blink of an eye, my pistol was level with my eye.

Bam!

The man went down.

Unfortunately, this led to his dozen or so friends noticing me—and so did Mr Ambrose. Cold, sea-coloured eyes bored into me.

'Mr Linton, get back!'

Ha! Not on your sweet wallet!

I only retreated a few steps, until I was just around the corner of the inn, then crouched down, half hidden behind the wall. Once more, I raised my gun.

Bam! Bam!

One more man went down.

Only one? Damn, I have to get more practise!

'There! That one! Get 'im!'

The other soldiers apparently didn't agree. They took aim, seeming quite determined to make sure I never again had the chance to practise shooting people. Spoilsports!

Bam!

'Again, you miserable louts!'

Bam!

I flattened myself against the wall—just in time. Something stung my arm. When I looked down, I saw a tear in my sleeve, and a small trickle of blood.

'Hey, you bastards! That was my best tailcoat! It was almost new!'

Really? *That* was my response? I really had to start spending less time with Rikkard Ambrose.

Be honest, Lilly. That's not very likely, is it? If you get out of this alive, that is.

Carefully peeking around the corner, I raised my gun again.

Bam!

Another soldier went down—but the others steadily continued to advance. *Damn!* Once they were around the corner, I'd be a sitting duck. I had to get out of here! I had to find some way to get to Mr Ambrose.

Just then, a door in the inn wall behind me swung open, and a portly Frenchman stuck his head through the crack.

'Au nom de Dieu, quelle est ce bruit—?'[44]

'Oh, hello.' I gave him my best I-love-Frenchmen-and-don't-mind-you-eat-frogs smile. 'I wonder...could I come inside?'

A shot whizzed over my head and blew the Frenchman's hat off.

'Merde!'

Jumping back inside, he slammed the door in my face, locked and bolted it.

---

[44] What in God's name is this racket—?

'Thanks so much!' I called after him.

Another '*merde*' came from inside in reply. I couldn't have said it better myself. I was in deep, deep *merde*.

Or...maybe not deep enough?

An idea struck. Whirling around, I dashed along the inn wall and into the stables, to the one place I might—just possibly—survive. *Merde. Merde, merde, merde, merde!*

Only moments after I had settled into my comfortable, wonderfully-smelling hiding place, half a dozen soldiers burst into the stables. I could hear the others outside, taking up positions to guard the entrance.

'Where is the little bastard?' One soldier asked in a thick cockney accent. If there had been any doubt that these weren't Frenchmen, it was gone now.

'Don't know, sarge.'

'Well, search! 'e can't 'ave gone far.'

The soldiers approached. I held my breath. And not primarily because of the soldiers.

Merde, merde, merde! Really very, very much *merde!*

The soldiers came even closer, and then, their rifles raised, they—

—they stepped past me.

I let out a sigh of relief. Then I silently cursed myself. That was the last bit of fresh air I had left!

''e's not in the horse boxes, sarge,' came a voice from somewhere behind me.

'Not in the haystack, either,' came another from the left.

'Keep searching! 'e can't have just vanished into thin air.'

Thin air? The air here is definitely getting thin, my friend.

I needed to breathe. But right now, breathing in did not seem like a good idea. I felt my face turning blue as the soldiers continued to ransack the stables. They seemed pretty determined to be thorough. So far they'd stayed away from my hiding place, for obvious olfactory reasons. But what if—

Bam!

'Bloody 'ell!' Whirling around, the sergeant raced to the door—and ducked just in time to dodge a bullet.

'It's those two bloody bastards!'

Mr Ambrose! He was still out there, totally outnumbered, probably desperate to get to me. Crap, crap, crap! If only I wasn't stuck in so much crap! I had find some way to help!

'You there!' The sergeant shouted to the men standing guard outside. 'Go take care of them!'

Six men.

Six against two.

I had lots of respect for Karim's killer instincts. And as for Mr Ambrose— well, he was Rikkard Ambrose. But still, those odds seemed just a little too risky. Particularly when dealing with professional mercenaries in the service of a certain lord.

What to do?

Well...

If I'd asked that question with my mind, there could have been many answers. I didn't, though. I asked my heart. And the blasted thing was already decided.

Help him!

A moment later, a large dollop of *merde* hit the closest soldier in the back of his *tête*. He stumbled forward, and had a nice little *tête-a-tête* with a horse's *derrière*. What do you know? I was getting the hang of this French thing after all.

'What the—arglmph!'

The soldier's comrades stared horrified at their muck-splattered companion getting intimate with an equine ass. It would be another second or two before they realized what was going on. A second or two was all I needed.

Bam! Bam!

'It's him! Get hi—'

Bam!

'—iiargh!'

Four rifles came up. I dived down behind the only cover I had.

Bam! Bam! Bam! Bam!

Splat! Splat! Splat! Splat!

Thank God for shit.

Now there's a sentence I had never thought I would ever use. Raising my revolver, I pointed it over the pile of refuse, aiming as well as I could without exposing myself.

Click!

What? No, no, no! Not click! It's supposed to go 'bam', dammit!

''e's out of ammunition! Get 'im!'

Merde!

And this time, I wasn't referring to horse crap.

I was just starting to fumble for more bullets when, from outside, I heard sounds approaching. But...that couldn't be, could it? It couldn't be...hoof beats? The entrance was still guarded by gunmen. Who would be crazy enough to ride at a line of rifleman at full gallop?

Oh no.

No, please, no.

Cries and shouts exploded outside. Gunfire roared. A moment later, the stable doors burst open, and what looked like a horse trough riding on top of a horse rushed inside. Then, the bullet-riddled horse trough was hurled aside, revealing Mr Rikkard Ambrose, eyes blazing like glaciers in the arctic sun. The two soldiers on whose heads he dropped the horse trough probably didn't appreciate the sight as much as I did.

Neither did the two soldiers who were still standing, apparently. They raised their rifles.

My hands moved in a flash. A new bullet was in the chamber before I had taken another breath. A split second later, it slammed into the first soldier's head. He dropped to the ground, dead as a doornail repurposed for coffin manufacture. His comrade cursed and, with his bayonet, lashed out at me. Or at least he tried to. With one swift tug on the reins, Mr Ambrose whirled his mount around, and its hooves lashed out, scything through the air. They slammed into the soldier's head, throwing him backwards, right into...

Well, let's just say the undertaker would have to do a lot of cleaning.

Suddenly, there was silence in the stable. Outside, we could hear the sounds of fighting still going on. Either Karim was on a rampage, or we had somehow received reinforcements. Knowing Karim, I was betting on the former. Still, right now, I didn't care. In that moment, there was only Mr Rikkard Ambrose and me, and the silent little space around us.

'What were you thinking, Mr Linton?' His voice was a spear of ice, his eyes swirling oceans of darkness. 'Risking your neck like that? What were you thinking?'

'I was thinking about you,' I told him.

'You...you...'

We moved at the same time. It was as if some inextricable force drew us towards each other. I dashed forward, he sprang down from his horse, ran towards me, and...

'...backed away?

'Ynk! Arg! Ng!'

Never before in my life had I heard Rikkard Ambrose utter such sounds. Concerned, I stepped forward.

'What's the matter? Are you all right?'

'I will be, as soon as you step away. What have you been doing to yourself?'

'Me?' I blinked, nonplussed, and took another step forward. 'Whatever do you mean? I–'

And then the penny dropped. Or should I say the road apple?

'Oh.' I cleared my throat. 'That.'

'Yes. *That.*'

I considered for a moment how best to answer—then smiled, batted my lashes like a prima donna and sidled closer. 'Do you like my new perfume? It's called *aux du cheval-merde.*'

Mr Ambrose gave me one of *those* looks. The looks that said 'you are an insignificant worm' to anybody else. The looks that said 'I love you' to me.

'I sincerely hope you did not pay very much for it.'

From outside, another gunshot sounded. We exchanged glances—and then started moving as one man.

God! Did I really just think that? I had to get back into a skirt pronto!

Outside, there was utter carnage and utter Karim. Three bodies of soldiers were already lying on the ground, with the two remaining ones cowering behind trees, trying to hold off the big Mohammedan and his fellow fighters.

Wait a minute...fellow fighters?

Yes, there were other people there. And they were on *our side*? Were they crazy, or had they just not met Mr Ambrose yet?

But then I caught sight of a big black hat, topped with red, white and blue, and I knew those weren't just passing strangers willing to help. Not at all. A grin spread across my face, and I turned to Mr Ambrose.

'You don't happen to have another horse trough, do you?'

'Pardon, Mr Linton?'

'A horse trough. Preferably one with water in it, this time? I have a feeling I should make myself a little more presentable.'

Mr Ambrose glanced over at the battlefield in front of the inn—then nodded, and led me behind the stables, where another horse trough stood next to a big puddle and wild clusters of hoof marks.

I threw him a censorious look. 'You know, you really shouldn't have pulled that foolish stunt with the horse trough. You could have been killed!'

He raised one eyebrow about half a millimeter. 'It's not the first time I risked my life for something I wanted.'

I froze. My gaze found his face. Suddenly, the distance between us seemed far too great.

'Mr Ambrose...I...'

'Don't.'

'What?'

'Don't look at me like that. Not while you're covered in horse manure.'

I cocked my head, batting my lashes. 'Oh? Why not?'

'Because the cleaning bill for my clothes will come out of your pocket.'

Right then and there, I almost considered it worth it. But then I heard shouts from around the corner of the house, and I realized the fighting was coming to an end. We didn't have time for this. Plenty of horse shit, but no time. Quickly, I ducked and stuck my face into the horse trough.

'Phhrrtt! Phhrz! Grgl!'

Holy Moly! How did horses manage to drink this stuff? It was ice cold, and the smell was hardly better than the stuff it was meant to remove. Well, at least it got me marginally cleaner. By the time the last shot had fallen, I was clean as a whistle. Maybe only by the standards of whistling sewer cockroaches, but none of us are perfect, are we?

'*Sahib!*'

I turned at the sound of the familiar voice. And there he was: at the head of a line of French soldiers I wouldn't be calling frogs while they had rifles and I only had a half-loaded revolver, Karim strode towards us, the fierce gleam of victory in his eyes. He came to a halt in front of Mr Ambrose, opened his mouth—and coughed.

'In the name of the...*What is that smell?*'

I put my hands on my hips. 'Hey! I just washed myself.'

'Karim.' Mr Ambrose stepped forward, gaining his bodyguard's attention. 'You were victorious?'

'Indeed, *Sahib*. Thanks in part to this gentleman.'

He gestured to the French officer beside him, and the man stepped forward, saluting. 'Good evening, *Monsieur* Ambrose. I've been sent to...*Bon Dieu!*' Pulling an embroidered silk handkerchief out of his pocket, he waved it in front of his nose. 'What in God's name is that smell?'

'I'm washing again, all right? I'm washing again!'

'I'm Mr Rikkard Ambrose.' Completely ignoring my diligent attempts to scrub behind my ears in the horse trough, my dear employer stepped forward and inclined his head. 'May I assume that you were sent here by a certain concerned politician?'

'You are as wise and discreet as His Excellency the minister intimated.' The French officer gave a small bow. 'Indeed, *Monsieur,* you are correct. His Excellency thought you might require some aid. And when he received your message—'

Sputtering and spraying water in all directions, I resurfaced from the horse trough. 'Message? What message?'

Glancing over at me without bothering to turn his head, Mr Ambrose raised one eyebrow infinitesimally. 'While we were at Jacques' charming establishment, I paid someone to take a message to a certain politician we met yesterday, asking for reinforcements. Didn't I mention that before?'

'No. Somehow you neglected to tell me that fact before I risked my neck in a harebrained dash to suicide!'

I glared at him, demanding to see some guilt on his face.

But this Mr Rikkard Ambrose. He didn't have a face, just a stone bust attached to his torso. Giving up, I plunged my head back into the horse trough. I'd set his ears on fire later!

'Blldiag blablbdaa lmalablablabldlaa?'

'Lblablda ddldkd dklal ak abblaoble.'

Who knew? The most incompressible language I had encountered so far on my travels wasn't French, Spanish, or even Portuguese, but my own, listened to from underwater with my head stuck inside a horse trough. Maybe all English speakers should walk around with horse troughs on their head. It might encourage them to become bilingual.

Before I could come to any deeper underwater philosophical conclusions, however, my air ran out, and I had to resurface. I came up just in time to hear the French gentleman enquire: '...correct in the assumption that your mission is of a time-sensitive nature?'

'Indeed.'

'Very well. I shall detain you no further, then. Do you need someone to take care of your wound?'

'Not currently, no. I have a very, very diligent nurse with me.'

'Nurse?' The French officer glanced around. 'Where is she?'

'She's hiding,' Mr Ambrose said, his face as deadpan as a recently murdered cooking pot.

'No wonder. Poor dear, she must 'ave been frightened to death by this massacre. Such matters are no place for delicate ladies. She's probably shivering in a corner somewhere.'

I felt a sudden desire to plunge *his* head into the horse trough. But before I could, the inn door opened and the innkeeper cautiously stuck his head outside. Once he saw that bullets were no longer flying, his caution evaporated instantly, and he burst into the open, gesticulating wildly.

'*C'est un outrage! Les citoyens honnêtes ne peuvent-ils pas aller de leurs affaires quo-tidiennes en paix en France de nos jours? Je vais me plaindre au maire! Je vais me plaindre au gouverneur! Je vais me plaindre au—*'[45]

'*À moins que vous ne souhaitiez vous plaindre à Sa Majesté le roi, vous feriez mieux de fermer la bouche tout de suite!*'[46]

The sharp voice of the French officer cut the man off. When he caught sight of the sabers, rifles, and uniforms, his eyes widened, and he retreated.

'Leave,' the officer advised Mr Ambrose. 'We can 'andle this. You have your own work to do. We'll take care of the bodies and make sure this little incident will not fall under further scrutiny.'

My dear employer nodded—about as much of a 'thank you' as you could expect to get from Mr Rikkard Ambrose. Marching over to the nearest horse, he swung himself onto its back before anyone noticed it wasn't his, and gave the animal the spurs.

'Come, Mr Linton!'

'Coming, Sir. I just—'

'And leave the horse trough!'

Sighing, I let go. I was just about to get my ears clean!

Grabbing my own horse, which—clever beastie!—had somehow actually managed to stay alive and present, I galloped after Mr Ambrose. Karim was on my heels, luckily for my feet in a metaphoric manner. We rode silently through the night, the rising moon now our only pursuer. Time in this silent, shadowy world seemed like a distant concept. We rode, and rode, and rode.

It came suddenly. One minute, we were riding along, and the next—

'There!'

Karim's arm pointed into the darkness. Even squinting, it took me a moment or two to make out what he was seeing—but when I did, there was no doubt we were at the right place. The coach was standing right in front of the inn. It was huge, and even through the shadows I could vaguely see the giant forms of the lions rising on their back paws to form the crest of the East India Company. Right next to it was the crest of the earl.

Reining in my mount, I came to a stop next to Mr Ambrose.

'What now?'

In the moonlight, his face looked as if chiselled from white marble.

'Now we do what we came to do.'

'And if it doesn't work?'

The only answer was silence.

---

[45] This is an outrage! Can't honest citizens go about their daily business in peace in France nowadays? I'm going to complain to the mayor! I'm going to complain to the governor! I'm going to complain to the—

[46] Unless you wish to complain to His Majesty the King, you had better close your mouth right now!

'Karim!'

The Mohammedan appeared beside us out of the shadows. 'Yes, *Sahib*?'

Opening his saddlebag with his one good arm, Mr Ambrose reached inside and pulled out the uniform that we had fought so hard to obtain.

'Here. Put this on.'

Karim looked as if he'd rather have swallowed a bucketful of *merde*, but he grabbed the uniform and vanished behind the nearest bush.

'Shy, are we?' I enquired sweetly.

No answer.

Rustle, rustle...

Scrape, scrape...

'*Sahib*?'

'Get on with it, Karim.'

'Yes, *Sahib*. It is only...how big was the soldier we took this from?'

'I have no idea, Karim. Get a move on!'

'Yes, *Sahib*. As you command, *Sahib*.'

Rrrip!

There was a moment of silence.

'Um...*Sahib*?'

'For heaven's sake, Karim, what is it now?'

'Do you perchance have needle and thread?'

'I think I might have one somewhere,' I lied. 'Should I come and see if I can help—'

'No! No, no everything is perfectly fine! Stay where you are!'

'Oh, but if you need help I'd be only too happy to—'

'No help required! I have everything under control!'

Rrrip!

'*Boo da boja Bhander Tutti!*'

'Everything still under control, Karim?' I enquired solicitously.

'Yes! Definitely!'

Scrape, Scrape.

Scratch.

'Ng! Arg!'

Scrape!

Finally, Karim emerged from behind the bush. And when I say 'emerged', I mean...well I wasn't exactly sure what I meant. He was walking rather funny.

'Feeling a bit tight around the waist?' I asked. 'I know the feeling from my corset.'

He threw me a look that promised thunder and vengeance. Then he stepped up to Mr Ambrose, and bowed. Or at least he tried to. He got about halfway down before his face twisted and he grabbed his crotch.

'Rrg! I'm ready, *Sahib*.'

'Good. You know what to do. And...Karim?'

'Yes, *Sahib*?'

'Don't let your trousers split.'

Muttering something incomprehensible in Punjabi, the Mohammedan swung back onto his horse. He wheeled the animal around and rode off into the forest.

'What is he doing?' I demanded. 'The inn is that way!'

'True. And what do you think, Mr Linton, would the governor-general think if he saw a messenger who is supposed to be arriving from India arrive from a direction that has no major ports within a hundred miles? Is the messenger supposed to have ridden all the way from India?'

'Oh. I hadn't thought of that.'

'Indeed.'

Even for one of his indeeds, that was indeed a particularly frosty indeed. Glancing over at him, I saw he was sitting unnaturally stiff in the saddle. Normally, this wouldn't have worried me, since everything about him from his soul to his handkerchief was unnaturally stiff. But considering the way he was clutching his arm...

'Are you all right, Mr Ambrose, Sir?'

'Certainly.'

'Ah, good. So it won't hurt if I do this,' I said and jabbed his arm. He nearly toppled off his horse.

'Nnrrg! Mr Linton!'

'Yes?' I blinked up at him, sweet and innocent as the driven snow after a yeti orgy.

'I'm not a pin cushion! Desist from prodding me this instant.'

'Oh. So you mean that did hurt after all? Should I take a look at it?'

Silence.

Then...

'No. No, everything is fine.'

That bloody stubborn son of a bachelor! At this rate, he was going to kill himself! And for what? Pride?

I was about to blister his ears with some choice phrases, when something strange happened. My hand reached out of its own accord and came to rest on his uninjured shoulder.

'What are you afraid of?' I asked. Gently. Without even using a single curse word. What was the matter with me? 'I'm here. I care. Don't you know that?'

There was another moment of silence, longer this time. Finally, he shifted, his good hand coming to rest on mine.

'I know. That's what scares me.'

'Why?'

He hesitated.

'You might have noticed that I'm not particularly open-handed, Mr Linton.'

'You don't say? I would never have noticed.'

Out of the corner of his eye, he threw me a look. I shut up.

'I've had to learn how to economize. Words. Money. Everything. I keep it all and give nothing away—because anything I give away is a weapon that can be used against me. But when you're close…I want to have things I never knew I needed. And I want to give parts of myself away I never knew I had.'

His fingers clenched around mine.

'You're dangerous, Mr Linton. Deadly dangerous. Especially when I'm vulnerable.'

Gently, I raised my free hand to touch his face. 'I would never do anything to hurt you, except demand a raise. You know that, don't you?'

His fingers tightened even more. 'I know. And you're not getting a raise.'

'Not even a shilling per week?'

'I love you.'

'I love you, too. Sixpence?'

'Can you help me?'

A quip about thruppence was on the tip of my tongue. But when his words reached my ears, my tongue froze, and so did my mind.

Mr Rikkard Ambrose was the hardest, strongest, most stubborn man I had ever met in my life—and for a girl who grew up in the house of Bufford Jefferson Brank, that's saying something! I couldn't remember him ever breathing the word 'help'. But now, here, alone in the darkness with me, he was asking.

'I'm about to fall off my horse, Mr Linton. Could you make up your mind?'

I squeezed his hand. That was the only answer he needed. Extending his healthy arm, he slipped it around my shoulder, and I felt a surge of warmth inside me. He was trusting me. He hadn't asked anyone else for this. He hadn't even asked Karim. He'd asked me. I wouldn't disappoint him. I would show him that I could—

That was the moment when he put his weight on me.

'Mmmph! Grrx!'

How shall I put it…Love can be a heavy burden.

'Lillian? Are you all right?'

'Oh yes,' I wheezed. 'Just peachy.'

Bloody stinking hell! How did he manage to get so heavy? If it had been any other man, I'd have said 'sweets and meats', but after several years in his employ, it was my firm belief that Mr Rikkard Ambrose subsisted on water and the smell of bank notes. I was just about to open my mouth and hint that maybe, just maybe, he was a little bit too heavy after all, when Mr Ambrose's fingers touched my cheek.

'Thank you, my little *ifrit*.'

My lips snapped shut. My spine straightened. Heavy? Who had said anything about heavy? I could do this. Ha! I could do this for two hours straight!

Just then, I heard a noise up ahead. Instantly, my eyes snapped to the spot in question and saw a giant figure on horseback break out of the forest and gallop towards the inn. I'd recognize that beard and headgear anywhere.

'It's time!' I whispered.

Mr Ambrose's arm tightened around my shoulder, and I felt warmth well up inside me once more. Sure, the warmth came from a two-ton furnace squashing me to death, but so what? It was a loving furnace that was relying on me.

A stable hand came out of the inn's stable as he heard the horse approach. When he saw the figure of Karim ride up at full gallop, he nearly toppled over onto his butt. I had to work hard to suppress a grin.

'Miss Linton...what's happening?'

My head snapped to the side. Mr Ambrose was referring to me as 'Miss'? He really had to be seriously injured! Staring at him, I saw a single drop of sweat run down his forehead. Crap! He never sweated. Never!

'Miss Linton? I asked you a question.'

Quickly, I glanced back towards the inn. Karim had picked up the stable hand and put him back on his feet. He seemed to be questioning the young man, who was too sensible and scared to object. The stable hand gestured up at the inn. Karim nodded, handed the servant his horse, and strode towards the door.

'He's going in. And...he's inside now. It looks like the governor-general really is here.'

'Good.'

Good? Not *adequate*? Holy moly, I had to get him to a doctor straight away! Was the wound infected? Had the infection already reached his brain?

But before I could start to worry too much, my eye was drawn back to the inn. A familiar mountainous figure passed one of the upper windows. And...yes! There was another man. Much slimmer, with the roasted look of a pale aristocrat who had spent a little too much time in the hot sun of India. Even from this distance, I thought I saw a muscle in Karim's jaw twitch. Then, slowly, as if his back had rusted, he sank into a bow. Extending his hand, he handed the governor-general some slim object.

'What is that thing Karim is giving him?'

'A...letter,' Mr Ambrose wheezed. Wheezed. Mr Ambrose. 'A letter with...the official seal of the East India Company.'

I stared at him. 'How on earth did you get your hand on an official seal of the East India Company?'

'I didn't. Karim has one.'

The words hung heavy in the air. Karim? But he...he couldn't have been...He couldn't...?

No. It was impossible.

Wasn't it?

'Don't.'

'What?' Blinking, I looked at Mr Ambrose. He was breathing heavily, but his gaze was steady as he looked at me.

'I can see the cogs moving in your head, Miss Linton. Don't ask. Not me, and most especially not Karim.'

'But—'

'Just don't. For me.'

Damn him! Why did he have to put it like that? Why couldn't he simply have ordered me around like usual? Then I'd have had no problem disobeying!

Sudden movement up in the inn drew my eyes and attention back to the window. The roasted aristocrat was rushing around, throwing things here and there, pulling on clothes and shouting commands I couldn't hear. Karim was still standing there, massive and threatening as a Himalayan mountain peak. The governor-general must not have suspected a thing, or he wouldn't be turning his back on the bodyguard like that.

Keep your fingers off your sabre, Karim! Come on. You can do it! Just a few more minutes.

Somewhere in the inn, a door slammed. Moments later, a sleepy fellow in a rumpled coachman's uniform rushed out of the front door and started dragging a couple of equally sleepy horses out of the stable.

Yes! It's working! Please, please let it work!

'Miss...Miss Linton?'

Instantly, my head whirled back to Mr Ambrose. 'Yes?'

'I think...I...'

Silence.

And not of the comforting, cold, spine-chilling type.

'Mr Ambrose?'

No answer.

'Mr Ambrose, stay awake!'

Silence.

'Stay awake, damn you! Stay with me.'

Still no answer.

All right. Maybe I needed a different strategy.

'Don't you dare waste time sleeping! There's work to be done!'

His eyelids fluttered. Yes!

'The early bird gets the worm! Early to bed and early to rise, makes a man healthy, wealthy and wise!'

One eyelid rose.

'Miss Linton?'

'Yes?'

'Stop trying to annoy me with silly proverbs.'

Taking hold of his chin, I raised his head until he had no choice but to look straight into my eyes.

'I'll annoy you as much as I damn well please if it helps keep you awake! Pull yourself together! You need a doctor, and I can't drag you back to Paris unconscious.'

'A *doctor*? Are you out of your mind? Do you have any idea how much medical professionals in Paris charge for—'

I kissed him. That shut him up, and probably would have the added benefit of keeping him from falling asleep. If it didn't, I honestly would have been rather miffed.

'Listen to me, you stubborn sack of money!' I growled against his lips. 'I'm going to get you back to Paris, and then I'm going to get the best, most expensive doctor for you I can get my hands on, and I'm going to pay him out of your pocket! That's what you get for being stupid enough to let yourself be shot! Understood?'

When he opened his mouth to fire back, I kissed him again—and he was silent.

I should employ this strategy more often.

Finally, I had to break away and gasp for air. Mr Ambrose was breathing heavily as well—but I didn't really think it was from my marvellous kissing skills. He was swaying back and forth on his horse, and I barely managed to keep him upright.

'Come on, Karim! Come on! Where are you? Get your butt back here!'

The door of the inn slammed. Out of the corner of my eye, I saw the figure of the governor-general hurrying towards his coach. Moments later, the coach started to roll down the road, back towards the port it had come from. The sight lifted a heavy burden from my shoulders. Unfortunately, there was another, even heavier one, already there.

'Miss...Miss Linton...I...'

'Come on, Mr Ambrose, Sir. Hold on! Karim will be here any minute!'

He started to sway more heavily, just as I heard hoof beats from the direction of the inn.

Hurry up, Karim! Hurry up! Hurry up!

Another big sway. I struggled, fighting to stay upright, and—

Thud!

'Mmmph!'

I lay on the ground for a moment, contemplating what a heavy burden love could be. Karim's voice tore me from my philosophical contemplations.

'*Sahib? Sahib*, where are you?'

I cleared my throat. 'Down here on the ground, Karim. Could you give me a hand?'

HEALING STONE

Back in Paris, I kicked out the first doctor who came to look after Mr Ambrose, and the second, too. The third I kept, because (a) he was the first one to speak English, and (b), he didn't propose to use leeches. I wasn't exactly a medical professional, but considering the massive amounts of blood my dear employer had already lost, I didn't really see the point of bleeding him some more. Besides—the doctor was already going to suck him dry with his bill. That would be hard enough for poor Mr Ambrose to handle.

If he survives, a tiny, scared voice in the back of my mind whispered. A voice I had never heard before.

I straightened my spine. Of course he'd make it! I wouldn't allow him to die!

'Well, doctor?' I demanded. 'Are you done yet?'

In response, the doctor looked up from his patient. He had a pincer-like instrument in his hand, and gripped between the pincers, I saw what looked little marble covered on tomato sauce. When my stomach realized what it really was, it rebelled.

'Nearly, *Monsieur*.' With a *plink*, the doctor dropped the bullet into a metal container. ''and me the bandages, if you please?'

Trying not to look at the prone form of Mr Ambrose on the bed, I handed him some strips of pristine linen—not ripped out of my shirt this time, but bought from the finest store in Paris. Mr Ambrose was going to be so furious.

Please let him be furious! Please, let him live to be furious!

Calmly taking the linen strips, the doctor used one to clean the wound, then wrapped it with another and tied the bandages with agile fingers. While he was still working, he glanced up at me out of the corner of his eye.

'*Monsieur*...Linton, was it?'

'Yes? And pay attention to what you're doing!'

'I am, *Monsieur*. I am. If I may ask, 'ow exactly did the patient sustain 'is injury?'

'A duel.'

'*Monsieur* Linton...' Tying the last knot, the doctor turned towards me. He picked the bloody bullet out of its container and raised it to eye-level. I had to swallow. 'Sis is not a pistol bullet. It comes from a rifle.'

My face remained stony. I had learned from the best. 'It was a long-distance duel.'

'*Monsieur* Linton, you cannot expect me to believe—'

'Do you want your fee, doctor?'

'Yes, of course, but—'

'Then get back to work and don't dare stop until Mr Ambrose is out of danger! Trust me, you do not want to know what *he* will do if Mr Ambrose does not survive.' I jabbed my thumb at Karim, standing in the corner of the room like a grim, turban-wearing sentinel. 'And you definitely do not want to know what *I* will do.'

The doctor's eyes flitted nervously between me and Karim. The big Mohammedan gave him his best you-are-about-to-decapitated-like-a-dog look. Quickly, the doctor turned back to his patient. He talked a lot less after that, and worked a lot faster.

Everything in me wanted to look away—but I forced myself to watch. I forced myself to observe every move, every little shift of his fingers. After the things Dalgliesh had done in the past, bribing a doctor definitely wasn't beyond him, and I wasn't going to let anything or anyone harm Mr Ambrose. However, the doctor did nothing but his job. He applied a second layer of bandages, covered Mr Ambrose with a thick quilt, and then pulled out a pencil to draw up a quick list.

'See to it sat you keep him covered, *Monsieur*. He 'as lost quite a lot of blood and might go into shock. If 'e does, send a messenger. I've left my card on the dresser. 'ere—' He tore the list off his notepad and handed it to me, 'is a list of suitable foods. Keep 'im on sis diet, and sat should support his convalescence.'

I glanced at the list, and made a quick mental calculations of how much this would cost.

Oh yes. This would support a *very* quick convalescence, definitely.

'I sink that's all for now.' The doctor was edging towards the door. For some mysterious reason, he seemed rather eager to get out of here. 'If you would be so kind, *Monsieur*...'

'Oh, of course.'

Reaching underneath the quilt, I slipped a hand into my dear employer's pocket, and pulled out that mysterious well of plenty, that hallowed object of mystery which was Mr Rikkard Ambrose's wallet. At the other end of the room, Karim made a garbled noise of protest—but when I sent him a look, he shut up and concentrated very hard on looking bodyguardly.

I raised the wallet, trying to act as if this was nothing special. And in a way, it wasn't, right? After all, he wanted me to be his wife. As his wife, everything that was his would be mine, wouldn't it?

Yes, and of course he's going to see it like that, too, eh?

Taking a deep breath, I opened the wallet.

Holy....!

Suddenly, I didn't feel quite as confident about the whole 'what's his is mine'-thing anymore. My pockets weren't nearly big enough!

I swallowed.

'How much, doctor?'

The doctor named a sum that, five minutes ago, would have seemed exorbitant to me. Now I just reached into the wallet, pulled out the smallest bill and handed it to him. 'Keep the change.'

'S-sank you, *Monsieur*! 'ow very generous.' Wide-eyed, he retreated to the door. His gaze was fastened disbelievingly to the bill in his hands. 'As I said, if you should have need of me, call me. Day or night, it does not matter. I shall always be at your disposal.'

And he vanished.

Which left me alone in the room with one unconscious Ambrose and one self-conscious bodyguard.

Lifting the quilt, I carefully slid Mr Ambrose's wallet back in its place. Then I turned towards Karim, looking at him like I never had before. Not with amusement or annoyance, not with anger or a little devil dancing in my eyes, but with an earnest, heartfelt plea.

'Karim? Please?'

The Mohammedan met my eyes for a long moment. Then, without a word, he nodded and left the room.

'Thank you,' I whispered into the empty air as I sank onto the bed beside Mr Ambrose.

I don't know how many of you have ever lain beside the man you love while he was unconscious, on the brink of death. The advantage with Mr Ambrose was that, as long as I closed my eyes and just held him tightly, I hardly noticed the difference to the waking version. Well... maybe that wasn't entirely true. He probably was a little less chatty while he was awake.

Still, lying there, not knowing whether he would ever wake up again...

'Please.' Grasping his hand and lifting it to my lips, I pressed a light kiss on its back. 'Please wake up.'

Silence.

Just in case, I peeked up to check if his eyes were open. With him, you never knew. But they were still firmly closed.

And even if he woke up, what then? It didn't mean he was out of danger. I had heard plenty of horror stories of people returning with a wound from the colonies, or from a simple hunting accident, and dying a miserable death weeks later when it started to fester.

Don't worry. Mr Ambrose would never waste that much time. If he kicks the bucket, it'll be quick.

'Shut up!' I told my inner voice and hugged him to me even more tightly.

'You're not allowed to leave me, understood? I forbid you!'

Silence.

Bloody stubborn son of a bachelor!

Slipping under the quilt, I snuggled up to him. I lay there as time slowly drifted by, unable to close my eyes for even a moment. Outside of the opera house, the first glimmer of dawn began to appear at the horizon. Paris awoke as the sun began to rise over the city. The noise of people and wagons starting to move through the streets drifted in through the thin glass panes. Church bells rang out, telling everyone who hadn't caught on yet that it was time to get up.

Still, Mr Ambrose did not wake.

Don't panic, Lilly. Don't you dare lose your head! He'll wake up in just a minute and start ordering you around. He has to!

But what if he didn't?

I'll have lost him. And I would have never really had him in the first place.

Why hadn't I grabbed fate by the balls? After all our adventures together, after knowing how I felt deep down for so long, why hadn't I just told him how I felt ages ago? We could have been...

The images flitting past my inner eye made me want to cry.

Yes, and of course that would accomplish so much. Pull yourself together, Lillian Linton! It's no use crying over spilled milk.

True.

But making sure I wouldn't spill any in the future? That was an entirely different matter.

Raising my chin, I gazed up at Mr Ambrose's stony face, memorizing its every edge and line. From now on, there would be no more hesitation. If I got him back, I wouldn't hide, wouldn't hold back anything. I was his, and he was mine, *basta*. The time for sneaking around behind other people's backs was over. I was going to stand up for him, stand up for us, and anyone who objected could go bugger themselves with a banana!

Which might actually be an interesting sight.

I'm going to marry this man. I'm going to give him all my heart. And then I'm going to browbeat him into funding a campaign for women's suffrage.

Smiling, I stroked a finger down his cheek.

But maybe I'll only tell him about that last part after we were married.

His eyelids fluttered.

I lay there for a moment, unmoving, staring at him. Had that really just happened, or had it just been my imagina—

His eyelids fluttered again.

160

Yes, yes, yes, thank you, God, Zeus, Odin and anybody else up there! Thank you, and please excuse that I don't believe in you!

'Mr Linton...w...w...'

'Yes?' Quickly, I leant forward, trying to catch his words. 'What do you need? Water?'

'W...why is my wallet lighter?'

It was then that I knew he was going to be all right.

~~**~*~*

It took time, of course. Much more time than was to Mr Ambrose's liking. But after I was sure that the danger of his wound festering was past, it was rather enjoyable to have him at my mercy. Alas, it wasn't a state that was to last for long. Three days after we arrived back in Paris, a messenger boy knocked at the door of the opera house.

'The minister is expecting us,' Mr Ambrose told me when he had perused the missive. 'It appears he's rather eager to know if he should expect a world-wide war to break out in the next couple of days.'

'But you can't go! You're still much too weak!'

The moment the words were out of my mouth, I could have kicked myself. I might as well have set his bed on fire.

'Weak?' The word was spoken softly. Coolly. Like the first whisper of an arctic storm approaching. 'Indeed, Mr Linton?'

'No! No, I didn't mean—'

Ignoring me, Mr Ambrose swung his legs out of the bed. Grabbing his hat off the nightstand, he pushed himself to his feet. I held my breath, watching him intently for any sign of weakness. But his legs were straight, his feet as steady as iron.

'Do I seem weak to you, Mr Linton?'

'No, Sir. Of course not, Sir.'

Because if I answer 'yes', you'll probably insist on marching all the way to the ministry and collapse from exhaustion.

'Adequate. Karim!'

The Mohammedan stuck his head in through the door. When he caught sight of Mr Ambrose standing, his eyes widened. '*Sahib!* You shouldn't be out of bed alrea—'

I shook my head vigorously. Karim's jaw slammed shut.

'What was that, Karim?'

'Nothing, *Sahib*. Nothing whatsoever.'

'Hm. Order a cab. We are going to the ministry.'

'Yes, *Sahib*. Immediately, *Sahib*.'

He vanished, and I gave Mr Ambrose a look. 'All right, all right. You can go. But you have to stop playing the stoic, do you hear? Tell me when it hurts!'

He lifted an eyebrow infinitesimally. 'Hurt? What, pray, are you speaking of, Mr Linton?'

I jabbed a finger into his side.

161

'Aarrr!'

'That,' I informed him, and grabbed my tailcoat from a hook on the wall. 'Come on. Let's go.'

The ride to the ministry didn't take long. I diplomatically refrained from pointing out that, under normal circumstances, Mr Ambrose would have eaten rusty nails rather than paying money for a cab. I even pretended to let him help me out of the coach, while *I* actually steadied *him*. What the heck was happening to me? Why was I suddenly being so nice to him?

It had to be this marriage-thing. It was messing with my head. I had to make a point of being nasty to him at least once a week, or all the fun would go out of life.

Minister Guizot awaited us in his cluttered office. I stood next to Mr Ambrose, inconspicuously supporting him, while Karim took up his post next to the door.

'*Bonjour, Monsieur* Ambrose. *Bonjour, Monsieur* Linton, and *Monsieur*...what was your name again?'

He gave Karim a questioning look.

Unfortunately, Karim was immune to questioning looks.

'Um. *Alors...Monsieur* Ambrose, my lieutenant already reported back to me and told me of the little altercation in front of the *Sainte Catherine* inn. Would you be so kind as to elaborate?'

Mr Ambrose looked as though he had to seriously consider the question. Understandable, in a way. He was neither elaborate, nor particularly kind. But finally he nodded and started recounting the events of a few nights ago. There were a lot fewer words, bullets and blood splatters than I would have used, but he got the gist across. When he reached the part where Karim put on the uniform and knelt to the governor-general, I saw the bodyguard stiffen.

'So that was it,' Mr Ambrose concluded. 'The governor-general left, and we simply returned to Paris.'

Yes, with you slung over the back of my horse like a pair of rock-filled saddlebags. Very simple indeed.

'You are sure he left?' the minister enquired, his forehead furrowed. 'He didn't see through your ruse and turn back at some point?'

For the first time since we entered, Karim spoke.

'He left. I made sure my description of the rebellion was quite...convincing.'

His voice sent a shiver down my back. And to judge by the look of the minister, I wasn't the only one.

'*Très bien.* Then I think our business is concluded, *non*? It 'as been a pleasure, gentlemen.'

The invitation to leave was quite evident. The minister's smile said, 'Thank you so much for helping. Now could you please get out of my country before you cause a miniature war with your nemesis?'

Giving a curt nod, Mr Ambrose turned towards the door. 'I shall send you my bill.'

The minister blinked. 'Bill? For what?'

'For keeping your country out of a war. You didn't think that would be for free, did you? *Au revoir.*'

And he marched out of the room.

The minister blinked—then glanced at me. ''e...'e cannot be serious, *non?*'

I gave the poor man a pitying look and patted his shoulder. 'Just pay. It'll be easier that way, trust me.'

'Stop dawdling, Mr Linton!'

'Oops. Duty calls. Excuse me.'

And I scurried out into the hall.

The three of us marched in silence until we reached the entrance hall. The sun was just rising as we stepped into the big empty space. Neither inside nor outside on the street many people were about. At the sight of the sun through the big windows, Karim stopped and gazed out, eastwards, towards the burning orb.

'One day, I'll bring news of rebellion in my homeland,' he told the sun. 'And it won't be fake.'

Mr Ambrose gazed at his loyal bodyguard for a moment. Then, stepping forward, he placed a hand on Karim's shoulder.

'The East India Company will be dealt with in time, Karim—as will Dalgliesh. You have my word.' Lowering his hand, he turned back towards the exit. 'But for now, I have other things to take care of.'

I raised an eyebrow. 'Things that are more important than the fate of a whole continent?'

'Yes,' he told me and took my hand firmly in his.

The whole cab ride back to the opera house passed in silence. And yet...I couldn't help the feeling that something was going on. Mr Ambrose exchanged more than one look with Karim. Then, halfway through the ride, he suddenly reached out and took my hand again.

'Mr Ambrose? What's the matter?'

He didn't answer.

About ten minutes later, the cab rolled to a stop in front of the opera house. During the whole ride, Mr Ambrose had not once let go of my hand. When the coach stopped and the door opened, he didn't loosen his grip. Instead, he stepped from the coach and held out his hand to guide me outside—not something a boss usually did for his trouser-wearing secretary. Something a man might do for his sweetheart. My heart was started pounding.

'Mr Ambrose?'

No answer. He pulled me through the front door, and started up the main stairs. I glanced back, and Karim, the bloody blighter, was standing next to the coach, arms crossed. What was going on? Karim went everywhere with Mr Ambrose! Why wasn't he coming with us?

'Mr Ambrose, what's going on?'

The only reply was silence. Cold, hard, all-encompassing silence.

I tried to tug my hand out of his—just out of habit. I might as well have tried to tug free from an iron clamp.

'Mr Ambrose, Sir? Why are you holding my hand?'

'To manipulate your direction of movement, Mr Linton.'

'I had sort of noticed that! Why?'

'Because I want to.'

'Where are we going?'

Silence.

'Where the heck are you leading me?'

More silence. Still, the question was answered a moment later when Mr Ambrose pushed open the doors in front of us and we entered the great hall of the opera house. It was completely empty and silent, and yet, for some reason, the lights of the stage were shining brightly, casting the whole scene into a warm glow. Step by step, Mr Rikkard Ambrose lead me up onto the stage. The red velvet of the curtain fell like a waterfall behind us, enveloping us in fiery warmth. In contrast, Mr Ambrose's eyes were like cool, dark oceans threatening to drag me under. Tightening his grip on my hand, he turned to face me head-on.

'Now are you going to tell me?' I demanded. 'What are you doing here?'

His only answer was more silence. But he didn't really need to say anything. It became pretty clear what he wanted when he reached into his pocket sank to one knee.

A BIG ONE ON THE FINGER

Holy Mother of Molys...

I stared down at Mr Rikkard Ambrose kneeling in front of me, and at the ring in his hand. The big, golden ring. Were my eyes deceiving me? This couldn't be real, could it?

'Upon consideration,' Mr Ambrose stated, 'I came to the conclusion that we should take this customary step to formalize relations.'

This was real. Only Mr Rikkard Ambrose would make such a breathtakingly romantic proposal.

This was real. *He* was real. He was mine. I swallowed and forced my dry mouth to open.

'Formalize away.'

Reaching up, he took my hand with a care that almost approached tenderness.

'Miss Lillian Linton, do you want to become my wife?'

With all my might, I squeezed a single word past the lump in my throat. 'Y-yes.'

'Good. Because you're going to.'

Had he just said good? *Good*? Not adequate?

Taking a firmer grip on my hand, he slipped the beautiful, big golden ring onto my ring finger. It went easily. In fact...a little bit *too* easily. It was a little bit too big.

I blinked.

No, not just a little bit…The bloody thing was large enough for three fingers at a time! Had Mr Ambrose gotten a knock on the head during the fight that had messed up his eyesight? Why else would he pick such a humongous ring that actually didn't look like an engagement ring, but much more like a…

I froze.

No.

No, he wouldn't. Not even *he* would dare to…

Slowly, I raised my eyes high, high above to where the theatre curtain hung from the ceiling, held by a number of big, glinting, gilded rings. At the very edge of the curtain, one ring was missing.

My eyes snapped back to Mr Ambrose, sparking with fury.

'You…you…'

'…are the love of my life?' he suggested.

'You miserable excuse for a miserly son of a bachelor! I…I…'

'Yes?'

'…I love you, dammit!'

'How gratifying.'

'But don't ask me why!'

'I was not planning to.' Rising to his feet, he dusted off his tailcoat and offered me a hand. 'Shall, we, Mrs Ambrose?'

Unable to keep the smile from my face, I slipped the ring over three of my fingers and took his hand. So what if it was crazy? It was us. The rest of the world could go bugger themselves!

'We shall.'

Our little scene was interrupted by slow claps. Startled, I glanced around, just in time to see Claudette ascending from the orchestra pit.

'*Perfait!* What a spectacle. It's a pity sat I cannot turn your story into an opera. Se audience would flee se city in droves and I could get a well-deserved holiday.'

Mr Ambrose gave the prima donna a cold look. 'I thought I gave orders for everyone to vacate the great hall.'

'*Pouah!*' Claudette made a dismissive gesture. 'In my opera house, I can do what I want.'

Mr Ambrose opened his mouth, probably to remind her of the little fact that it was actually *his* opera house, but I squeezed his hand, and—wonder of wonders—he closed his mouth.

'So, *ma petit*, you are truly leaving?' The prima donna regarded me with warmth in her eyes. 'Too bad. Life is more fun wis you here. I haven't seen so much drama offstage since I was romanced by an actor from the royal seatre.'

'Yes. I should be getting home, back to my family. And besides…' Letting the sentence trail off, I glanced up at Mr Ambrose.

Claudette smiled. 'I understand.'

You do? Then please explain it to me, because I sure as hell don't!

I was going to get married. I was going to get married, and leave behind my home and my sisters—everything I had ever known. It was a terrifying thought. And I should have been terrified. But…

I glanced up at Mr Ambrose again.

The only thing I could think was: *How can I be terrified as long as I have him on my side?*

'You're *leaving?*'

The agonized cry came from the door.

Oh God. Not *that*.

Footsteps rushed closer, and a moment later, Claudette was shoved aside by a wide-eyed Emilia Harse.

'Oh. Um, hello Miss Ars— I mean, Miss Harse.'

'Why, Mr Linton?' Oh God. Her eyes were shining. Was she going to cry? Please, don't let her cry! 'Why are you leaving me?'

'I, um...am getting married.'

'*What?*' Now there definitely wasn't any water in her eyes—fire, rather. 'Who is it? Who is the little hussy that stole you away from me?'

Beside me, Mr Ambrose stiffened.

Trust me, you'd rather not know.

'A, um...Argentinian belly dancer.'

'What?' demanded Miss Harse.

'*What?*' demanded Mr Ambrose. I could feel his icy stare bore into the back of my neck. Hm. Interesting. Maybe I should have him do a belly dance for me someday.

'Yes, exactly. A beautiful Argentinian belly dancer,' I confirmed, stepping on Mr Ambrose's foot. 'We've been carrying on a scandalous affair for months, didn't you know? And now I've finally decided to get divorced from my current wife so I can marry her and move to China.'

'You...you...'

'Scoundrel? Rogue?'

'...man!'

Ouch! Now there was an insult that really hurt. But I guessed my problems with Miss Emilia Harse were over once and for all.

'Come, come, my dear!' Claudette slung a consoling arm around her protégé's shoulders. 'That scoundrel isn't worthy of you. You deserve a real man!' Over her shoulder, she winked at me. Devious little witch! I was going to miss her. A speck of moisture appeared at the corner of my eye.

As the two singers departed, Mr Ambrose cleared his throat. 'Miss Linton?'

I sighed. 'Yes, yes. I know. It's no good crying, is it? After all, I'm going to see her again someday.'

'That, and you could take your heel off my toes.'

'Oh.' Hurriedly, I lifted my foot. 'Sorry.'

Extending his hand, Mr Ambrose took hold of me. 'Shall we go?'

I nodded. 'Yes. Let's go home.'

'I have a better idea.' Pulling me towards him, Mr Ambrose captured my face between his hands and looked deep into my eyes. 'Let's make one. Together.'

~~**~*~*

166

The sun stood high over Paris when our coach rolled through the northern gate. I gazed back at the city for a moment—then turned to look at the road ahead. It was well-paved, and busy with many travellers and wagons. It looked to be an easy road.

As for my own personal road into the future...

Well, that would be a little more difficult.

What's so difficult about it? asked a little voice in my head. *You love him. You're going to marry him. Basta.*

True. But my congenial feelings towards Mr Ambrose might not be shared by everybody. The only time he and my best friend Patsy had actually met, he had eviscerated her in a debate about women's rights, ridiculed her from atop a podium and sent her packing. I doubted very much that she had fond memories of the event. And as for my family...

Ella would be ecstatic, of course. She'd be ecstatic if I married a scarecrow as long as the scarecrow in question was kind, loving and devoted husband. But Anne and Maria would be vicious. And while I didn't particularly care for their opinions, I wasn't looking forward to their jibes. For years, I had told everyone that I would never marry, that I didn't need any man.

And now?

Had I changed that much?

No. He's not any man. He's Rikkard Ambrose.

It wasn't I who had changed. It was us. He was still him, and I was still me. But together, we were something new. Something better.

And I could convince Patsy of that, surely.

Probably.

Maybe?

'What's the matter, Mr Linton?'

Turning towards Mr Ambrose, I gave him a bright smile. 'Nothing. Nothing whatsoever. I was just wondering...what do you normally do if you offend someone? Would you consider an apology?'

'Certainly. If it is well-delivered, I might even accept it.'

It took a moment for the meaning of his words to sink in. When it did, I gave a groan, covering my face with both hands. 'I'm so going to be skewered with a parasol.'

The drive to Calais was over disturbingly quickly. As we stepped out of the coach, we were greeted by flocks of screeching seagulls. One of the braver ones tried to use Mr Ambrose as a toilet, but quickly changed its mind when he sent a frosty look her way.

'Do you think we'll get cabins on a ferry at such short notice?' I enquired.

'One cabin. Just one.' His gaze bored into me, making me shiver to the bone— as well as other, more interesting parts.

'Really? You plan to introduce me to the ship's steward as your significant other in this getup?' I tugged at one leg of my trousers and smirked. 'We can try, if you want. It would be amusing to see the poor man's face.'

Mr Ambrose's little finger twitched. His jaw worked, but no sound came out. Reaching out, he squeezed my hand.

I don't want to be apart from you.

I squeezed back.

I know.

It was amazing how much silence could say.

'Let's get this over with,' Mr Ambrose announced. 'The quicker we're back in England, the better.' And he marched off towards the ticket counter.

The clerk behind the counter was sitting with his chin in his hands and his eyelids at half-mast in a way that was either deeply philosophical or half-asleep. In either case, he didn't have much attention to spare for Mr Ambrose. My dear employer wrapped sharply on the table, gaining about a quarter of the man's attention. He yawned.

'Do you 'ave reservations?'

'No. But I have this,' Mr Ambrose told him and placed the title deed of his shipping company on the counter.

The man blinked.

He blinked again.

Then his chin slipped out of his hand and slammed onto the desk. It landed only inches away from the title deed. Horrified, the man jumped to his feet and hurried around the desk.

'M-my apologies, *messieurs*. If there is anysin' I can do for y—'

'A cabin. Now.'

'Yes, certainly, certainly. Please follow me. Right sis way, *messieurs*.'

The journey back across the channel passed quietly. However, there wasn't a single storm or shipwreck, nor even an encounter with a stowaway. There was a slight disturbance when *someone*—of course I had no idea who—tried to enter my cabin at night, only to find out head-first that I had locked the door.

Thud!

'Ow!'

Rolling over, I pulled the blanket up under my chin and smiled into the pillow. I was really looking forward to my wedding night. Anticipation was a wonderful feeling.

Outside, *someone* uttered a low curse and stomped off into the night.

When a few days later we landed at Dover, the bruise on Mr Ambrose's forehead had almost vanished. Stepping towards the gangway, I extended my hand to him.

He took it.

'How are going to do this?' My voice was little more than a whisper. Inside my head, though, there was shouting.

I'm getting married. Married. Bloody married!

'Well, the traditional way is for the suitor to approach the parents or guardians of the lady in question and ask for her hand.'

'What?' My hand clenched into a fist instinctively, crushing Mr Ambrose's fingers. I whirled around to face him. He didn't even blink. 'No way! I'm not some prize to be given away! I'm my own woman. I'm going to go to my aunt and uncle and tell them I'm getting married, and that's it!'

His cool gaze was implacable. There wasn't a hint of emotion on his face and he leaned forward and calmly spoke one authoritative word.

'No.'

'No?' I narrowed my eyes. 'What do you mean, n—'

One elegant finger against my lips cut me off abruptly. Leaning even closer, Mr Ambrose captured my face in his hands.

'You are not going to tell them. *We* are. Tradition be damned.'

Never had I loved him as much as I did in that moment. So I showed him. Standing up on my tiptoes, I threw my arms around his neck and kissed him for all I was worth. Granted, it wasn't much, counted in pound sterling, but so what? This, right here in his arms, was where I belonged.

Only when shocked gasps came from behind me did I remember that, while I was still wearing trousers, the rest of the world might disagree.

Oops.

Letting go of Mr Ambrose, I took a hurried step back. That didn't exactly soothe the nerves of the onlookers, however. A small crowd of our fellow passengers had gathered on the deck to stare down at us. One elderly gentleman's face slackened so his monocle fell and hung dangling from its chain. A lady gave a gurgling noise and keeled over backwards, hitting the planks of the deck with a *thunk*.

'Oh. Um...hello there.' I waved at the audience—then hurriedly glanced at Mr Ambrose. 'You don't happen to have a fast coach standing by, do you?'

'I have something better.'

Mr Ambrose waved his hand imperiously. Immediately, a towering shadow fell upon the onlookers.

'Yes, *Sahib*?'

'We were just leaving, Karim. Do you think these ladies and gentlemen have anything to say against that?'

Turning towards the other passengers, Karim gave them a look. A look at his sabre and pistol, to be precise. I had never seen so many heads shake so fast.

'No, *Sahib*.'

'Adequate. Let's be on our way.'

Side by side, we strode down the gangplank. Down on the docks, Karim cleared his throat. 'Should I hail a cab, *Sahib*?'

'I think we'll walk,' I said before Mr Ambrose could bring himself to pry his lips apart. I winked at him, 'It's so much more economical.'

Karim blinked. Whatever he had expected, an order from me definitely wasn't it. 'Um...*Sahib*?'

Mr Ambrose raised one eyebrow infinitesimally. 'You heard her.'

'Yes, *Sahib*! Certainly, *Sahib*.'

Karim inclined his head, and we started down the street. After a few steps Mr Ambrose seemed to notice the giant grin on my face.

'What are you so exuberant about, Mr Linton?'

'Oh, nothing, really. I just realized that once we're married, Karim will have to do what I say.'

'Whatever it is you are thinking, Mr Linton—no.'

I heard a sigh of relief from behind me.

'No? Are you sure?' I fluttered my eyelashes at him.

It had zero effect.

'Indeed I am. You shall have to plot your vengeance on my bodyguard another way,'

I realized what he was thinking and gifted him with a brilliant smile. 'Oh, no, no! I wasn't going to do anything to Karim.'

'You weren't?'

'No, of course not! I would never make him do a handstand in a tutu, or strap him down and let half a dozen children tickle his feet for three hours, or anything like that!'

'For something you never intended to do you seem to have spent an inordinate amount of time thinking about it, Mr Linton.'

'Well, a girl has to amuse herself somehow, doesn't she?'

Mr Ambrose did not deign to reply to that. For a while, we walked in silence. In my head I started counting down.

Five...four...three...two...one—

'So...what *was* it that you were thinking?'

I grinned.

'Well...I was just running down my list of enemies in my head. There are a few friends of my demon-brood sisters Ann and Maria, for instance, who would really benefit from a visit by a seven-feet-tall sabre-swinging giant. It might improve their character.'

'Indeed.'

I stopped in my tracks. Mr Ambrose continued walking for a few more strides before he noticed I was not at his side any longer and turned, his head cocked.

'Mr Linton?'

'Did you...did you just *agree* to let me use your bodyguard to terrorize my enemies?'

'Certainly. If he is not otherwise engaged.'

I let that sink in for a moment—then I dashed forward and threw my arms around him.

'I'm so glad I'm going to marry you!'

He stiffened—then, after a moment, relaxed and put his arms around me.

'Likewise.'

Suddenly, I remembered where I was and what I was still wearing. Hurriedly, I slid out of Mr Ambrose's arms and jumped back. But the staring crowd and rude comments I expected weren't forthcoming. In fact, there wasn't even a single curious bystander staring at us.

'Where is everybody?'

Mr Ambrose glanced around. He didn't seem particularly perturbed by the empty street.

'Working?' he suggested.

I raised an eyebrow. 'On a Sunday afternoon?'

'It's where I would be.'

'We'll have to have a talk about that once the formalities are over and done with.'

'We can have it now. I won't stop working. There. I talked. We're done.'

'I think we also need to look at your definition of "talk".'

Apparently not deeming this worthy of a reply, Mr Ambrose pointed down the street, and we proceeded. I still threw confused glances right and left at the empty street, but as we approached Uncle Bufford's house, my thoughts became more and more preoccupied with what I was going to say. Or rather, how I was going to get Aunt Brank to shut up long enough to be able to say anything.

Dump a bucket of cold water on her?

No, that would just make her screech louder.

Gag her?

Maybe with Karim's help I could do it. But then...it would probably not make her a lot more receptive to what I had to say. And my birthday was still a long way off. I technically still needed a guardian's permission to marry.

Well...

There would be one way to ensure her cooperation. But...

I glanced at Mr Ambrose.

'How should I introduce you?' I asked, cautiously. 'As Mr Ambrose, or Lord Ambrose, Heir to The Honourable The Marquess Ambrose?'

His mouth slammed into a thin line. His face turned from marble to granite.

'Mister. Always just mister.'

'It might help smooth the way if—'

'No.'

'But—'

'No.'

All right. That was one avenue closed.

If only I could get to Uncle Bufford first. As soon as I showed him Mr Ambrose's bank balance he'd be happy to get him as a son-in-law without asking his name. Most likely, he wouldn't even ask about age, size, sex or species.

He might ask what kind of man he is, though.

Yes. He really might. My grumpy uncle and I had gotten to know each other quite well during the last year or two. He might actually care about my happiness. The challenge would be getting to him. Aunt Brank was a tough coconut to crack.

Time seemed to pass far too fast. One moment, we were walking away from the docks, the next, we turned the corner and saw my uncle's house farther down the street.

Mr Ambrose stopped, and turned me towards him.

'Do you have a change of clothes somewhere?'

I nodded. Somehow, my mouth was too dry for an actual answer.

'Adequate. You go change and prepare them for my arrival. I will take a brief trip to Empire House to dress appropriately for the occasion. I shall return directly.'

'Dress appropriately? You mean you actually own a *second tailcoat*?'

Looking most superior, Mr Ambrose straightened his lapels. 'No. But I can have this one ironed.'

A smile spreading across my face, I reached up to touch his face. 'You do that. I'll be waiting for you.'

He nodded, and started to turn. My hand on his shoulder stopped him.

'And...'

'Yes?'

'Hurry up. I'm not good at waiting.'

'Neither,' Mr Ambrose told me and took hold of my face, 'am I.'

And he kissed me, there, right in the middle of the street. Nobody was watching. The street was still beautifully, wondrously empty. After a long, long while, he let go. His dark, sea-coloured eyes bored into mine for a moment.

'Until later.'

And with that, he turned and vanished into the London fog.

Gathering all my courage, I turned, too, and headed towards the garden wall. As I unlocked and slipped through the familiar little gate into the back garden, a feeling of unreality came over me. Could it really be that I was doing this for the very last time? That soon, I wouldn't be Miss Lillian Linton anymore? That instead, I would be Mrs Lillian Ambrose?

Well...the last part isn't necessarily decided yet. After all, why should you be the one to change your name?

Hm...what would Mr Ambrose say to becoming Mr Rikkard Linton?

Nothing, probably. A whole lot of ice-cold, very explicit, very determined nothing.

Smiling, I slipped into the garden shed. Married life was going to be interesting.

As quickly as I could, I changed into my (slightly dusty) spare female outfit. Then, like a condemned woman going to meet the aunt squad, I marched to the front door and knocked.

No response.

Well, that wasn't really that odd. You could usually brush your teeth, write a sonnet and do a few cartwheels in the time it took Leadfield, our ancient butler, to reach the door. But...this time I didn't even hear a hint of the slow, lopsided gate of the dear old mummified fellow.

'Hello?'

I knocked again.

Nothing.

For the first time, then, it really sank in: the streets around me were empty. Completely empty. How often did that happen in London, even on a Sunday? No, *especially* on a Sunday! People should be heading to the public parks in droves. Instead, an unnatural silence hung over the city. Trust me, by now I was an expert on unnatural silences.

'Hello? Hello! Is anyone in there? Answer me, dammit!' I started pounding on the door. 'Open up right now!'

Finally, footsteps hurried down the corridor. The latch clicked, and the door slowly slid open just wide enough to let me see a little slice of a face on the other side. It was not my aunt's.

HOMECOMING SURPRISE

'Maria? What are you doing at the door? Where is Leadfield?'

'L-Lilly?'

'You're not sure? That hurts my feelings. I distinctly remember you telling me once you'd recognize my ugly mug from sixty paces.'

'N-no! It can't be you! Go away!'

She tried to slam the door on me. She honestly tried to *slam the door* shut *right in my face!* Luckily, you don't spend a year working for Rikkard Stubborn-As-A-Rock Ambrose without learning a thing or two about persistence. My foot wedged itself in the door before I even had time to think about it.

'No! Don't come in! Leave! I don't want to get sick!'

The barrage of words I had been about to unleash died on my lips.

Sick?

My eyes flicked from left to right, once again taking in the empty streets, the closed shutters, the barred doors. A cold shiver went down my back. And unfortunately, it wasn't because Rikkard Ambrose was standing behind me.

'Maria, it's really me. It's me, Lilly! Open up!'

'My stupid sister has run way! She isn't here! She can't be!'

'I'm back. That happens when people return, you know. And I'm as healthy as a horse. Now open the door!'

For a moment, nothing but silence came from the other side of the door.

'How do I know this really is Lilly?' Maria's suspicious voice finally reached my ears. 'You sound like her, but—'

'Open the door this minute, you bloody little nitwit, or I'll kick it down and stab you with my parasol!'

There was another moment of silence.

'All right. It *is* you.'

Slowly, the door creaked open.

'Lilly! Good God, Lilly, where have you been all this time?'

I waved her question away. 'Never mind that now. What's going on here? Where are Uncle and Aunt?'

Maria swallowed.

'Up in the North of England.'

What? All that bloody anxiety for nothing? I had composed over five different speeches to explain my marriage machinations on the way here, and now it was all for nothing? Crap! 'Do you think that if they were here we'd still be stuck here? We should have left the city days ago! But you know Uncle Bufford! He left us enough money for water and dried bread crusts, but not for coach tickets out of the city, let alone the rent of a place somewhere safe in the country!'

'What do you mean, somewhere safe? Why did they leave? What happened?'

'An...an old army friend of uncle's died, and they went up to the funeral. But then...then...'

Trembling, she sank against the wall.

Maria, trembling? And worse, not trying to insult or harass me? Dear God. Things had to be bad.

'Then people started dying.'

'An epidemic?' I squeezed past around the lump in my throat. 'What kind?'

'How should I know? I'm no doctor!'

'Yes, but you have eyes, and you can read the paper.'

'The newspaper?' She wrinkled her oh-so-delicate nose. 'That's unladylike!'

With difficulty, I resisted the temptation to slap some sense into her. Considering how thick her head was, the sense would probably not reach the inside of her skull even if I slapped her all the way to Birmingham.

'You have to know something!'

Maria's eyes lowered. Her voice was nothing but a whisper when she said, 'Cholera. They say it's cholera.'

I felt the blood drain from my face.

'Is everyone still all right here? None of you are feeling ill, are you?'

'Well...until recently, yes. But...'

Something clenched tight around my heart.

'But what?'

'Well, a few days ago, Ella started feeling poorly and...'

She probably said more after that. Knowing Maria, a lot more, and most of it useless chatter. But I didn't hear anything besides one name.

Ella.

Dear Lord, not her! Please, not her!

'Where is she?'

My voice sounded far, far away, as if it belonged someone else. A very capable, determined someone.

'Well, in her room, but...'

'Bring me to her right now!'

'I, um...'

I suddenly felt very cold.

'Maria? You have been taking care of her, haven't you? Tell me you've been taking care of her!'

My sister crossed her arms in front of her chest.

'She's sick! Everyone says cholera is caused by bad air! I can't risk to—'

Taking a step closer, I pinned her to the wall with a look I had learned from a certain someone. As I had the voice.

'Take. Me. To. Her. Now.'

Never in my life had I seen my sister move that fast. In fifteen seconds we were at Ella's door. Maria hesitated.

'Open it,' I ordered.

She reached for the knob and she pushed open the door. Stepping inside, we saw Ella lying sleeping on the bed, and a butt sticking out of the open window.

Wait just a minute...

A *butt?*

A moment later, it was followed by a back, and then...

'You!'

At Maria's gasp, the young man tumbled backwards into the room he'd been trying to climb into. He rolled around and I stared down into the slightly guilty, but far more determined face of Edmund Conway.

'Mr Conway!' Maria exclaimed. 'What are you doing in here? This is a lady's room! That's most improper!'

It was decided. Karim would be paying my sister a visit—with a *really* big sabre.

'Maria?' I said in my most civilized, calm, I'm-going-to-murder-you-in-two-seconds tone. 'Shut up and get out. Now.'

She opened her mouth to shoot back an indignant reply—then realized she might be breathing contagious air, and reconsidered.

'I was leaving in any case. Have your fun, Lilly. Just you wait till Aunt gets home. You'll get what's coming to you!'

A really, *really* big sabre.

'I don't doubt it. I look forward to it.'

Huffing, she exited the room, leaving me alone with the piano-tuner on the floor.

Edmund looked up at me. I met his eyes.

'You've been visiting her regularly, haven't you?'

He raised his chin, stubbornly. 'Yes, I have! And I don't care what you say, I'm going to continue to come here.'

'No, you're not.'

'Yes, I—'

'Because you and your parents are coming with us.'

He blinked. For a moment, he looked at me as if the piano in his head needed re-tuning. 'Err...come? Where?'

'Anywhere! Away from here.' I pierced him with a look. 'You don't imagine I'm going to let my little sister stew in her misery here? If this sickness is really caused by infected air, she needs to get out of here pronto!'

'L-Lill?'

Both our heads snapped around to the bed.

'Ella! You're awake!'

Both Edmund and I started forward at the same time. I beat him to the punch, but only because he tripped over his own legs while trying to scramble to his feet. Falling to my knees beside the bed, I grabbed Ella's hand.

'Lill? Is that really you?'

I hardly recognized her voice. It was rough and dry like old sandpaper. Schooling my face to not betray a hint of my shock, I leaned over her.

'You really needn't have gone to all this trouble, you know,' I told her. 'You could have just sent me a postcard saying how much you missed me. You needn't have caught yourself some silly illness just to get my attention.'

Ella laughed. Or at least she tried to. Rapidly, it devolved into a rattling cough. I winced.

'I'm so glad you're back, Lill.'

'So am I. I've got big plans ahead of me, and I'm going to need you. So you'd better stop all this silly lying about and coughing right now and get better. That is an order, understood?'

She gave that dry laugh again, obviously thinking I was joking.

Well, aren't you?

Hm...

Maybe I had spent just a little too much time with Mr Rikkard Ambrose.

'I'm glad you've got plans for the future, Lill.' Ella squeezed my hand. 'But I'm afraid you'll have to manage without me. It's getting worse day by day.'

'What does the doctor say?'

Silence pervaded the room.

'Ella? A doctor *has* been to see you, right?'

She glanced down at her hands. 'Well...'

'I tried!' Edmund stepped forward, his eyes fastened to Ella like romantic superglue. 'But there's an epidemic in the city! Doctors' prices have shot through the roof. All I could afford was some quack from the East End who wanted to bleed her. Besides, even if I did have the money, I would have no idea whom to ask! Good doctors are few and far between. I don't have the kind of funds or connections you'd need to get someone from Harley Street.'

'You're right,' I agreed, rising to my feet. 'You don't.'

'Lill?' Ella eyed me suspiciously. 'You've got that look on your face. What are you planning?'

'Well, let me put it like this...if there were a way to get you away from here— not just you, Ella, but Edmund, his mother, his father, Lisbeth, Gertrude, oh, and Anne and Maria, curse her rotten eyeballs, and find all of you a nice place in the country for the time being with doctors to look after you, and all you could possibly need to get well again, what would you say?'

Ella blinked up at her. 'Well, I'd say that is a nice fantasy, but—'

'Good. We leave in half an hour.'

Turning, I marched out of the room. I suppose I should have stayed, should have explained, but I couldn't stay a second longer in that room. Seeing Ella like that, her cheeks sunken in, wrinkles around her eyes as if she had aged ten years in a day...

Don't think about it! Not now! Action now. Thinking later. Crying never. Because tears won't be necessary. Nothing is going to happen to Ella.

At least not if I could help it.

'Leadfield!'

Slow footsteps approached. After a moment or three, the aged butler stuck his head out of the kitchen.

'Yes, Miss?'

He didn't seem particularly surprised I was back. Well...that was about to change.

'Call the family. We're leaving.'

The butler's eyes widened. 'Leaving?'

'Yes.'

'For a walk in the park? I don't know if under the current conditions that is a particularly wise—'

'No. We're leaving town. Ring the gong. Tell everyone to be dressed and down here in a quarter of an hour. We're closing up the house.'[47]

He opened his mouth—but then he met my eyes, and closed it again.

'Yes, Miss!'

Maybe I hadn't spent too much time with Mr Ambrose after all. Maybe it was just enough. Listening to him giving orders could be quite educational.

'Is your nephew here, Leadfield?'

'Yes, Miss!'

'Send him to rent a coach—no, two—from the closest stable. Big ones. We'll need coachmen, too.'

'Coaches? But Miss, I don't think your uncle left enough money to—'

He broke off when I reached into my pocket and dumped a purse into his hand.

'That should be more than enough.'

'Yes, Miss!'

'I'll be going out. I expect everything to be ready when I return.'

'Certainly, Miss!'

And he hobbled off as fast as a racing snail.

I turned and marched out of the front door. I had things to attend to. My family weren't the only people I needed to get safely out of town. Only minutes later, I arrived at Patsy's mother's house. I knocked.

It took a while before the door opened. And when it did, it wasn't my female steam engine of a best friend on the other side, but a dignified, grey-haired butler.

'Miss Linton. What a pleasure to see you.'

'I'd like to see Miss Patsy, please. Could you announce me?'

'I'm sorry to disappoint you, Miss, but Miss Patsy is not at home. She and her mother went to Bath for a few weeks.'

'Bath? How long has she been gone?'

'More than a fortnight, I believe, Miss.'

'And my other friends? Eve? Flora?'

'As far as I know, she asked them to accompany her, Miss.'

Of course she had. It wasn't like Patsy to leave anybody out. I bet she scoured the whole of London for me before giving up on me. I felt a sudden twinge of guilt. I should have let them know where I was. But the main thing was that they were out of danger, blissfully ignorant of what was going on.

'All right, thank you. If Patsy comes back, please let her know I asked after her, and...' Pulling a piece of paper out of my pocket, I scribbled a hurried note, explaining Ella's condition. '...give her this, will you?'

---

[47] Wealthier households in Victorian England used to have a gong which was rung by the butler to call the family together, usually to meals.

'Certainly Miss. Good day.'

'Good day to you, too.'

The door closed in my face and I whirled around, marching back towards home. I was just about to turn into the street where my uncle's house stood when something tall and black came around the corner fast.

'Ouf!'

'Ng!'

I slammed face-first into a hard chest, and suddenly was pressed up against a familiar ten-year-old mint-condition tailcoat.

'You. Oh my God, I nearly forgot! I must explain, I...'

A single finger touched my lips, silencing me. A moment later, he pulled me into his arms and gave me the hardest, best, most rib-cracking hug I had ever had in my life.

'No need.' He pulled my face against his chest. 'I heard.'

'There's an epidemic...and...and...Ella...'

'Shh. I know. I know.'

For a while I just stood like that, silently letting him rock me in his arms. But it wasn't long before I remembered where I was, and who was waiting for me at home.

'Let go, please?'

He instantly released me. I stepped back, feeling slightly dizzy.

Slowly, I glanced up at him. It was in this moment that I realized: this was it. This was real. This was the first time when this thing between Mr Ambrose and me would be put to the test. Would he stand by me? Or would he do what I'd come to expect of men—nothing?

I opened my mouth.

'Mr Ambrose, I—'

His finger once again covered my lips before I could say another word. Hard, sea-coloured eyes bored into me.

'The coaches you ordered have arrived. I had a talk with the stable owner. You will have the best horses and coachmen, at, I am assured, a very reasonable discount rate. They will take you straight to the town of Bath. I hear that the air there is healthy, and room, board and doctors come cheap.'

'You heard that, did you?' One corner of my mouth quirked up. 'I heard they cost a fortune.'

He met my eyes implacably. 'Not if you own them.'

I opened my mouth to point out that you couldn't 'own' a doctor—then closed it again. With Mr Rikkard Ambrose, you could never be entirely sure. And right now, I was thoroughly glad for it.

'Here.' He pressed a small piece of paper into my hand. 'Have the coachmen take you to this address. Everything will be taken care of.'

I managed a small smile. 'Including the bill?'

'Don't push it, Miss Linton.'

Standing up on my tiptoes, I pressed a light kiss on his cheek. 'I love pushing it. You should know that by now.'

'I know.' A strong hand enveloped mine and squeezed, hard. 'Take care of yourself. I don't intend to foot your hospital bill.'

'Don't worry. I'll be careful. And you...'

'I'll be there.'

I let out a breath that, up until that moment, I hadn't noticed I was holding.

'Lilly? Lilly!' The demanding voice of my sister Anne cut through the London fog like an extremely annoying knife. 'Lilly, where are you?'

'Until we meet again, Miss Linton.' Stepping back, Mr Ambrose tapped his hat in goodbye. A moment later, he had disappeared into the mist.

'Lilly! What in God's name—ah!' Anne suddenly appeared beside me. Suspiciously, she glanced from left to right. 'Who was that you were talking to?'

'Me?' I did my best to look as innocent as a cherub with a really big figleaf. 'There's no one here but us.'

'Why are you lurking around in the street? And what is this nonsense I hear about us leaving?'

Raising my chin, I looked straight into her eyes. 'It isn't nonsense.'

'We can't leave! We have no money, no coaches, no—'

She was interrupted by a rumble. The mist before us parted, revealing the huge forms of two dark blue coaches rolling down the street. And on the box, holding the reins...

Dear Lord.

The best horses and coachmen, at a very reasonable discount rate.

You could say that again. Leave it to Mr Rikkard Ambrose to find a way to cut corners even when my sister was maybe lying on her deathbed.

Pulling on the rains, the driver of the first coach brought his vehicle to a halt. A moment later, he slid from the box and landed with a heavy thud directly in front of me, tight uniform, turban, beard and all.

'May I help you with your luggage, Miss?' Karim asked in the tone of a cannibal torturer enquiring 'May I eviscerate you with my bare hands?'

'Waaah!'

Stumbling back, Anne raised a trembling hand to point at the gargantuan man in front of her. I noticed he had not deemed it necessary to put aside his sabre while putting on his coachman's uniform.

'That...that is a...'

'Yes?' I asked, politely.

'What kind of coach stable did you get *him* from?'

'The best you'll ever find. Now come on. Get your things. We're leaving.'

'But...but...you can't just...you're not in charge here! You don't have the money, the authority, the...'

Ignoring her, I turned to Karim. 'The luggage will be down in the hall of the house in ten minutes. Anything that's not there by then you don't need to collect.'

Anne gave an outraged yelp. Karim nodded. I could have sworn I almost saw the ghost of a smile flicker around the corner of his mouth.

'Yes, Miss.'

Leaving Anne standing in the street, I marched into house. Leadfield was just busy trying to break his back by attempting to drag a huge suitcase down the stairs.

'Here, let me.'

Grabbing the thing, I hauled it down the last few steps.

'Thank, you Miss Lillian. Some of your sisters have a, um...interesting conception of packing quickly.'

'I bet they do.'

'What about Miss Ella's things? I don't think she will be able to pack for herself.'

'Don't worry about Ella. I have a feeling that a little piano-tuning brownie already took care of that.'

Leadfield blinked. 'Miss?'

I just winked and started up the stairs. Upstairs, Edmund had already packed a bunch of Ella's things into a suitcase, valiantly ignoring the weak protests coming from the bed.

'Lil! There you are! Will you tell that thick-headed fiancé of mine to stop packing?'

'No.' I patted Ella on the shoulder. 'My head is pretty thick too, you know.'

'But we can't possibly be going anywhere! We don't have the money.'

'Just trust me.' For one moment, I held her shadowed eyes. Long enough to show her I was serious. Long enough for me to see how serious her condition was. How had her face gotten this pale? 'I'm going to take care of everything.'

With a little help.

A year ago, that thought would have made me angry, would have made me want to do it all on my own. Today, it just made me feel warm inside.

'But...but...'

'Please.' Edmund stepped up beside me and took my little sister's hand. 'Let her help. Please.'

'Well...I...' She hesitated—then nodded. 'All right.'

Breathing a sigh of relief, Edmund squeezed her hand and stepped back. 'Thank you.' He glanced at me, his eyes hard. 'You'd better be able to keep all your fine promises. If not...'

'Edmund!' Ella exclaimed.

I grinned. 'I like you,' I informed the young piano tuner, and, turning to Ella, added, 'You can keep him.'

She gave me a terrifyingly weak smile. 'Thank you very much.'

'You're welcome. Come on, Romeo.' Grabbing a packed suitcase, I pushed open the door. 'Let's load up.'

Edmund grabbed a suitcase, too—then turned back, and squeezed Ella's hand one last time. 'We'll take care of you. Just rest. I'll be back to fetch you in just a moment.'

'Oh no you won't! You and your spindly arms are not carrying my little sister down those rickety old stairs.'

He frowned. 'Do you have a man better suited for the job?'

A grin spread over my face. 'As a matter of fact, I do. Wait for me in the hall, will you?'

Striding outside, I looked around until I spotted a hulking figure next to the second coach, just lifting a huge suitcase onto the roof.

'Ah, Karim, my little bundle of joy.' Beaming, I stepped towards him. 'I have a special task for you.'

A LADY TAKING CHARGE

'This is very kind of you, Mr...Karim, was it?'

'Hrmph.'

'What an interesting name. And an interesting hat. I've never met a coach-man with a turban before.'

'Hm.'

'Or with that kind of accent. Where did you say you were from, again?'

'Hrm.'

'But, really, this isn't necessary. I'm quite sure if someone supported me I could walk down the stairs on my own two feet quite easily. Just—'

Ella shifted, bringing it home to Karim all too clearly that he was carrying a female dressed only in her nightgown in his arms. The poor man. He looked about to expire. Maybe I should offer my sympathies?

Karim's eyes found me and bored into me.

Well...maybe better not. Inconspicuously, I sidled out of the room. Outside, Edmund was waiting with the expression of a young man whose fiancée was currently in the clutches of an unknown seven-foot-tall bearded giant.

'Um...Miss Linton?'

'Yes?'

'Do you think it was wise to ask the gentleman from the coach stable to...um...you know...'

'Know what?'

Edmund gave up. 'Is Ella all right?'

I patted his shoulder. 'Perfectly all right. She'll be down here in a minute.'

'Err...In one piece?'

'Probably. She might be a bit squashed, though.'

'It's absolutely scandalous!' Maria exclaimed. 'Touched by some kind of savage from God only knows where! It's indecent, that's what it is!'

'Indecent?' I gave her a bright smile. 'Why, you should have said so before! Of course, if he's indecent, you're perfectly welcome to walk all the way to Bath instead of letting him drive you. Doesn't that sound like fun?'

Maria opened her mouth—and shut it again.

It wasn't long before Karim arrived downstairs with his precious load. With the care usually reserved for crown jewels, he deposited my little sister in the first of the carriages, and Edmund, Lisbeth, Gertrude and I climbed in after her. Edmund's parents, meanwhile, who had been staring at me with a strange mix of puzzlement and awe ever since their son had dragged them out of the house to tell them about the free holiday they were about to get, went to keep Anne and Maria company in the other coach, so at least someone in there would behave like an adult.

With a *click*, the coach door closed behind us.

'Am I dreaming?' Ella whispered as she gazed out at the elegant coach drawn by four of the fastest horses in London. 'Or is this really happening?'

I pinched her.

'Ouch!'

'The latter,' I informed her jovially. 'Sit down and relax. Would you like a piece of solid chocolate?'

'Lil...how?' Shaking her head, she stared at me as if she were seeing me for the very first time. And maybe, in a way, she was. 'How is this possible?'

I glanced out of the window, back towards the house. Through the mist, beyond the second coach travelling behind us, I thought I could just about make out the dark outline of a tall man, staff in hand, top hat sitting atop his head. Another carriage rolled up beside him. With one swift move, he pulled open the door and swung himself inside.

I smiled.

'Anything is possible, Ella. Anything.'

'Where to?' Karim called from outside.

I glanced down at the note clutched tightly in my hand.

'Bath. Straight there. No stops.'

'As you wish. Gee-up!'

The whip snapped, and the coach rolled forward.

~~**~*~*

'You can't be serious!'

Maria's voice roused me from my slumber. It was only then I realized—we had stopped. Quickly, I glanced outside and saw that the sun was already setting. No wonder. Karim might have driven like the devil, but still, Bath was over a hundred miles away from London. Outside the coach stretched a beautiful park with slim, decorative trees, beds of fiery red roses, and gentlefolk in their finery walking, laughing and playing games. Beyond the park, the picturesque town stretched all the way to the horizon, bathed in the light of the fiery sunset.

I knew this view. I'd seen it once, in a book. But no. He couldn't possibly own *this* place, could he? Not even he was that wealthy!

'You have to be joking!' That was Maria again. 'You expect us to camp in the park? What kind of hair-brained scheme have you cooked up this time, Lilly?'

'The other window, Maria,' I said, not quite capable of believing it myself. 'Look out of the other window.'

She did.

'Oh my holy...!'

Nothing more. Nothing but awed silence.

'What is it?' Frowning, Edmund leaned across the coach to the other window and raised the blinds. He sucked in a breath.

'You're not serious!'

I smiled. So I had been right. 'As an acquaintance of mine would say, I'm not in the habit of making jokes.'

Outside the window rose the biggest building any one of us had ever seen. Bigger than Empire House. Bigger than Buckingham Palace even. Over five-hundred feet long, it curved along the edge of a beautiful park in an effortless crescent, providing a perfect view of a small forest and the town beyond. Between tall columns, dozens of shiny white doors were set into the elegant Georgian façade at regular intervals. We were standing right before the central entrance, right in front of a door over which a sign proclaimed *The Country Queen Hotel.*

'The Royal Crescent,' Edmund whispered. 'The bloody Royal Crescent!'

'Dear me.' One corner of my mouth twitched in amusement. 'Swearing? I didn't know you had it in you. Congratulations.'

He didn't seem to be in a joking mood. Turning towards me, he looked at me seriously. 'What is the meaning of this, Miss Linton? You can't possibly afford this place! Heck, I doubt even your uncle could afford to stay here for more than a night or two, and he'd beggar himself in the process!' He glanced at the pale, sleeping Ella in the corner, then looked back at me, accusation in his eyes. 'Why did you drag us all the way to this place? We can't stay here.'

The doorman standing in front of the fancy white door seemed to be of the same opinion. Stepping forward, he gave me a onceover, his eyes sliding haughtily over my worn dress and hastily thrown-over coat.

'Do you have a reservation, Miss?'

He was answered by a heavy *thud* from behind him. When he turned, he found himself facing a barrel of a chest covered in beard as thick as a carpet.

'She does not need a reservation,' Karim said. 'Have the staff take the luggage up to the Royal Suite.'

Recognition sparked in the doorman's eyes. Not just recognition of Karim, but most importantly, recognition of whom he worked for. Hurriedly, he took a step back, bumping into the coach.

'Y-yes. Of course. I'll be right back, Miss, um, I mean My Lady. Please be so kind as to wait here. It won't take a moment.'

And he dashed off into the hotel lobby.

Everyone stared. Everyone. Gertrude. Lisbeth. Edmund. Even Anne and Maria were hanging out of their coach's windows to gawk, and several passers-by had stopped to gape at the exchange. At first, they stared at Karim. But then, after a moment or two, all the eyes turned inextricably towards someone else.

Me.

I waved.

'Don't worry.' I told Edmund, patting him on the shoulder. 'I have a feeling they're going to be very hospitable to us.'

Karim opened the door for me, and I climbed out of the coach.

'Hospitable' turned out to be something of an understatement. As soon as the hotel manager spotted Karim, he knew which way the wind was blowing. I had the distinct pleasure to have, in front of all of my sisters, the keys to the royal suite handed to me on a literal silver platter. Maria was so green with envy she could have stepped out on the lawn and turned invisible. You could tell she was dying to ask why the heck the whole world suddenly treated me, her misfit misbegotten minx of a sister, as if I were the Queen of England, but she couldn't bring herself to. Not in front of other people.

I might have enjoyed the colour of her face considerably more if Ella's face hadn't been a similar unhealthy shade, and most definitely not from jealousy.

'A-are we h-here?' my little sister murmured, blinking in the sudden light of the entrance hall. Karim was supporting her on one side, Edmund on the other.

'Yes, Ella.' Smiling, I stepped closer and squeezed her shoulder. 'No more travelling. We've arrived.'

'But where....' Raising her eyes, she blinked up at the giant chandelier illuminating the hotel lobby. 'Oh my goodness.'

'Ladies and gentlemen?'

A bellhop appeared before us, bowing so low his nose nearly scratched the floor.

'Your rooms are ready. If you would be so kind as to follow me?'

'My sister isn't feeling too well,' I told him. 'Please send someone for a doctor immediately. I'd like him to attend her first thing in the morning.'

'Certainly, Miss. But, if I may ask, what if no doctors happen to be free tomorrow?'

'They had better be free. Arrange it.'

The bellhop stared at me—until one of his colleagues leaned over and whispered something in his ear. Blanching, the young man bowed and retreated towards the steps. 'Certainly, Miss! I will send a messenger off directly. If you will follow me, I'll show you to your rooms so the young lady can rest. We have some beautiful, easily accessible rooms on the ground floor with a view of the park available.'

And he dashed off.

Once again, I felt all eyes upon me. Anne and Maria were staring at me as if they saw me for the very first time, and didn't like what they saw.

'Who are you?' Anne demanded. 'And what has happened to Lilly?'

I graced them with a smile. 'The staff will show you to your rooms. Ask them to prepare something if you are hungry. I won't be joining you. I'll have to see to it that Ella is settled in.'

And I marched off. Behind me, the lobby exploded into whispered conversation.

With the help of several members of the staff, it didn't take us long to reach Ella's room. It was a delightful, airy space. A fire was crackling in the hearth, casting a warm glow on the beige wallpaper. Outside the windows, the lights of the town were shimmering in the distance.

'Well?' I asked, bending down far enough to look straight into Ella's tired eyes. 'What do you think?'

'It's wonderful,' she whispered, managing a weak smile. 'And I'm not just talking about the room. The way you handled those people downstairs...Lil, what's happened to you? You've always been more confident than I could dream of, but this...it was amazing.'

'Just you wait till tomorrow.' Gently, I stroked her tangled hair, trying to force a smile onto my face. Nothing inside me wanted to smile right now. Not while she was looking this pale. But for her I would try. For my little sister I'd try anything. 'I'm going to move mountains if that's what it takes to get you well. We're going to get you the best doctor in all of England.'

'But you can't possibly afford—'

'I can. Trust me.'

She looked at me with eyes far more penetrating than an invalid was supposed to have. 'What aren't you telling me, Lil?'

'Tomorrow.' I squeezed her hand. 'I'll tell you tomorrow. *After* we get you the country's best doctor, and the best medicine money can buy.'

'That's not n-necessary. I'm already feeling much b...bet...'

Her head drooped.

'Ella? Ella! What is it?'

'Lil...I...'

Before she could utter another word, Ella slumped forward, unconscious.

PRETTY FLOWERS AND THEIR USES

When we'd first arrived at the Royal Crescent, I'd been hopeful. I thought that we had found a place where Ella could recover. A place where my family would be safe. By the next morning, I wasn't so sure of that anymore.

'Lill! Lill, I—unng!'

Ella's cry woke me up in the middle of the night. Shooting up from the cot I had insisted be brought into her room, I hurried over to her bed.

'What's wrong? Are you—Ella!'

She was lying on her side, convulsing and shuddering. Her hands were clamped over her stomach, and probably not because she felt peckish.

'Lilly, I...'

She couldn't bring herself to say it. That was no problem. After two years with Mr Ambrose, I was an expert in silent conversation. Striding over to the corner, I grabbed a beautiful enamelled vase filled with lilies, and held it under her nose.

'Here.'

'Lil! I can't possibly—'

'Oh yes you can. They won't mind. Trust me, I'm a Lilly, and I'd be honoured to have you puke all over me.'

Another fit shook Ella, but to judge by the noise coming from her throat, this time it wasn't coming from the urge to vomit.

'Dammit, Lilly! Not fair! Don't...can't laugh...not now!'

A smile tugged at one corner of my mouth. 'Did I hear you right? Did you, Miss Ella of Properville in the County of Politetington just curse? How shocking! Now go ahead and puke on the lilies.'

'You...youuumphrgxxmphrrrg!'

Delicately, I looked away while Ella provided some flowers with fresh fertilizer. When the noise finally began to subside, I glanced down. Ella was staring up at me, her eyes wide with fear.

'What's happening to me?'

'I don't know.'

But I promise you, I'll do my damnedest to find out! Even if that means I have to drag every single doctor in Bath to you by the scruff of his neck!

I didn't say that out loud, though. For some strange reason, threats of violence against innocent bystanders had never had the same soothing effect on my little sister as on me. Instead, I just knelt down and took her in my arms.

'Lill, don't! What if whatever I've got is catching?'

I smiled at her grimly. 'Then I'd better find a bloody good doctor, hadn't I?'

Things didn't improve during the night. Ella's stomach was more busily rebelling than William Wallace and Spartacus put together. After half an hour, I had to ask for another vase, and then another. The maid was truly touched I liked her room decoration so much I got her in the middle of the night to bring me more.

'Here you go,' I told Ella, handing her the newest vase.

'Lill – why does that one have flowers in it, too?'

I shrugged. 'I thought as long as you had to vomit, you might as well enjoy the view.'

'Thanks so murgrxmph...!'

'You're welcome.' I smiled a half-hearted smile and reached forward to pull her hair out of her face.

Sometime around three o'clock, the vomiting finally let up—but not for lack of trying. There simply wasn't anything left to deposit in flower vases. I sat by my little sister's bedside, holding her clammy hand as dry heaves wracked her and shudders ran up and down her body.

'What's wrong with me?' she whispered into the darkness.

They hadn't told her?

One look in her face was enough to answer the question. No, they had not told her! I opened my mouth to utter the dreaded word—but then hesitated. Could I be really sure? After all, I was no doctor. How could I know for certain what sickness had grabbed hold of her?

'I don't know.' *Please don't let it be what I think it is. Please!* 'Here.' Reaching for a carafe of water on the nightstand, I brought it to her lips.

'But it would just come up again!'

'Trust me. If my suspicions are correct, you'll need it. And if they aren't...well, then at least the flowers will have been watered.'

'Has anyone ever told you have a wonderful bedside manner?'

'Why, thank you. Now, down the hatch, little sister.'

Obediently, she drank. About five minutes later, the flowers were getting a shower. Thus, it went on for most of the night. When, finally, Ella sank into an uneasy slumber, I was about ready to drop. Hardly able to move my limbs, I slunk over to my cot and sank onto the wonderfully, wonderfully soft mattress I would have been complaining about only a few hours earlier. My head had hardly touched the pillow when my eyes started to slide shut and sweet dreams began to enf—

Plink!

—bloody hell! What now?

Plink! Plink!

The window. Some numbskull son of a nitwit was throwing stones at the window in the middle of the night and robbing me of my last few hours of sleep! With steam clouds of rage practically coming from my ears, I marched over to the window. Oh, the tortures I would inflict upon the silly little brat who thought he'd try to amuse himself by playing a practical joke on me! I'd dunk him in fondue and roast him over an open fire! I'd drag him to the nearest boat and ship him to a desert island! I'd...I'd...well, I didn't exactly know yet what I was going to do, but it was going to be something fabulously nasty!

Reaching the window, I wrenched it up and stuck my head outside. The cool night air only fanned the flames of my rage. Below, I saw something shift in the darkness.

'You there!' I hissed. 'Yes, you, you miserable little pipsqueak! Have you got any idea what time it is, you little pest? Just you wait until I'm down there! I'll give your backside a tanning so you won't be able to sit down for a month!'

'It would be interesting to see you try,' came a cool, familiar voice from below.

I closed my mouth.

Oh.

Um.

'Mr...Ambrose?'

'Indeed. And my backside is currently unavailable.'

Heat rose to my face.

Heck, wait just a minute! Why was I feeling embarrassed? It was *him* that had some explaining to do.

'What are you doing at my window? This is your bloody hotel! Don't you know where the front door is?'

'My knowledge of hotel-door placement is impeccable. However, since my introduction to your family has been postponed for the present time, I thought it prudent to use more circuitous methods of communication. How is she?'

I was tired. I was ready to drop. But in that moment, I forgot all my anger. He came to me, he woke me up, and the first thing he did was ask after my little sister. I could have kissed him.

'I'm coming!'

'Wait, Miss Linton! There's a d—'

Thud!

'Ouch! Grx!'

187

'—itch under the window.'

Pushing myself into a sitting position, I groaned. 'Thrice blasted architect!'

Suddenly, arms were around me, helping me to stand. Sure, dexterous hands started picking twigs and leaves out of my hair.

'I do not think the late John Wood the Younger would appreciate your expletives, Miss Linton.'[48]

'John Wood the Younger can go and—'

My voice cut off when he pulled me against his chest, encasing me in warmth, love, and everything else I thought we would never find. It was too much. The weight of the whole day came crashing down on me all at once, and I collapsed against him. Maybe I even cried. I let it happen. In the darkness of the night, nobody could see. He would never let anyone see. He just held me, silent strength wrapping around me like a cloak.

'How is she?'

'H-how do you think?'

'That bad.'

'When can we get a doctor?'

'I've had my people searching for the very best specialist all day. The man is currently some dozen miles to the north.'

'Is he willing to come?'

'Willing has nothing to do with it. He'll be there first thing in the morning.'

That should probably have worried me. Instead, I just smiled in blissful relief.

'I told the hotel staff—'

'Don't worry about the staff. They have been briefed on the situation—or at least as much as they need to know. They will do anything you say, and if they don't...'

The ominous way in which he ended the sentence said more than a thousand words. I squeezed him, hard.

'Thank you.'

'Don't thank me. This counts as your next ten years' worth of holidays.'

Still squeezing him, I smiled against the thin cotton of his tailcoat. 'I surmised as much, Sir.'

I felt his lips brush against the top of my head, and suddenly, the bone-crushing need to fall over and sleep which I'd felt all night lifted from my shoulders. I had him to lean on. Who needed a bed, anyway?

Beds...rooms...

That reminded me of something.

---

[48] John Wood the Younger, son of (unsurprisingly) John Wood the Elder, was the architect of the Royal Crescent and many other buildings in the city of Bath. The Royal Crescent is an intriguing piece of architecture. Presenting an elegant, unified, crescent-shaped façade at the front, at its back one can see that it is actually composed out of many individual houses arranged in a crescent shape right next to one another. It is generally considered one of the most significant examples of Georgian Neo-Classical architecture in the United Kingdom.

Blinking the sleep out of my eyes, I glanced up at him. 'What about my other sisters? I've been so busy with Ella that I completely forgot about them. Are they settled in? Do you know if they've been showing symptoms, too?'

'Your two oldest siblings are well.' He cocked his head thoughtfully. 'As for the twins, Anne and Maria—I'm not certain. They might be ill. They certainly looked somewhat ill when they were shown to their quarters in the broom cupboard.'

A slow grin spread across my face. 'The...broom cupboard? Really?'

'Indeed.'

'You really know how to make a girl feel better.'

'Yes.' Suddenly, one of his fingers was underneath my chin, lifting it up. For one moment I felt his dark, sea-coloured eyes bore into me—then he bent down towards me, and—

He made me feel better.

Much, much better.

~~**~*~*

The next morning, I awoke to the sweet music of my sister puking out of the window.

'Decided that the flowers outside deserved some fertilizer to, did you?' I enquired, gently grasping her trembling shoulders, supporting her.

'Something like that,' she croaked. 'Besides, the vases are full.'

To judge by the smell in the room, she was right. Oh well...time to take a leaf out of Mr Ambrose's book, I guess. My turn to do some waste-disposal. Grabbing the first vase, I stepped towards the door—then hesitated, glancing back at Ella, who was still hanging out of the window.

'Will you be all right, or should I help you get back into bed?'

'Go, go.' She waved me off with a weak smile. 'I can still take three steps across the room.'

Reassured, I pulled open the door and started heading down the corridor. I was just about to start down the first set of stairs when a chambermaid with a feather duster came out of an unoccupied room to my left and stopped to stare at me.

'My goodness, Miss! What are you doing with that thing? Please, let me help you.' Rushing forward, she took the vase out of my arms.

'Thanks,' I panted, flexing my fingers. 'That thing is pretty heavy.'

'Why did you carry it out yourself? Just ring, and one of us will be there right away to help you.'

'Yes, I know. It's just, well...' For lack of words, I gestured at the vase.

'Yes, I see what you mean.' Critically, the chambermaid regarded the flowers. 'They do seem sort of wilted, don't they? Strange. I had Betty put in new ones only yesterday. And is it just me, or do they smell kind of funny?'

'It's not just you,' I assured her.

'Well, no problem, Miss. I'll have the flowers replaced immediately.'

'Thank you, but...err....actually, I would like to have the whole vase replaced.'

'The vase?'

'Preferably with a tub.'

'A...tub. You want a tub full of flowers.'

'Well, no. Flowers are not strictly necessary. But you can put them in if you like.'

She blinked at me, obviously weighing the orders she had been given to obey my every whim against the possibility that I was completely cuckoo. Finally, the orders won. Several hundred years of British Monarchy and more than one batshit-crazy king will do that to people.

'Yes, Miss. A tub. Right away, Miss.'

I was just about to turn back, when the face of a bellhop appeared around the corner further down the stairs.

'Miss Linton? Miss Linton! There's a gentleman down at the front desk asking for you.'

My heart made a leap. A gentleman? Hadn't Mr Ambrose said he wanted to stay in the background for now?

'What does this gentleman look like?'

'Older, grey-haired, with a big nose and a bigger opinion of himself.'

I frowned. That didn't sound like anyone I knew.

'He says his name is Dr Brooks.'

'Doctor? Why the heck didn't you say so at once?' Pushing the maid aside, I raced down the stairs. The bellhop had just enough time to jump out of the way before I barrelled past him. I didn't stop until I reached the lobby. Panting, I slowed and looked around. Where...

There!

He was standing at the front desk, just like the bellboy had sad, impatiently tapping his foot, a black bag held in his left hand, and a grumpy, ruffled expression on his face, as if he'd been thrown out of bed at three in the morning—which, if I knew Mr Ambrose, he had.

'Dr Ross!' Rushing towards him, I extended my hand. 'I'm so glad you've come.'

'That makes one of us,' he grumbled, eying me through heavy-lidded eyes. 'I had a bearded giant with a sabre pounding on my door this morning and threatening to decapitate me if I didn't drop everything and come attend to a special patient halfway across the country, so I hope whoever it is, they're at death's door, Miss, or I shall be doubling my fee.'

I attempted a smile. It didn't quite work. 'You'll pardon me if I don't share that hope, Dr Ross. It's my little sister.'

The disgruntled look instantly disappeared from the doctor's face and in that moment I knew that Mr Ambrose and his not-so-merry-men had done as he'd promised. They'd found me a real doctor. One who cared about his patients.

'Where is she?'

'Upstairs.'

190

Without wasting another word, Dr Ross swept up the stairs. I followed right on his heels. We had just turned around a corner and were heading towards Ella's room when a maid rushed out of the door, her face as pale as a ghost. She caught sight of me.

'Oh, Miss! I swear, it wasn't my fault, Miss! I just came in to see if she wanted anything, and I found her like that!'

My heart froze. 'Like what?'

The maid didn't answer. She just raised one trembling hand and pointed through the open doorway. Pushing past the doctor, I rushed forward into the room and found Ella lying on the floor, halfway between the window and the bed. She wasn't moving.

DISORDERLY ORDERS

'Ella!'

Was that my voice screaming? It sounded so distant. Like a stranger from a foreign land.

'Out of the way! Let me check!'

Someone pushed past me. Who...? Of course. The doctor. He knelt by Ella's side, feeling her pulse.

'She's alive! Help me get her onto the bed!'

Some part of me, the part that refused to faint when proper ladies should be out cold on the floor having smelling salts waved under their delicate noses, rushed forward and grabbed Ella's feet. But most of me just watched, detached, as my body went through the motions.

'Good! Now, on three. One, two...three!'

With the maid looking on anxiously from the doorway, we lifted Ella onto the bed. Was she breathing? Oh my God, please let her be breathing! Let her be alive!

'Help me turn her onto her back. Good! Now give me that pillow over there. We have to get her legs up, improve the circulation.'

Without thinking, I followed the doctor's instructions.

Thank God he's here! Thank God I have someone capable who knows what to do!

'Well done. Now, open her dress!'

My hands froze.

Scratch that! I got an old lecher!

Hands on hips I sent him a fiery glare. 'Doctor! This is my sister! You can't seriously think I would let—'

'—me open the corset so she can breathe easier?' he cut in. 'Yes, I think that. In fact I think it would be a really good idea to do it right now.'

Oh.

Ears turning red, I started unbuttoning Ella's dress. 'Turn your back!' I grumbled.

'I've seen ladies in the nude before, Miss. It's part of my job.'

'Well, this lady damn well isn't! Turn your back. And as for you,' I shot at the maid who was still standing in the doorway, 'be so kind as to close the door, will you?'

'Oh. Of course, Miss. I'll be outside if you need anything.'

'Thank you.'

I looked at the doctor, my eyes determined. Sighing, he turned around.

'Hands over your eyes. Now!'

'Miss Linton, I really don't think—'

'Hands over your eyes, or I'm fetching the big fellow with the beard and sabre!'

Instantly, the doctor put his hand over his eyes. The moment I was sure he could see nothing, I started to open Ella's dress. It wasn't as if I didn't believe him when he said he was a professional. It was simply that I knew my little sister. And I knew the silly, lovable little goose would die of shame if she knew some stranger had seen her like this.

'And I'm not going to go to all this trouble saving your life just to have you keel over dead afterwards,' I told the unconscious Ella sternly. 'Do you hear? You're going to survive! Survive, dammit!'

All I got in response was silence. And not the comforting kind I was used to.

Quicker than I'd ever managed to do it with my own, I unlaced and removed her corset. After I buttoned her dress back up, I tapped the doctor on the shoulder.

'She's ready. You can turn around.'

Instantly, he went to work. From a corner of the room, I watched as he pulled various instruments from his bag and started to examine Ella. He listened at her chest with some strange kind of tube, lifted one eyelid to shine a candle in her eyes and did various other things that, in my opinion, had about as much medical value as wiggling your toes. But it must have told him something, because, he rose with a contented sigh and nodded.[49]

'I don't think the fall was caused directly by her illness or did any lasting damage. She probably just fainted from exhaustion because of a lack of sleep and that infernal corset. Those things should be outlawed!'

'I'm with you on that. But let's postpone the political rally till tomorrow, shall we? Right now, I want to know what is wrong with my little sister. Please.'

The doctor's face darkened. 'I have my suspicions. But I need to talk with the patient first. To ask her a few questions. Could you ask the maid to bring us some smelling salts?'

'Coming, Miss!' came a voice from outside the door, followed by receding footsteps.

How nice.

---

[49] For anyone who might be interested: shining a light in your eyes is done by doctors to test your pupillary light reflex. If your pupil contracts when intense light shines in your eyes, the doctor knows that the most important nerves in your eye are working correctly.

The helpful eavesdropper was back two minutes later, face flushed and a little lilac bottle clutched in her hand. Taking it, I handed to the doctor who stepped up beside Ella's bed and bent over her.

'Would you come here, Miss? Stand like this. I think it's best if she sees a familiar face when she wakes up. I wouldn't want to alarm her.'

'Of course.'

Quickly, I took up a position at the head of the bed. The doctor uncorked the little bottle, and immediately, a strong scent pervaded her room. He waved the bottle under Ella's nose, and she twitched, letting out a pitiful little moan.

'What...how...'

Her eyes fluttered open—and widened, when she caught sight of the strange man leaning over her.

'Who are you? What are you doing here? I—?'

Feebly, she tried to pull away. I grasped her shoulder, holding her in place and leant over her.

'Shh. Everything is all right, Ella. This is Doctor Ross. I called him to have a look at you. When we came up we found you lying on the floor.'

'On the floor...? I don't remember...'

'You were unconscious.'

I saw the flicker of fear in her eyes, and pulled her against me. 'It's going to be all right, Ella. Everything is going to be all right. Doctor Ross will take care of you.'

She hesitated—then nodded. Gently, I let go and let her sink back onto the pillow.

'Emanuel Ross, MD.' Doctor Ross made a curt bow. 'May I ask your name, Miss?'

'E-Ella. Ella Linton.'

'A pleasure to make your acquaintance, Miss Linton, even in these disagreeable circumstances. Do you feel well enough to answer a couple of questions? There are some things about your condition I must know before I can make my diagnosis.'

Again, that flicker of fear flashed in Ella's eyes. She clearly wasn't too eager to find out what was wrong with her. But while she had always been a little timid, a coward she was not. Raising her chin, she nodded. 'Go ahead, doctor. Ask all you need.'

The nosy side of me – the one that took up ninety per cent of the available surface – wanted to join the maid outside the door and listen. It wasn't as if this would be the first time I listened in on my little sister. But somehow, I couldn't bring myself to do it. Not here. Not now. Not when she might have to bare things that she wouldn't want anyone, not even me, to know about. So I left the room and shooed the maid away with orders to prepare a good, hot, strong broth for Ella. Let the doctor do his doctoring. I'd help in any other way I could.

Anxiously, I paced up and down in front of the door. From inside, I heard nothing but low murmurs. Again and again, I was tempted to press my ear against the door and find out what the heck was happening—but I resisted. Somehow. Miraculously. The wait dragged on endlessly. I felt as if I had already worn grooves into floor from all my marching up and down—and yet, it couldn't have been more than ten minutes since I left them alone. It felt like ages.

What's taking them so long? What's bloody happening in there? What's wrong with her?

Finally, the murmurs stopped. A moment later, the door opened and the doctor stepped out, a serious expression on his face.

'And?' I demanded. 'What is it?'

'Under normal circumstances,' the doctor told me, 'my Hippocratic oath would forbid me from sharing that information with you. But since you are the main caregiver and have a hulking giant with a big sabre at your command who would cut my head off if you told him to, I think I will make an exception in this case.'

Well, well. What a wise man.

'I'm not a hundred percent certain yet what your sister's sickness is. It may just be a stomach bug. The symptoms would fit. It could all be over soon.'

His words didn't make me feel any better. His face was still as grim as death.

'Could?' I demanded, picking up on the key word. 'What do you mean, *could*? What else could it be?'

The doctor hesitated.

Please don't let him say it! Please!

'What else? Tell me!'

His face hard, he met my eyes. 'Cholera.'

The word nearly knocked my legs out from under me.

'Y-you're not serious.'

'I'm afraid I am. But at the present moment, it is only a possibility. I might be wrong in my suspicions.'

'Might?' Disregarding every rule of proper manners Aunt Brank had ever drilled into my head, I grabbed him by the lapels. 'What do you mean, might? How likely is it? Tell me!'

He didn't answer. Gently freeing himself from my hold, he pulled a card out of his tailcoat pocket and handed it to me.

'Call me if she begins to exhibit symptoms of diarrhoea.'

I grabbed the card.

'And then? What should I do then?'

He looked at me with so much kindness in his old eyes that it was almost too hard to bear. 'Pray.'

And with that, he turned and strode down the corridor.

I didn't take the doctor's suggestion. Ella was the praying type. I, on the other hand, had always taken a more practical approach. So, instead of appealing to the almighty, I force-fed my little sister chicken soup and held her head while she threw most of it up again. I made her drink warm tea and washed the sweat from her face with damp linens. The hours dragged on and on.

A knock came from the door.

'Yes?'

Karim stuck his turban through the door. His head followed a moment later.

'The kitchen staff tells me they're about to serve lunch. Do you wish to come down and—'

'No.'

'I would watch over her while you ate and—'

'No.'

Karim looked distinctly uncomfortable. 'I, um...was instructed to ensure that you ate and rested sufficiently.'

'I see. And did the person who instructed you perchance wear a ten-year-old mint-condition tailcoat?'

'They did.'

I considered for a moment—then smiled. 'But he also instructed you to follow all my orders, didn't he?'

'Yes...?'

'Very well then. I order you to disregard his orders. All of them. Past, present and future.'

This left the poor man looking distinctly discombobulated. If I hadn't been so hellishly scared for Ella, the constipated expression on his face might have made me laugh. When he looked as if steam was about to come from under his turban, I finally took pity on him.

'If you have one of the maids bring me something up, will that satisfy our mutual acquaintance? I just...' I glanced over at Ella. 'I can't leave her. Not now.'

Mine and Karim's eyes met and there was a rare moment of understanding between the two of us. He nodded.

'Family comes first. I shall have them bring something up immediately.'

Ten minutes later, I had a lavish meal in front of me, that had probably taken ten people to prepare and would take another ten to eat. A faint smile played around the corner of my mouth. The hotel manager apparently was taking his instructions to take care of me very seriously. Not surprising, considering from whom those instructions had come.

You're not alone Lilly. He's here. He cares.

The thought was almost enough to give me hope. Plus – so far, Ella hadn't shown a single symptom of diarrhoea. Her vomiting had even gone down a little, and she'd been able to eat some more broth. If things just stayed like that, if nothing went wrong—

'Lill!'

My head snapped up, away from the food. Ella had a panicked expression on her face and was trying to get out of bed. Just the effort to stand made her tremble.

'What are you doing? Lie back down!'

'I can't! I've got to—'

Her eyes strayed towards the toilette. Eyes in which fear shone bright.

No. No, please no.

'I...I...oh!'

Ella convulsed. A moment later, a dark stain began to spread across her bed.

A Beautiful Bowl of Carrots

Ella spent the next half hour on the toilet, while I spent the time inconspicuously carrying a soiled mattress out of a busy hotel in the middle of the busiest season. Oh, the joys of a holiday in the country!

Next, I went to have a little chat with the hotel manager. A maid was kind enough to point me in the direction of his office. Following her instructions, I soon stood before mahogany double doors with a golden door knocker. I raised my hand and knocked.

'Come in,' came a man's voice from beyond.

I pushed open the door and entered an opulent room full of plush leather armchairs, bookshelves filled with old books, and paintings in golden frames. A year or two ago, such opulent surroundings might have intimidated me. Now, I knew what real wealth and power looked like. Striding past all the pretentious opulence, I planted myself in front of the manager's desk and gazed down at him.

'We have things to discuss.'

'Ah.' He swallowed nervously. 'Miss Linton. Your sister's ailment...it is serious, then?'

'Yes.'

'Oh. I, um...should I...well...'

It was almost amusing, watching him squirm while he tried to think of a diplomatic way to ask whether we had to be put under quarantine. Under normal circumstances, I had no doubt Ella and I would already be out in the street, far away from any other hotel guests we might infect—never mind he didn't even know yet what sickness we were dealing with, and whether it was contagious. Fear was contagious, and fear would have been enough.

Except, in this case, there was something more frightening than some unnamed sickness.

'I spoke to Mr Ambrose last night,' I told him.

The manager's face lost quite a bit of colour.

'Y-you did?'

'Yes. He told me how adequate your services in support of me and my family have been thus far.'

The manager managed a tremulous little smile.

'Adequate. How wonderful.'

'He also said he would be...displeased were you to waver in your helpful attitude.'

'I see.' The manager cleared his throat. 'Um, Miss Linton?'

'Yes?'

'May I ask what kind of sickness your sister has contracted?'

I gave him a long, hard look.

'Helpful, remember? Not nosy.'

'Yes, Miss! Certainly, Miss.'

'Let's just say that for the time being, it would be best if your personal did not enter the top floor of the hotel. Tell them that my sister is recuperating from a nervous breakdown and must under no circumstances be disturbed.'

'Yes, Miss.'

'Have the staff leave meals in front of the door and knock. From time to time, I might send down lists of items I need. I expect deliveries to be made promptly and completely. Do we understand each other?'

Defeated, he inclined his head.

'Yes, Miss.'

'The first item I require is a fresh mattress.'

'A...mattress, Miss?'

'Yes.

'Of course, Miss. Straight away, Miss.'

My heart pounding, I turned and marched out of the room. Only when I was outside, I sank against the wall, trembling.

It had worked! He'd actually let us stay. Through sheer determination and a pinch of Rikkard Ambrose, it had worked! Slowly, a grim smile spread across my face.

I think I'm going to like being powerful.

Then the smile withered as I remembered that all the money or connections in the world would not make a jot of difference to Ella. Yes, I could get her the best doctors, the best care—but ultimately, her life lay in the hands of fate.

Straightening, I made my way back towards Ella's room. It was time I checked on her. I probably shouldn't have left her alone in the first place. But I had to have that talk with the manager.

Please don't let her have passed out again. Please.

I breathed a sigh of relief when I opened the door to Ella's room and found her lying on the chaise lounge, paler and more exhausted than before, but undeniably conscious. Her eyes met mine.

'Could I have something to drink?' she croaked, her eyes flitting to the bathroom door. 'I feel rather...dried up and empty.'

For some reason, I found it hard to answer. So I just nodded, filled a glass with water and handed it to her with shaking hands.

'Thank you.'

'Y-you're welcome.'

I waited in silence as she drank. She didn't manage more than a couple of gulps before handing the glass black to me. Our eyes strayed once again towards the privy door.

'You know what this means?' I nodded towards the door, unable to say it aloud. 'The doctor told you?'

Ella glanced away. 'Yes.'

I stepped forwards to take her in my arms—but quickly, she threw her hands up. 'No! Don't touch me! Don't come any closer! It's bad enough that you're in here with me. I won't allow you to risk any more infection.'

One of my eyebrows rose. 'Try and stop me. You're not exactly in prime wrestling condition right now. I'm going to take care of you, whether you like it or not.'

'You...you're impossible! Why do you always have to be so stubborn?'

I grinned at her. 'It's one of my most endearing qualities.'

She opened her mouth, probably to tell me how 'endearing' she found my endearing qualities, but was cut off by a knock at the door.

'Hello?' came an all-too-familiar voice from outside. The little colour that had still been in Ella's face drained away like juice from a leaky bowl. 'May I come in?'

I opened my mouth and was about to say 'Yes, Edmund, go ahead', when Ella clapped her hand across my mouth.

'Nng? Whh arr yo toshng mmm?' I protested.

'Shut up shut up shut up!' she hissed.

'Yo rr tching mmee. Wot abot rsk ff infexnn?'

'To heck with infection!' she hissed. 'Please don't let him in! Don't let him see me like this.'

'Wot mm I saposssd to tll hm?'

'Anything! Anything except the truth that I'm lying here, unable to control the need to—!' She blushed like a virginal volcano before its very first explosion and cut off. 'Just lie! Lie like the dickens! You're good at that.'

My, my. It seemed my little sister was taking a walk on the wild side. And all while she was lying in bed unable to stand or control her digestive organs. Impressive.

Gently removing her hand from my mouth, I rose.

Another knock came from the door. 'Miss Linton? Ella? May I enter?'

Ella sent me a last pleading look.

Rising to my feet, I strode to the door—then tore it open, slipped out and slammed it shut again before Edmund could get a peek inside. Dear me. I would never have thought that years of practise slamming doors in my suitors' faces would come in this handy.

'Miss Linton! Thank God!'

Poor Edmund was a sorry sight. To judge by the rings under his eyes, he hadn't slept all night, but it was the look in his eyes that was most disturbing. There had always been an underlying certainty about Edmund from the moment he'd met my sister. He'd known who he was and where he was going. But now...?

That certainty was gone.

'Please, Miss Linton, may I see her?' he asked.

Damn! Damn you, Ella, for making me say no to that sad puppy-dog face!

I magicked a grin onto my face. 'I'm afraid not right now. She's, um....resting.'

'Oh. Well, um...' He shifted from one foot to another. 'Then may I have a word with you? I heard the doctor was here, and...'

He didn't have to say any more. The desperation in his eyes spoke volumes. Volumes of touching, if not particularly original, romantic poetry about red roses, blue violets and words starting with 'L'.

'I can't tell you what they talked about.' Gently taking him by the arm, I tried to lead him away—but he wouldn't budge. 'You know that such things are confidential. Just between a doctor and his patient.'

'And you, apparently.'

Yes, but I'm a nosy busybody.

'I'm her sister.'

'And I'm the man who loves her more than life itself. Please, Miss Linton.' Grabbing my hand, he moved forward. For a moment, I was puzzled as to what he was up to—then watched aghast, as he sank to his knees. 'Please. I don't need any details. I don't care about confidentialities. I just want to know if she is going to be all right. Please.'

'Get up!' I hissed, self-consciously glancing down the corridor.

'No. Not until you've answered.'

'What if someone comes? It bloody looks as if you're proposing to me!'

A weak smile tugged on one corner of his lips. 'Sounds to me like a good motivation to answer.'

The devious little...! Maybe I had underestimated Ella's prospective bridegroom. But the poor fool didn't reckon with the lion lurking in the shadows. If Mr Ambrose somehow got wind of this little scene, which, with his army of spies, I wouldn't put past him, Edmund Conway would be tied up and on a ship to Timbuktu before he could say, *'Je ne parlais pas Francais.'*

I had to do something. And quick!

'Get up! Get up I said!'

He didn't move.

'I'll tell you what's wrong with her, all right? Just get up off the floor!'

'You will?' He jumped to his feet eagerly.

'Yes, um...' I cleared my throat, desperately trying to search my mind for something to say. 'The reason I was reluctant to mention anything about Ella is...is...'

...that she is in deep, deep crap right now, too literally to think about. That she might die, and she doesn't want to hurt you.

'...is that it's something rather delicate. A, um...female complaint.'

He blinked. 'Female complaint? So she's not suffering from the epidemic that has been rampaging through London?'

'Oh, no!' *If by 'no' you mean 'yes'.* 'She's suffering from something completely different. A female nervous disorder named...what did the doctor call it again... *Potius Stercoritis.*'[50]

Edmund's eyes went wide. 'Oh my God! Is it dangerous?'

'Oh, no, not at all!'

And I should know. After all, I invented it just now.

---

[50] 'Embarrassing shit' sickness.

'But it is very exhausting and requires the strictest rest. Otherwise, it could turn into *Egoiacentemexcogitatositis*, and that is deadly.'[51]

Edmund paled. 'Heaven help us!'

'Don't worry. There are a number of things we can do to prevent that from happening.'

'What? What, tell me!'

'Well, on doctor's orders, Ella must be visited by as few people as possible—preferably close female relatives. They are least likely to disturb the delicate balance of humours and aggravate the *Potius Stercoritis*.'[52]

'Certainly, certainly.' He nodded eagerly. 'I'll keep my distance. I promise. What else? Please, Miss Linton, let me help! I'll do anything!'

'Um, well...the doctor said...the doctor said that carrots would help.'

'Carrots?'

I nodded energetically. 'Oh yes. When peeled, they give off a certain aroma that is particularly beneficial for anybody suffering from *Potius Stercoritis*.'

'Wonderful! Tell me more! What else did the doctor say?'

Bloody hell! Why did this fellow have to be so damn steadfast, persistent and concerned for my sister's well-being? Why couldn't he be a witless fool, or a heartless bastard just like all the other men who had tried to marry her? That would make this situation so much easier to deal with.

Desperately, I looked from right to left, searching for anything sensible to say. To my left hung a painting of a decorative ocean scene, showing two fishing boats sailing into a harbour. 'Err...ship planks!'

'Pardon?'

Edmund blinked.

'Ship planks,' I repeated, more confidently. 'Preferably old and worm-eaten. Stuck under the pillow they are an excellent cure against *Potius Stercoritis*. And so is seaweed, if applied externally in moderate quantities and mixed with lugworms.'

'Really?' Edmund stared into empty air for a moment, then blinked. 'Lugworms? Amazing what kind of advances modern medicine makes nowadays. I would have never considered using those as medicine.'

Congratulations. You are a moderately sane person.

---

[51] 'Finding-out-I'm-lying' sickness.

[52] Humour, in this case, is not referring to anything comical, but to the medical theory of Humourism. Before doctors developed the germ theory and discovered that viruses and bacteria spread sicknesses, the most widespread theory was one stemming from Ancient Greece which proposed that there are four temperaments, each of which is linked to one of four bodily fluids, and sicknesses are caused by an excess of one or more of these bodily fluids. This is the theoretical reasoning behind leeches being used in medieval and ancient medicine: blood was considered to be associated with the sanguine humour, and if doctors diagnosed you as being excessively sanguine, they would bleed you.

'Don't you worry.' Taking my hand, he gave it a gentle squeeze. 'I'll take care of it. And I won't try to come in again. I won't disturb Ella unnecessarily. I would never do anything to jeopardize her health.'

Then he whirled and hurried down the corridor.

'Where are you going?' I called after him.

'I'll be back!' he yelled, and without another word disappeared around the corner. I stared after him, confused. Where was he off to?

Oh well, it wasn't really any of my business. Besides, I had more important things to care about. Turning away, I went back into Ella's room.

'How did things go?' Ella croaked.

I looked at her, long and hard.

'A lot better than I think they're going to go from here on out.'

Over the day, Ella's condition rapidly deteriorated. The doctor was called back, and when he left the room this time, there was no mistaking the grim expression on his face.

'I'm afraid there's no doubt this time,' he said. 'It's cholera.'

I clawed at my dress to keep my hands from shaking. 'What can we do?'

'Not much, I'm afraid. Make sure to give her plenty of water. If you don't, she'll dry up and die as if she is stranded in the middle of a desert.'

'What else?' I took a step forward. 'Please, doctor, there must be more I can do!'

'Well...' He hesitated. 'My colleague, Dr Lindstrom, has had not inconsiderable success with adding sugar and salt to water in equal quantities. According to him, it does not cure the sickness, but it does lessen the likeliness of death. The hypothesis hasn't yet been subjected to clinical trial, though.'

'Can it hurt?'

'No.'

'Then I'll do it. What else?'

Sadly, he shook his head. 'There is nothing else, Miss Linton. As yet, the origins of cholera are a mystery to modern science. As long as we don't know what causes it, we have no way of combatting the disease.'

In the back of my mind, I wondered what Mr Ambrose would say to making a sizable donation to medical research. Maybe I had better wait with that suggestion till after the wedding.

'And what,' I asked, my mouth going dry, 'about the risk of infection?'

The doctor glanced down at the gloves he was wearing.

'Well, Miss Linton...are you the one who has been taking care of your sister?'

'I am.'

'Then maybe you should not get close to anybody over the next few days. Just to be sure.'

Translation: he didn't have a clue how the sickness spread. Inside my chest, a cold vice clamped tight around my heart. I hadn't thought I would feel afraid. Not when it was my sister's life at stake. In the past, I wouldn't have hesitated an instant to put my life on the line for Ella.

A picture of Mr Ambrose's hard face appeared in front of my inner eye.

In the past, you didn't have nearly as much to lose.

Edmund mostly refused to budge from Ella's door. He didn't say a word about going in, didn't once try to disturb her, but he sat out there like a house-trained little dragon in front of the entrance to his personal horde. Every so often I'd catch him throw longing glances at the door. It was almost enough to make me want to let him inside—except I couldn't. I had promised Ella I wouldn't. And besides, if what the doctor had hinted about the risk of infection was true, it was best for him to stay far, far away from Ella, or her heart might be just as broken has her body soon.

The same goes for you, Lilly. You should be nowhere near her.

The voice of reason in my head was loud and clear. It sounded very much like Ella. She took every opportunity to tell me to go and leave her to suffer in misery.

'You're still healthy,' she croaked, convulsing as a tremor shook her body. 'Th-there is no reason for you to fall sick, too. Go! It's only reasonable.'

'Is that so?' I enquired, dipping a cloth in cold water and wiping her forehead. 'Well, then I guess it's fortunate that I've never been very reasonable.'

'Lilly! I'm serious.'

'Too bad. I could use a good joke right about now.'

'I don't want you to catch this,' Ella whispered, reaching out for my hand—then abruptly drawing her fingers back. 'It's not right. You have your whole life in front of you.'

'Really? I must be careful I don't trip over it.'

'Besides, the things you have to do to care for me...' Ella blushed. 'It's not right!'

I shrugged. 'I've cleaned you up before.'

'That's when I was three and we were potty training!'

'And to think you still haven't gotten the hang of it. You really are a slow learner, aren't you?'

I wasn't entirely sure how I was still able to joke right now. I only knew that I had to. If I stopped, I would think about what was happening, and I would fall apart. Besides, if anything kept Ella's mind off the pain she had to be suffering, it was worth it. Even if I annoyed the heck out of her.

'Lill?'

'Yes?'

I was waiting for another protest or plea for me to leave. Instead, just words came.

'Thank you.'

Glancing up, I gazed into my little sister's eyes, and for once, they weren't looking away in embarrassment. They were gazing straight into mine. I swallowed around the lump in my throat.

'You're welcome.'

'If anything happens to me...if I don't...you know... you'll break it to Edmund gently, won't you?'

I shook my head vehemently. 'No.'

'Lilly! Please, I—'

'I won't break anything to him, because nothing is going to happen to you! You're going to pull through this, do you hear?' Grabbing her by the chin, I forced her to look at me. 'That boy has been camping out in front of your door practically every minute since we arrived. He's worried so sick he's practically sicker than you are! What do you think will happen if you die?'

Ella gave me a weak mile. 'Are you honestly trying to guilt me into surviving?'

'Abso-bloody-lutely, if that's what it takes!'

'I don't think it works like that, Lill.'

'It does if I say it does! Now eat your broth and concentrate on getting better!'

'Yes, Ma'am.'

In spite of my clear orders, the stubborn girl's condition refused to improve. By the time evening had arrived, I had changed her linens half a dozen times and was about ready to drop dead from exhaustion. And Ella...well, she looked as if she already were dead from exhaustion. Her skin was dry and cracked, her hands feeble, and even her eyes, usually shining in a blue as bright as the summer sky, had dulled to the colour of brackish water.

She's still breathing! As long as she's breathing, there's hope!

But was there? A human needed other things besides air to live. Food. Water. A body that wasn't rebelling against anything and everything.

Finally, around ten pm, Ella dropped into an uneasy sleep, and I stepped out of the room into the corridor, dragging in a deep breath. I hardly remembered what clean air smelled like. Were the people who believed that disease spread through bad air correct? If so, Ella was doing her very best to spread it. But somehow, I couldn't quite believe that theory. If bad smells spread sickness, my Uncle Bufford's socks should have been the origin of the world's greatest plague. So far, my aunt hadn't succumbed to the Black Death on laundry day.[53]

Blinking at the corridor in front of me, I frowned. I was so exhausted I hadn't noticed at first, but...something was wrong with this picture. Where was Ella's staunch little watchdog? Edmund had hardly moved one inch away from the door since he'd heard the doctor's diagnosis. Had he given up already? If he'd forsaken my sister...!

Before I could even finish the thought, I heard someone quickly approaching from around the corner. A moment later, Edmund appeared at the end of the corridor, a big smile on his face and an even bigger bowl in his hands.

'I've got them! I've got them, Miss Linton! It took me a while, but I didn't give up! The very best quality, and peeled, too.'

'Pardon?'

For a moment, I considered whether someone had peeled his brains out of his skull. What was he babbling about?

---

[53] This was also part of pre-modern medical theory. The idea that bad-smelling air caused sickness is quite ancient, which was why, for example, in medieval Europe, people lit fires to cover the odour of plague victims, hoping it would hinder the spread of the disease.

My confidence in Edmund's sanity wasn't exactly reaffirmed when, a moment later, he came to a halt in front of me and pressed a giant bowl full of carrots into my hands.

'Err...thank you?'

'Real beauties, aren't they?' he beamed. 'I walked three miles to get the very best quality from a nearby farmers' market.'

'Good for you.'

'Do you think they'll help?'

'Help?'

'With the *Potius Stercoritis*.'

'The wha—oh!' It took my exhausted mind a moment or two to remember. When I did, I nearly wanted to burst out laughing. But I was far too tired. So, instead, I picked one of the carrots out of the bowl and took a bite. Hey, why not? I hadn't had the chance to eat in a while.

'Hm...not bad.' I took another bite. 'Not bad at all.'

Edmund's smile widened. 'Really? You think they'll help?'

'Definitely. You wouldn't happen to have a ham sandwich, too, would you?'

'Why? Could that also help against *Potius Stercoritis*?'

I took another bite. Who would have ever guessed carrots could be so delicious? 'Most definitely.'

'I'll go get it right away!'

'Don't be sparing with the ham.'

'I won't, I promise! I'll be back in a moment!'

Smiling, I looked after the young man as he dashed away, and then took another bite of carrot. Love was such a beautiful thing.

If it survives.

No. I couldn't think like that, or I would break down. Ella would survive. I would survive, and then I would...

Plink.

The sound was muffled by the door, but I recognized it instantly. Forgetting all about ham sandwiches, I pulled open the door and raced across the room to the window. Pulling it open, I stuck my head out into the cool night air. Beneath me, a familiar tall, dark figure waited in the darkness.

'Come,' he ordered.

I felt a tug at my heart. 'I can't. I...I might have caught the disease. I can't come near you until—'

'Miss Linton?'

'Yes?'

'Get your *derrière* down here *right now*.'

'I thought you had promised not to give me any more orders.'

'That wasn't an order,' he said, and held out one hand. 'Please.'

COLD, HARD COMMITMENT

Please?

Please?

Had I heard correctly?

Most likely not. My ears were probably playing tricks on me, or some owl was testing its ability to imitate Mr Ambrose's voice. Still, I once again felt that painful tug on my heart, and this time, it tugged in his direction. Before I knew what I was doing, I had swung my leg over the sill and was clambering outside. The moment I reached the ground, I rushed towards him. I only came to a stop a few feet away, drinking in the sight of him like an explorer in some distant land, who'd been looking for the fountain of youth and finally reached his goal.

I've been waiting for this all day, I realized. *This moment is what's been keeping me going.*

That realization should have worried me, probably. Up until recently, it would have scared the crap out of me to be so dependent on another person, especially a man. Now, however, I didn't give a flying fig, because I saw the same need in his eyes.

We're in this together.

He took a step forward.

And suddenly, the spell broke and I was brought back to reality with an uncomfortable jolt. We weren't together. And we couldn't be until this was over.

'Stop!' Quickly, I raised a hand and took a step backwards. 'I've got to tell you something! The doctor was here again. He said... he said that Ella...'

'I know,' Mr Ambrose cut me off.

'Then you know you can't come any closer. If you do—'

He took another step towards me.

'No!' I jumped back, my eyes wide with fear. 'Aren't you listening? I might be infected, too! Nobody knows how the sickness is transmitted! It could be through contact, and you'd be—'

I was cut off when he grabbed me, and his lips claimed mine.

It was a kiss unlike any we'd shared before. Before, every kiss had always been about need, or want, or even love. This was none of that. This was a kiss of belonging. It screamed *You are mine and I am yours*, and didn't brook any argument. Not that I felt in the mood to argue. My arms came up around him, clutching him to me with a force I hadn't thought my tired limbs capable of. His arms enfolded me, and they didn't feel hard and cold. They felt like coming home.

Silly girl! Do you know if he even has a home? For all you know, he sleeps on a straw mat in his office!

Well, if he did, I hoped it was broad enough for two. Because I was not letting go. I would never let go!

'You crazy, crazy man!' I whispered against his lips. 'How could you do something so stupid?'

'I prefer the word "determined", Miss Linton.'

'Sure you do.'

He silenced me by reclaiming my mouth. He kissed me hard and deep and, and crazy and determined, and a hundred other ways I wouldn't know how to name. Every second filled me with more love and desire, and most of all more pain. Because with every moment I touched him, the likelihood that he'd be infected grew exponentially. Yet I simply couldn't make myself let go. Even if his arms hadn't been like a wonderful vice around me—I needed him right now. I needed him like I needed air to breathe. So I closed my eyes and sank into the kiss, forgetting everything but him and me and us together.

Finally, he released me. When I had enough strength back in my wobbly legs to stand on my own and was able to open my eyes, I found him staring down at me, coldly and implacably. In other words—just like I loved him.

'Why?' I whispered.

Why risk this? Why kiss me?

He cocked his head. 'I believe the vows we intend to speak say "till death do us part", do they not? You ought to know by now, Miss Linton—I don't speak words I do not mean.'

His words sank into me like balm into an open wound. Grabbing him, I hugged him fiercely.

'Neither do I.'

His arm came around, stroking my hair and pressing my face to his chest. It was a fiercely protective gesture.

I've found someone I can rely on. Always.

The thought made me want to kiss him again. So I did. Why the heck not? I couldn't infect him twice in a row, could I?

When we broke apart again, he took my face in both hands and forced me to look him straight in the eyes. I wasn't about to complain about the view.

'How is she?'

A sliver of pain stabbed into the happiness that filled my heart.

'Bad. Very bad. I'm not sure...I'm not sure she—'

His forefinger on my lips silenced me. 'Sh. She will.'

'How do you know?'

'Because you won't give up until she's well again. And neither will I.' One finger gently stroked down my cheek. 'You look exhausted. How long is it since you've last slept?'

'Says the man who did an experiment to see whether one can go without sleep altogether.'

He gave me a cool look. 'It was a perfectly reasonable experiment.'

'Then let's just say I'm repeating it.' I grinned up at him. 'It's always good to check the results of an experiment, right?'

Mr Ambrose did not look amused.

'Are you familiar with the expression "working yourself into an early grave", Miss Linton?'

'Indeed I am, Sir. I feel its suitable use has been grossly exaggerated. Besides,' I gave a helpless little shrug, 'who's there to help?'

'Me.'

I stared at him, mouth open.

'W-what?'

'I am certain I spoke at a perfectly audible volume, Miss Linton.'

'B-but...you can't...the risk...'

His hand took a firm hold of my chin, forcing me to meet his gaze head-on. 'Was I not clear enough earlier? Need I repeat my demonstration for it to be more convincing?'

'Yes, please, right away for the next half hour.'

'Miss Linton! Be serious!'

'Who says I'm joking. I'm a sceptic by nature and need a lot of convincing.'

He promptly pressed a very, very convincing kiss on my lips.

'I'm not a man who shies away from risk,' he growled. 'If I were, I wouldn't be where I am today, with more power in my hands than most men can imagine! Some things are worth fighting for, and when the fight comes, you face it head-on.'

'But...but she...is...you know.'

'I've mucked out plenty a stable in my time. It won't be that different.'

Holy moly. He really meant it. He was really willing to go in there with me and care for Ella through all the risk, the muck and the things you didn't want to face but had to. Ignoring for the moment that he had, with his customary tact, compared my little sister to a horse, this was the most romantic and loving thing he had ever done.

'Thank you!' Throwing my arms around him, I hugged him to me fiercely. 'Thank you.' Never had I meant these two words more than in this moment. I held on for long, long moments—then let go and looked up into his stormy eyes.

'But I can't accept.' He opened his mouth to say something, but I quickly held up a finger. 'Not because of you. I want your help. God, how I want it. But Ella...' I gazed at him, asking to understand. 'I can't do that to her. Letting someone else see her like that, someone whom she hasn't even met yet...I can't hurt her like that. Please understand.'

He considered—then gave a curt nod. 'Understood.'

I breathed a sigh of relief—which was abruptly cut short when he grabbed my chin again. 'As long as you understand that I won't have you working yourself into an early grave.' Dark, sea-coloured eyes burrowed into me. 'I have plans for you, Miss Linton. Plans that require you to be above ground. I will have Karim monitor the situation. If you do not take care of yourself, I will come in and take charge of things, a proper introduction to your family be damned! Do you understand?'

I nodded, unable to get anything past the lump in my throat.

'Adequate.' One last time, his lips claimed mine in a fierce kiss. 'Then do not let me detain you.'

And, stepping back, he vanished into the shadows.

I returned to my room and settled myself in a chair next to the sleeping Ella. In spite of her laboured breathing, I felt a little bit of hope blossom in my chest. How could I not feel hopeful with Mr Rikkard Ambrose on my side? Somehow, we would pull through this. And when we did, Edmund would bring my little sister joy instead of carrots. I'd make sure of that.

Reaching for a book, I leant back and began to read to keep myself awake. I didn't want to leave Ella unsupervised in her current condition. Still, it was becoming harder and harder to keep my eyes open. With every page I turned, my eyelids became heavier and heavier. But I couldn't fall asleep. I couldn't fall...couldn't...

The book hit the floor with a *thud*.

~~**~*~*

I jerked awake, my whole body aching from a night spent in an armchair. My mind still fuzzy, I tried to focus on the world around me. What had woken me so suddenly? Everything seemed to be peaceful and quiet, and—

I froze.

Too peaceful and quiet.

My head whirled around and I saw Ella lying on the bed, stiff, pale and lifeless.

'No! Ella! Ella!'

Grabbing her by the shoulder, I started to shake her. Her cracked lips parted, letting out a soft moan.

She was alive! Alive!

Just barely.

My eyes flitted over her cracked lips, her parchment-like skin and eyes that staid tearless in spite of the pain she had to be suffering. She was drying up.

'Oh my God, Ella, I'm so sorry! I should never have fallen asleep!' Rushing over to the jug on the window sill that held water mixed with sugar and salt as per the doctor's instructions, I quickly filled a cup and lifted it to her lips. Giving another groan, she turned her head away, but I held her in place firmly.

'I'm sorry, Ella, but you have to. It's the only thing keeping you alive right now.'

With what seemed to be a monumental effort, she opened her eyes. They looked half dead already. The will to live had long fled.

'What if I don't want to?'

'Then do it for Edmund.'

A moment passed—then her trembling lips parted and I tipped the jug just enough for a little of the liquid to trickle into her parched mouth.

It wasn't enough. It wasn't nearly enough. No matter how much I begged and pleaded and pestered, I was never able to get as much fluid into her as fled her body at the same time under the onslaught of the sickness. Desperate, I sent Karim to fetch the doctor, and to the doctor's credit he came instantly, but except for mixing me up a stronger version of the liquid I'd been feeding my little sister anyway, with a few special additions of his own, there wasn't much he could do.

'I'm sorry, Miss Linton,' he told me, shaking his greying head. 'I wish I had an answer to your prayers. But so far, a cure for cholera has eluded modern science. Do you, um...' Nervously, he glanced over at the prone form of Ella on the bed. 'Do you wish for me to stay and help care for her?'

Not for the first time, I was impressed at how intimidating Mr Rikkard Ambrose could be. This man knew better than most how dangerous and infectious cholera could be. Yet he still offered to stay and help. Because of his impeccable ethics? I didn't think so.

'For thirty minutes or an hour, if you could,' I said, giving him a weak smile. 'Could you? Just Keep an eye on her and feed her? I need to close my eyes for a moment, or I'm going to collapse.'

'Certainly, Miss Linton. I'll wake you when it's time.'

He kept his word. Promptly on the hour, he awoke me and took his leave. I was marginally more functional, but even with an hour or so of sleep under my belt, I still felt as if a horse had sat on me.

Still, one look at Ella told me that no matter how I might feel, she had to feel a hundred times worse. I hardly recognized my little sister. Oh, her body was there, her shell—but the spirit had drained right out of her along with every drop of water. She stared at me out of sunken, hopeless eyes.

'Lill?'

I swallowed. 'Yes?'

'If...' she coughed, and groaned from the pain. 'If I dictate you a letter, will you give it to Edmund?'

The words echoed in the room that was far too small to have an echo. She might as well have shouted at me or kicked me in the stomach. Her meaning was painfully, horrendously clear.

'Why don't you just tell him yourself what it is you want him to know,' I growled, leaning forward. 'When you're well again!'

You probably weren't supposed to be angry at a loved one on their deathbed, but dammit, I couldn't help it! I wanted nothing more than to kick her off her deathbed, break it into a thousand pieces and find her something more comfortable to lie on.

'I think...' she coughed again. This time the fit lasted longer. It was horrible, dry coughing without a drop of moisture anywhere in sight. 'I think we have to admit that's unlikely to happen, don't you?'

'No! I think nothing of the kind!'

'Lill...'

A trembling, dry little hand reached out to touch mine. I gripped it fiercely. Too fiercely, probably. But if it hurt her, Ella didn't let it show.

'I'm going to die,' she whispered. 'I can feel it in my bones...the sickness eating away at me. I don't think I'll last long now.'

'What a load of horse crap!' I clenched her hand even tighter. 'You're going to live, dammit, do you hear me? Bloody live!'

'Your bedside manner gets more charming day by day.'

'You can't go!' Leaning forward, I stared into her eyes, not commanding now but pleading shamelessly. 'What about Edmund? You love him, God knows why! You can't leave him behind!'

Pain flashed in her eyes for a moment—but then it vanished, to be replaced by a strange, otherworldly peace. Something I wouldn't understand if I lived to be a hundred.

'I'll see him again eventually. Death isn't the end.'

'It bloody is for me! If you're dead, you're gone!'

Smiling, she gave my hand a little squeeze. It was all she was capable of. 'You don't need me, Lill. You've never needed me. You always were the strongest of us.'

'Of course I bloody need you, you feckless little idiot! I...I...'

My hands trembling, I wrestled with myself. I hadn't wanted to do this—but now I had no other choice! I had pulled out all the stops. I only had one weapon left in my arsenal.

'Bloody hell, yes I need you!' I told her from between clenched teeth. 'If there's ever been a time I needed you, it's now! You...' I swallowed. My heart was pounding like an army drum. The moment of truth had finally come. With enormous effort, I managed a tremulous smile. 'You wouldn't want to miss the big event, would you?'

Slowly, I slipped my trembling hand into my pocket. When it came out again, there was a glinting ring on my ring finger.

REVELATIONS-

Ella blinked.

And blinked again.

And a third time.

'Err...Lill?'

'Yes?'

'Why do you have a curtain ring around your finger?'

I glared at her. She might be my favourite sister and about as near to death as a person could get outside of a mausoleum, but nobody insulted my engagement ring! It took a moment or two for the truth to dawn on her. When it finally did, her eyes went wide as wagon wheels.

'You...no! You don't mean that you...'

'Yes.'

'Lill! You...you...'

'...you'll get better?' I finished, giving her a stern look.

'Yes! Yes, of course I will.'

'And you won't fool around with Edmund before the wedding? I need a maid of honour.'

'Lill!'

I grinned. 'Just making sure. Although I guess you could always be my vixen of honour. Has an interesting ring to it.'

Ella blushed up to the roots of her hair, and the sight warmed me. She still had life in her! She still had fight in her! And I would make sure she didn't give up.

'Here.' Grabbing the water cup from the nightstand, I held it up to her lips. 'Drink.'

For just a moment, she hesitated—then our eyes met. We looked at each other for a long, long moment. Her eyes filled with warmth and one lone, single little tear spilled out of her eye and ran down her parched cheek.

'I'm so happy for you, Lill.'

And she started to drink.

It was by no means over. The cholera burned as hot in Ella's poor body as ever, turning it into a desert that soaked up every drop of water and spat out things I'd rather not think about, let alone smell. But the light was back in her eyes, and the fight back in her body. She drank whenever I told her to, and once her throat was greased, the questions started.

'Who is he, Lill?'

I raised an eyebrow. 'Who?'

She glared at me. Or at least tried to. It was quite adorable watching my sweet little sister try and glare.

'You know perfectly well who I mean! You haven't shown a jot of interest in a single man since you've been tall enough to not need Leadfield to get you books from the upper shelves in the library! And now you tell me you're engaged to be married? Who is he? What kind of man would catch your interest?'

Even though she didn't say it, I heard the part she thought: *and what kind of man would be that suicidal?*

I grinned.

'Well, you'll just have to get well again to find out, won't you?'

'*What?*'

'You heard me, little sister.'

'This is cruel and unusual punishment!'

'No. This is effective therapy. The bridesmaids' dresses I have in mind for Anne and Maria will be cruel and unusual punishment.'

'Just tell me! Please!'

'Open your mouth, will you? It's time to drink. One gulp for Lilly, one gulp for the mysterious bridegroom, another gulp for Lilly, another gulp for the mysterious bridegroom...'

'Lill!'

'Yes?'

'Just a little hint! Please! I'm dying here!'

I grinned. Because even though she'd spoken the words I most feared to hear in the world, for the very first time, she didn't really sound as if she meant them.

'All right.' I nodded graciously. 'One little hint.'

'Yes? Yes?'

I considered carefully. What could I tell her about Mr Rikkard Ambrose without giving away who he was?

'His tailcoat is ten years old,' I told her.

Ella looked at me, aghast. 'Ten ears? Good Lord, the poor man must be destitute!'

I snorted into my sleeve. Ella, God bless her, mistook it for a sob.

'There, there.' Lifting a trembling hand, she patted my arm. 'The money isn't what matters. No matter how poor he is, if he loves you, he must be a good man. I'm sure the two of you will be happy together. If Uncle Bufford gives his consent, that is. I don't think he'll be very enthusiastic when he hears you intend to marry a man in such circumstances.'

'Oh, I don't know. He might surprise you.'

She gave me a warm smile. 'Bless you, Lill. It's good of you to think so well of him.' The smile melted into a frown of worry. 'But you really should be on your guard. Don't spring the news on him. It might come as a shock.'

'Oh, I'm quite certain it will.'

She patted my arm again. 'Don't worry. I'll be there to help. Together we'll convince him. And I'll talk to your man, too. I'll tell him that even if he hasn't got two pennies to rub together, I will always love him like a brother.'

'I'm sure he will be delighted to hear that. Here, take another swallow, will you?'

'Only if you tell me more about him. Where is he from? How did the two of you meet?'

'Later. Once you're better.'

She opened her mouth to protest and, not being one to waste an opportunity, I put the glass to her lips and started pouring before she could say a word. Reluctantly, she started to swallow, glaring at me over the top of her glass.

I smiled. Curiosity. Not the most typical of cures, but so what? Ella was my sister after all. It definitely would have worked on me.

The last drops of water vanished between Ella's lips. I lowered the glass, and quickly, she opened her mouth to speak.

'Here,' I said and shoved a piece of carrot between her lips. '*Bon appetit.*'

'Mmph! Mm mph gmph!'

'Yes, delicious, aren't they?'

Reaching over to the nightstand, I let my hand hover over the bowl of carrots for a moment—then shifted to the left and reached into the bowl full of ham sandwiches instead. Edmund really was such a loving, caring man. He would make a good husband for Ella. I'd have to visit them for lunch once they were settled.

Over the next few days, Ella slowly but surely began to improve. More and more often, she was able to keep down her food. Her skin ceased to resemble dried old parchment, and life came back into her eyes. As for the amount of *merde* I had to smuggle out of her room on a regular basis—that was still considerable. More than once, I wished I had Mr Ambrose's talent for waste disposal. Still, as Ella's general condition improved, those symptoms also slowly started to abate.

'Miss Linton?'

I looked up. I had just come out of Ella's room with a bag of...well, smelly things that I'd rather not think about, when Edmund came around the corner and strode toward me, a broad smile on his face, hiding something behind his back.

'I've found one, Miss Linton! It took me really long, but I've finally found one!'

'Um...one what?' I enquired, trying to hide the crappy bag behind my back.

'This!'

With a triumphant grin, he held out his hands, presenting me with—

'Rrrrng! What the heck is that?' I hadn't thought it possible for there to be anything that smelled worse than the bag I was currently carrying. I had been wrong. The mouldy piece of wood Edmund was holding out to me smelled as if a whale had used it as a privy. It looked like it, too. Squashed and cracked in multiple places, it was covered with cracked shells, grime, tar, and other delightful things you come across if you go for a nice swim in a dirty harbour basin.

'A ship plank!' Edmund was beaming as if he was one of Father Christmas's elves. 'Mouldy and rotten, too, just as you ordered. It wasn't easy to find. Do you know how far away Bath is from the coast? Plus, you won't believe how many ship captains object to your chopping off a piece of their ship, even if it's just a tiny small one.'

'Oh, I think I might believe that.'

'Well, anyway, I finally found one who allowed me to take this for a fee.' He lifted the plank proudly. 'Will you put it under Ella's bed, Miss Linton?'

I gazed at him and his hopeful puppy dog expression.

'Right away,' I lied and took the plank. Why not? My hands would need to be scrubbed with bleach anyway.

'Thank you. Thank you, Miss Linton. What would I do without you?'

Stick mouldy planks under your fiancée's bed, probably?

I really would have to drop in on them occasionally once they were married, just to check whether someone had tried to sell the poor fellow some all-healing snake oil or get him to invest in an expedition to rediscover a lost ancient south-African silver mine.

'I'll bring her this right away,' I lied.

'How is she?'

Anxiety was written all over his face with letters so big even a blind analphabetic bat could have read it.

'Much better,' I assured him, grateful that this time it was the absolute truth. 'The carrots helped a lot.'

'Really?' he perked up. 'Should I bring more?'

'Um...I think more ham sandwiches would be better. They were even more effective.'

He nodded earnestly. 'I'll go make some straight away.'

'Bless you. You're a good man, Edmund. And...'

'Yes?'

'Never buy anything from a salesman, or invest in anything before asking Ella.'

He blinked—then nodded. 'Err...all right. I'll see you later, Miss. Later.'

'Till then.'

I watched him recede down the corridor, then looked down at the two objects in my hand. I might be able to sneak out with the sack, in spite of the odour. But the mouldy ship plank? I didn't think I should try to march through the lobby with that. Not unless I wanted to visit the local loony bin. But there was always more than one way to solve a problem. One: solve it yourself. Two, and far better: unload it on someone else.

Turning around, I strode back into the room. From her bed, Ella blinked as she saw me striding by with my new load.

'Err...am I hallucinating?'

'Unfortunately no.'

'Are you sure?' She eyed the plank dubiously. A bit of seaweed was still dangling off the edge. 'I could be having a relapse.'

'Trust me,' I huffed, pushing up the window and leaning out, 'you aren't.'

Outside, the air was moderately fresher than in the room. Still, the odour of the seaweed, combined with the exquisite perfume of *l'eau de la merde* issuing from the sack, managed to make even the fresh morning air smell like a big pile of horse shit. Trust me, I know what I'm talking about.

Slipping two fingers between my lips, I whistled. Karim, who was standing guard a little farther down the wall, turned and glanced up at me.

'Yes?'

'Catch!'

The big Mohammedan ducked just in time to avoid being brained by a mouldy ship plank. His hands shot out to grab the thing, and, stumbling, he tumbled into the nearest flower bed. Yellow tulips. How fitting.

'Have a care, Prince Fragrant Yellow Flower!' I called down to him, grinning broadly. With a little bow, I let the sack drop, too, and it landed with an unappetizing noise next to the flower bed. 'We would not want you to injure your majestic royal self.'

Karim sent me up a look that could kill at twenty paces. Luckily, I was at least twenty-five away.

'What,' he enquired, raising the plank, 'is that?'

'Oh, just a little present.'

'A present? A *mouldy ship plank*?'

'Oh yes. Some people say they're very good for your health.'

He gave me a long, long look—the kind of look you give a person when you decide how best to chop their head off. 'Is your brand of madness hereditary, woman? Because if so, I shall advise the *Sahib* to reconsider his marriage offer.'

'Don't worry.' I grinned down at him. 'My madness is undoubtedly and uniquely me.'

With that, I leant back into the room and shut the window. When I turned, Ella was staring at me, eyes wide.

'There's a *prince* outside my window?'

I sighed. Edmund and Ella really were meant for each other.

~~**~*~*

With every passing day, Ella improved. My hope soared, and along with it, Ella's ravenous desire for answers. While she had still been weak, I'd been able to placate her. But now that she was able to sit on her own again and wasn't spending half the day producing masses of *merde*, there was no stopping her.

'It's that army fellow, isn't it? Captain Carter?'

I shook my head.

'No.'

'Are you sure?' Ella sent me a suspicious look over the top of her glass. 'He didn't ask you?'

'Oh, he asked me. I turned him down.'

She spat her water all over her covers. 'You *what*?'

'Turned him down. You know, down, the opposite of up?'

'When was this?'

'Last year, shortly before Christmas.'

'But...but he...he's...' Raising her hands, she indicated the captain's impressive measurements. 'Half of the girls I know would kill to get his hands on him.'

'They might just have to. He's on another continent fighting rebels right now.'

'Oh.'

She considered my words. Then she glanced up at me out of the corner of her eyes. 'You really must love this other man.'

I held her eyes. 'I do.'

'How is he doing? Are his money troubles bad?'

My darling little sister. Even with curiosity eating her up from the inside, she still thought of others before herself. It was an admirable trait. It was also pretty darn funny in this case.

'I think he's doing all right,' I said, trying not to start giggling like a headcase.

'I see. But...' Slipping a hand under her pillow, she pulled out her purse and fished out a coin. 'Give him this when you next see him, will you? With my best wishes for his future.'

'You have no idea how much this means to us,' I told her with a totally one hundred percent straight face. 'You are the best sister I could wish for.'

'Oh, Lill!' Throwing her arms around me, she hugged me close. 'I'm just so happy that you've finally found someone.'

'Me too.' I squeezed back. 'Me too.'

'There's only one thing that's missing to make everything perfect,' she sighed.

'And that is?'

'His name!'

Grinning, I slipped out of her embrace and reached for the mug.

'I think it's time for another cup to drink, don't you? We wouldn't want the doctor to get angry.'

She sent me another glare. Over the last few days, my little sister had gotten surprisingly good at glaring. Maybe, if I kept up the suspense, she'd even let a curse slip eventually. Hope springs eternal, as Alexander Pope used to say.[54]

But, actually, was there a reason to still keep it from her? In the beginning I had refused to tell her, clinging to my irrational belief that anything, even curiosity, might help keep her alive. But she was well on her way back to health by now. There was no reason not to tell her about Mr Ambrose. After all, she had never met him and would have no preconceived notions. It wasn't like with my best friend, Patsy, who had encountered him one day in Green Park at a women's rights demonstration and...

Well, the less said about that meeting, the better.

So, one day, after I'd let her dangle for a few more days just for the fun of it, I drew up a chair next to her bed, sat myself down and took her hand.

'Ella?'

'Yes? It's not time to drink again, is it? Honestly, Lil, I'm full! I feel like a blowfish.'

'No, you've drunk enough for now, as the vicar said to the bishop barking at the moon on the tavern roof. I'm not here about that.'

'No? Then what is it?'

'Well...' I gave her an innocent smile. 'I remember you wanting to know the identity of a certain someone...'

Instantly, her hand latched onto me like a kraken's tentacle. 'Yes? Tell me!'

'Very well, if you insist.' Sitting up straight, I took a deep breath. 'You might have heard of him before, so it might come as a little bit of a surprise. Just don't get overexcited, will you? No one else knows yet, and I would like to refrain from telling them until we're back in London.'

'Yes, yes! Now tell me already!'

'All right. The man I'm engaged to is—'

Behind me, the door to the room flew open. In the mirror beside the bed, I could see three formidable figures standing in the doorway, armed with parasols. Eve, Flora, and in the front, looking as if someone had just waved a red flag in front of her and her bull-instincts were kicking in, stood my best friend, Patsy.

'Engaged? Who is *engaged*?'

---

[54] The phrase 'hope springs eternal' comes from the poem *An Essay on Man* by 18th-century poet Alexander Pope. The part of the poem around the quotation goes like this:

Hope springs eternal in the human breast;
Man never is, but always to be blessed:
The soul, uneasy and confined from home,
Rests and expatiates in a life to come.

-HIT!

'It's Lilly!' Ella, the little traitor, exclaimed, beaming brightly. 'She's finally met the right man. I'm so happy!'

Patsy's face betrayed that she, too, was experiencing some intense emotion. However, happiness would probably not have been the right way to describe it.

'Is that so?' Her eyes sparkled like the stars on the night before Armageddon. 'How fabulous.'

'Ah. Um. Patsy.' I cleared my throat. 'So...the hotel manager found you?'

'Yes, he did.' She took a step forward, her parasol swinging menacingly. 'Just in time, apparently.'

'S-so nice of you to drop by. Won't you take a seat? Would you like something to eat? A cup of tea?'

'No, no.' She waved. 'Don't let me interrupt. You were at "the man I'm engaged to is..."'

...the man who defeated you in a rhetoric battle and humiliated you in front of several hundred people in a public park?

But I didn't say that. Unwise though it may seem, considering the last two years' events, I hadn't yet taken out a life insurance policy on myself.

'*Sahiba?*'

I glanced to the door behind Patsy, already knowing who it would be. Never in my life had I been this glad to see that beard and turban, and the man who accompanied them everywhere! If there was one person who could take on Patsy and survive the battle, it was Karim.

I was so derailed by her sudden appearance that it took me a moment to realize – *Did I just hear him call me Sahiba?*

'These females made their way upstairs, it appears, against the staff's express instructions.' The big Mohammedan stalked into the room. 'Do you wish for them to be removed?'

'Excuse me?' Patsy puffed out her chest, which was bad news for her poor corset. 'I will not allow myself to be manhandled! You touch me, and I'll have the law on you!'

'I,' Karim said with an expression as deadpan as a pan in in a graveyard at the funeral of a fellow pan, 'am so terribly afraid.'

Patsy turned purple and started sputtering like a defective teakettle. She was about to reach for her parasol, when I hurriedly jumped to my feet.

'Um, Patsy? Allow me to introduce you to Karim. He was kind enough to drive Ella and me here. Without him, we probably wouldn't have managed to escape the epidemic.'

Patsy's hand froze halfway to her parasol. She eyed Karim suspiciously.

'Are you sure?'

'Yes. Quite sure.'

'Damn!' Sighing, Patsy let her hand drop. 'I guess I can't skewer him today, then.'

'You won't be able to tomorrow, either, woman,' Karim shot back.

'Don't count on it, goatface!'

Karim gave her a look. The kind of look he'd probably learned from his employer.

Please don't insult her back! Please! If you do, I won't be able to vouch for the consequences.

He didn't. He did something far worse.

'I am above bandying words with mere women,' he told her. And with that, he turned around and marched out of the room. Patsy stood there, mouth open, her face slowly turning a nice, explosive tomato colour. I could almost see the fuse sticking out of her head, shortly about to blow.

'That...that...that...'

'Man?' I suggested

Patsy made a noise somewhere between a growl of a tiger and the trumpet of a charging regiment of cavalry. Grabbing her parasol tightly in both hands, she marched after Karim, slamming the door after her. Breathing a sigh of relief, I sank against the wall. Catastrophe averted! At least for now. Sooner or later, I would have to come clean to my best friend. But if possible, I'd like to do it in an open field with no easily breakable things around, like vases, siblings, or buildings.

When I opened my eyes again, I found Eve and Flora staring at me, eyes wide open and mouths no less so.

'*Engaged?*'

With a lopsided little smile, I raised my hand to show the big ring dangling loosely from my ring finger.

Eve's eyebrows shot up. 'Good God! How big is he?'

My ears turned fire-red—which was probably not the smartest move. Eve's eyebrows shot even higher, and a twinkle appeared in her eyes.

'Lilly? Is there something you'd like to tell us?'

I cleared my throat. 'Um, well, I...'

A devilish grin spread across Eve's face. Flora and Ella meanwhile, bless them, looked perfectly puzzled.

'Well, Lilly? Answer my question. How *big* is he?'

'He, is, um...quite tall.' I cleared my throat again. 'Yes. Quite tall indeed.'

'Especially when standing up?'

I kicked Eve against the shins.

'I'll tell you all you wish to know.' *Or, at least, all I can say without making my little sister faint.* 'But first...how about some tea and biscuits?'

~~**~*~*

I gazed out the window into the sunset, for the first time in many days taking time to appreciate how beautiful it was.

Especially since Ella will see more of them. Many more.

Night was falling, and my heart knew what that meant. It fluttered in eager anticipation at the knowledge. Any moment now. Any moment...

Plink!

'What was that?' Ella sat up in her bed, alarmed.

'Nothing, nothing.' I waved my hand and pulled up the window, sticking one leg out into the night. 'Go back to sleep.'

'Lilly! What are you...*oh*.'

I winked at her. 'Exactly.'

Her eyes went wide. 'He's...out there? He came for you?'

'He's been here the whole time.'

Her eyes warmed and, reaching out a hand, she squeezed mine. 'I'm so glad you've found yourself a good, kind man.'

I just about managed to stifle my laughter. Mr Rikkard Ambrose good and kind? But who was I to disabuse her of her notions if it helped her sleep with a smile on her face? Plus...Mr Ambrose actually occasionally could be kind. To me. Just not to himself or anybody else.

'Can I meet him? Please? Please?'

'No chance!' I grinned evilly at Ella. 'You're still recuperating. You need to stay in bed.'

'You're wicked!'

'And proud of it. Don't worry. There'll be plenty of time later.'

With that, I slid out the rest of the way, pulled the curtains shut to prohibit peeking, and closed the window. When I turned, it wasn't difficult to make out Mr Ambrose's dark silhouette against the burning sunset.

'Miss Linton.' He greeted me with a tip of his top hat that said more than a thousand smiles from another man. 'I gather that matters have somewhat improved?'

In answer, I threw myself at him, hurling my arms around his neck and clinging to him like a limpet. 'She's going to survive! She's going to survive! She's going to survive!'

'It appears my sources of information were correct, then.'

'Yes, indeed, Sir,' I managed through my tears. 'They were absolutely correct.'

'Adequate. Then you can cease staining my suit with your ocular fluids.'

I promptly wiped away my ocular fluids. Still, more tears kept coming. Glancing up at his stony visage, I hesitated. I didn't know how he would take this. Finally, I took a deep breath and just spoke two words.

'She knows.'

Mr Ambrose hadn't gotten to where he was by being slow on the uptake.

'Your sister?'

'Yes.'

'About us?'

'Yes. I...I told her in the hope it would help her recover. I thought it would give her hope.'

'So I gather you didn't mention too many details about me, then?'

I grinned. 'No. I wanted her to recover, not to have a heart attack.'

'How flattering.'

'Speaking of flattery...' Reaching into my pocket, I pulled out something small that glinted in the light of the sinking sun. 'Here. This is for you.'

I dropped it into his hand. Mr Rikkard Ambrose stood there, wordlessly staring down at the penny lying on his palm. It was by no means the only time I'd seen him silent, but one of the few I'd seen him dumbstruck.

Finally, he raised his gaze to meet mine. 'Your idea of a dowry, is it?'

'No. It's from my little sister. A gift for you.'

He blinked—then looked down at the penny again, as if trying to solve the mysteries hidden in its depth. Finally, he shrugged and pocketed it. 'Well, if she is trying to secure my affections as a future sister-in-law, she certainly has made the right start. Tell her to send more next time.'

'I will.'

'I accept bills in all currencies and denominations, checks, bonds, gold, jewels, and property deeds of all kinds.'

'I'll be sure to let her know.'

For a few moments, we gazed at each other in silence. Moments during which, miraculously, Mr Ambrose didn't pull out his pocket watch and complain about wasted time. Could it be that his definition of 'wasted' had slightly altered during recent months?

Finally, he asked, 'And the others? Do they know?'

'Not as much as Ella, but...yes. They know there's someone.'

'So it's finally happening.'

I knew what he meant. After all the years of denial and secrecy, it was hard to believe that soon, I would be marching down the aisle to meet him at the altar. There was a tiny part of me that was wondering whether this was all actually happening, or whether it was just a dream.

Time to reassure myself.

'Come here,' I said, and grabbed him by the lapels.

He didn't waste a moment. Before I knew it, his lips were on mine and taking everything I offered and more, with no possibility of a refund. We kissed and kissed and kissed. When I finally came up for air, it was just for a moment, to drag in a much-needed breath. But when I pulled him close again, he placed a finger on my lips, stopping me.

'Wait.'

'Wait?' I grinned up at him 'Waiting is for time-wasters, Sir.'

His face remained expressionless, and so did his eyes. Slowly, the grin melted from my face. 'What's wrong?'

'I didn't just call you out here to ask about your sister. There's news.'

My heartbeat picked up. 'News about wedding planners?'

'No. News about Dalgliesh.'

Ice spread through my veins at hearing the name. 'What?'

'I've been receiving interesting reports from Europe and India. After that business in France, I asked to be updated by my agents on all the latest developments regarding Dalgliesh's power base. What happened in Paris...' Mr Ambrose shook his head. 'It was an incredibly risky operation, even for a man of Dalgliesh's audacity. If he'd been found out...well, let's just say the French would have had a use for all those guillotines left over from the revolution. Normally, Dalgliesh would never risk his own neck. To go to such extremes he must have been under an extraordinary amount of pressure.'

My brow creased. 'What could pressure a man like Dalgliesh? Present company excepted, of course.'

'That's what I thought. Then I contacted my agents, and they had most interesting things to report. It appears that Dalgliesh is having increasing troubles within his own power base. Things are stirring in India. The people aren't willing to slave for the British anymore. The various principalities are starting to realize that they are one people, and quite a large one at that. Things are beginning to move.'

'Not in a direction His Lordship approves of, I gather?'

'Not at all.' Mr Ambrose gazed into the distance, his face more cold and inscrutable than ever. Not for a million pounds would I have been able to guess what thoughts, plans and stratagems were going through his head right then. Abruptly, his eyes snapped back to me and burned into me with icy intensity. 'Which means that now we must be more vigilant than ever. A snake is most dangerous when it's injured.'

'But also most vulnerable.'

'Indeed.'

'Well, then.' I held out my hand. 'Is it time to attack?'

With an icy gleam in his eyes that told me I didn't want to be in the shoes of Lord Daniel Eugene Dalgliesh, he took my hand.

'Yes. But first...' Pulling me toward him, he grabbed me and pressed a hot, hard, swift kiss on my mouth. 'Time to go to London. We have a wedding to attend.'

KNOCK, KNOCK

It took a few days before we could return to London. Mr Ambrose had insisted on dispatching one of his not-so-merry men to the city to check if the epidemic was passed before he would let me within fifty miles of the capital. Explaining to my friends and family why exactly they had to wait for word from a man they didn't know existed, employed by another man whose name they didn't yet know, wasn't easy, but, accomplished truth-bender that I was, I managed.

One thing was noticeable, however: with the exception of Ella, nearly everyone suddenly treated me differently. Edmund was almost worshipfully grateful for all I'd done for his beloved. He would have put his coat down for me to walk on over puddles if the weather hadn't been so consistently sunny and dry. Lisbeth and Gertrude as well as Edmund's parents looked at me with a sort of shocked awe, probably caused by the reverence of the hotel staff and the fact that somehow, inexplicably, I suddenly seemed to be in charge of everything. Patsy was angry as hell. Not at me so much as at the fact that she couldn't bring herself to hate my prospective suitor. I had shared with her the little detail that he'd been instrumental in saving Ella's life, and she had looked at me as if she'd swallowed a lemon.

'Really? Are you sure?'

'Yes.'

'So...I shouldn't whack him over the head with my parasol, or push him into a duck pond?'

'No.'

'Damn!'

Eve was constantly peppering me with questions, and Flora had caught the wedding fever and was doing her best to plan a wedding for me, or maybe two or three in one go while she was at it. Only Anne and Maria were truly reliable. They hated my guts just like before. Only a lot, lot, more. Relatives you can truly depend on are such a comfort, aren't they?

Finally, the day of departure arrived.

'Are you sure you're well enough? We could wait another few days and—'

'Stop fussing, Edmund,' Ella ordered with a smile that said she'd like nothing better than for him to continue. 'I'm fine. And besides...' She glanced at me. 'We should get home. We've got things to take care of.'

I squeezed her hand. It was warm and smooth, nothing like the paper-dry skeleton fingers of only a week or so ago.

'Well, let's go then.' Nodding to Karim, I strode toward the door—which he promptly held open for me. Mr and Mrs Conway exchanged looks. Anne and Maria exchanged scowls.

'You came with two coaches, didn't you?' Patsy asked. 'Will we all fit, or should I hire an extra?'

'Oh, I think we'll fit.' I grinned. 'And if not, you can always sit next to Karim on the box. I'm sure he'd love the company.'

Before either of the two could dismember me with their looks, I slipped into the nearest coach.

Under the stern eyes of Karim, it didn't take long for the hotel staff to load our luggage onto the coaches. Soon, he swung himself onto the box—of the coach Patsy was sitting in, as it happened. Trying not to smile, I leaned back into the plush seat.

'Gee-up!'

The coach jerked and started rolling forward. Smoothly, we slid along the palatial façades of Bath. As soon as we reached the outskirts of the town, riders appeared on both sides of the coaches—plain-dressed men in black and grey, with sharp eyes and forgettable faces.

Maria glanced out of the window, shifting nervously. 'Who're they?'

I smiled. 'Insurance.'

The others exchanged looks, but none of them knew quite what to say.

Around mid-day, I knocked against the coach roof with my parasol.

'Stop, please!'

The coachman veered off to the side and brought the coach to a halt at the side of the road. Pushing open the door, I slid out. One of the riders galloped up and brought his mount to a stop right beside me.

'What is it, Miss?'

'This.' Raising my parasol, I pointed at a picturesque little inn beside the road. 'It's time for lunch, don't you think?'

The rider cleared his throat. 'We have instructions to proceed with all deliberate speed, Miss.'

'And that we are,' I told him with a smile, 'to the nearest inn, in order to have lunch. Please help the other ladies out of the coach.'

The man hesitated, glancing back, then forward again, as if looking for some invisible authority.

'He's not here,' I informed him with a cool smile. 'I am.'

The rider made a decision. 'Yes. Lunch, Miss. Immediately, as you say.'

'Thank you.'

Still smiling, I turned back towards the coach—only to find every single occupant staring at me with eyes wide open.

'Who do those men think you are?' Anne demanded. 'The Queen of England?'

'Don't be ridiculous.' I waved her away. 'The Queen isn't nearly as pretty as I am.'

And I strode towards the inn.

~~**~*~*

The inn was a charming little place. As soon as I stepped in, the innkeeper greeted us with a big smile.

'Welcome, ladies and gentlemen, welcome! What brings you out onto the road on such a fine morning?'

'We're returning from a little holiday in Bath,' I said, thinking it best I didn't mention the word 'cholera'.

'How nice. Won't you take a seat?'

He pulled back a chair, and I was just about to say 'Yes, thank you,' when a big shape filled the doorway. The smile slipped from the innkeeper's face.

'I'm sorry miss, but we don't allow *his* kind in here.'

I turned to see Karim standing in the doorway, gazing at the innkeeper with narrowed eyes.

'Don't allow...' I repeated.

'He'd put all my customers off their food. You can go and eat with the servants out back. Go on.' The innkeeper waved a hand at the bodyguard. 'Off with you.'

The bigoted son of a....!

Reflexively, my whole body stiffened. So did Karim's hand around the grip of his sabre. The innkeeper didn't seem to notice. Ah. So the man wasn't just bigoted, he also was blind and stupid.

Karim took a step forward—but I raised a hand and stepped between him and the landlord. I wouldn't allow Karim to behead the man. After all, why should he have all the fun?

'You don't allow "his kind" here, do you?' I repeated slowly.

'Nay.' The innkeeper spat out of an open window, oblivious to the warning lights flashing in my eyes. 'Those damn towelheads can go to where they come from!'

Rage welled up inside me. That was it! Karim might be a grumpy, irritating son of bolder, but in his own, bearded, heavily armed way, he was as much part of my family as Ella, Eve or Patsy. Nobody got to give him insulting nicknames except me!

'Sir?' I said, smiling and taking a step forward. 'Do you perchance have a room where we could talk privately for a bit? Five minutes would do.'

'Hm. Well, we could step into the back room if you insist. But I don't think—'

'Just five minutes, Sir. That's all I'll need.'

'All right. If you must. Follow me.'

'Oh, and just one thing?'

'Yes?'

'How thick are the walls in this place? Can one usually hear what's going on in the next room?'

The innkeeper tugged up his apron. 'Do you mean to insult me, Miss? My inn is built solidly, and I'll ask you not to imply anything different.'

'Excellent. After you, Sir.'

I stepped into the room. The door closed behind us.

Four minutes and thirty-seven seconds later, the door opened again and I stepped out, followed by a pale, somewhat unsteady innkeeper.

'Y-you can stay,' he mumbled in the direction of Karim's shiny shoes.

'And...?' I suggested.

'A-and I'm sorry about what I called you earlier. I shouldn't have said it, and I apologize, and...and...'

I nodded encouragingly. The innkeeper made a face. 'And all your meals will be on the house as my personal apology.'

Picking up a menu, Karim perused the prices. He didn't thank me. He didn't say anything about what had just happened. For a long moment, silence hung between us. Then, glancing up, he raised one bushy eyebrow. 'Maybe you are the right one for him after all.'

Everybody else exchanged confused glances. I didn't care. I grinned from ear to ear, so broadly it nearly split my head in two.

Eve tugged at my sleeve. 'What the heck is he rambling on about?'

My grin broadened even more. 'You'll understand soon. Come. Let's sit down and eat.'

It was one of the best meals of my life, not least because it was completely free and eaten in the company of my friends and family, who were, thank goodness, all safe and healthy. But the food itself was excellent, too. Just goes to show: you can be an arrogant, prejudicial asshole and still be a good cook.

'Another helping of pie, Miss?' the innkeeper asked, stepping up to the table with a gloomy expression on his face.

'Yes, thank you. How very kind.'

'For me as well,' Karim said with a smile that showed all his teeth. 'It really is excellent.'

'How wonderful,' the innkeeper groaned and trudged off.

Once again, the others at the table—except Edmund and Ella, who were in their own private, pink little world—gave me those strange looks that I'd been getting a lot recently Was it really so strange to them to see me taking charge?

You've grown, Lilly, I realized. *Ever since that moment when you first stepped into the office of a certain business magnate in London, you've done a whole lot of growing.*

Grinning, I stabbed my fork into a piece of roast beef. After all, a growing girl needed her food.

After dinner, Ella looked more than a little drowsy. So I ordered for the horses to be stabled, and Edmund and I helped her up to a comfy bedchamber, where soon she was snoring the day away. I had to admit, I was feeling more than a little sleepy myself. I hadn't quite realized how much caring for Ella day after day after day had taken out of me. I had just enough strength left to find myself a bed before I collapsed and sank into warm, wonderfully downy darkness.

When I awoke, warm, red light filtered in through the windows. Yawning, I stretched. Dear me. I had slept half the day away. And that with Mr Ambrose waiting for me back in London. Hopefully he'd been patient and—

'Well rested?' came a cool voice from behind me.

Mr Ambrose patient?

Yep. I should probably have known better.

I turned to see a familiar tall, dark figure leaning against the door.

'Oh. Um.' I cleared my throat. 'Yes, thank you.'

'I cannot exactly say the same.' Eyes glittering with a frost that would have sent sane people running, but only made me want to grab him and never let go, he stepped towards me. 'I was already in London, preparing a speech for my first encounter with your guardians. Imagine my surprise when one of my men arrived to inform me that my bride-to-be and her retinue were merrily feasting at a countryside inn, still several dozen miles from the city.'

'It was lunchtime,' I pointed out.

Mr Ambrose waved that argument away with the supreme confidence of a man who survived on money fumes alone.

'I was *waiting for you*,' he told me, his gaze burrowing into me with heart-wrenching intensity. I had to swallow to be able to speak.

'I wasn't about to starve myself and my family! Especially not my sister who, incidentally, is still recuperating from cholera. I may be in love, but I'm not daft. Unlike some people, I can distinguish between the two.'

'You...you...!'

Without the slightest warning, he pounced. His arms came around me, pulling me up against him in a crushing embrace.

'I love you!'

'For being late?' I whispered against his lips. 'Dang! I wish I'd known that earlier. That would have been useful to know on work days during the last two years.'

He gave me a look telling me what exactly he thought of my humour—then kissed me again, long and hard.

'You shouldn't be here,' I gasped.

'Correct,' he agreed. 'We should both be in London.'

'That's not what I meant! I thought we agreed that we'd talk to my uncle and aunt before....'

'We did. I came in the back way.'

'What for?'

Stormy, sea-coloured eyes captured mine. 'To remind you of what's waiting for you. And for this.'

One last time, he kissed me. Then he let go and pushed open the door, revealing a red-faced Karim standing guard outside.

'Don't leave me waiting too long, Miss Linton. Knowledge is power is time is money.'

And with that, he was gone.

~~**~*~*

Our coaches rolled into good old London town early next morning. A strange sense of *déjà vu* overtook me as we rattled over the cobblestones towards my uncle's house. I half expected the door to be answered by my sister, giving me the news of Ella's sickness, although she was sitting right beside me, smiling brightly at Edmund. It felt just like it had back then, with the eerie quiet, and the—

'Lillian Linton! What in God's name are you up to? Taking off like that, and then dragging the whole family away from home for one of your hair-brained schemes? Get into the house this instant, young lady, before I come out and drag you inside by the ear!'

I winced.

Ah. Not so eerily quiet after all. Though, perhaps, the deadly silence of an epidemic would have been preferable.

'Coming, my dear Aunty!' I called and forced a smile onto my face. Showtime. I nodded to the others in the coach. 'Wish me luck.'

Ella squeezed my hands. 'Good luck.'

Eve nodded. 'Break a leg.'

'No.' Anne smirked. 'Break *both* legs.'

'And both arms,' Maria added.

'Thanks so much,' I shot back. 'Dislocate your shoulder and crack your skull at the next opportunity, won't you?'

Sliding out of the coach before she could fire back—or before I could let my fear get the better of me and make me run away back to France—I started towards the house. My aunt, the fiery dragon of doom, was awaiting me at the front door.

I raised a hand and waved. 'Hello there.'

To judge by the expression on my aunt's face, she was not impressed with my good manners.

'Into the house, straight away! I've got a few things to say to you, young lady!'

I cleared my throat. 'I'm sure you do. But before you do, could I have a word with Uncle Bufford? I've got something to tell him that—'

'Inside! Now!'

Hm. That went well, didn't it?

Behind me, I heard the giggles of Anne and Maria.

Just you wait, you two. Just you wait until today is over...

Ducking my head just in case my aunt was equipped with her trusted carpet-and-niece beater, I slunk into the house. She hadn't used that thing since I'd turned fourteen and big enough to wrestle with her, but right now, I wouldn't put it past her.

Inside the house, I tried to turn. 'Listen, Aunt, there are a few things you should probably know—'

'Move! Into the drawing room with you, you disobedient chit!'

Something prodded me in the back. The end of the carpet beater? Or had my aunt gotten herself a bayonet complete with firing squad?

'But I have to tell you that I'm—'

'You're a good-for-nothing runaway, that's what you are! Drawing room! Now!'

For once in my life, I did as ordered. Once I had reached the drawing room, I turned around. My sisters had assembled in the entryway, in front of the front door that Ella, thank the Lord, had closed behind her. It was bad enough that my whole family apparently intended to stay to witness my evisceration. It wasn't exactly necessary for our entire street of neighbours to listen in, as well.

'Now, Aunt.' Straightening, I took a step towards her. 'Listen here—'

'No! *You* listen, you miserable excuse for a proper young lady!' Oh boy, she was on full steam. I nearly could see it coming out of her ears. Her eyes were blazing, and...yes. There it was. Mr Carpet Beater. Hello. So nice to see you after all this time. How have you been? Feeling lonely without my *derrière*?

'You...you....' Arms, shaking, Aunt Brank raised the carpet beater. I was too well-mannered to point out that, in her excitement, she was holding it the wrong way round. 'You are a disgrace to the family!'

I raised an eyebrow about half a millimetre. 'Indeed?'

'You...you...insufferable little...!'

Ah. So it's just as annoying for other people as it is for me. Good to know.

'Your uncle and I did all we could for you! We took you in, clothed you, fed you—'

'...with cold potatoes and unsalted porridge.'

'Silence! We clothed you, fed you, instilled in you the good manners and virtues a true lady should possess, and tried to teach you all the accomplishments you would need to succeed in life—'

'...like handling a carpet beater?'

'Like proper decorum!' Aunt Brank screeched, waving her carpet beater through the air like a madwoman and sending a nearby vase crashing to the ground. 'Like composure! Like good manners!'

'Ah. Those,' I said and cautiously stepped away from the shards of the shattered vase.

'All we asked for in return was for you to make an good match. With all the advantages we gave you, it should have been easy to find someone to marry. But did you do it? No! Did you even try? No!'

'Aunt, before you go on, I think I should tell you that—'

'Silence! Don't you dare disrespect your elders, girl! It's past time you behaved like a proper lady!' my aunt screeched and stomped on the shards of broken porcelain, scattering them all through the living room.

I just nodded. Normally, I wouldn't have been eager to listen, but my aunt had never tried to teach me *this* kind of proper lady behaviour before. I had to admit, it was a pleasant change, and I was willing to listen and find out how vase-smashing and foot-stamping would be valuable lessons for my future.

'We took you to ball after ball! We introduced you to countless gentlemen! But you never even tried! Instead, you ran off doing God only knows what and put the entire family's reputation at risk! And was once enough for you? Oh no, you had to do it again, and again, and again over Christmas of all times, and you even dragged your uncle into this, somehow getting his permission for your hair-brained schemes and ventures! And now, apparently, it's not enough for you to run off alone anymore, is it? No, you take along the whole family, dragging them into whatever it is you're up to!'

'Aunt—' Ella began behind her, probably to mention a few little things like, oh, I don't know, perhaps the cholera epidemic? But Aunt Brank raised a hand, silencing her instantly. Probably because it was the hand holding the carpet beater.

'So you've dragged more of the family onto your side with your madness, have you?' My aunt's beady little eyes pierced me where I stood, pinning me to the spot. 'Well, you can't play that game with me, young lady! I won't tolerate your shenanigans any longer. We're going to put an end to this once and for all! You're going to do what you should have done years ago—marry! And this time, there won't be any balls and choices for you, Lillian Linton! No more officers and knights vying for your hand! I don't give a darn who it is I hand you over to, as long as you're out of the house! You're going to marry the next darn man who knocks at the door, no matter if it's the greengrocer, the shoeblack, or a bloody beggar, do you hear?'

I opened my mouth to reply—when a knock came from the door.

All heads turned.

'Who could that be?' Lisbeth asked, frowning.

Aunt Brank didn't waste time with asking question. Carpet beater still in hand, she whirled around, marched towards the door and ripped it open.

'Yes?'

There was a moment of silence. Very cool, very familiar silence. Mr Ambrose's icy gaze rested for a moment on the carpet beater, then slowly rose to my aunt's face.

She dropped the carpet beater.

He inclined his head about a millimetre.

'W-who are you?' she demanded, raising her chin to glare at him. 'What do you want?'

'My name,' he said, sending back an arctic stare that had her retreating down the hall, 'is Rikkard Ambrose.' Removing his top hat and gloves, he stepped into the house without bothering to wait for an invitation and surveyed the small, sparse entryway with the supreme confidence of a general entering newly conquered territory. 'I think it's time you and I had a little talk.'

THE END

MEETING OF MISERS

'My name is Rikkard Ambrose. I think it's time you and I had a little talk.'

My aunt's mouth dropped open.

'R...Rick...Rickard...A-Ambrose?'

One look at her face was enough for me to see—she knew who he was. Of course she did. My aunt had kept a list of London's most eligible bachelors since my sisters and I were old enough to hold our own spoons. There was no way she wouldn't know the name of the man who stood unchallenged at the very top.

'*The* Ri...Rickard Ambrose?'

'No. Not Ririckard. Rickard.'

Neatly folding his gloves, he slipped them into his tailcoat pocket, and, hanging the top hat on the hat stand, stepped into the hallway without wasting time on asking first.

'You are Hester Mahulda Brank, I presume?'

'Y-you've heard of me?'

Mr Rikkard Ambrose glanced at me.

'Oh yes.'

My aunts shrivelled vulture face flushed with pleasure. I didn't she had noticed that glance in my direction, or the ominous emphasis on his words.

Just then, footsteps approached from the drawing room.

'Aunt Brank?' Maria stuck her head out into the hallway. 'Aunt Brank, what's the commotion? Who is i—'

That was the moment she spotted Mr Ambrose.

'Grrgmmph.'

'Quite the unusual name, I must say.' Mr Ambrose inclined his head about half a millimetre. 'Greetings, Miss Grrgmmph. My name is Rikkard Ambrose.'

'Ri-Rickard Am...Ambrose...'

'Hm. Deficient hearing seems to be common in this family.'

'P-please excuse our behaviour.' Aunt Brank sank into the deepest curtsey I had ever seen her make. 'We were simply taken aback by having the chance to great such an eminent personage as yourself in our humble home. It is quite an honour.'

'Yes. It is.'

'Maria? What's the hold up?' Anne appeared behind her twin sister and tapped on her shoulder. She received no reaction whatsoever. 'Maria? What's the matter? What are you staring at? Who—grk!'

Dear me.

Mr Ambrose did have a talent for abruptly silencing people, didn't he?

Normally, watching my twin demon sisters wasn't one of my favourite hobbies. But right now, it was well worth it. Smirking, I leaned against the wall and decided to enjoy the show. This was promising to be a most entertaining afternoon.

'Lillian Linton! What are you doing, slouching against the wall with that silly smile on your face? Can't you see we have an important guest? Go and fetch some refreshments, quick!'

'That won't be necessary,' Mr Ambrose cut in. 'In fact, it would be counter-productive for her to leave. The reason I've come here today is that I have a matter to discuss with your husband. A matter regarding Miss Lillian.'

'R-regarding Lillian?' Never had I seen my aunt go so pale so fast. By the looks of it, I should go fetch smelling salts, not refreshments. 'Please, Mr Ambrose, whatever she's done, we'll make sure she pays for the damage!'

Thank you so much for the trust and faith you put in me, Aunt. It really means a lot.

'Lillian, you bad, bad girl!' Turning to me with fury blazing in her eyes, Aunt Brank waved her hand in my face. I was only glad she'd let go of the carpet beater, or I might have been laid flat. 'How dare you insult a personage like Mr Rikkard Ambrose? Don't you know anything? He is one of the most important people in the entire empire! Why, it is even rumoured that he has connections to the royal family!'

You mean the fellows whose wedding we attended? That royal family?

'You miserable little unfilial girl! You're simply hopeless! Stupid! Worthless! And anyone who says different deserves to be flogged, tarred, feathered, and driven out of town!'

Oh, they do, do they? Demonstratively, I tried *not* looking at Mr Rikkard Ambrose. Now that's something I'd like to see.

'Why in goddness's name are you smirking, you worthless wench?' Shaking her head, my aunt turned back to Mr Ambrose. 'I simply do not know what to do with her. Please, Mr Ambrose, whatever this unfilial niece of mine has done to deserve your ire, she'll do anything to appease you! We'll do anything!'

'You will?' He cocked his head. 'I see. That simplifies matters. Then let me marry her.'

'Of course, Sir! You may punish her in any way you—wait, *what*?'

I had seen my aunt stunned with shock plenty of times. The first time I had stuck a frog into her shoe, for instance. Or that one memorable occasion on which Uncle Bufford had actually gone so far as to *come down for breakfast* and *say 'good morning'* to her. But never ever in my life had I seen her so utterly flabbergasted as right then.

They said getting married would bring a girl the greatest joy of her life.

What do you know? They'd actually been right.

'P-pardon? Mr Ambrose, I think I heard you incorrectly. *What* did you say?'

Uh-oh...

I couldn't help but grin into my hand.

His arctic eyes narrowed infinitesimally. 'Did I not mention that I do not like to repeat myself? I said I wish to marry her. As in contract matrimonial relations? That is the reason for my coming here today.'

'Marry?' She asked once more, faintly. 'Lillian?'

Clearly, she was having trouble imagining any reasonably sane male putting those two words in the same sentence.

One of my sisters raised their hands. 'Err...are you sure you have the right house, Sir? I think another Lillian lives that way, five houses down the road. She's thirty-five and has a clubfoot, but she's a very nice girl.'

Thank you very much for your vote of confidence!

'What,' Mr Ambrose enquired, his icy gaze sweeping the room, 'did I just say about repeating myself?'

Everyone instinctively took a step backwards and bowed their heads. Everyone but me, that is. My sisters didn't fail to notice the straightforward, completely unintimidated way I looked at Mr Rikkard Ambrose, perhaps the most powerful man in the entire British Empire. Their faces instantly changed complexions. Lisbeth and Gertrude went pale. Ella flushed with joy. And as for Anne and Maria, they couldn't have been more green with envy if they'd been frogs in my aunt's shoes.

They were slowly starting to realize: this was real. And it had been, for quite some time. And nobody had noticed.

'No way!' Anne whispered. 'No way! It's really true? It can't be! There's simply no way that a miserable little fussock like you could catch—'[55]

Mr Rickard Ambrose's eyes snapped to her in a flash. Her words dried up mid-sentence in a croak.

'You were saying?' he enquired, cocking his head.

'N-nothing.' Shaking her head wildly, she began to retreat. 'I wasn't saying anything.'

'Indeed. That is what I thought.'

'P-please forgive us, Mr Ambrose.' My aunt made a hurried curtsy. 'This has come as quite a shock to all of us! We had no idea...' She turned her head towards me and was about to throw me a venomous glare when she realized that, under the current circumstances, that might not be the wisest thing to do. 'Dear me. Here I am prattling on, and I haven't even offered you refreshments yet. Where are my manners?'

Mr Ambrose met her attempt at an ingratiating smile with an arctic look immune to ingratiating, bootlicking, and probably a dozen poisons besides. 'I wouldn't know. How many years has it been since you've seen them last?'

'Err...um...well, I think I'd better fetch refreshments now. Leadfield, please show the gentleman into the drawing room. Girls, hurry up and help me! And as for you, Lillian—'

'She,' Mr Ambrose said, 'is coming with me.'

'Ah. Um. Right.' Aunt Brank gave him another smile as sincere as a promise made on April Fool's day. 'I was just about to suggest that.'

'Doubtlessly.'

A bent and wrinkled Leadfield, who seemed to be walking even more excruciatingly slowly than normally, held open the door to the drawing room, and my aunt stepped towards the door, only to be overtaken by Mr Ambrose, who strode straight to her favourite chair and sat down.

'Err...please take a seat,' Aunt Brank said.

---

[55] Fussock—a victorian insult for well-padded ladies.

232

He cocked his head about one millimetre. 'I already have. Now, will you go inform the head of the household of my arrival? I would like to make him give his blessing to this arrangement immediately.'

'Err...surely you mean *ask* him to give his blessing?'

Leaning forward, Mr Ambrose gave her a very long, very marrow-freezing look. 'Do I look like the type of man who says things he does not mean?'

'Err...no! I didn't mean to imply...'

'Your face looks a little bit red, dear aunty,' I asked, the picture of a concerned niece drawn by an extremely devious cartoon artist. 'What's wrong? Feeling flustered? Would you sit down? This must be such a great joy to you, knowing that your greatest dream will finally come to fruition and your dear niece will be happily married.'

'Yes,' my dear aunty ground out between clenched teeth as she speered me with her dagger-like eyes. 'Such a...joy.'

'I can see that. You look like you could explode from delight.'

'Well...yes. Then I'd better go and...and...'

'Explode outside?' Mr Ambrose nodded. 'Adequate idea. And do not forget to fetch the man of the house.'

'No, Sir! Certainly not, Mr Ambrose, Sir.'

And she fled from the room.

Left behind was me, Mr Ambrose, and my flabbergasted collection of frozen statues, also known as 'sisters'.

Reaching for one of cup of teas Leadfield had brought, I took a sip. 'Nice weather today, isn't it?'

'Indeed,' said Mr Ambrose.

No one else said a thing. They all just kept staring at the two of us as if watching a zebra and tiger snuggling in the zoo.

'Hm.' Rising to his feet, Mr Ambrose tugged on his tailcoat. 'This is taking too long. I shall see what is the matter!'

And he strode out of the room.

The door closed behind him.

I started counting in my head.

Three.

Two.

0—

'*What the everloving figs!? Lilly, what the heck is going on here?*'

My sisters Anne and Maria appeared in front of me, like fallen angels of vengeance. All that was missing were the tails and pitchforks. Although at least the flames of hell in their eyes were there.

'What do you mean?' I asked, batting my eyelashes like a professional cricket player.

'Don't give us that innocent routine! What is this charade supposed to be? What the heck is your connection to...to that man? How...why...what...?'

'I believe he already stated it, didn't he?' I raised an eyebrow. 'We're getting married.'

'How can this be?' she growled. I heard the unspoken part at the end. *How can it be you lowly little insect, and not me?* 'It's impossible! This is a fake! It's impossible for something like this to happen without any of us knowing!'

'Oh,' Ella picked that moment to say in an innocent and sublimely effective tone I couldn't hope to match, 'I knew.'

Maria nearly swallowed her own tongue.

I knew there was a reason why Ella was my favourite sister.

'You *what*?'

Instantly, everyone's attention turned to Ella. My dear, innocent little sister sat there, sipping her tea with her little finger sticking out, the perfect image of a lady. I, personally, always mixed up my little finger with my middle finger.

'You didn't?' Ella's eyebrows rose oh-so-innocently. 'Wasn't it so obvious? I've seen the sign for. oh…about four years.'

Impressive! Since that's before I actually met him.

My dear little sister had impressive hidden skills. Lying like a rug apparently being one of them.

'Four years?'

My dear sisters' eyes were almost popping out of their heads.

'Oh yes. He sent her love letters all the time.' She gave a meaningful sigh. 'I still remember that one he sent from Paris…such touching words of love!'

Ah yes. The one that said 'stop wasting ink'.

By this point, Anne and Maria's heads were nearly ready to explode. Taking turns and helping each other as all good sisters should, they manged to simultaneously glare at me and Ella. 'From Paris? He sent her *love letters* from *Paris*?'

'Oh yes.' Ella took another sip of tea. 'Just before she went to visit him there and he proposed.'

This year, I decided, I was going to have to get Ella something really spectacular for her birthday.

'P-proposed? In Paris?'

'Oh yes. Where was it again, Lilly?'

'On the stage of an opera house,' I cheerfully proclaimed. '*His* opera house.'

Looking at Maria's face right there and then, for the first time I realized why the expression 'green-eyed monster' was used to refer to jealousy.

'Why!' My dear older sister's fist slammed onto the table. 'Why you? It's impossible! Not a bloody pudgy gibface[56] like yo—'

'Maria! Control yourself!' Gertrude admonished. She was a quiet girl and very rarely played the eldest sister card. But right now, her eyes were sparkling with danger.

But, apparently, Maria didn't give a flying fig. 'Why would I? You know as well as I do she's the worst of all of us! She's wilful, unladylike, ignorant about anything a girl of good birth ought to know, and as for her looks, well…' She cast a look at me, and then at the mirror on the wall that clearly said *Compare specimen A and B and tell me you don't realize what I mean.*

---

[56] A Victorian expression for an ugly person.

'I realize what you mean,' Ella said, sweetly. 'Unlike you, she actually has some.'

'You...! You little...!'

Bravo, Ella!

I was feeling less and less anxious about leaving this house and leaving her behind. Apparently, my little sister had grown quite a bit recently, and was more than capable of taking care of herself.

But even Ella could not hold my twin sister's wrath long. The soon-to-be-married elephant in the room was just too tempting to ignore.

'You!' They both whirled towards me. 'It's all your fault! Tell me! How did you do it? What did you do to ensnare him?'

'Hm, let me think...' I tapped my chin, thoughtfully. 'What was it called again...ah, yes! 'Being nice'. That was one of the things I did. You should try it once in a while. And...what was the other one gain? Oh yes! 'Having a brain'! That was useful, too, and—'

'You...!'

Eyes lit with rage, Anne and Maria charged towards me. Unable to restrain herself, Anne reached out to grab me by the collar, and—

—and with his inimitable sense of timing, Mr Rikkard Ambrose pushed open the door.

Anne froze.

'Something wrong?' He raised an eyebrow, just one millimetre.

Anne backed off as if her hand had been seared. A smile as sincere as a succubus's marriage vow appeared on her face. 'N-no! Of course not. I was just about to hug her and congratulate her!'

'Indeed?'

'Yes! It's been such a wonderful surprise!' He smile widened. 'The two of us should have a long chat later. Now that we're going to be relatives, we should get to know each other better.'

Icy eyes scrutinized my sister for one long moment. Then...

'No. We shouldn't.'

Sometimes, I really, really loved Mr Rikkard Ambrose.

'Seems like your uncle isn't available at the moment,' he said, turning to me. Reaching into his pocket, he withdrew his silver pocket watch and let it snap open. 'I have an appointment with the head of a turnip farm in Cheshire in half an hour. Let matters rest here for today. I can come back another day and finish this asking for your hand business.'

On the other hand, there were moments like *this one*.

But before I could leap forward and try to suffocate my dear fiancée, an angel rushed inside to save the day.

'Oh no, Mr Ambrose, you mustn't!' Aunt Brank dashed into the rooms, her arms flailing like a frantic windmill. 'You mustn't!'

Angels come in the unlikeliest shapes and sizes.

'I must not?'

'I just spoke to my husband! He will be happy to speak with you. Please, come right this way.'

'Hm. Very well.' He held out his hand towards me, and before even thinking about it, I took it. 'Let's go, shall we?'

My heart made a leap. This was it! The big moment. I wasn't of age yet. Not quite. If I wanted to marry this man, as much as I detested the fact, I needed another man's permission. Of course, I could always wait a few months, but...

Out of the corner of my eyes, I glanced at Mr Rikkard Ambrose's sublime profile.

Nah. Waiting was out.

'Let's go!' I said and, together, my husband-to-be and I marched towards the stairs, following my aunt. Slowly, we ascended the stairs, the old wood beneath our feet creaking ominously. We came to a stop at the dark door at the end of the landing.

'Husband?' Clearing her throat, she knocked at the door. 'I've brought Mr—
'

'Ah,' a familiar growl came from inside. 'The madman is here, is he?'

'Husband!'

'Do you have to remind me, woman? It's painful enough every day when I see that ring on my finger. Get the two of them in here!'

'Y-yes.'

Aunt Brank opened the door, and I stepped through before she managed to realize she was actually politely holding the door for me. Her suddenly souring face as I stepped past was a fabulous sight.

Unfortunately, it was superseded by the grim face of Uncle Bufford, sitting behind his desk with his fingers steepled. Mr Ambrose followed me into the room and the door closed with a click behind us.

'Hm. Hello, Girl.'

'Hello.'

Uncle Bufford's eyes flicked to Mr Ambrose.

'You are...?'

'I,' he informed uncle Bufford, 'am the man who is going to marry your niece Lillian.'

'Confident? Good, good.' His brows furrowed. 'If you can back it up, that is. Name?'

Mr Ambrose's eyes flashed with the pride of a man who knew his name meant something. 'Rikkard Ambrose.'

'Hm. That one.'

'Yes.'

'I see.'

'Indeed.'

Yes...this conversation was about as full of scintillating rhetoric as I had expected.

'You seem like a gentleman.' Uncle Bufford leaned forward. 'But this little girl is very precious to me. So you understand I have to make sure...'

'Yes.'

I couldn't help but feel moved. Precious? I was precious to him?

'So,' he growled, 'how much are you willing to pay for her?'

Precious?

Precious!

That dastardly old badger...! I...

I felt Mr Ambrose's hand holding me back.

He cocked his head. 'I thought it traditionally is the duty of the bride's family to pay a dowry?'

'I've never been particularly fond of traditions that empty my wallet. So...' Small black eyes sparkling, eh leaned forward. 'How. Much. Will. You. Pay. For. Her?'

Ambrose regarded him coolly for a moment or two—then leaned forward, too, meeting his gaze. 'Not a penny.'

My mouth dropped open. But before anything could come out of it, he grabbed my hand and, stepping forward, continued, 'Because I know her. Because she is free to choose. I cannot offer money to buy what you don't own. I will only marry her because she wants to, not because you allow it.'

I felt a lump rise in my throat. He...he just said the most wonderfully romantic thing he had ever uttered in his life to me. And he did it while being as miserable a skinflint a skinflint as ever. That was the man I loved!

'Harrumph.' Uncle Bufford's did his very best to hide it under his bushy eyebrows, but I saw the glint of approval in his eyes. 'So it's like that, is it?' He gazed at Mr Ambrose out of narrowed eyes. 'Are you at least going to pay for the ceremony?'

I grinned. *Translation: you have my blessing.*

'No. Are you?'

Translation: thank you.

Well...I was being optimistic about that one.

'No.'

'Hm.'

'Hm. Hm. We appear to be at an impasse.'

'Indeed?'

'Yes. I completely approve of you, yet I cannot agree to the match as long as you remain stubborn on this issue.'

Mr Ambrose considered for a moment. 'How about we split the costs fifty-fifty?'

'Sounds sensible. However, I have paid for her room and board for more then a decade. The costs of that should be subtracted from my share, which would leave you owing me, let me see...' Reaching for an abacus, he swiftly shifted a few different-coloured beads around, then looked up. 'Roughly two-hundred pounds sterling, ten shillings and sixpence.'

The answer came swift and decisive. 'Unacceptable.'

'I'm afraid that is a non-negotiable condition.'

'Then we are indeed at an impasse.'

'Indeed.'

'Hm.'

'Hm. Hm.'

I grinned. 'I can see the two of you are going along great!'

Two heads turned, and two cool gazes bored into me, silently asking *What is this deranged female talking about?*

My grin widened, and, folding my arms behind my neck, I leaned back in my armchair. 'By all means, do continue. I have a feeling I'm going to enjoy this.'

'You are supposed to be fearful and anxious to obtain my blessing,' Uncle Bufford grumbled.

I continued to grin, unabashed. 'Sorry to disappoint.'

'You don't *look* sorry.'

'Oh my. Indeed?'

His small dark eyes scrutinized me for a long moment. 'You look...happy.'

The grin on my face slowly morphed, until a soft, sincere smile was left, unlike any I could remember having on my face before. 'I am.'

'Hm.' His jaw worked for a moment—then he glanced at Mr Ambrose. 'Maybe we can discuss who shall take care of the wedding costs at a later date.'

Giving me a long look, Mr Ambrose's hand squeezed mine. 'Agreed.'

'So...' Reaching out, I took his gnarled old hand. 'Will you give it to me? For free?'

He knew what I meant. His jaw worked, and, after a moment of intense struggle, he nodded.

'You have my blessing.'

A WARNING TO THE GRIM REAPER

Chapter 33, 'Cold, Hard Commitment' from Mr Ambrose's Point of View

I stood there, in the garden, gazing up at the window pane at the back of the hotel. The window pane that blocked my way to *her.*

I knew it was a waste of money to pay for this much glass. I should just have left the windows empty instead, customer complaints be damned!

Well, no matter. This problem was easily resolved.

Bending down, I picked up some gravel from the path that ran behind the building and hurled it against the window.

Plink.

I waited.

And waited.

And waited another long, long moment.

By Mammon! Three entire moments of waiting? This whole 'love' thing was really getting out of hand!

Or at least that's what I thought until she opened the window and I saw her face.

For one long second, we gazed at each other in silence, I ordered.

'Come,' I ordered.

Her face twisted in a way that made me want to tear the wall down, as well as any other obstacles that stood between us. 'I can't. I...I might have caught the disease. I can't come near you until—'

My eyes narrowed. 'Miss Linton?'

'Yes?'

'Get your *derrière* down here *right now*.'

'I thought you had promised not to give me any more orders.'

'That wasn't an order,' I told her, and held out one hand. 'Please.'

She stared at me for long, long moment—then, in a blink, swung her legs over the window sill and slid down, dashing towards me. She only came to a stop a few yards away from me.

Still too far. Much too far.

I gazed at her, unable to take my eyes away. Every second counted.

This isn't time wasted, I realized. *This is the best way to spend time there ever was.*

I took a step forward.

And she abruptly jerked back.

'Stop!' Quickly, she raised a hands to block my path. 'I've got to tell you something! The doctor was here again. He said... he said that Ella...'

'I know,' I cut her off. *As if, after paying his bills, I'd let that quack off without squeezing every little bit of information out of him.*

'Then you know you can't come any closer. If you do—'

As if I care!

I took a determined step forward.

'No!' She leapt back, her eyes wide with fear. Fear for me. 'Aren't you listening? I might be infected, too! Nobody knows how the sickness is transmitted! It could be through contact, and you'd be—'

With you. Wherever you go.

I could have said it aloud, I suppose. Instead, I chose a much more expedient method. Grabbing her face tightly in my hands, I pulled her towards me and claimed her lips with mine.

You are mine! My lips spoke without speaking. *You are mine and I am yours!*

She stiffened for just a moment—then softened. Her arms came up around me, pulling me tightly against her with a force I hadn't thought her capable of. In return, my arms enfolded her, determined never to let go.

'You crazy, crazy man!' I felt her whisper against my lips. 'How could you do something so stupid?'

I cocked my head, challenging her. 'I prefer the word "determined", Miss Linton.'

'Sure you do—mmm!'

I kissed her once again. Kissed her with all the ferocity and determination I could muster. So what if I died? I could have died in the gold rush. I could have died tracking through the dessert. I could have died on the seas a thousand times. And still, I had done it! Profit vs Risk. That's all there was to it. Profit vs risk. If the former outweighed the latter, you stride ahead and destroy anything in your path!

I gazed into her eyes for a long, long moment.

And in this case, the profit most definitely outweighs the risk.

Cholera be damned!

I released her after how long I neither knew nor cared. She took a slightly wobbly step backwards, her eyes still closed in bliss, and when she finally opened them, they were the colour of warm chocolate.

'Why?' she whispered.

I could read the rest of the question in those chocolate eyes of hers.

Why risk this? Why kiss me?

I cocked my head. 'I believe the vows we intend to speak say "till death do us part", do they not? You ought to know by now, Miss Linton—I don't speak words I do not mean.'

In those warms eyes of hers, suddenly, a fire was lit. Reaching out, she grabbed hold of me and held me close. I did not object.

'Neither do I.'

Adequate.

My arms slid around her and I stroked her hair, gently pulling her face against my chest. She cuddled into me, and I felt a tug deep in my chest.

At this point, I was 99% sure it was not heartburn. Not that I would ever waste the money on a doctor's appointment to make sure.

If this is heartburn, I can live with it. I want to.

I kissed her again. And again. Apparently, I had managed to make her loose her reticence. When we broke apart again, I took her face in both hands and turned her so I could look straight into her eyes.

And what I saw in there made me want to punch something.

Pain.

Deep, terrible pain.

Under normal circumstances, I would simply eliminate the one who'd put it there. But in this case, that would probably be...inadvisable.

I felt a muscle in my cheek twitch.

'How is she?'

The pain flared, and I knew that I'd guessed right.

'Bad. Very bad. I'm not sure...I'm not sure she—'

I pressed a finger on her lips, cutting her off. 'Sh. She will.'

'How do you know?'

Because I'll buy the underworld and evict her if she doesn't!

However, a little voice at the back of my mind, a voice that sounded suspiciously like my little siter, told me that might not be the entirely correct thing to say.

'Because you won't give up until she's well again,' I told her instead. 'And neither will I.' With a single finger, I gently stroked her cheek. 'You look exhausted. How long is it since you've last slept?'

'Says the man who did an experiment to see whether one can go without sleep altogether.'

I gave her a cool look. 'It was a perfectly reasonable experiment.'

'Then let's just say I'm repeating it.' She gave me that infernally impudent grin that should have infuriated me. Should have, but didn't. 'It's always good to check the results of an experiment, right?'

My eyes narrowed infinitessimaly.

'Are you familiar with the expression "working yourself into an early grave", Miss Linton?'

'Indeed I am, Sir. I feel its suitable use has been grossly exaggerated. Besides,' she shrugged, looking entirely too vulnerable for a moment, 'who's there to help?'

I didn't even think. I just soke.

'Me.'

She stared at me, mouth open.

'W-what?'

'I am certain I spoke at a perfectly audible volume, Miss Linton.'

'B-but...you can't...the risk...'

Grabbing hold of her chin, I forced her to meet my gaze head-on. 'Was I not clear enough earlier? Need I repeat my demonstration for it to be more convincing?'

'Yes, please, right away for the next half hour.'

'Miss Linton! Be serious!'

'Who says I'm joking? I'm a sceptic by nature and need a lot of convincing.'

Well...who was I to reject an attractive offer? Tightening my grip, I pulled her towards me for a long, deep, and in my personal opinion, very convincing kiss.

'I'm not a man who shies away from risk,' I growled. 'If I were, I wouldn't be where I am today, with more power in my hands than most men can imagine! Some things are worth fighting for, and when the fight comes, you face it head-on.'

'But...but she...is...you know.'

'I've mucked out plenty a stable in my time. It won't be that different.'

I stared implacably into her eyes until I saw the realization spread over her face. *Yes. I really mean it.*

With her, I always meant what I said—even without a signed contract.

'Thank you!' Suddenly, her arms were around me, and she was hugging me, hugging me fiercely and fiery. 'Thank you.'

I felt a strange, warm fealing rising inside me nad, once again, I was 99% sure it was not fever. She held me for long, long moments that felt far too short—then let go and looked up into my eyes.

'But I can't accept.' I opened my mouth to object, but before I could, she held up a finger to silence me. Silence *me*? My eyes flashed. 'Not because of you. I want your help. God, how I want it. But Ella...'She gazed up at me, her gaze a plea for me to understand. 'I can't do that to her. Letting someone else see her like that, someone whom she hasn't even met yet...I can't hurt her like that. Please understand.'

Understand?

Understand?

She was in trouble! I could help! Why would I stand back and...!

I met her vulnerable, wide-open eyes again.

Damnation.

Swallowing, I gave a curt nod. 'Understood.'

She was about to breathe a sigh of relief—when I I grabbed her chin once more, and speared her with my gaze. 'As long as you understand that I won't have you working yourself into an early grave. I have plans for you, Miss Linton. Plans that require you to be above ground.' I leaned forward, just enough to let her see the glitter of danger in my eyes. 'I will have Karim monitor the situation. If you do not take care of yourself, I will come in and take charge of things, a proper introduction to your family be damned! Do you understand?'

She nodded, unable to speak a word.

'Adequate.' One last time, I claimed her lips in a fierce kiss. No, not just a kiss—a brand, marking what was mine. 'Then do not let me detain you.'

And with that, I whirled around and marched away, glaring into the shadows. I felt...felt so...what was this strange thing called? When you were foolish enough to have no power? So...helpless!

By mammon! Grim reaper, you had best stay away from her—or else!

...THE MIDDLE...

ABOUT THE AUTHOR

 Robert Thier is a German historian and writer of historical fiction. His particular mix of history, romance, and adventure, always with a good deal of humour thrown in, has gained him a diverse readership ranging from teenagers to retired grandmothers. For the way he manages to make history come alive, as if he himself lived as a medieval knight, his fans all over the world have given him the nickname 'Sir Rob'.

For Robert, becoming a writer followed naturally from his interest in history. 'In Germany,' he says, 'we use the same word for story and history. And I've always loved the one as much as the other. Becoming a storyteller, a writer, is what I've always wanted.'

Besides writing and researching in dusty old archives, on the lookout for a mystery to put into his next story, Robert enjoys classical music and long walks in the country. The helmet you see in the picture he does not wear because he is a cycling enthusiast, but to protect his literary skull in which a bone has been missing from birth. Robert lives in the south of Germany in a small village between the three Emperor Mountains.

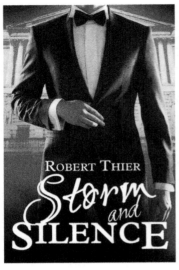

Storm and Silence

Freedom – that is what Lilly Linton wants most in life. Not marriage, not a brood of squalling brats, and certainly not *love*, thank you very much!

But freedom is a rare commodity in 19th-century London, where girls are expected to spend their lives sitting at home, fully occupied with looking pretty. Lilly is at her wits' end – until a chance encounter with a dark, dangerous and powerful stranger changes her life forever...

The award-winning first volume of the *Storm and Silence* series! Winner of the *People's Choice Award* and *Story of the Year Award* 2015.

ISBN-10: 3000513515   ISBN-13: 978-3000513510

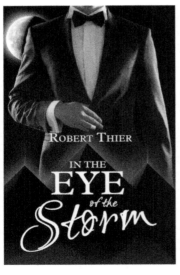

In the Eye of the Storm

Egypt... land of romance, mystery, and exploding camels. Lilly Linton thought she'd be ready for anything after one month of working for her boss – cold, calculating businessman Rikkard Ambrose. But when they embark on a perilous hunt through the desert, she has to face dangers beyond anything she has encountered before: deadly storms, marauding bandits, and worst of all, a wedding ring!

Can the desert's heat truly be enough to melt the cold heart of Britain's richest financier?

The long-awaited second volume of the acclaimed *Storm and Silence* series.

ISBN-10: 3000513515   ISBN-13: 978-3000513510

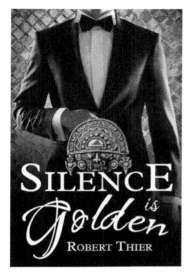

Silence is Golden

Silent. Cold. Chiselled perfection. That is Rikkard Ambrose, the most powerful business mogul in Great Britain.

Free-spirited. Fiery. Definitely *not* attracted to the aforementioned business mogul. That is Lilly Linton, his personal secretary and secret weapon.

The two have been playing a cat and mouse game for months. So far, Lilly has been able to fight down and deny her attraction to Mr Ambrose. But what happens when suddenly, the dark secrets of his past begin to surface and they are forced to go on a perilous journey into the South-American jungle? A journey they can only survive if they band together?

Volume three in the award-winning *Storm and Silence* series.

ISBN-13: 978-3962600587

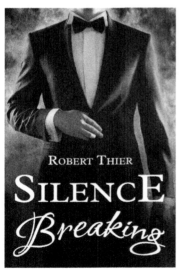

Silence Breaking

Family - the most important thing in the world, right? If it's your own, maybe. But if it's the family of the incredibly powerful, incredibly alluring businessman with whom you've been conducting a secret office affair, and they don't yet know about the affair, things are a little bit different.

Life is about to get real for Lilly Linton. All those stolen moments behind closed doors, those secret kisses and whispered words are about to catch up with her. As she and her boss, business-magnate Rikkard Ambrose, travel north to his parents' palatial estate, she is about to discover whether she has the strength to step out of the shadows and change her fate forever.

Volume four of the award-winning Storm and Silence series.

ISBN-13: 978-3962600594

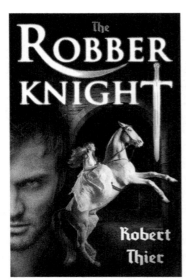

The Robber Knight

When you are fighting for the freedom of your people, falling in love with your enemy is not a great idea.

Sir Reuben, the dreaded robber knight, has long been Ayla's deadliest enemy. She swore he would hang for his crimes. Now they are both trapped in her castle as the army of a far greater enemy approaches, and they have only one chance: stand together, or fall. Welcome to *The Robber Knight*—a tale full of action, adventure, and romance.

Special Edition with secret chapters revealed and insights into Sir Reuben's mysterious past.

ISBN-10: 1499251645   ISBN-13: 978-1499251647

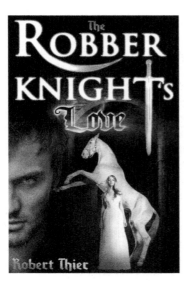

The Robber Knight's Love

Ayla has uncovered a terrible secret: the man she loves is in fact her worst enemy. As a mighty army gathers to destroy her and her people, she must ask herself: will he join them to destroy her? Must she cut him out of her heart to survive?
Or is there another way—a way to forgiveness and...love?

Special Edition with secret chapters revealed and insights into Sir Reuben's mysterious past.

ISBN-10: 3000536590   ISBN-13: 978-3000536595

WARNING! Fairy Tales

WARNING! Please be advised that this is not a bedtime story about sparkly fairies and pink unicorns. This book may contain graphic descriptions of poisoned apples and witches' ovens. It is not appropriate for supernatural beings under the age of 377 (excluding vampires and werewolves).

DISCLAIMER: Wicked Witches Inc. and Evil Stepmother Enterprises are not responsible for any maiming, mass murder or permanent insanity resulting from the reading of this book.

The first volume of Robert Thier's *WARNING! Fairy Tales* series.

ISBN-10: 3000547118   ISBN-13: 978-3000547119

WARNING! Fairy Tales 2

WARNING! Please be advised that big bad wolves, wicked witches, and harmless-looking little girls are roaming the pages of this book. It may contain graphic descriptions of wolf teeth and grandmothers with big ears. This book is not appropriate for supernatural beings under the age of 388 (excluding anyone wearing a red hood).

DISCLAIMER: *Wicked Witches Inc.* and *Evil Stepmother Enterprises* are not responsible for wolf bites, vampirism or witch curses incurred during the reading of this book.

The second volume of Robert Thier's *WARNING! Fairy Tales* series.

ISBN-13: 978-3962600013

WARNING! Fairy Tales 3

HEALTH WARNING! Reading this book may cause sudden attacks of magical metamorphosis. It may cause a fast and furry transformation into a beast, a troll, a vegetable, or, in a worst-case scenario, a cute little blue bird. No curse-breaking via kiss of true love guaranteed.

DISCLAIMER: *Beastly Beasties Inc.* and the *Royal Society of Enchanted Princes* are not responsible for any acquaintances, personnel and/or random bystanders accidentally transformed into furniture. Furniture polish and feather dusters must be purchased separately.

The third volume of Robert Thier's *WARNING! Fairy Tales* series.

ISBN-13: 978-3962600020

Internet & Social Media

Website: www.robthier.com
Twitter: http://twitter.com/thesirrob
Goodreads: www.goodreads.com/author/show/6123144.Robert_Thier

Printed in Great Britain
by Amazon

25695022R00148